U0134765

TOEIC®
Listening and Reading Test Official Test-Preparation Guide

Vol. 6

TOEIC® 聽力與閱讀測驗官方全真試題指南 VI

2018年3月題型更新，首本官方應考必備書

Acknowledgements

We would like to acknowledge The Institute for International Business Communication (IIBC), Tokyo, Japan, for providing the original content for this book for translation.

前言

TOEIC® 聽力與閱讀測驗是由 *ETS®* 在 1979 年，針對母語非英語人士所研發的英語能力測驗。由於各領域國際交流及商務往來日益頻繁，英語在世界各國職場中扮演的角色亦更加重要。TOEIC 系列測驗目前可於全世界 160 個國家施測，至少為 14,000 個以上的企業客戶、教育單位及政府機構所採用。TOEIC 測驗分數不僅具備信度及效度，也具有國際流通度，足以體現考生在實際溝通情境中的英語文能力。因此，是企業員工英語能力管理標準，也是學校的英語文教學管理工具。

ETS 一直在檢驗，TOEIC 聽力與閱讀測驗是否能反映當今英語溝通的現況？測驗是否能確實評估考生現在或將來所處環境中需要的英語能力？隨時代演進，日常生活中或國際職場上英語使用及溝通方法不斷改變，為了因應這些變化，ETS 更新部分 TOEIC 聽力與閱讀測驗的題型，納入過去十年間經常使用的溝通用語，以求符合真實的現況。日、韓兩國從 2016 年 5 月開始實施更新題型（詳情請參考第九頁），台灣於 2018 年 3 月開始實施。

台灣地區過去曾發行五本官方全真試題指南《*TOEIC®* Official Test-Preparation Guide》，2017 年為了因應題型更新，乃出版第六本官方全真試題指南，供讀者及語言教學機構充分運用。本書包含了兩份試題（共 400 題），內容均照 ETS 製作的試題標準型態編寫，MP3 音檔中所收錄的聲音亦完全比照正式測驗規格，對於考生而言，是準備考試及熟悉更新題型內容的有效練習工具。

為了精確了解自己的英語文能力現況，讀者在做過本書的試題後，可以根據書中所附的分數換算表計算出參照分數。對於不甚了解的試題，可參閱翻譯及題解，聽力測驗題解中另加註英、美、加、澳等四國口音，讓讀者更能掌握不同英語系國家的發音腔調，進而有效調整學習的方法及進度。

我們也期盼讀者能藉由本書充分理解 TOEIC 聽力與閱讀測驗的特色，在面對實際測驗時，順利發揮應有的實力。而中英語雙語版的官方指南，係因應華人地區考生普遍反映的需求而製作，希望能更方便讀者查考。

本書中文版的編輯及翻譯責任歸屬於 *TOEIC®* 臺灣區總代理忠欣股份有限公司編輯委員會，而非美國 ETS，因此翻譯內容如有任何不當或疏漏之處皆由編譯團隊負責，敬祈專家、學者不吝指正。

TOEIC® 臺灣區總代理　忠欣股份有限公司

邵作俊　謹識

目錄

關於*TOEIC*®測驗

TOEIC 測驗簡介

TOEIC 測驗全名為 Test of English for International Communication，是針對母語非英語人士所設計之英語能力測驗，測驗分數反映受測者在國際生活及職場環境中的英語溝通能力。TOEIC 測驗並不要求一般生活及職場情境常用英語以外的專業知識或字彙。TOEIC 系列測驗包括 TOEIC 聽力與閱讀測驗、TOEIC 口說與寫作測驗、*TOEIC Bridge*® 測驗。

TOEIC 系列測驗能夠評量個人是否能真實的在全球職場環境與生活情境中使用英語溝通，是全球通用的英語能力標準。目前可於全球 160 個國家施測、至少為 14,000 個以上的企業客戶、教育單位及政府機構所採用，不僅可以協助人資部門打造高效能的國際人才團隊；求職者也相信 TOEIC 測驗能夠幫助他們提升國際移動力，在競爭激烈的求職市場中脫穎而出。

TOEIC 系列測驗能全方位評量聽、讀、說、寫四項英語技能，並能夠針對不同考生語言能力的優勢和弱勢提供分析，這點有助於企業的關鍵徵才及職務派遣決策。另外，由於 TOEIC 測驗的施測流程標準化，企業人資部門可運用 TOEIC 測驗成績做為員工英語能力管理工具，包括招募、國內外人事派遣、訓練、晉升的參考。TOEIC 測驗在各校園中也常被用作升學加分證照、大學英文免修門檻、英語教學分班及診斷測驗、國際溝通英語能力證照測驗等用途。

TOEIC 聽力與閱讀測驗本身沒有所謂的「通過」或「不通過」，而是將受測者的能力以聽力 5 ～ 495 分、閱讀 5 ～ 495 分、總分 10 ～ 990 分的分數來呈現。分數所代表的能力基準是固定不變的，也就是說，只要英語能力沒有變化，分數就會維持不變。測驗內容主要並不是要檢測專業知識或素養的英語能力，而是要檢測職場情境或日常生活中的英語溝通能力。這項測驗還採用「全球標準」，排除了不了解特定文化就無法理解的內容，讓所有人都能公平地接受檢測。

關於研發製作單位——*ETS*®

ETS 是目前全球規模最大的非營利教育測驗及評量單位，專精教學評量及測驗心理學、教育政策之研究，在測驗及教學研究領域上居於領導地位。擁有教育專家、語言學家、統計學家、心理學家等成員，研發的測驗及語言學習產品包括：*TOEFL iBT*® 測驗、*TOEFL ITP*® 測驗、*TOEFL Junior*® 測驗、*TOEFL*® *Primary*™ 測驗、TOEIC 聽力與閱讀測驗、TOEIC 口說與寫作測驗、TOEIC Bridge 測驗、*SAT*®、*GRE*® 測驗等，及英文寫作軟體 *Criterion*®、TOEIC 官方線上課程 TOEIC Official Learning and Preparation Course、互動式英語線上學習系統 English Learning Center 及 TOEFL iBT 官方全真試題線上模擬測驗 *TOEFL*® Practice Online。

本書使用方法

本書收錄的兩套 *TOEIC*® 聽力與閱讀測驗全真試題，長度皆和實際測驗相同，分別包含 200 道題目。在練習測驗之後，還提供題目的中文翻譯、詳細題解、答案表及參考分數計算方法。

題型範例

為了讓考生對 TOEIC 聽力與閱讀測驗的問題形式能有基本的認識，在練習測驗前面，本書也提供了題型範例，以及例題的中文翻譯與詳細題解。在實際測驗中，聽力測驗與閱讀測驗的問題各有 100 題，聽力測驗的範例內容收錄在 MP3 音檔中。

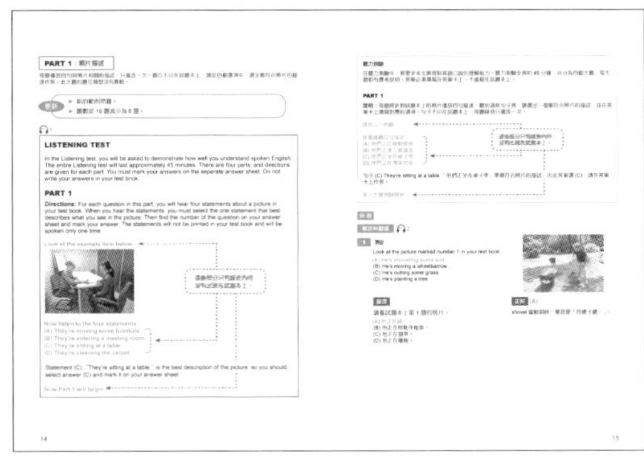

▲ 聽力測驗

▲ 閱讀測驗

全真試題（Test 1、Test 2）

全真試題的內容與實際測驗一樣，聽力測驗有 100 題，閱讀測驗有 100 題，測驗時間同樣約為 120 分鐘。請利用第 36 頁後所附的答案卡作答。

聽力測驗的內容收錄在 MP3 音檔中，可至密碼卡中所提供的網站上下載，長度約為 45 分鐘。做完聽力測驗後，請不要休息，繼續進行閱讀測驗，測驗時間為 75 分鐘。請試著在限制時間 120 分鐘內，盡量完成所有題目。

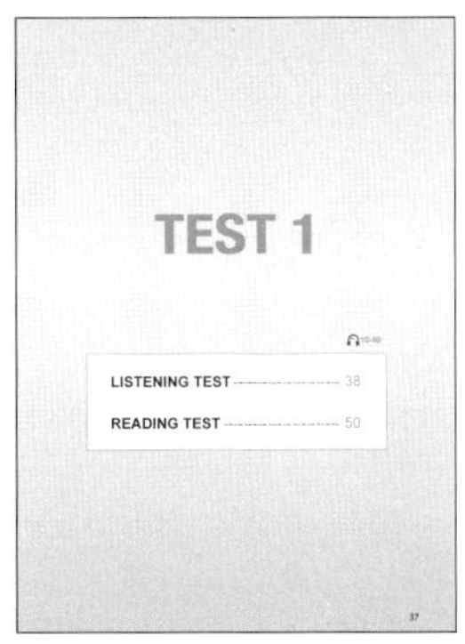

▲ 全真試題

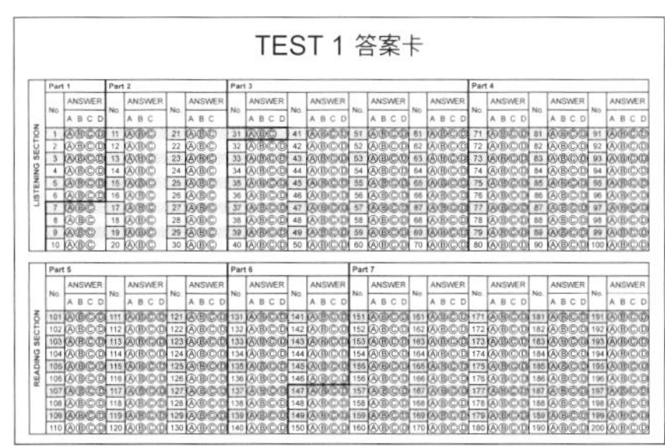

▲ 答案卡

分數的計算

測驗完畢後請以《解答篇》第 125 及 257 頁所提供的解答核對答案，並依據《解答篇》第 122 頁的參考分數計算方法及第 123 頁的分數換算表，算出參考分數。

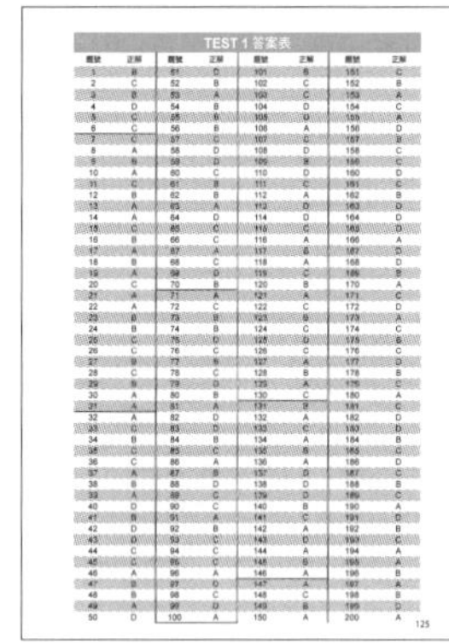

TEST 1 答案表

題號	正解	題號	正解	題號	正解	題號	正解
1	B	51	D	101	B	151	C
2	C	52	B	102	C	152	B
3	B	53	A	103	C	153	A
4	D	54	B	104	D	154	C
5	C	55	B	105	D	155	A
6	C	56	B	106	A	156	D
7	C	57	C	107	C	157	B
8	A	58	D	108	D	158	C
9	B	59	D	109	B	159	C
10	A	60	C	110	D	160	D
11	C	61	B	111	C	161	C
12	B	62	B	112	A	162	B
13	A	63	A	113	D	163	D
14	A	64	D	114	D	164	D
15	C	65	C	115	C	165	D
16	B	66	C	116	A	166	A
17	A	67	A	117	B	167	D
18	B	68	C	118	A	168	D
19	A	69	D	119	C	169	B
20	C	70	B	120	B	170	A
21	A	71	A	121	A	171	C
22	A	72	C	122	C	172	D
23	B	73	B	123	B	173	A
24	B	74	B	124	C	174	C
25	C	75	D	125	D	175	B
26	C	76	C	126	C	176	C
27	B	77	B	127	A	177	D
28	C	78	C	128	B	178	B
29	B	79	D	129	A	179	C
30	A	80	B	130	C	180	A
31	A	81	A	131	B	181	C
32	A	82	D	132	A	182	D
33	C	83	D	133	C	183	D
34	B	84	B	134	A	184	B
35	C	85	C	135	B	185	C
36	C	86	A	136	A	186	D
37	A	87	B	137	D	187	C
38	B	88	D	138	D	188	B
39	A	89	C	139	D	189	C
40	D	90	C	140	B	190	A
41	B	91	A	141	C	191	D
42	D	92	B	142	A	192	B
43	D	93	C	143	D	193	C
44	C	94	C	144	A	194	A
45	C	95	C	145	B	195	A
46	A	96	A	146	A	196	B
47	B	97	D	147	A	197	A
48	B	98	C	148	C	198	B
49	A	99	D	149	B	199	D
50	D	100	A	150	A	200	A

125

▲ 答案表

參考分數計算方法

TOEIC® 聽力與閱讀測驗分數是使用統計的方法，將原始分數轉換成評量分數。藉由換算程序，即使是不同測驗，所得出的分數意義是相同的。因此，某次測驗得分 550 分，和另外一次測驗得分 550 分，表示英語能力相當。

完成練習測驗後，依照下列步驟可計算出參考分數。

步驟一：請參考第 125 及 257 頁的答案表，分別計算出聽力測驗與閱讀測驗的答對題數。各部分的答對題數，即為原始分數。

步驟二：請用第 123 頁的分數換算表，找到原始分數對應的評量分數範圍。例如，聽力測驗的原始分數是 45，換算出來的評量分數範圍就是 140 分到 225 分。

步驟三：各部分換算出來的評量分數範圍加總後，就是 TOEIC 聽力與閱讀測驗的總分。

此分數換算表是為了練習測驗而製作，不能使用於實際 TOEIC 聽力與閱讀測驗的分數計算。

122

分數換算表

聽力測驗		閱讀測驗	
原始分數範圍	評量分數範圍	原始分數範圍	評量分數範圍
96 – 100	485 – 495	96 – 100	455 – 495
91 – 95	445 – 495	91 – 95	410 – 490
86 – 90	400 – 475	86 – 90	380 – 455
81 – 85	360 – 450	81 – 85	350 – 430
76 – 80	330 – 420	76 – 80	315 – 405
71 – 75	300 – 385	71 – 75	290 – 380
66 – 70	265 – 355	66 – 70	260 – 355
61 – 65	235 – 330	61 – 65	235 – 325
56 – 60	210 – 305	56 – 60	205 – 300
51 – 55	185 – 275	51 – 55	175 – 270
46 – 50	165 – 250	46 – 50	155 – 235
41 – 45	140 – 225	41 – 45	125 – 205
36 – 40	115 – 195	36 – 40	105 – 170
31 – 35	95 – 165	31 – 35	85 – 140
26 – 30	80 – 135	26 – 30	65 – 115
21 – 25	65 – 110	21 – 25	55 – 90
16 – 20	35 – 90	16 – 20	45 – 75
11 – 15	10 – 70	11 – 15	30 – 55
6 – 10	5 – 60	6 – 10	10 – 45
1 – 5	5 – 50	1 – 5	5 – 30
0	5 – 35	0	5 – 15

123

▲ 參考分數計算方法及分數換算表

TOEIC®聽力與閱讀測驗題型更新說明

為何 ETS® 要更新 TOEIC 聽力與閱讀測驗題型？

由於英語的使用現況有所改變，ETS 的測驗及試題內容也必須跟進。ETS 想要確保 TOEIC 聽力與閱讀測驗能反映出時下語言之使用情形，並檢驗受試者目前或未來在真實生活情境中所需的語言技巧，2016 年 TOEIC 聽力與閱讀測驗之題型更新即包含近十年來使用頻率更高的溝通用語。

TOEIC 聽力與閱讀測驗有什麼改變？為什麼？

為確保測驗符合考生及成績使用單位之需求，ETS 會定期重新檢驗所有測驗試題。2016 年 TOEIC 聽力與閱讀測驗題型更新，反映了全球現有日常生活中，社交及職場之英語使用情況，測驗本身維持其在評量日常生活情境或職場情境英語的公平性及信效度，其中一些測驗形式有改變，然而，測驗的難易度、測驗時間或測驗分數所代表的意義並未變動。

題型

聽力測驗（Listening Section） 測驗時間：約 45 分鐘			
大題	內容		題數
1	照片描述	Photographs	6
2	應答問題	Question-Response	25
3	簡短對話	Conversations 13 conversations with 3 questions each	39 (3x13)
4	簡短獨白	Talks 10 talks with 3 questions each	30 (3x10)
Total			100

閱讀測驗（Reading Section） 測驗時間：75 分鐘			
大題	內容		題數
5	句子填空	Incomplete Sentences	30
6	段落填空	Text Completion	16 (4x4)
7	單篇閱讀	Single Passages 10 reading texts with 2–4 questions each	29
	多篇閱讀	Multiple Passages 5 sets of double or triple passages with 5 questions per set	25
Total			100

試題型態

Q：為什麼 *ETS*® 選擇將文字簡訊和即時通訊納入 *TOEIC*® 聽力與閱讀測驗考題中？

A：文字簡訊和即時通訊反映真實世界職場溝通的變化。有越來越多來自世界各地、不同據點的人一起工作，此類型的溝通在全球化工作場域中變得更加普遍。

Q：文字簡訊和即時通訊會使用網路用語、縮寫或簡寫字詞嗎？

A：雖然某些題目以文字簡訊或即時通訊的形式呈現，其內容不會使用網路用語、縮寫或簡寫字詞。由於不是所有的縮略語在世界各地皆通用，縮略語可能因區域或文化差異而有不同的理解。為了確保對全體考生的公平性，簡略的表達方式不會納入測驗中。

Q：TOEIC 聽力與閱讀測驗中使用的四國口音：美國、英國、加拿大和澳洲，比例上是否會有變化？

A：不會，這四國口音仍繼續以平均分配方式呈現。

優勢

Q：實施題型更新對於考生及成績使用單位有什麼優勢？

A：2016 年 ETS 實施之題型更新是為了符合英語使用上的改變，以及個人於日常生活及全球化工作環境普遍溝通情形。實施題型更新之 TOEIC 聽力與閱讀測驗所增加的題目內容能真實反映現今英語的使用，例如：從上下文掌握文意、整合及連結不同來源的文字訊息、能夠理解線上交談的非線性溝通內容，以及兩名以上談話者的對話內容。

與過去版本相較，題型更新後的 TOEIC 聽力與閱讀測驗可幫助考生藉由準備考試的過程中，充分練習上述必備能力，並驗證自己的溝通技巧是否符合現今的全球職場工作環境，進而應用於現實生活中，順利達到溝通目的。各採用機構則可放心地透過此測驗成績，評量出國際職場所需的各種致勝關鍵英語能力。

考題難易度

Q：TOEIC 聽力與閱讀測驗題型更新後難度是否改變？

A：否，TOEIC 聽力與閱讀測驗難度維持不變。題型更新經過測驗研發專家團隊的精心設計，以確保在難度、測驗長度、考題總數、計分量尺及測驗品質都跟過去版本無異。因此，TOEIC 聽力與閱讀測驗題型更新後之成績是可與過去的測驗成績相互對照比較的。

Q：聽力及閱讀的長度是否會有所改變？

A：雖然部份考題類型及出題形式有做調整，但整體而言，測驗的難度或是聽力及閱讀的長度都維持不變。

2016 年題型更新後，對話的句子變得更短且易懂。有出現圖片的考題，其文字描述也會較簡短淺顯。此外，每篇簡短對話或簡短獨白的內容都有長度限制，因此與過去測驗中的對話及談話考題大致相同。

Q：作答需參照圖片（如：標誌或圖表）的考題時，是否會運用到英語以外的能力與技巧？

A：日常生活中，不論是聽或讀都需要先了解溝通時的整體情境。例如，在現實生活裡，說話的一方很可能在聽話跟說話的同時，邊查看電子郵件或圖表，在這種情境下，就一定得理解口頭傳達的訊息與文字傳達的訊息有何關聯。

考生會看到的圖片都非常精簡，其中出現的文字或數字量也有限。每道圖片題（包括圖表裡出現的文字及題目中的敘述文字）作答所需的閱讀量，與過去測驗中的簡短對話及簡短獨白考題大致相同，考生並不需任何額外的技巧理解考題中出現的地圖或圖表。

Q：TOEIC 聽力與閱讀測驗更新題型後，閱讀某些長度較長的問題是否需花更多時間？

A：閱讀測驗整體閱讀需求量並無改變。以內容含有三篇相關文章的閱讀題組而言，試題的平均總字數不會超過內容含有兩篇相關文章之閱讀的平均總字數。

成績解讀

Q：成績意義是否與題型更新前相同？

A：聽力測驗之能力項目從原本的四項增為五項，新增項目為：考生是否能了解說話者談話目的或明白句意或句子中隱含意義的能力。

更新題型能幫助測量上述的能力評估標準，以提供考生與成績使用者更多有用的評估資訊，同時也能讓考生更清楚自己的強項與弱項，以便能更有效地設立未來英語學習目標。

Q：TOEIC 聽力與閱讀測驗對應歐洲語言共同參考架構（Common European Framework of Reference, CEFR）的等級，是否改變？

A：TOEIC 聽力與閱讀測驗對應歐洲語言共同參考架構之等級參照維持不變，可參考 ETS 官方網站：https://www.ets.org/s/toeic/pdf/toeic-cefr-flyer.pdf

題型範例

Sample Items

為了讓考生瞭解 *TOEIC*® 聽力與閱讀測驗的出題類型，以下將介紹 29 題例題。

- ▶ 實際應考時的試題本上，每大題一開始都會有英文應考說明（Directions）。為了輔助學習，本書特別附上中文翻譯。
- ▶ 每大題均以更新題型為主。
- ▶ 以下例題的題號連續，與實際應考情況不同。

詳細內容

TOEIC 聽力與閱讀測驗的聽力測驗共分為四個大題，閱讀測驗共分為三個大題。

聽力測驗：共 12 題例題

大題	題型	頁數	新型態考題的問題範例	
Part 1	照片描述	14-15	———	
Part 2	應答問題	16-17	———	
Part 3	簡短對話	18-21	No. 7~9 No. 8	聆聽並根據三人的對話回答問題 根據對話中所隱含的意思進行提問
Part 4	簡短獨白	22-23	No. 10~12	根據圖表與對話內容的連結回答問題

閱讀測驗：共 17 題例題

大題	題型	頁數	新型態考題的問題範例	
Part 5	句子填空	24-25	———	
Part 6	段落填空	26-27	No. 18	從選項中選出一個完整句子填入短文
Part 7	閱讀測驗	28-35	No.19~20 No.24 No.25~29	多方即時訊息對話的閱讀理解問題 引述文章部分內容測驗考生是否理解談話者之意 將句子歸置於正確段落 三篇相關文章的閱讀理解問題

PART 1：照片描述

每題播放四句與照片相關的描述，只播放一次。題目不印在試題本上，請從四個選項中，選出最符合照片的描述作答。此大題的題目類型沒有異動。

▶ 新的範例問題。

▶ 題數從 10 題減少為 6 題。

 1

LISTENING TEST

In the Listening test, you will be asked to demonstrate how well you understand spoken English. The entire Listening test will last approximately 45 minutes. There are four parts, and directions are given for each part. You must mark your answers on the separate answer sheet. Do not write your answers in your test book.

PART 1

Directions: For each question in this part, you will hear four statements about a picture in your test book. When you hear the statements, you must select the one statement that best describes what you see in the picture. Then find the number of the question on your answer sheet and mark your answer. The statements will not be printed in your test book and will be spoken only one time.

Look at the example item below.

這些部分只有錄音內容，
沒有出現在試題本上。

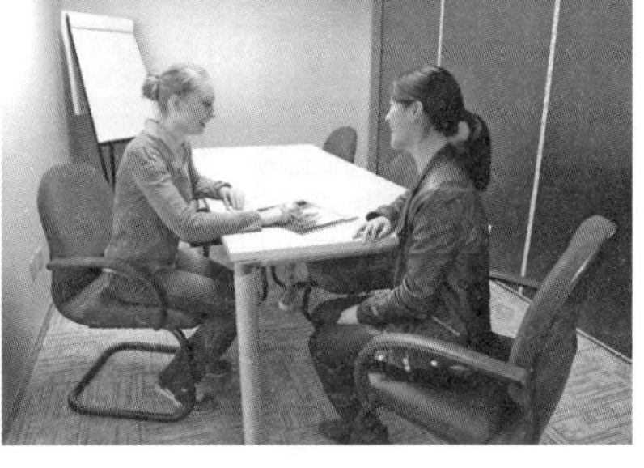

Now listen to the four statements.
(A) They're moving some furniture.
(B) They're entering a meeting room.
(C) They're sitting at a table.
(D) They're cleaning the carpet.

Statement (C), "They're sitting at a table," is the best description of the picture, so you should select answer (C) and mark it on your answer sheet.

Now Part 1 will begin.

聽力測驗

在聽力測驗中，將要求考生展現對英語口說的理解能力。聽力測驗全長約 45 分鐘，共分為四個大題，每大題都有應考說明。答案必須填寫在答案卡上，不能寫在試題本上。

PART 1

說明：每題將針對試題本上的照片播放四句描述，聽到這些句子時，請選出一個最符合照片的描述，並在答案卡上填寫對應的選項。句子不印在試題本上，每題錄音只播放一次。

請見以下例題：

接著請聽四句描述。
(A) 他們正在搬動傢俱。
(B) 他們正進入會議室。
(C) 他們正坐在桌子旁。
(D) 他們正在清潔地毯。

這些部分只有錄音內容，沒有出現在試題本上。

句子 (C) They're sitting at a table.「他們正坐在桌子旁」是最符合照片的描述，因此答案選 (C)，請在答案卡上作答。

第一大題測驗開始。

例題

解說和翻譯  2

Look at the picture marked number 1 in your test book.
(A) He's shoveling some soil.
(B) He's moving a wheelbarrow.
(C) He's cutting some grass.
(D) He's planting a tree.

翻譯

請看試題本上第 1 題的照片。
(A) 他正在鏟土。
(B) 他正在移動手推車。
(C) 他正在割草。
(D) 他正在種樹。

正解 (A)

shovel 當動詞時，意思是「用鏟子鏟…」。

PART 2：應答問題

每題播放一個問句或直述句與三個答句，只播放一次。題目和選項不印在試題本上，請根據問題選出最適合的答案。此大題的題目類型沒有異動。

- ▶ 題數從 30 題減少為 25 題。
- ▶ Part 2 沒有例題。

3

PART 2

Directions: You will hear a question or statement and three responses spoken in English. They will not be printed in your test book and will be spoken only one time. Select the best response to the question or statement and mark the letter (A), (B), or (C) on your answer sheet.

Now let us begin with question number 2*. ← 這部分只有錄音內容，沒有出現在試題本上。

* 實際考試題號為 7。

2. Mark your answer on your answer sheet.
3. Mark your answer on your answer sheet.

PART 2

說明：每題將以英語播放一個問句或直述句，以及三個答句。題目和選項不印在試題本上，每題只播放一次。請選出最適合該問句或直述句的回答，並在答案卡的 (A)、(B) 或 (C) 上選填作答。

測驗第二題開始。 ← 這部分只有錄音內容，沒有出現在試題本上。

解說和翻譯  4

2 Q: A:

How well does Thomas play the violin?

(A) Sure, I really like it.
(B) Oh, he's a professional.
(C) I'll turn down the volume.

翻譯

湯瑪斯的小提琴拉得有多好？

(A) 當然，我非常喜歡。
(B) 喔，他是專家。
(C) 我會把音量調小。

正解 (B)

相對於 How well...?「…有多好？」的提問，回答「他是專家」的 (B) 最為適當。

3 Q: A:

Martin, are you driving to the client meeting?

(A) Oh, would you like a ride?
(B) Nice to meet you, too.
(C) I thought it went well!

翻譯

馬汀，你會開車去跟客戶碰面嗎？

(A) 喔，你想要搭便車嗎？
(B) 我也很高興認識你。
(C) 我以為進展很順利。

正解 (A)

根據「是否開車去跟客戶碰面」的提問，可以推測出對方可能想要搭便車。ride 表示「搭乘（汽車）」。

PART 3：簡短對話

每題播放一段對話與數個問題，只播放一次，且對話不印在試題本上。閱讀試題本上的問題和選項後，從四個選項中選出最適合者作答。此大題的題目類型有以下幾種異動。

更新

- ▶ 部分題型將出現兩人以上的對話內容（參考 No. 7-9）。
- ▶ 根據對話者的談話背景或對話中所隱含的意思進行提問（參考 No. 8）。
- ▶ 根據圖表與對話內容的連結回答問題（參考 Part 4 的 No. 12）。
- ▶ 題數從 30 題增加為 39 題。

 5

PART 3

Directions: You will hear some conversations between two or more people. You will be asked to answer three questions about what the speakers say in each conversation. Select the best response to each question and mark the letter (A), (B), (C), or (D) on your answer sheet. The conversations will not be printed in your test book and will be spoken only one time.

例題 未更動的題目類型

4. Where do the speakers work?
   (A) At a hotel
   (B) At a department store
   (C) In a restaurant
   (D) At a call center

5. What does the man ask about?
   (A) How many people have applied for a promotion
   (B) If a manager is in the lobby
   (C) Whether a position is available
   (D) When new shifts will be assigned

6. What does the woman say the man should be prepared to do?
   (A) Handle customer complaints
   (B) Work within a budget
   (C) Get to know local clients
   (D) Work evening hours

PART 3

說明：每題將播放兩人或兩人以上的對話內容，每段對話會有三個提問，對話只播放一次，且對話不會印在試題本上。請根據題目選出最適合的選項，並在答案卡的 (A)、(B)、(C) 或 (D) 上選填作答。

解說和翻譯

 6

Questions 4 through 6 refer to the following conversation.

M: Oh, hi Yolanda—❶I'm surprised to see you at the front desk this late. Don't you usually work at the hotel in the morning?

W: Actually, I'm going to be working the evening shift for a while; I'm covering for a front-desk supervisor who was just promoted, but only until the hotel hires a permanent replacement.

M: Oh, so ❷there's a front-desk supervisor position open? I've been looking for a chance to take on a managerial role. Are they still accepting applications?

W: Yes, and ❸if you don't mind working evening hours, I think you have a good chance at the job. I'd contact the manager right now, though---she's starting interviews this week.

請參考以下的對話回答第 4 題至第 6 題。

男： 女：

男：喔，嗨，Yolanda，這麼晚了還在櫃台看到您真讓我驚訝。妳通常不都是早上才在飯店工作的嗎？

女：事實上，我這陣子都要值晚班，櫃台主任最近升職了，所以我來代班，直到飯店找到能長期工作的人接手。

男：喔，那麼，目前櫃台主任的職務有空缺囉？我一直在找機會擔任管理階層的工作。現在還接受應徵申請嗎？

女：是的，若你不介意上晚班，我想你有很大的機會獲得這份工作。我現在就跟經理聯絡吧，她這周就要開始面試了。

4 翻譯

說話的人在哪裡工作？

(A) 飯店
(B) 百貨公司
(C) 餐廳
(D) 客服中心

正解 (A)

從❶的 the front desk、work at the hotel 等可判斷。

5 翻譯

男子詢問了關於什麼的事？

(A) 有多少人申請升職
(B) 經理是否在大廳
(C) 某職位是否有空缺
(D) 何時分派新的輪班時間

正解 (C)

從❷there's a front-desk supervisor position open?「櫃台主任的職務有空缺嗎？」可得知。

6 翻譯

女子說男子應該要有什麼樣的準備？

(A) 處理顧客投訴
(B) 在預算範圍內工作
(C) 認識當地客戶
(D) 值晚班

正解 (D)

對於有意申請櫃台主任一職的男子，女子描述了❸「若你不介意上晚班，我想你有很大的機會獲得這份工作」。

例 題 聆聽並根據三人的對話回答問題

7. What is the conversation mainly about?
   (A) An enlargement of office space
   (B) A move into a new market
   (C) An increase in staff numbers
   (D) A change in company leadership

如同 21 頁指示說明中的 **with three speakers**，這裡是三人的對話場景（說明只以錄音播放，不印在試題本上）。

8. Why does the woman say, "I can't believe it"?
   (A) She strongly disagrees.
   (B) She would like an explanation.
   (C) She feels disappointed.
   (D) She is happily surprised.

針對對話中的所隱含的意思進行提問。
* 這種題目類型也出現在 **Part 4** 的簡短獨白中。

9. What do the men imply about the company?
   (A) It was recently founded.
   (B) It is planning to adjust salaries.
   (C) It is in a good financial situation.
   (D) It has offices in other countries.

< 更為自然的對話表現 >

在聽力測驗中，對話內容經常會以母音省略（elision, 如 going to 變成 gonna），或不完整的句子（fragment，如「Yes, in a minute」、「Down the hall」、「Could you...?」等省去主詞和動詞的句子）呈現。

比方說在 22 頁 No. 10-12 的對話中，第二句就出現了 But before we start, a few administrative details.「但在我們開始前，有些行政上的細節（要說明）」這樣的表現，將 a few administrative details 前的 we have 省略了。

解說和翻譯

 7

Questions 7 through 9 refer to the following conversation with three speakers.

請參考以下三人的對話回答第 7 題至第 9 題。
男：澳／加　女：美

M:（澳） ❶Have you two taken a look at the progress they've made upstairs on the office expansion? ❷It looks great!

男：你們兩個有看到樓上辦公室的擴建進展嗎？看起來棒極了！

W: I know! I can't believe it! And the offices up there have amazing views of the city.

女：對啊！我真不敢相信！而且上面的辦公室有很棒的都市景觀。

M:（加） I wonder which division will move up there when it's finished.

男：不曉得完工後會是哪個部門搬上去。

W: I heard it's the research department.

女：我聽說是研究部門。

M:（澳） Ah, because they have the most people.

男：啊，因為他們人最多。

W: Probably. I'd love to have an office on that floor, though.

女：可能吧。要我也很樂意在那層樓有間自己的辦公室。

M:（加） Yeah. Well, ❸the company must be making good money if they're adding that space!

男：沒錯，嗯，公司會增加那個空間，一定是賺了不少錢！

M:（澳） ❹I think you're right, there!

男：我想這你說得沒錯！

7 翻譯

這段對話主要跟什麼有關？
(A) 擴大的辦公空間
(B) 進入新市場
(C) 增加員工人數
(D) 公司領導階層的改變

正解 (A)

❶中有 office expansion「辦公室擴建」，後續內容也圍繞在同樣話題上。

8 翻譯

為什麼女子要說「I can't believe it」？
(A) 她強烈反對。
(B) 她想要一個解釋。
(C) 她感到失望。
(D) 她感到驚喜。

正解 (D)

第一名男子用❷It looks great! 來表示對樓上擴建的想法，接著女子說 I know!「我知道、對啊」表示同意，接著又說了這句話，由此判斷答案為 (D)。

9 翻譯

從男子說的話可以推論出關於公司的什麼事？
(A) 公司是近期創立的。
(B) 公司計畫要調整薪水。
(C) 公司的財務狀況良好。
(D) 公司在其他國家有分公司。

正解 (C)

其中一名男子說了❸「公司會增加那個空間，一定是賺了不少錢」後，另一名男子說了❹表示同意。

PART 4：簡短獨白

每題只播放一次簡短的獨白，後面接連會有幾個提問。獨白內容不印在試題本上，請閱讀試題本上的題目和問題，然後從四個選項中選出最適合者作答。此大題的題目類型有以下幾種異動。

更新
- ▶ 根據圖表與對話內容的連結回答問題（參考 No.12）。
- ▶ 根據獨白內容所隱含的意思進行提問（參考 21 頁 Part 3 的 No.8）。
- ▶ 題數維持 30 題。

8

PART 4

Directions: You will hear some talks given by a single speaker. You will be asked to answer three questions about what the speaker says in each talk. Select the best response to each question and mark the letter (A), (B), (C), or (D) on your answer sheet. The talks will not be printed in your test book and will be spoken only one time.

例題 包含根據圖表與對話內容的連結回答問題的題型

Program	
Presenter	**Time**
Ms. Carbajal	1:00-1:50
Mr. Buteux	1:55-2:45
BREAK	2:45-3:00
Mr. Chambers	3:00-3:50
Ms. Ohta	3:55-4:45

題目部分包含圖表

10. Where most likely is the speaker?
    (A) At an award ceremony
    (B) At a musical performance
    (C) At a retirement celebration
    (D) At a training seminar

11. What are listeners asked to do?
    (A) Stay seated during the break
    (B) Carry their valuables with them
    (C) Return any borrowed equipment
    (D) Share printed programs with others

12. Look at the graphic. Who will be the final presenter?
    (A) Ms. Carbajal
    (B) Mr. Buteux
    (C) Mr. Chambers
    (D) Ms. Ohta

根據圖表內容回答的題目類型。
* 這類提問也會出現在 **Part 3** 的簡短對話中。

PART 4

說明：每題播放一篇獨白，後面會有三個相關的問題，請根據獨白選出最適合的選項，並在答案卡的 (A)、(B)、(C) 或 (D) 上選填作答。獨白內容不印在試題本上，每題只播放一次。

解說和翻譯

 9

Questions 10 through 12 refer to the following talk and program.

W: ❶We're happy to see you all at this seminar this afternoon—we have a lot of useful information to cover. But before we start, a few administrative details. There will be one break, half way through the afternoon. You can leave your laptops here if you leave the room—there will always be someone in here—❷but do keep your money and phones or...ah...other small electronic devices with you. Don't leave them at the tables. And please note that there's an error in your printed program: ❸there will be a change—a switch—in times for the last two presenters. Ms. Ohta has to leave a little early today.

請參考以下的對話與節目表回答第 10 題至第 12 題。

女：很高興能在下午這場研討會中見到大家——我們將介紹許多實用的資訊。不過，在我們開始之前，有些行政上的細節要說明。下午到了中場時，將有一次休息時間。您若想要離開，可以將筆電留在這裡——這裡都會有人——但請隨身攜帶您的錢和手機，或是，嗯，其他小型的電子設備，不要將它們放置在桌上。另外請注意，紙本的節目表上有個錯誤：最後兩場講者的時間將有所異動——場次交換——Ohta 女士必須提早離開。

10 翻譯

說話者最有可能在哪裡？

(A) 頒獎典禮
(B) 音樂表演場合
(C) 退休慶祝活動
(D) 訓練研討會

正解 (D)

從❶的 this seminar「這場研討會」，以及 we have a lot of useful information to cover「我們將介紹許多實用的資訊」可判斷。

11 翻譯

聽眾被要求做些什麼？

(A) 休息時間要坐在原位
(B) 隨身攜帶貴重物品
(C) 歸還借用的設備
(D) 跟他人分享紙本的節目表

正解 (B)

❷中有「請隨身攜帶您的錢和手機」的描述。

12 翻譯

節目表	
講者	時間
Ms. Carbajal	1:00-1:50
Mr. Buteux	1:55-2:45
休息	2:45-3:00
Mr. Chambers	3:00-3:50
Ms. Ohta	3:55-4:45

請看此表。最後的講者是誰？

(A) Ms. Carbajal
(B) Mr. Buteux
(C) Mr. Chambers
(D) Ms. Ohta

正解 (C)

由於❸描述了「最後兩場講者的時間將有所異動——場次交換」，所以 (C) Mr. Chambers 為正確解答。

以下開始是閱讀測驗，實際應考時，到了聽力測驗的最後會播放「This is the end of the Listening test. Turn to Part 5 in your test book.」（聽力測驗結束，請翻到試題本上第五大題。）此時便可以開始作答。（不得跨區作答）

PART 5：句子填空

每題須從四個選項中選出最適合者作答以完成句子，此大題的題目類型沒有異動。

更新 ▶ 題數從 40 題減少為 30 題。

READING TEST

In the Reading test, you will read a variety of texts and answer several different types of reading comprehension questions. The entire Reading test will last 75 minutes. There are three parts, and directions are given for each part. You are encouraged to answer as many questions as possible within the time allowed.

You must mark your answers on the separate answer sheet. Do not write your answers in your test book.

PART 5

Directions: A word or phrase is missing in each of the sentences below. Four answer choices are given below each sentence. Select the best answer to complete the sentence. Then mark the letter (A), (B), (C), or (D) on your answer sheet.

例題

13. Customer reviews indicate that many modern mobile devices are often unnecessarily -----.
    (A) complication
    (B) complicates
    (C) complicate
    (D) complicated

14. Jamal Nawzad has received top performance reviews ----- he joined the sales department two years ago.
    (A) despite
    (B) except
    (C) since
    (D) during

閱讀測驗

在閱讀測驗中，考生將會閱讀各類文體的內容，並回答不同類型的閱讀理解問題。閱讀測驗全長 75 分鐘，共分為三個大題，每大題都有應考說明。考生應在有限時間內盡量作答。

答案必須填寫在答案卡上，不能寫在試題本上。

PART 5

說明：以下每個句子都缺少了一個單字或片語，每題有四個選項，請從選項中選出最適合者以完成句子，然後在答案卡 (A)、(B)、(C) 或 (D) 上選填作答。

解說和翻譯

13 **翻譯**

顧客評價顯示許多現代化行動裝置通常並不一定要很複雜。

(A) 複雜化（名詞）
(B) 使複雜（第三人稱單數動詞）
(C) 複雜（原形動詞）
(D) 複雜的（形容詞）

正解 (D)

由於空格前面出現 be 動詞的 are，可知空格處需要補語，因此選 (D) complicated「複雜的」。副詞 unnecessarily「不必要地」用來修飾後面空格的文字。

14 **翻譯**

Jamal Nawzad 自從兩年前加入業務部門後，一直獲得最高的業績評價。

(A) 儘管…（介係詞）
(B) 除了…（連接詞）
(C) 自從…（連接詞）
(D) 在…期間（介係詞）

正解 (C)

空格前後的句子都有 < 主詞 + 動詞 >，可得知這裡需要連接詞。從文意判斷，選 (C) since「自從…」最為合適。

PART 6：段落填空

每題須從四個選項中選出最適合者作答，使整篇文章完整。

▶ 新增將完整句填入短文的題型（參考 No.18）。
▶ 題數從 12 題增加為 16 題。

PART 6

Directions: Read the texts that follow. A word, phrase, or sentence is missing in pasts of each text. Four answer choices for each question are given below the text. Select the best answer to complete the text. Then mark the letter (A), (B), (C), or (D) on your answer sheet.

例題 **Questions 15-18 refer to the following e-mail.**

To: Project Leads
From: James Pak
Subject: Training Courses

To all Pak Designs project leaders:

In the coming weeks, we will be organizing several training sessions for --15-- employees. At Pak Designs, we believe that with proper help and support from our senior project leaders, less experienced staff can quickly --16-- a deep understanding of the design process. --17--, they can improve their ability to communicate effectively across divisions. When employees at all experience levels interact, every employee's competency level rises and the business overall benefits. For that reason, we are urging experienced project leaders to attend each one of the interactive seminars that will be held throughout the coming month.

--18--.

一篇短文會有四個提問，問題出現在短文後。

Thank you for your support.

James Pak
Pak Designs

15. (A) interest
(B) interests
(C) interested
(D) interesting

16. (A) develop
(B) raise
(C) open
(D) complete

17. (A) After all
(B) For
(C) Even so
(D) At the same time

18. (A) Let me explain our plans for onsite staff training.
(B) We hope that you will strongly consider joining us.
(C) Today's training session will be postponed until Monday.
(D) This is the first in a series of such lectures.

將完整句子填入短文的題型。

PART 6

說明：請閱讀以下短文，每篇短文都缺少了一個單字、片語或句子。短文後的每個問題都有四個選項，請選出最適合者完成短文，並在答案卡 (A)、(B)、(C) 或 (D) 上選填作答。

解說和翻譯 **請參考以下的電子郵件回答第 15 題至第 18 題。**

收件人：專案組長們
寄件人：James Pak
主旨：研修課程

致所有 Pak 設計公司的專案組長們：

在未來幾周，我們將為感興趣參加的員工安排數場研習會。在 Pak 設計公司裡，我們相信，只要有資深專案組長的適當協助與支持，經驗較為不足的員工們都將對設計過程有更深入的瞭解。同時，他們也能增進自己的能力，好在跨部門之間更有效地溝通。當各位經驗不同的員工們能有所互動時，每位員工的能力都將得以提升，而公司整體的營運也將有所獲益。基於此原因，我們鼓勵資深的專案組長們參加每場於下個月舉辦的互動研討會。
* 誠摯地希望您認真考慮加入。

感謝您的協助。

James Pak
Pak 設計公司

* 為 18 題的內文翻譯

15 **翻譯**

(A) 使（人）感興趣（原形動詞）
(B) 使（人）感興趣（第三人稱單數動詞）
(C) 感興趣的（形容詞）
(D) 有趣的（形容詞）

正解 (C)

能修飾空格後面 employees 的是形容詞 (C) 或 (D)，從文意判斷要選 (C) interested。

16 **翻譯**

(A) 發展
(B) 提升
(C) 打開
(D) 完成

正解 (A)

空格後面的受詞為 a deep understanding「深入的瞭解」，從文意判斷最適合的動詞為 (A) develop。

17 **翻譯**

(A) 畢竟…
(B) 為了…
(C) 即便如此
(D) 同時

正解 (D)

從空格前後的文意判斷，都是專案組長參加研討會的益處，所以選 (D)。

18 **翻譯**

(A) 讓我說明對於員工實地訓練的計畫。
(B) 誠摯地希望您認真考慮加入。
(C) 今天的訓練研習會將延至周一。
(D) 這是系列講座裡的第一場。

正解 (B)

鼓勵參加研習會的電子郵件結尾以 (B) 最為合適。

PART 7：閱讀測驗

這一大題將出現各類的文章書信，除了過去單篇與雙篇文章的理解問題外，也增加了三篇文章的題目。請閱讀題目，再從四個選項中選出最適合者作答。

更新

- ▶ 加入多方即時訊息對話的閱讀理解問題（參考 No.19-20）。
- ▶ 引述文章部分內容，測驗考生是否充分理解談話者之意（參考 No. 20）。
- ▶ 部分文章中會標記數字，考生需將句子歸置於正確的段落（參考 30 頁的 No.24）。
- ▶ 三篇相關文章的閱讀理解問題（參考 33 頁的 No.25-29）。
- ▶ 題數從 48 題增加為 54 題。

PART 7

Directions: In this part you will read a selection of texts, such as magazine and newspaper articles, e-mails, and instant messages. Each text or set of texts is followed by several questions. Select the best answer for each question and mark the letter (A), (B), (C), or (D) on your answer sheet.

例題 **Questions 19-20 refer to the following text message chain.**

SAM BACH 11:59
My first flight was delayed, so I missed my connection in Beijing.

SAM BACH 12:00
So now, I'm going to be on a flight arriving in Kansai at 18:00.

AKIRA OTANI 12:05
OK. Same airline?

SAM BACH 12:06
It's still Fly Right Airlines. It will be later in the day but still in time for our client meeting.

AKIRA OTANI 12:06
I'll confirm the arrival time. Do you have any checked bags?

SAM BACH 12:10
I do. Would you mind meeting me at the door after I go through customs?

AKIRA OTANI 12:15
Sure thing. Parking spots can be hard to find, but now I'll have extra time to drive around and look.

SAM BACH 12:16
Yes, sorry about that. See you then!

19. What is suggested about Mr. Bach?
    (A) He has been to Kansai more than once.
    (B) He currently works in Beijing.
    (C) He is on a business trip.
    (D) He works for Fly Right Airlines.

20. At 12:15, what does Mr. Otani mean when he writes, "Sure thing"?
    (A) He has confirmed the arrival time of a flight.
    (B) He is certain he will be able to find a parking place.
    (C) He agrees to wait at the door near the customs area.
    (D) He knows Mr. Bach must pass through customs.

針對談話者表現意圖的提問

PART 7

說明：在這個部分考生將閱讀如雜誌、新聞報導、電子郵件和即時訊息等各類內容。每篇或每組文章後面都有數個題目，請從選項中選出最適合的答案，並在答案卡 (A)、(B)、(C) 或 (D) 上選填作答。

解說和翻譯 **請參考以下的即時訊息回答第 19 題至第 20 題。**

SAM BACH 11:59
我最初的航班延遲了，導致我在北京錯過轉機航班。

SAM BACH 12:00
所以，現在我要搭 18:00 抵達關西的航班。

AKIRA OTANI 12:05
好，同一家航空公司嗎？

SAM BACH 12:06
還是 Fly Right 航空，時間上會稍微晚一點，但還是趕得及參加客戶會議。

AKIRA OTANI 12:06
我會確認抵達時間。您有任何托運行李嗎？

SAM BACH 12:10
有，您可以跟我在通過海關後的門口碰面嗎？

AKIRA OTANI 12:15
沒問題。雖然停車位不好找，但我現在有更多時間可以開到附近看看。

SAM BACH 12:16
對，很抱歉，到時見了！

19 **翻譯**

關於 Bach 先生我們可以知道什麼？

(A) 他不只一次去過關西。
(B) 他目前在北京工作。
(C) 他正在出差。
(D) 他替 Fly Right 航空工作。

正解 (C)

從 Bach 先生一開始的兩個訊息中可得知，他是在北京轉機要前往關西。在那之後 12 點 06 分的訊息中，說明了「趕得及參加客戶會議」，所以可以知道是在出差。

20 **翻譯**

Otani 先生在 12 點 15 分時寫下了的「Sure thing」是什麼意思？

(A) 他已確認了航班的抵達時間。
(B) 他很確定能夠找到停車位。
(C) 他同意在靠近海關附近的門邊等候。
(D) 他知道 Bach 先生必須通過海關。

正解 (C)

Sure thing 是對於他人要求給予承諾的表現，因 Bach 先生在前面提出「您可以跟我在通過海關後的門口碰面嗎」的要求，所以選 (C)。

例題 **Questions 21-24 refer to the following information.**

Noticeboard Space Available to Community Groups

Mooringtown Library is pleased to invite local community groups to use the free advertising space on its new noticeboard, located outside the front entrance of the library. Space on the board is available for up to four weeks at a time.

Notices must be approved in advance at the library's front desk and must meet the following requirements. All content must be suitable for public display. The notice must be written or printed on standard-quality paper with dimensions of either 8.5 in. x 11 in. or 5.5 in. x 8.5 in. The desired start and end date for display should be written in the front bottom right corner. —[1]—. Any notices that do not meet these requirements will not be considered and will be discarded —[2]—.

—[3]— Submissions are now being accepted at the Mooringtown Library front desk. Please have the actual notice, in the format in which you would like it to appear, with you when you arrive. Within one business day, you will receive a call confirming that your notice has been added to the board —[4]—.

Mooringtown Library
www.mooringtownlib.co.au

21. What is indicated about advertising space on the Mooringtown Library noticeboard?
    (A) It is available at no charge.
    (B) It can be used for any length of time.
    (C) It is open to all area businesses.
    (D) It is intended mainly for sporting events.

22. What is NOT a stated requirement for a notice to be placed on the board?
    (A) It must be of a particular size.
    (B) It must be marked with posting dates.
    (C) It must be reviewed beforehand.
    (D) It must be signed by a librarian.

23. What should an advertiser bring to the library when making a submission?
    (A) An outline of proposed content
    (B) A final version of the notice
    (C) A completed submission form
    (D) A letter from an organization

24. In which of the positions marked [1], [2], [3] and [4] does the following sentence best belong?
    "The name and telephone number of the person posting the notice must be clearly marked on the back."
    (A) [1]
    (B) [2]
    (C) [3]
    (D) [4]

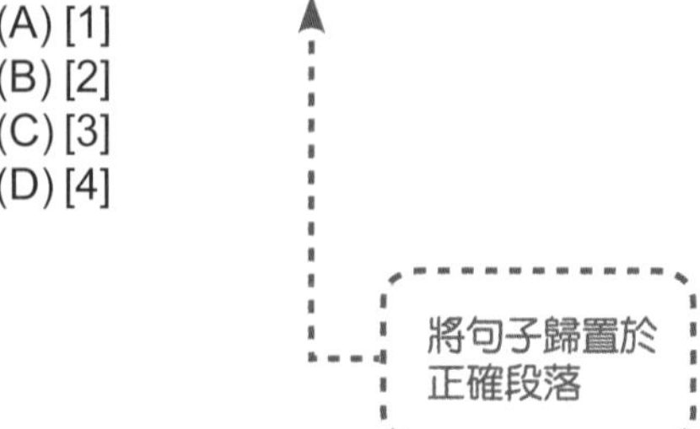

解說和翻譯 **請參考以下訊息回答第 21 題至第 24 題。**

社區團體可使用的公告空間

Mooringtown 圖書館很高興地邀請在地社區團體，使用位於圖書館前門外新佈告欄上免費的廣告空間，公佈欄上的空間每次可供使用四周時間。

公告必須事先在圖書館櫃台獲得許可，同時必須符合下列條件。所有內容必須適合公告大眾，並以手寫或印刷方式，載明於 8.5 x 11 吋或是 5.5 x 8.5 吋的標準紙張上。請將希望展示公告的開始與結束時間寫在正面右下角，* 公告人的姓名與電話號碼必須清楚寫在背面。任何不符合以上條件的公告將無法納入考量而被棄之不用。

Mooringtown 圖書館櫃台現在已開始接受公告申請，請攜帶您希望呈現的公告格式正本前來。您將在一個工作天之內接到電話，確認您的公告已被加入公佈欄。

Mooringtown 圖書館
www.mooringtownlib.co.au

* 為 24 題的內文翻譯

21 **翻譯**

關於 Mooringtown 圖書館公佈欄的廣告欄位，從文中可以得知什麼？

(A) 它可以免費使用。
(B) 它可以無限期使用。
(C) 它開放給所有領域的企業使用。
(D) 它主要供體育活動使用。

正解 (A)

在第一段第一句中出現了 the free advertising space「免費的廣告空間」的說明。

22 **翻譯**

對於放在公佈欄上的告示，哪一項不是必要條件？

(A) 它必須是特定尺寸。
(B) 它必須註明張貼時間。
(C) 它必須經過事前審閱。
(D) 它必須有圖書館員的簽名。

正解 (D)

公告的條件出現在第二段中，其中並未提到需要圖書館員簽名。

23 **翻譯**

若有人要提交公告，應該要帶什麼去圖書館？

(A) 提交內容的大綱
(B) 公告的最終版本
(C) 填寫好的提交表單
(D) 某企業團體的信件

正解 (B)

第三段第二句有「請攜帶您希望呈現的公告格式正本前來」。

24 **翻譯**

下列句子最適合出現在 [1]、[2]、[3] 或 [4] 的哪個位置？

「公告人的姓名與電話號碼必須清楚寫在背面。」

(A) [1]
(B) [2]
(C) [3]
(D) [4]

正解 (A)

插入的句子內容為公告條件，說明公告背面需記載的資訊，因此放在公告正面應記載資訊後的 [1] 最為合適。

例題 **Questions 25-29 refer to the following advertisement, online shopping cart, and e-mail.**

1. 廣告

Sparky Paints, Inc., makes it easy to select the right colors for your home. Browse through hundreds of colors on our Web site, www.sparkypaints.com. Select your top colors, and we'll send free samples right to your door. Our color samples are three times larger than typical samples found in home-improvement stores and come with self-adhesive backing, allowing you to adhere them to your walls so you can easily see how colors will coordinate in your home. When you're ready to begin painting, simply select your chosen colors online, and we'll ship the paint of your choice to arrive at your home within 3-5 business days, or within 2 business days for an additional expedited shipping fee.

*Actual colors may differ slightly from what appears on your monitor. For this reason, we recommend ordering several samples in similar shades.

2. 線上購物車

www.sparkypaints.com/shoppingcart

Order Summary #3397 **Customer:** Arun Phan

Item	Size	Quantity	Price
Caspian Blue SP 237	n/a	1	$0.00
Deep Sea Blue SP 298	n/a	1	$0.00
Stormy Blue SP 722	n/a	1	$0.00
Misty Gray SP 944	Gallon	2	$50.00
Tax (8 percent)			$4.00
Expedited shipping			$18.99
Total			$72.99

Proceed to Checkout

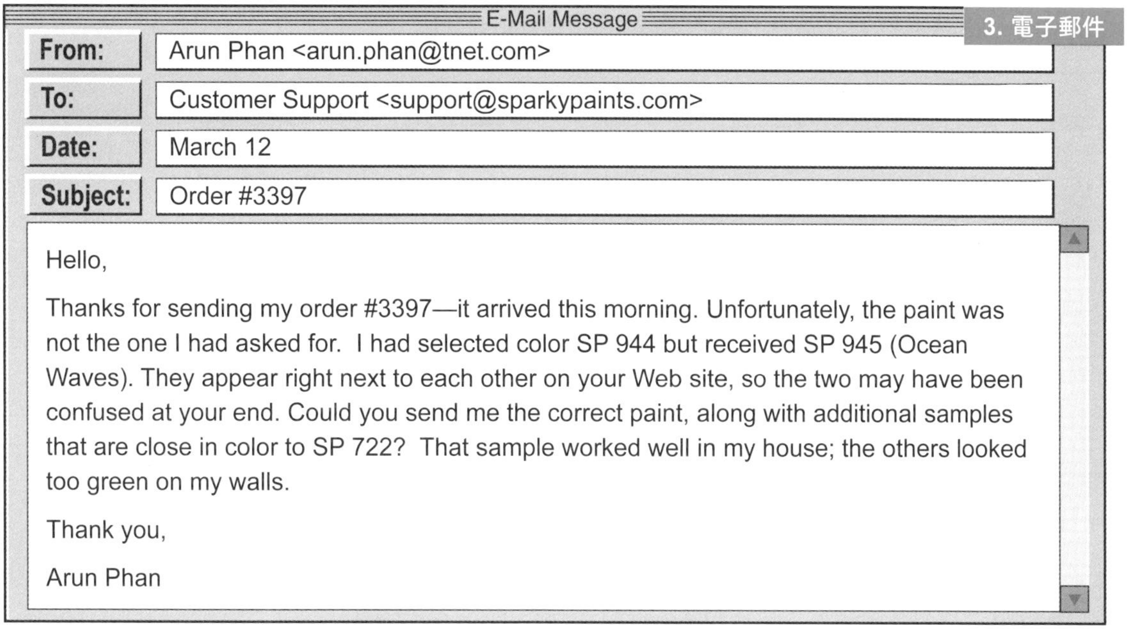

E-Mail Message

3. 電子郵件

From: Arun Phan <arun.phan@tnet.com>

To: Customer Support <support@sparkypaints.com>

Date: March 12

Subject: Order #3397

Hello,

Thanks for sending my order #3397—it arrived this morning. Unfortunately, the paint was not the one I had asked for. I had selected color SP 944 but received SP 945 (Ocean Waves). They appear right next to each other on your Web site, so the two may have been confused at your end. Could you send me the correct paint, along with additional samples that are close in color to SP 722? That sample worked well in my house; the others looked too green on my walls.

Thank you,

Arun Phan

25. In the advertisement, the word "top" in paragraph 1, line 2, is closest in meaning to
    (A) maximum
    (B) favorite
    (C) important
    (D) upper

26. What are Sparky Paints customers advised to do?
    (A) Apply an adhesive to color samples
    (B) Visit a store to compare paint colors
    (C) Adjust the color on their computer monitors
    (D) Order samples of several similar colors

27. What is most likely true about order #3397?
    (A) It arrived within two business days.
    (B) It included an extra sample.
    (C) It was shipped in February.
    (D) It contained four gallons of paint.

28. Which color does Mr. Phan indicate that he likes?
    (A) Caspian Blue
    (B) Deep Sea Blue
    (C) Stormy Blue
    (D) Misty Gray

29. What problem did Mr. Phan mention in his e-mail?
    (A) He received the wrong item.
    (B) He was charged the wrong price.
    (C) The delivery time was too long.
    (D) The instructions were too confusing.

根據三篇相關的文章作答

解說和翻譯 **請參考以下的廣告、線上購物車和電子郵件回答第 25 題至第 29 題。**

Sparky 油漆公司讓挑選家裡的色彩變得更為輕鬆，您可以在我們的網站上 www.sparkypaints.com 瀏覽數百種色彩，挑選出您想要的顏色，我們會將免費樣品送到您家。我們的色彩樣品較一般家居裝潢店裡的樣品大上三倍，並附有自黏背板，讓您可以將樣品黏附在牆上，清楚地看到該色彩與您家中的搭配程度如何。當您準備好開始油漆時，只要在網上選擇您挑好的顏色，我們便會在三到五個工作天內，將您挑選的油漆送到家中。若是支付額外快送運費，則可於二個工作天內寄達。

* 實際顏色可能與您在電腦螢幕上看到的略有色差，因此我們建議您挑選數種顏色相近的樣品。

www.sparkypaints.com/shoppingcart

訂購清單 #3397 **顧客：Arun Phan**

商品	尺寸	數量	價錢
裡海藍 SP 237	不適用	1	0 元美金
深海藍 SP 298	不適用	1	0 元美金
暴風藍 SP 722	不適用	1	0 元美金
霧色灰 SP 944	加侖	2	50 元美金
稅（8%）			4 元美金
快送運費			18.99 元美金
總金額			72.99 元美金

結帳

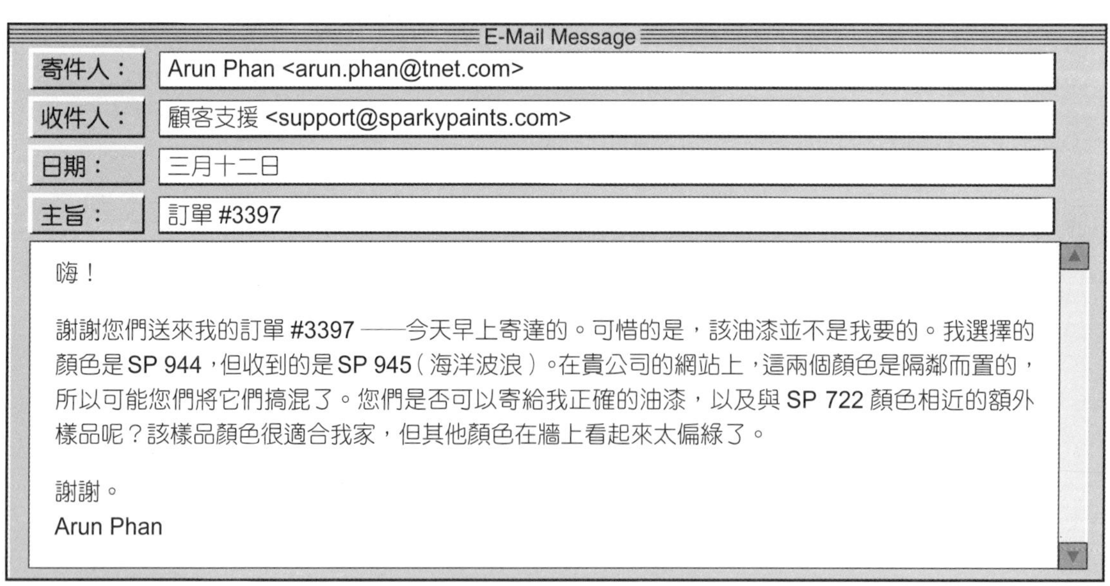
E-Mail Message

寄件人：Arun Phan <arun.phan@tnet.com>

收件人：顧客支援 <support@sparkypaints.com>

日期：三月十二日

主旨：訂單 #3397

嗨！

謝謝您們送來我的訂單 #3397 ——今天早上寄達的。可惜的是，該油漆並不是我要的。我選擇的顏色是 SP 944，但收到的是 SP 945（海洋波浪）。在貴公司的網站上，這兩個顏色是隔鄰而置的，所以可能您們將它們搞混了。您們是否可以寄給我正確的油漆，以及與 SP 722 顏色相近的額外樣品呢？該樣品顏色很適合我家，但其他顏色在牆上看起來太偏綠了。

謝謝。
Arun Phan

25 翻譯

在第一篇的廣告中，第一段第二行的「top」一字意思最接近以下的

(A) 最大量的
(B) 最喜歡的
(C) 重要的
(D) 上面的

正解 (B)

top 的意思是「最好的」，在文中指「對顧客來說最好的」，也就是「顧客最喜歡的」。

26 翻譯

Sparky 油漆公司的顧客被建議要做些什麼？

(A) 在色彩樣品上塗黏著劑。
(B) 拜訪店家好比較油漆顏色。
(C) 在電腦螢幕上調整顏色。
(D) 訂購數種顏色相近的樣品。

正解 (D)

在第一篇的廣告中，最後有註記「建議您挑選數種顏色相近的樣品」。

27 翻譯

關於 #3397 的訂單，以下何者最有可能是真的？

(A) 這批貨在兩個工作天內送達。
(B) 這批貨包含了一份額外的樣品。
(C) 這批貨是在二月運來的。
(D) 這批貨包含了四加侖的油漆。

正解 (A)

在第一篇廣告的本文最後，出現了「支付額外快送運費可在二個工作天內將油漆送達」。而在第二篇的線上購物車中，可看見支付了 Expedited shipping「快送運費」的項目，由此可推斷訂購貨物會在二個工作天內送達。

28 翻譯

Phan 先生喜歡的是哪種顏色？

(A) 裡海藍
(B) 深海藍
(C) 暴風藍
(D) 霧色灰

正解 (C)

在第三篇電子郵件的第五、六句中，Phan 先生要求對方額外提供與 SP 722 相近的顏色樣品，並說了「該樣品顏色很適合我家」。再透過第二篇線上購物車的內容可得知，SP 722 是 (C) Stormy Blue。

29 翻譯

Phan 先生在電子郵件中提到了什麼問題？

(A) 他收到錯誤的商品。
(B) 他被收取錯誤的金額。
(C) 送貨時間太久。
(D) 說明太令人困惑。

正解 (A)

第三篇電子郵件中的第二句，出現了「該油漆並不是我要的」。

收錄兩套完整全真試題聽力測驗，音檔音軌獨立，可用電腦、手機播放

請輸入網址

https://publishing.chunshin.com.tw/download/TOEIC_LR_OG6

或用手機掃描QR Code，輸入下載碼後，即可下載MP3音檔聆聽。

下載碼： 13a052b1e5

桌上型或筆記型電腦下載

1. 請在瀏覽器輸入上述網址，進入本書音檔下載網頁。
2. 在右方的空白方框內輸入「下載碼」後，點擊「登入下載」。
3. 閱讀「音檔下載使用同意書」並點選「同意」後，點擊右方「下載」按鈕，開始下載。
4. 下載檔案解壓縮後，即可在解壓縮後的資料夾中看到聽力測驗題目MP3音檔，請對照書中目錄或題號旁的耳機圖示，依圖示的數字找到對應的題目。

手機或平板電腦下載

1. 掃描QR Code或於瀏覽器輸入上述網址，進入本書音檔下載網頁。
2. 輸入「下載碼」並點擊「登入下載」。
3. 閱讀「音檔下載使用同意書」並點選「同意」按鈕。
4. 下載
   - **iOS裝置**：請點擊「下載」，待下載完成後，至資料夾中的「下載項目」，點擊所下載的zip檔解壓縮。
   - **Android裝置**：請點擊「下載」，選擇儲存路徑並下載後，至「下載管理員」或儲存路徑，點擊所下載的zip檔解壓縮。
5. 在解壓縮後的資料夾中看到聽力測驗題目MP3音檔，請對照書中目錄或題號旁的耳機圖示，依圖示的數字找到對應的題目。

※注意事項

1. 不支援Windows XP、Windows 7、Windows 8、Internet Explorer（IE）所有版本。
2. 每組「下載碼」可跨裝置、跨平台使用，共能下載5次。
3. 音檔下載有任何疑問，請來信客服信箱：publishing@examservice.com.tw

TEST 1

MP3 10-90

 10

LISTENING TEST

In the Listening test, you will be asked to demonstrate how well you understand spoken English. The entire Listening test will last approximately 45 minutes. There are four parts, and directions are given for each part. You must mark your answers on the separate answer sheet. Do not write your answers in your test book.

PART 1

Directions: For each question in this part, you will hear four statements about a picture in your test book. When you hear the statements, you must select the one statement that best describes what you see in the picture. Then find the number of the question on your answer sheet and mark your answer. The statements will not be printed in your test book and will be spoken only one time.

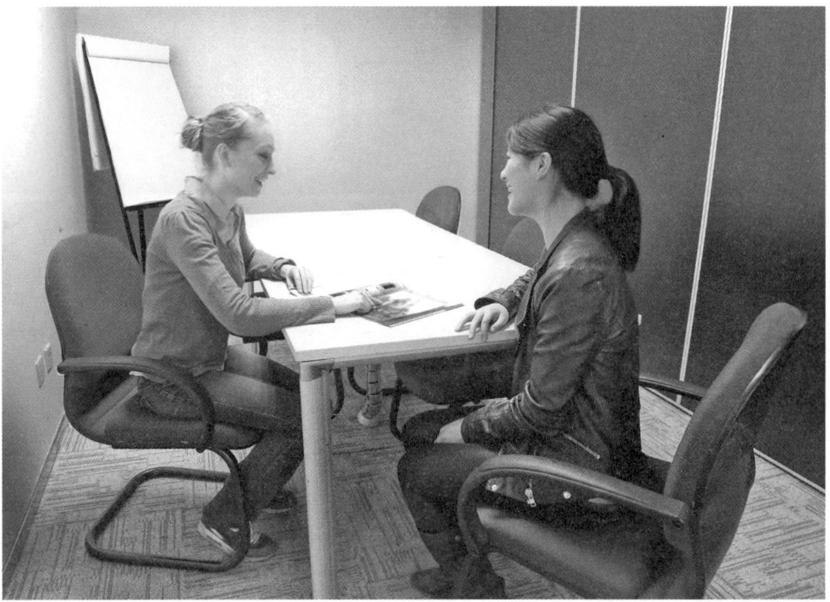

Statement (C), "They're sitting at a table," is the best description of the picture, so you should select answer (C) and mark it on your answer sheet.

1.

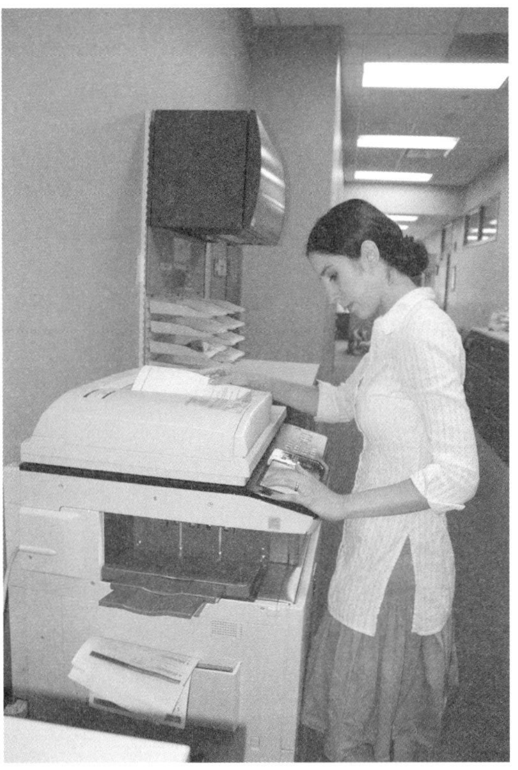

2.

Go on to the next page.

3.

4.

5.

6.

Go on to the next page.

 17

PART 2

Directions: You will hear a question or statement and three responses spoken in English. They will not be printed in your test book and will be spoken only one time. Select the best response to the question or statement and mark the letter (A), (B), or (C) on your answer sheet.

7. Mark your answer on your answer sheet.
8. Mark your answer on your answer sheet.
9. Mark your answer on your answer sheet.
10. Mark your answer on your answer sheet.
11. Mark your answer on your answer sheet.
12. Mark your answer on your answer sheet.
13. Mark your answer on your answer sheet.
14. Mark your answer on your answer sheet.
15. Mark your answer on your answer sheet.
16. Mark your answer on your answer sheet.
17. Mark your answer on your answer sheet.
18. Mark your answer on your answer sheet.
19. Mark your answer on your answer sheet.
20. Mark your answer on your answer sheet.
21. Mark your answer on your answer sheet.
22. Mark your answer on your answer sheet.
23. Mark your answer on your answer sheet.
24. Mark your answer on your answer sheet.
25. Mark your answer on your answer sheet.
26. Mark your answer on your answer sheet.
27. Mark your answer on your answer sheet.
28. Mark your answer on your answer sheet.
29. Mark your answer on your answer sheet.
30. Mark your answer on your answer sheet.
31. Mark your answer on your answer sheet.

43

PART 3

Directions: You will hear some conversations between two or more people. You will be asked to answer three questions about what the speakers say in each conversation. Select the best response to each question and mark the letter (A), (B), (C), or (D) on your answer sheet. The conversations will not be printed in your test book and will be spoken only one time.

32. Where most likely is the conversation taking place?
(A) In a clothing store
(B) In a furniture factory
(C) In a restaurant
(D) In a dry-cleaning shop

33. What is the problem?
(A) Some merchandise has been lost.
(B) Some clothing is the wrong size.
(C) An item is damaged.
(D) An order has not arrived.

34. What does the man offer to do?
(A) Issue a refund
(B) Reduce a price
(C) Speak to a manager
(D) Check the inventory

---

35. Where most likely does the woman work?
(A) At an airport
(B) At a bicycle shop
(C) At a train station
(D) At a taxi stand

36. Why is the man calling?
(A) To find out the hours of operation
(B) To schedule a service
(C) To reserve a ticket
(D) To inquire about a delay

37. What does the woman say will cost extra?
(A) Transporting a bicycle
(B) Traveling during rush hour
(C) Changing a reservation
(D) Upgrading to business class

---

38. What does the man want to do?
(A) Sign up for membership
(B) Use a computer
(C) Make a telephone call
(D) Borrow some materials

39. Who most likely is the woman?
(A) A librarian
(B) A security guard
(C) A software developer
(D) A salesperson

40. What does the woman say she will give the man?
(A) An application form
(B) An Internet address
(C) A business card
(D) A temporary password

---

41. What does the woman mention about the Selwin 6?
(A) It is easy to use.
(B) It is an earlier model.
(C) It is well designed.
(D) It is very popular.

42. What does the man request?
(A) A warranty
(B) A reimbursement
(C) A replacement part
(D) An instruction manual

43. What does the woman offer to do?
(A) Reset a password
(B) Explain a policy
(C) Check part of an order
(D) Send a link to a Web site

Go on to the next page.

44. What are the speakers discussing?
(A) A real estate loan
(B) A ride-sharing initiative
(C) A company budget
(D) A hiring plan

45. What does the man say about the office space?
(A) It has become too small.
(B) It is in a good location.
(C) The rent has gone up.
(D) The lobby is outdated.

46. What would the speakers like employees to do?
(A) Help pay for parking
(B) Work a weekend shift
(C) Vote on a policy change
(D) Create training materials

---

47. Why does the woman talk to the man?
(A) To offer him a ride
(B) To invite him to an event
(C) To discuss a work assignment
(D) To ask for his assistance

48. What does the woman say is important?
(A) Reviewing a schedule
(B) Arriving by a certain time
(C) Parking nearby
(D) Checking a ticket

49. What does the man agree to do?
(A) Join a group
(B) Help with some work
(C) Calculate a cost
(D) Reserve some seats

---

50. What type of service does the woman's company provide?
(A) Career counseling
(B) Home improvement
(C) Garden landscaping
(D) Web site design

51. What does the man say he wants to do tomorrow?
(A) Make a payment
(B) Review a document
(C) Redecorate an office
(D) Meet with a consultant

52. What information does the woman request?
(A) The size of a room
(B) The name of the man's friend
(C) The number of people in a group
(D) The start date of renovations

---

53. Why did the man come to Miami?
(A) To see some relatives
(B) To open a business
(C) To do some sightseeing
(D) To take cooking classes

54. What does the woman mean when she says,"we could use some help in the kitchen"?
(A) She enjoys her work in the kitchen.
(B) She may have work to offer the man.
(C) The restaurant is undergoing changes.
(D) Some staff need further training.

55. What will the woman do next?
(A) Make a reservation
(B) Look for an employee
(C) Show the man a menu
(D) Take a customer's order

---

56. Where do the speakers most likely work?

(A) At a research laboratory
(B) At a construction company
(C) At a nature park
(D) At a real estate agency

57. What does the man mean when he says, "I've been meaning to contact them"?

(A) He is looking forward to discussing a project.
(B) He needs to clarify a statement.
(C) He is aware he needs to do something.
(D) He has forgotten to contact a client.

58. What will the woman include in her e-mail?

(A) An updated list of assignments
(B) Results from a recent customer survey
(C) An estimate of additional costs
(D) An explanation for a delay in setting a date

---

59. What are the speakers mainly discussing?

(A) Ways to reduce a travel budget
(B) Places to visit in Vancouver
(C) Possible locations for a conference
(D) Plans for an upcoming business trip

60. What problem do the speakers have?

(A) Their business cards have not arrived.
(B) Their reservations are for the wrong dates.
(C) Their transportation arrangements are not complete.
(D) Their client in Vancouver is unavailable.

61. What does the woman suggest they do?

(A) Cancel an order
(B) Contact a hotel
(C) Prepare a speech
(D) Postpone a decision

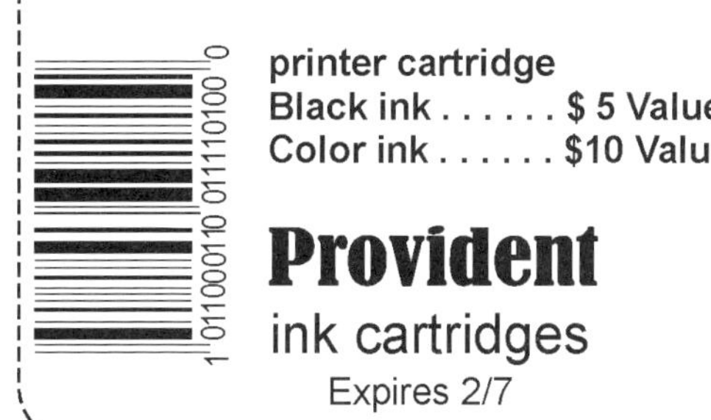

62. What problem does the woman mention?

(A) An item she purchased is defective.
(B) She cannot locate a product.
(C) A sale price seems incorrect.
(D) An expiration date has passed.

63. What does the man say recently happened?

(A) Merchandise was rearranged.
(B) Flyers were distributed.
(C) An order was delayed.
(D) A service was discontinued.

64. Look at the graphic. What discount will the woman most likely receive?

(A) $2
(B) $5
(C) $7
(D) $10

TEST 1

Go on to the next page.

Office Directory

1st FL: HLT Company

2nd FL: Noble Incorporated

3rd FL: Romano Construction

4th FL: Grayton and Sons

65. Who most likely are the speakers?
(A) Carpet installers
(B) Interior designers
(C) Cleaning staff
(D) Office receptionists

66. Look at the graphic. Where is the man currently working?
(A) On the first floor
(B) On the second floor
(C) On the third floor
(D) On the fourth floor

67. What are the speakers probably going to do next?
(A) Move a table
(B) Fix a machine
(C) Look at some plans
(D) Make a conference call

Name	Comment
1. Carol Lee	Dirty seat
2. Jean Harvey	No discount
3. Eun-Jung Choi	Web site down
4. Kinu Iizuka	Late to destination

68. Where do the speakers most likely work?
(A) At a shipping company
(B) At an engineering firm
(C) At a taxi company
(D) At a railway station

69. Look at the graphic. Which customer are the speakers discussing?
(A) Carol Lee
(B) Jean Harvey
(C) Eun-Jung Choi
(D) Kinu Iizuka

70. What will the speakers do next?
(A) Look at fuel prices
(B) Review customer complaints
(C) Update staffing schedules
(D) Organize training programs

PART 4

Directions: You will hear some talks given by a single speaker. You will be asked to answer three questions about what the speaker says in each talk. Select the best response to each question and mark the letter (A), (B), (C), or (D) on your answer sheet. The talks will not be printed in your test book and will be spoken only one time.

71. What type of service does the speaker provide?
(A) Food preparation
(B) Cooking lessons
(C) Grocery delivery
(D) Nutritional counseling

72. What information does the speaker need from the listener?
(A) The time of a lunch
(B) The location for a delivery
(C) The size of an order
(D) The theme of a banquet

73. When should the listener return the call?
(A) Later today
(B) Tomorrow
(C) Next week
(D) In one month

---

74. Why is the listener going overseas?
(A) To attend a sales conference
(B) To manage an office
(C) To meet some clients
(D) To go on a tour

75. What does the speaker plan to do first?
(A) Organize a business dinner
(B) Reserve airline seats
(C) Purchase some merchandise
(D) Contact a moving company

76. What does the speaker have to confirm?
(A) Travel dates
(B) Account information
(C) A passport number
(D) Vaccination requirements

---

77. What is the main purpose of the event?
(A) To celebrate successful sales
(B) To exhibit course projects
(C) To advertise a clothing store
(D) To recruit new teachers

78. According to the speaker, what can be found in the leaflet?
(A) Dates of future shows
(B) Names of event organizers
(C) Information about materials
(D) Instructions for enrollment

79. What is scheduled to happen at the end of the event?
(A) A celebrity will appear on stage.
(B) Some creations will be sold at auction.
(C) A reception will be held in a different room.
(D) Students will answer questions about their work.

---

80. What is the purpose of the announcement?
(A) To review a budget proposal
(B) To discuss an upcoming merger
(C) To explain some survey results
(D) To introduce new staff members

81. What does the woman mean when she says, “And why wouldn’t we”?
(A) She supports a decision.
(B) She hopes to relocate.
(C) She wants listeners to share their opinions.
(D) She feels concerned about a shipment.

82. What does the woman ask listeners to do?
(A) Attend a training
(B) Sign some paperwork
(C) Gather a list of questions
(D) Review some information online

Go on to the next page.

83. What does Hamson College specialize in?

(A) Teacher training
(B) Industrial design
(C) Computer programming
(D) Business management

84. According to the advertisement, what do students like about Hamson College?

(A) The quality of the instruction
(B) The flexible scheduling
(C) The low tuition costs
(D) The work experience opportunities

85. What will happen on August 17?

(A) A reading group will meet.
(B) Students will graduate.
(C) An information session will be held.
(D) The registration period will end.

---

86. Why is the woman calling?

(A) To express her gratitude
(B) To ask for a favor
(C) To discuss an assignment
(D) To report some good news

87. What does the woman imply when she says, "You have got to tell me where you found the recipe"?

(A) She wonders if some ingredients are local.
(B) She would like to make the dish herself.
(C) She needs a restaurant recommendation.
(D) She cannot find a recipe in a cookbook.

88. Why is the woman looking forward to Monday?

(A) She is going to see a play.
(B) She is taking a friend to lunch.
(C) Some results will be available.
(D) A new project will start.

---

89. According to the speaker, what is happening today?

(A) An ad campaign is being launched.
(B) A store is opening a new branch.
(C) A product is being released in stores.
(D) A clearance sale is beginning.

90. What does the speaker mean when he says, "From the look of it, you'd think they were giving the phones away"?

(A) The store's advertising is misleading.
(B) Some products are no longer in stock.
(C) There are a lot of customers waiting at the store.
(D) There are many good bargains at the store.

91. According to the speaker, what feature of the Aria 7D is most attractive?

(A) Its water resistance
(B) Its affordable price
(C) Its colorful patterns
(D) Its slim design

---

92. What does the speaker want to focus on this year?

(A) Increasing staff numbers
(B) Targeting smaller businesses
(C) Reducing operating costs
(D) Attracting new clients

93. What does the speaker request help with?

(A) Greeting clients
(B) Collecting payments
(C) Gathering data
(D) Locating résumés

94. What will the listeners receive by e-mail?

(A) A work schedule
(B) A confirmation number
(C) A sample report
(D) An employee roster

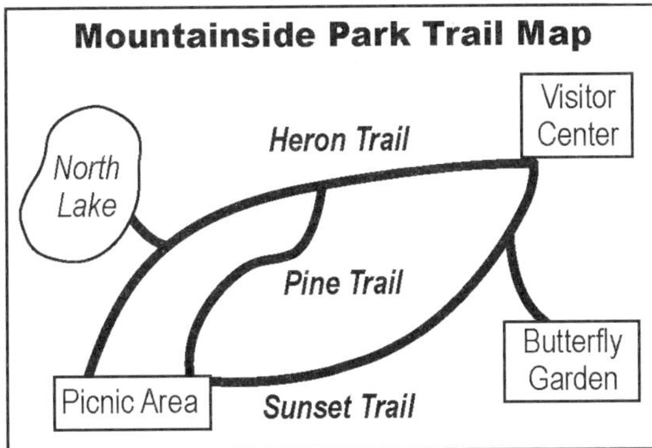

95. Who most likely are the listeners?
(A) Maintenance workers
(B) Bus drivers
(C) Tourists
(D) Park rangers

96. Look at the graphic. Where will the listeners be unable to go today?
(A) The North Lake
(B) The Picnic Area
(C) The Butterfly Garden
(D) The Visitor Center

97. What does the woman encourage the listeners to do?
(A) Bring a map
(B) Check the weather forecast
(C) Store their belongings
(D) Use sun protection

ORDER FORM

Item	Order more?	Quantity to Order
Drafting tables		—
Whiteboards		—
Desk chairs	✓	9
Adjustable lamps		—

98. Look at the graphic. Which department filled out the order form?
(A) Maintenance
(B) Accounting
(C) Human Resources
(D) Public Relations

99. What does the speaker anticipate may happen?
(A) A project may not be completed on time.
(B) Some measurements may be incorrect.
(C) An order may be too small.
(D) There may not be enough available items.

100. What is the listener asked to do if she finds an error?
(A) Contact her manager
(B) Submit a form
(C) Make a correction
(D) Keep a record

This is the end of the Listening test. Turn to Part 5 in your test book.

Go on to the next page.

READING TEST

In the Reading test, you will read a variety of texts and answer several different types of reading comprehension questions. The entire Reading test will last 75 minutes. There are three parts, and directions are given for each part. You are encouraged to answer as many questions as possible within the time allowed.

You must mark your answers on the separate answer sheet. Do not write your answers in your test book.

PART 5

Directions: A word or phrase is missing in each of the sentences below. Four answer choices are given below each sentence. Select the best answer to complete the sentence. Then mark the letter (A), (B), (C), or (D) on your answer sheet.

101. New patients should arrive fifteen minutes before ------- scheduled appointments.

(A) themselves
(B) their
(C) them
(D) they

102. The ------- version of the budget proposal must be submitted by Friday.

(A) total
(B) many
(C) final
(D) empty

103. Ms. Choi offers clients ------- tax preparation services and financial management consultations.

(A) only if
(B) either
(C) both
(D) not only

104. Maya Byun ------- by the executive team to head the new public relations department.

(A) chose
(B) choose
(C) was choosing
(D) was chosen

105. Belvin Theaters will ------- allow customers to purchase tickets on its Web site.

(A) yet
(B) since
(C) ever
(D) soon

106. AIZ Office Products offers businesses a ------- way to send invoices to clients online.

(A) secure
(B) securely
(C) securest
(D) secures

107. Because several committee members have been delayed, the accounting report will be discussed ------- than planned at today's meeting.

(A) late
(B) latest
(C) later
(D) lateness

108. According to the revised schedule, the manufacturing conference will begin at 9:00 A.M. ------- 8:00 A.M.

(A) now
(B) when
(C) due to
(D) instead of

109. While the station is undergoing repair, the train will proceed ------- Cumberland without stopping.

(A) aboard
(B) through
(C) quickly
(D) straight

110. Dr. Morales, a geologist from the Environmental Institute, plans to study the soil from the mountains ------- Caracas.

(A) out
(B) next
(C) onto
(D) around

111. If you have already signed up for automatic payments, ------- no further steps are required.

(A) even
(B) additional
(C) then
(D) until

112. Confident that Mr. Takashi Ota was ------- more qualified than other candidates, Argnome Corporation hired him as the new vice president.

(A) much
(B) very
(C) rarely
(D) along

113. Poleberry Local Marketplace takes pride in carrying only ------- processed dairy products from the region.

(A) nature
(B) natures
(C) natural
(D) naturally

114. All of Molina Language Institute's ------- have three or more years of experience and a valid teaching credential.

(A) instructed
(B) instruction
(C) instructing
(D) instructors

115. The restaurant critic for the *Montreal Times* ------- the food at Corban's Kitchen as affordable and authentic.

(A) ordered
(B) admitted
(C) described
(D) purchased

116. The Merrywood Shop will hold a sale in January to clear out an ------- of holiday supplies.

(A) excess
(B) overview
(C) extra
(D) opportunity

117. Zoticos Clothing, Inc., has acquired two other retail companies as part of a plan to expand ------- Europe and Asia.

(A) each
(B) into
(C) here
(D) already

118. According to the city planning director, Adelaide's old civic center must be ------- demolished before construction on a new center can begin.

(A) completely
(B) defectively
(C) plentifully
(D) richly

119. An accomplished skater -------, Mr. Loewenstein also coaches the world-champion figure skater Sara Krasnova.

(A) he
(B) him
(C) himself
(D) his

120. Sefu Asamoah is an innovative architect who is ------- the traditional approach to constructing space-efficient apartment buildings.

(A) challenge
(B) challenging
(C) challenged
(D) challenges

TEST 1

Go on to the next page.

121. Because of ------- regarding noise, the hotel manager has instructed the landscaping staff to avoid operating equipment before 9:30 A.M.

(A) complaints
(B) materials
(C) opponents
(D) symptoms

122. For 30 years, Big Top Prop Company has been the premier ------- of circus equipment for troupes around the world.

(A) providing
(B) provision
(C) provider
(D) provides

123. Chris Cantfield was ------- the outstanding candidates considered for the Thomas Award for exceptional police service.

(A) on
(B) among
(C) during
(D) up

124. Please instruct employees with questions concerning the new payroll policy to contact ------- or Ms. Singh directly.

(A) my
(B) mine
(C) me
(D) I

125. Although the author ------- presents the purchase of real estate as a safe investment, she later describes times that it might be risky.

(A) highly
(B) afterward
(C) quite
(D) initially

126. The research released by Henford Trust ranked automobile companies according to sales ------- and financial position.

(A) performed
(B) performing
(C) performance
(D) performer

127. An insightful ------- in the *Boston Daily Post* suggests that offering opportunities for professional development is a valuable method of motivating employees.

(A) editorial
(B) novel
(C) catalog
(D) directory

128. The Web site advises customers to review their orders carefully as it is difficult to make changes ------- an order is submitted.

(A) following
(B) once
(C) right away
(D) by means of

129. Well-known journalist Kent Moriwaki published a book in May ------- a compilation of quotes from interviews with various artists.

(A) featuring
(B) featured
(C) feature
(D) features

130. ------- delays in the entryway construction, the Orchid Restaurant in Chongqing will reopen and provide an alternative entrance until all work is complete.

(A) Furthermore
(B) Assuming that
(C) Regardless of
(D) Subsequently

PART 6

Directions: Read the texts that follow. A word, phrase, or sentence is missing in parts of each text. Four answer choices for each question are given below the text. Select the best answer to complete the text. Then mark the letter (A), (B), (C), or (D) on your answer sheet.

Questions 131-134 refer to the following e-mail.

To: Sunil Pai <sp8410@xmail.co.uk>

From: Fabrizio Donetti <customerservice@palazzadesign.co.uk>

Date: Friday, 1 July

Subject: Order #491001

Dear Mr. Pai:

Thank you for your recent order. -------(131.) the tan linen suit you ordered is unfortunately not available in your size at this time, we do have the same style in stock in light gray. -------(132.).

If you order now, we can offer you a 15% discount on the suit, as well as free shipping on your -------(133.) order, so you could have the items by next week. If you are interested, please e-mail our customer service department and reference the order number above.

We apologize for any inconvenience this may cause you. We -------(134.) forward to serving you and providing you with fashionable apparel in the future.

Sincerely,

Fabrizio Donetti

Customer Service Representative

131. (A) After
(B) Although
(C) Even
(D) When

132. (A) We could send you one of these right away.
(B) Thank you for returning them.
(C) These will be available early next season.
(D) You may exchange your new suits for a larger size.

133. (A) ready
(B) general
(C) entire
(D) thorough

134. (A) look
(B) looked
(C) were looking
(D) had been looking

Go on to the next page.

Questions 135-138 refer to the following notice.

For the first time, the Oakville Library is conducting a survey to learn how it can better -------
135. the needs of the public. The information gathered from the survey responses will help guide -------
136. five-year plan. -------
137. .

The survey can be completed online at www.oakvillelibrary.org/survey. Visitors can also pick up a -------
138. of this form at the circulation desk on the first floor. Library patrons are strongly encouraged to complete the survey. The Oakville Library is open Monday to Friday from 10:00 A.M. to 8:00 P.M. and Saturday and Sunday from 1:00 P.M. to 5:00 P.M. For more information, call 555-0130.

135. (A) met
(B) meet
(C) meeting
(D) meetings

136. (A) its
(B) his
(C) your
(D) theirs

137. (A) The questions are the same as those used five years ago.
(B) Patrons of the library are welcome to the event.
(C) Membership will be renewed after five years.
(D) This plan covers programming, services, and materials.

138. (A) placement
(B) showcase
(C) magazine
(D) copy

Questions 139-142 refer to the following notice.

-------(139.) . Starting this April, the North-South express train will no longer be stopping at Green Street Station. This will affect the express service only; local train service will continue uninterrupted to all stations on the North-South line, -------(140.) Green Street Station. Please speak with a conductor or visit our Web site if you have any questions.

Additionally, we would like to remind passengers to be -------(141.) to others at all times. An increasing number of passengers are expressing irritation with the level of -------(142.) . Please remain mindful of those around you and keep mobile phone use at a minimum when you ride the train.

Thank you for your cooperation and for riding Montego Metro.

139. (A) Montego Metro is announcing fare increases.
(B) Note that Green Street Station will soon close.
(C) New station facilities are available on this line.
(D) Please be advised of a change to train service.

140. (A) regarding
(B) including
(C) added to
(D) given that

141. (A) adjacent
(B) incompatible
(C) polite
(D) frequent

142. (A) noise
(B) expense
(C) precision
(D) personnel

TEST 1

Go on to the next page.

Questions 143-146 refer to the following letter.

Ms. Seema Nishad
Yadav Engineering Ltd.
7100 B-4 Pratap Bazar
Ludhiana 141003

Dear Ms. Nishad:

I am writing to invite you to participate in the India Materials Engineering Association's (IMEA) trade show this year. As always, the event will provide ------- (143.) opportunities for networking.

Many vendors have already reserved booths. However, there are other ways to ------- (144.) your company. Those who sponsor a meeting or provide refreshments receive special acknowledgment in the program.

Enclosed please find information regarding the trade show. It includes pricing ------- (145.) for reserving a booth, placing ads, and sponsoring an event, in addition to a list of past participants.

------- (146.). If you have questions, please contact me by e-mail.

Sincerely,

Manik Chaudhary
IMEA Vendor Coordinator
chaudhary@matengineer.org.in
Enclosure

143. (A) extend
(B) extends
(C) extensively
(D) extensive

144. (A) promote
(B) monitor
(C) construct
(D) negotiate

145. (A) markets
(B) details
(C) labels
(D) receipts

146. (A) We hope you decide to join us this year.
(B) We have placed your ad in the brochure.
(C) Your participation in the event will be at no cost.
(D) Your presentation is scheduled for the first day.

PART 7

Directions: In this part you will read a selection of texts, such as magazine and newspaper articles, e-mails, and instant messages. Each text or set of texts is followed by several questions. Select the best answer for each question and mark the letter (A), (B), (C), or (D) on your answer sheet.

Questions 147-148 refer to the following job announcement.

CORPORATE TRAINER WANTED

San Francisco-based Logistos Advisors, Inc., is seeking an energetic person with strong public-speaking skills to serve as a temporary replacement for an employee who is away on leave. Logistos delivers training classes on Internet security to large financial institutions and retail businesses worldwide. The successful applicant will be responsible for assisting with training sessions throughout Latin America. Although the sessions are delivered in English, proficiency in Spanish is necessary for the job. At least one year of experience as a corporate trainer in any field is highly desirable. The work assignment is for six months, the first two weeks to be spent at the Logistos headquarters for initial training. Interested candidates should submit a cover letter and résumé to hr@logistosadvisors.com by March 1.

147. What is NOT a stated requirement for the job?

(A) Experience working at a financial institution
(B) Ability to speak more than one language
(C) Willingness to travel internationally
(D) Public speaking skills

148. How long will the job last?

(A) Two weeks
(B) One month
(C) Six months
(D) One year

Go on to the next page.

Questions 149-150 refer to the following text message chain.

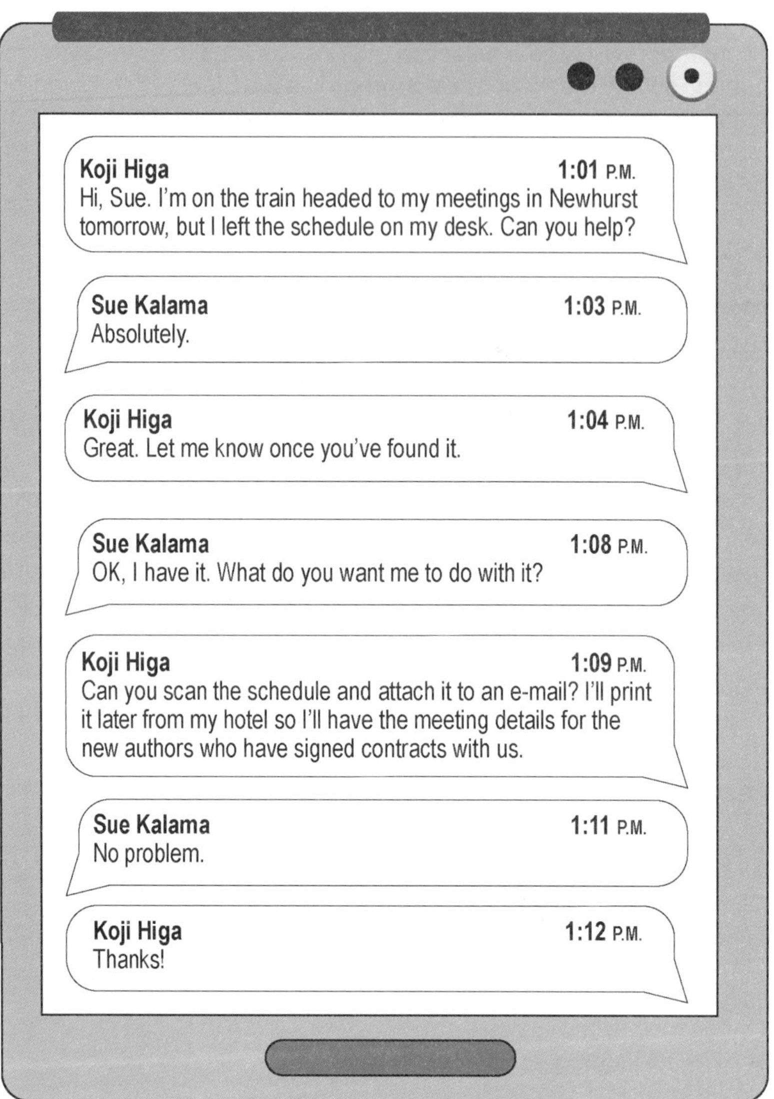

Koji Higa 1:01 P.M.
Hi, Sue. I'm on the train headed to my meetings in Newhurst tomorrow, but I left the schedule on my desk. Can you help?
Sue Kalama 1:03 P.M.
Absolutely.
Koji Higa 1:04 P.M.
Great. Let me know once you've found it.
Sue Kalama 1:08 P.M.
OK, I have it. What do you want me to do with it?
Koji Higa 1:09 P.M.
Can you scan the schedule and attach it to an e-mail? I'll print it later from my hotel so I'll have the meeting details for the new authors who have signed contracts with us.
Sue Kalama 1:11 P.M.
No problem.
Koji Higa 1:12 P.M.
Thanks!

149. At 1:03 P.M., what does Ms. Kalama mean when she writes, "Absolutely"?

(A) She is happy that Mr. Higa contacted her.
(B) She is willing to assist Mr. Higa.
(C) She is certain that Mr. Higa is correct.
(D) She is leaving her meeting now.

150. For what type of business does Mr. Higa most likely work?

(A) A publishing company
(B) A hotel chain
(C) A travel agency
(D) An office supply store

Questions 151-152 refer to the following document.

Browning's Shoe Repair

Order number: VG12983 **Drop-off date:** November 5

Customer: Janice Goldblatt **Contact number:** (873) 555-0143

Shoe description
Style: Lady's dress shoe **Size:** 7 **Color:** Black

Requested repair: Fix broken heel **Ready by:** November 14

Repair assigned to: Jack Burris

Notes:
Apply 10% frequent customer price reduction. Order will be picked up by Harry Silver.

151. Who most likely is Mr. Burris?
(A) Ms. Goldblatt's assistant
(B) A department store salesperson
(C) An employee at Browning's
(D) A delivery person

152. What does the document indicate about Ms. Goldblatt?
(A) She is ordering a new black dress.
(B) She will receive a discount.
(C) She will visit Browning's on November 14.
(D) She is attending a special event on November 5.

Go on to the next page.

Questions 153-154 refer to the following e-mail.

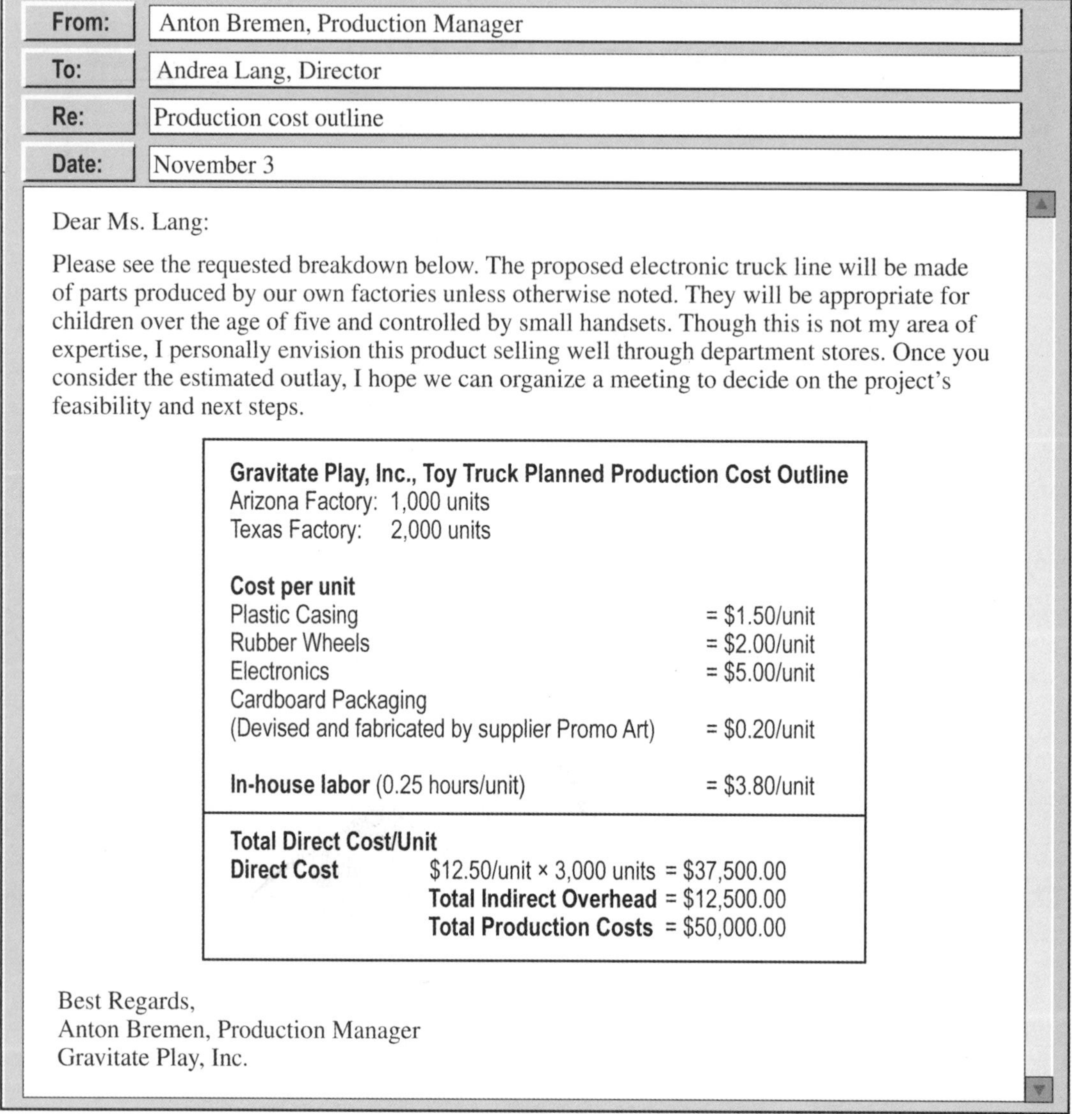

From:	Anton Bremen, Production Manager
To:	Andrea Lang, Director
Re:	Production cost outline
Date:	November 3

Dear Ms. Lang:

Please see the requested breakdown below. The proposed electronic truck line will be made of parts produced by our own factories unless otherwise noted. They will be appropriate for children over the age of five and controlled by small handsets. Though this is not my area of expertise, I personally envision this product selling well through department stores. Once you consider the estimated outlay, I hope we can organize a meeting to decide on the project's feasibility and next steps.

Gravitate Play, Inc., Toy Truck Planned Production Cost Outline
Arizona Factory: 1,000 units
Texas Factory: 2,000 units

Cost per unit	
Plastic Casing	= $1.50/unit
Rubber Wheels	= $2.00/unit
Electronics	= $5.00/unit
Cardboard Packaging (Devised and fabricated by supplier Promo Art)	= $0.20/unit
In-house labor (0.25 hours/unit)	= $3.80/unit

Total Direct Cost/Unit		
Direct Cost	$12.50/unit × 3,000 units	= $37,500.00
	Total Indirect Overhead	= $12,500.00
	Total Production Costs	= $50,000.00

Best Regards,
Anton Bremen, Production Manager
Gravitate Play, Inc.

153. Why is Mr. Bremen writing the e-mail?
(A) To ask for a review of proposed costs
(B) To report a problem with product pricing
(C) To argue for increasing an existing budget
(D) To support a bid from a product manufacturer

154. What is indicated about the product packaging?
(A) It is decorated with colors appropriate for children.
(B) It is made from recycled department store packaging.
(C) It is designed and produced by an outside vendor.
(D) It is an important component of the end product.

Questions 155-157 refer to the following article.

New Tasteemix Flavor a Big Hit

By Deepanjali Jaddoo

PORT LOUIS (2 February) — Three weeks ago, Helvetia Food Industries (HFI) announced the introduction of a new flavor of its popular Tasteemix breakfast cereal—coconut cream. — [1] —. HFI also announced that the product would be available for a limited time only, sending Tasteemix enthusiasts from Argentina to Zambia into a buying frenzy.

All six major grocery distributors here in Mauritius confirmed that they had received a large supply of coconut cream Tasteemix shortly after the new product was introduced on 8 January. — [2] —. Both wholesalers expected it to be gone by the end of the day.

"HFI's current campaign is reminiscent of the one it waged four years ago when it introduced its strawberry-cinnamon cereal," said Bina Perida, a professor of marketing at Port Louis Business College. "Then, as now, HFI announced a product as being offered for a limited time only, resulting in that item's rapid disappearance from shelves in grocery stores across the globe." — [3] —.

On 5 April, HFI's accountants will review the company's first-quarter earnings. Based on the initial sales, market watchers are confident that HFI's expectations will be met. — [4] —.

155. What is indicated about Tasteemix cereals?

(A) They are distributed internationally.
(B) They are made in a factory in Mauritius.
(C) They are HFI's main source of revenue.
(D) They were first marketed four years ago.

156. What is reported about HFI?

(A) It has no more Tasteemix cereal in stock.
(B) It hired a consulting firm to do its accounting.
(C) It expects this year's earnings to be better than last year's.
(D) It previously offered a product for a limited time only.

157. In which of the positions marked [1], [2], [3], and [4] does the following sentence best belong?

"Yet as of yesterday morning, only Vendibles and Foodiverse reported that they had any of the item left in stock."

(A) [1]
(B) [2]
(C) [3]
(D) [4]

TEST 1

Go on to the next page.

Questions 158-160 refer to the following memo

MEMO

Date: May 15

We would like to announce the upcoming retirement of Ken Esser. Mr. Esser began his 30-year career here at The Terra Fund as a wildlife ranger in the California Wildlife Park. He has held seven different positions, eventually becoming the general director of conservation for all West Coast Wildlife Parks. He has been in this position for the past 15 years, leading with vision and commitment. Now at the age of 65, he is leaving us for a well-deserved retirement.

The board of directors has voted to give him a Lifetime Achievement Award and will present him with a commemorative plaque at the staff meeting next Friday. Following the staff meeting, we invite all employees to stay for a reception to honor Mr. Esser and his great contributions. If you would like to write a farewell note to Mr. Esser, please stop by Andrew Braun's office to sign a book that will be presented at the reception.

158. In what field does Mr. Esser work?

(A) Youth education
(B) Historical archiving
(C) Nature conservation
(D) Urban development

159. For how many years has Mr. Esser worked at The Terra Fund?

(A) 7
(B) 15
(C) 30
(D) 65

160. What will NOT be given to honor Mr. Esser?

(A) A reception
(B) An award
(C) A book
(D) A photo album

Questions 161-164 refer to the following online chat discussion.

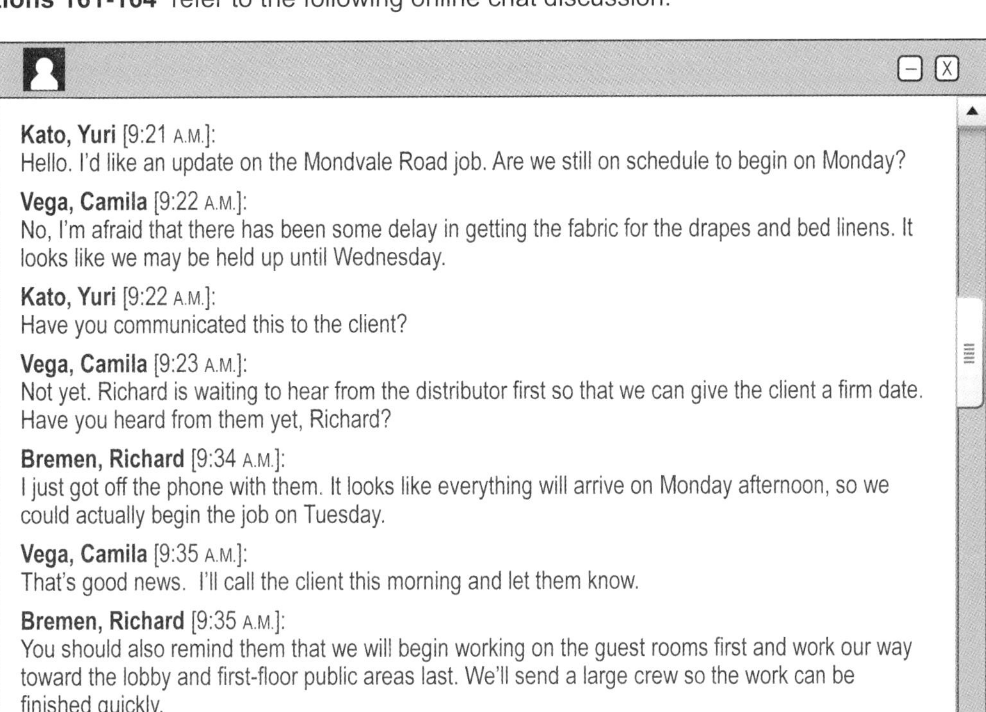

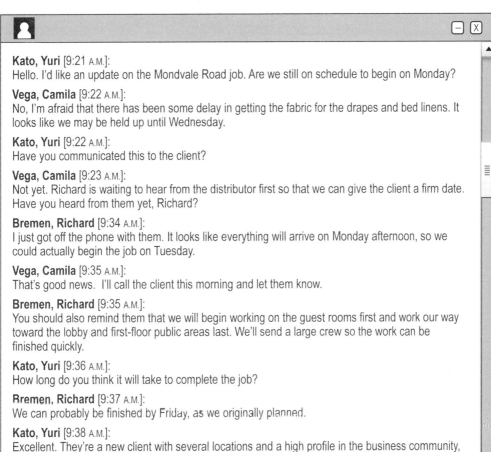

Kato, Yuri [9:21 A.M.]:
Hello. I'd like an update on the Mondvale Road job. Are we still on schedule to begin on Monday?

Vega, Camila [9:22 A.M.]:
No, I'm afraid that there has been some delay in getting the fabric for the drapes and bed linens. It looks like we may be held up until Wednesday.

Kato, Yuri [9:22 A.M.]:
Have you communicated this to the client?

Vega, Camila [9:23 A.M.]:
Not yet. Richard is waiting to hear from the distributor first so that we can give the client a firm date. Have you heard from them yet, Richard?

Bremen, Richard [9:34 A.M.]:
I just got off the phone with them. It looks like everything will arrive on Monday afternoon, so we could actually begin the job on Tuesday.

Vega, Camila [9:35 A.M.]:
That's good news. I'll call the client this morning and let them know.

Bremen, Richard [9:35 A.M.]:
You should also remind them that we will begin working on the guest rooms first and work our way toward the lobby and first-floor public areas last. We'll send a large crew so the work can be finished quickly.

Kato, Yuri [9:36 A.M.]:
How long do you think it will take to complete the job?

Bremen, Richard [9:37 A.M.]:
We can probably be finished by Friday, as we originally planned.

Kato, Yuri [9:38 A.M.]:
Excellent. They're a new client with several locations and a high profile in the business community, so I want things to go smoothly. I'm sure there will be more work with them in the long run if all goes well.

161. What kind of business does the client most likely own?
(A) A shipping company
(B) A fabric manufacturing factory
(C) A hotel chain
(D) A design firm

162. When will the crew begin work?
(A) On Monday
(B) On Tuesday
(C) On Wednesday
(D) On Friday

163. What will Ms. Vega most likely do next?
(A) Deliver a shipment of drapes
(B) Organize a large work crew
(C) Call the fabric distributor
(D) Contact the client

164. At 9:38 A.M., what does Ms. Kato mean when she writes, "in the long run"?
(A) She is pleased that the client is located nearby.
(B) She is proud of her company's history of high-quality performance.
(C) She believes that the work will be more expensive than expected.
(D) She thinks that there could be additional work with the client in the future.

Go on to the next page.

Questions 165-167 refer to the following instructions.

Perrybridge Office Furniture

Office Workstation Installation Manual

General Notes

- Always use the tools specified in the instructions when installing.
- Use eye protection when working with tools.
- Ensure that your work area is clean and clear of any potential obstructions to the installation.
- Wash hands before beginning the installation process.
- Parts weighing more than 15 kilograms are marked Heavy. Use two or more people when lifting or moving these items.
- Elements marked DS have one or more delicate surfaces. Handle these carefully to avoid scratching.
- If you have any questions, please see our Help section on perrybridgeoffice.com before contacting us through our online form. To receive the installation instructions in a language not available in this manual, please contact us at 497-555-0101.

165. What is described in the general notes?

(A) How to connect cubicle walls
(B) How to measure the office space
(C) How to operate the required tools
(D) How to prepare an area for installation

166. According to the instructions, what should people do before beginning to work?

(A) Wash their hands
(B) Make sure no parts are scratched
(C) Record the weight of each part
(D) Clean their tools

167. Why are people advised to call the listed number?

(A) To order additional parts
(B) To schedule a product installation
(C) To report a defective product
(D) To acquire a different version of the manual

Questions 168-171 refer to the following e-mail.

From:	<DDrabik@lowmaster.co.ca>
To:	<New Employees List>
Subject:	Welcome
Date:	May 28

The Lowmaster Toronto office is pleased to have such a promising group of new employees become part of our consulting team. Please review the company policies listed below and familiarize yourself with some important locations on our campus.

Personal computers may not be used to complete company work. If you need to work outside your offices in Dempsey Hall, visit the Information Technology Department to request a security-enabled laptop. Their office is located in the Russ Building in R-135.

The identification badges you received at orientation must be worn at all times; they provide access to the buildings on campus. If your identification badge is misplaced, contact the Security Desk immediately. The Security Desk is located in the Hadley Building in room H-290 and can be reached at extension 8645.

The cafeteria is located on the first floor in the Russ Building and is open until 2:30 P.M. The lounge in D-108 in Dempsey Hall is especially convenient for your breaks. Coffee, tea, juice, and light snacks are available in the lounge until 6:00 P.M. daily.

Brandt Library is located behind the Russ Building and can be accessed by way of the raised walkway connecting the two.

Finally, if you expect a package or important mail, you may notify the Shipping and Receiving Office at extension 8300 or stop by room R-004 in the basement of the Russ Building.

Sincerely,

Donald Drabik

168. What is the purpose of the e-mail?

(A) To assign work spaces to employees
(B) To explain employee compensation policies
(C) To arrange a company meeting
(D) To provide details to recently hired workers

169. The word "promising" in paragraph 1, line 1, is closest in meaning to

(A) pledging
(B) likely to succeed
(C) suggesting
(D) recently hired

170. Where is the Information Technology Department located?

(A) In the Russ Building
(B) In the Hadley Building
(C) In Dempsey Hall
(D) In Brandt Library

171. According to the e-mail, what is provided to all employees?

(A) A mailbox
(B) An approved laptop
(C) An identification badge
(D) A library card

Go on to the next page.

TEST 1

Questions 172-175 refer to the following letter.

Orangedale Press
54 Thompson Street
Sausalito, CA 94965
www.orangedalepress.com

September 19

Mr. Richard Tomase
89 Moreland Drive
Portland, OR 97205

Dear Mr. Tomase:

We at Orangedale Press are delighted that you have agreed to work with us again on an update of your book *Global Traveling: A Consumer's Guide*. Rest assured that we understand the ongoing paradigm shift in our field and are pleased that we can amend your previous contract with us to account for these changes. — [1] —. Since the original *Global Traveling* received such a warm reception in its target markets, we want to ensure that the updated version faithfully meets the needs and expectations of both new and returning readers. This new version will include electronic editions of your book in order for it to be more easily distributed and bring in the widest possible audience. — [2] —. All other provisions of the previous contract will remain unchanged, except for the adjustment to your royalty fees as we discussed.

— [3] —. The updated agreement is enclosed. Please initial the marked paragraphs if you approve, and then sign and date it. I would appreciate it if you could return it to me by October 1. — [4] —. Also, if you have not yet returned the author information form that my assistant mailed to you, you can send that in at the same time.

Thank you for attending to this matter in a timely manner and for your great contributions to the field of travel publishing. We value our authors, and we are honored to continue licensing the books we publish in both traditional and emerging formats.

Please contact me if you have any questions or concerns at all.

With very best regards,

Kathryn Lloyd

Kathryn Lloyd
Director, Orangedale Press

Enclosure

172. Why did Ms. Lloyd send the letter to Mr. Tomase?

(A) To request that he review a book
(B) To inquire about an itinerary
(C) To determine if he will sign some books
(D) To explain a modification to an agreement

173. What did Ms. Lloyd send with the letter?

(A) A revised contract
(B) An author information form
(C) An advance copy of a book
(D) A collection of book reviews

174. The phrase "attending to" in paragraph 3, line 1, is closest in meaning to

(A) planning to go to
(B) discovering of
(C) taking care of
(D) being present at

175. In which of the positions marked [1], [2], [3], and [4] does the following sentence best belong?

"A new chapter on travel in East Asia is also sure to draw much interest."

(A) [1]
(B) [2]
(C) [3]
(D) [4]

Go on to the next page.

Questions 176-180 refer to the following e-mail and document.

From:	Kana Saito <ksaito@kmail.com>
To:	Customer Service <CS@lantiauto.com>
Subject:	Request for information
Date:	September 16

To Whom It May Concern:

I currently lease a car from your company. However, I recently accepted a job in Memphis City, and I am going to start taking the bus. My lease agreement is number LA508. It is a month-to-month lease that automatically renews on the same day each month.

My new job starts on Tuesday, September 28, so ideally I would return the car to you on Monday, September 27. However, if the renewal date is earlier than that Monday, I would rather return the car at the end of the current month's contract and make other transportation arrangements until my new job starts.

Please let me know on what exact day of the month my lease ends and when I need to return the car.

Thank you

Kana Saito

List of Current Month-to-Month Lease Agreements

Agreement Number	Car Model	Cost per Month	Final Contract Date for Each Month
LA502	Cartif	$199	7
LA508	Sylvon	$211	25
LA513	Thundee	$159	28
LA519	Grayley	$249	14

*For lease termination, cars must be returned by 4 P.M. on the final contract date. Otherwise, the lease will automatically be extended for one additional month.

176. Why did Ms. Saito send the e-mail?

(A) To request a car rental
(B) To resign from a position
(C) To get information about a lease
(D) To inquire about available parking

177. What is suggested about Ms. Saito?

(A) She wants to sell her car.
(B) She lives near a train station.
(C) She has recently moved to a new city.
(D) She currently drives to work.

178. What type of car does Ms. Saito drive?

(A) A Cartif
(B) A Sylvon
(C) A Thundee
(D) A Grayley

179. When should Ms. Saito go to Lanti Auto?

(A) On September 7
(B) On September 14
(C) On September 25
(D) On September 28

180. What is indicated about month-to-month agreements?

(A) They may expire at 4 P.M. on the final contract date.
(B) They are available for one year at most.
(C) They all cost $199 per month.
(D) They include the cost of maintenance.

Go on to the next page.

Questions 181-185 refer to the following Web page and e-mail.

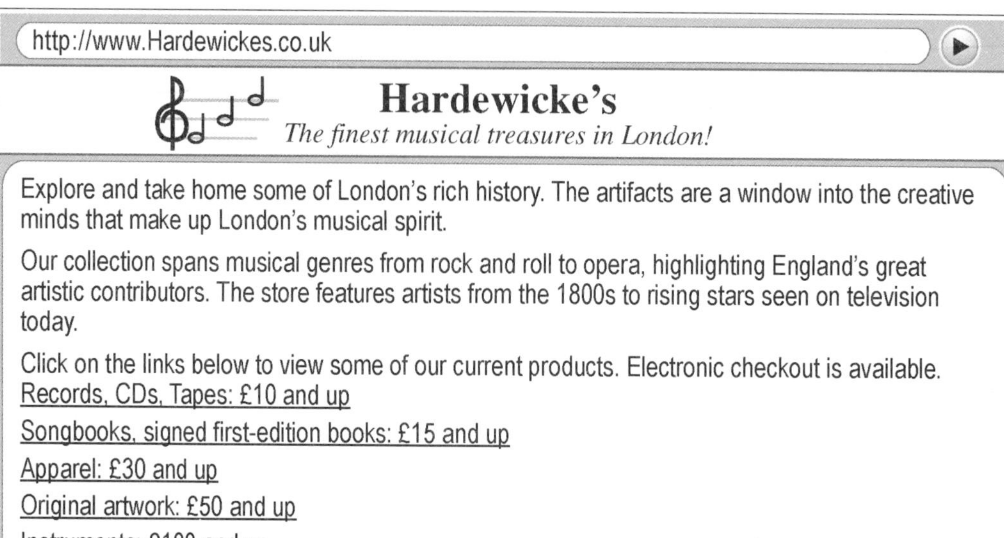

http://www.Hardewickes.co.uk

Hardewicke's

The finest musical treasures in London!

Explore and take home some of London's rich history. The artifacts are a window into the creative minds that make up London's musical spirit.

Our collection spans musical genres from rock and roll to opera, highlighting England's great artistic contributors. The store features artists from the 1800s to rising stars seen on television today.

Click on the links below to view some of our current products. Electronic checkout is available.

Records, CDs, Tapes: £10 and up

Songbooks, signed first-edition books: £15 and up

Apparel: £30 and up

Original artwork: £50 and up

Instruments: £100 and up

We have even more in our shop, and the best pieces are often bought before they make it to the Web site! For the full experience, please visit us.

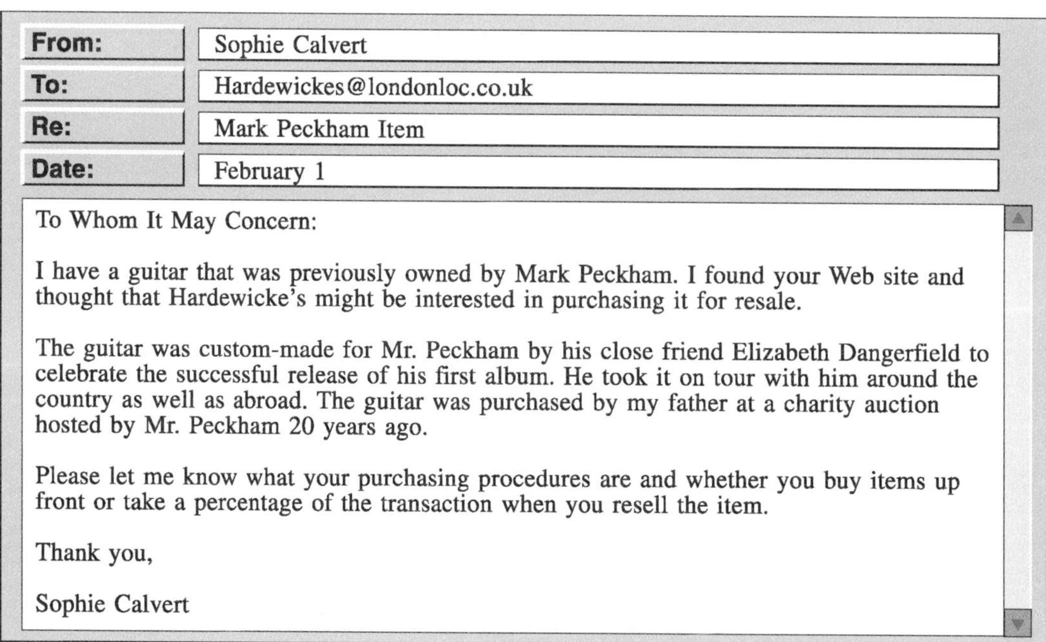

From: Sophie Calvert

To: Hardewickes@londonloc.co.uk

Re: Mark Peckham Item

Date: February 1

To Whom It May Concern:

I have a guitar that was previously owned by Mark Peckham. I found your Web site and thought that Hardewicke's might be interested in purchasing it for resale.

The guitar was custom-made for Mr. Peckham by his close friend Elizabeth Dangerfield to celebrate the successful release of his first album. He took it on tour with him around the country as well as abroad. The guitar was purchased by my father at a charity auction hosted by Mr. Peckham 20 years ago.

Please let me know what your purchasing procedures are and whether you buy items up front or take a percentage of the transaction when you resell the item.

Thank you,

Sophie Calvert

181. What is NOT suggested about Hardewicke's?

(A) It has items from many different years.
(B) Its products represent numerous types of music.
(C) It guarantees the lowest prices on records and songbooks.
(D) It features products from English musicians.

182. What is indicated about Hardewicke's?

(A) It was started by a musician.
(B) It plans to host a performance by Mr. Peckham.
(C) It advertises at concerts.
(D) It sells items directly from its Web site.

183. What is the lowest price Ms. Calvert's item would most likely sell for at Hardewicke's?

(A) £10
(B) £30
(C) £50
(D) £100

184. What is suggested about Ms. Calvert?

(A) She saw Mr. Peckham perform in England.
(B) She owns an item made by Ms. Dangerfield.
(C) She has previously worked with Hardewicke's.
(D) She would like to make a donation to her father's charity.

185. What does Ms. Calvert ask about?

(A) The price of an instrument she saw at the store
(B) The procedure for renting a concert space
(C) The process for selling items to Hardewicke's
(D) The history of an item she wants to purchase

Go on to the next page.

Questions 186-190 refer to the following list, schedule, and e-mail.

Books by James Trozelli

The History of Jeans
Where did it all begin? Trozelli visually chronicles the evolution of jeans through the centuries, from working wear to high fashion.

Look Past the Runway
Trozelli captures the creative process of some of the top designers from New York City to Paris. Spanning almost twenty years, the book is filled with Trozelli's photographs and shows what goes on in fashion houses before designs are ready for the runway.

Growing Into Clothes: My Story
An amusing memoir about growing up in the fashion world. Trozelli writes about his unconventional upbringing in New York City with parents who began as fashion models before launching their own design label.

Yards of Talent: A Decade of Style
A collection of Trozelli's images spanning a decade of fashion and revealing what was in style, what was out of style, and then what was back in style again.

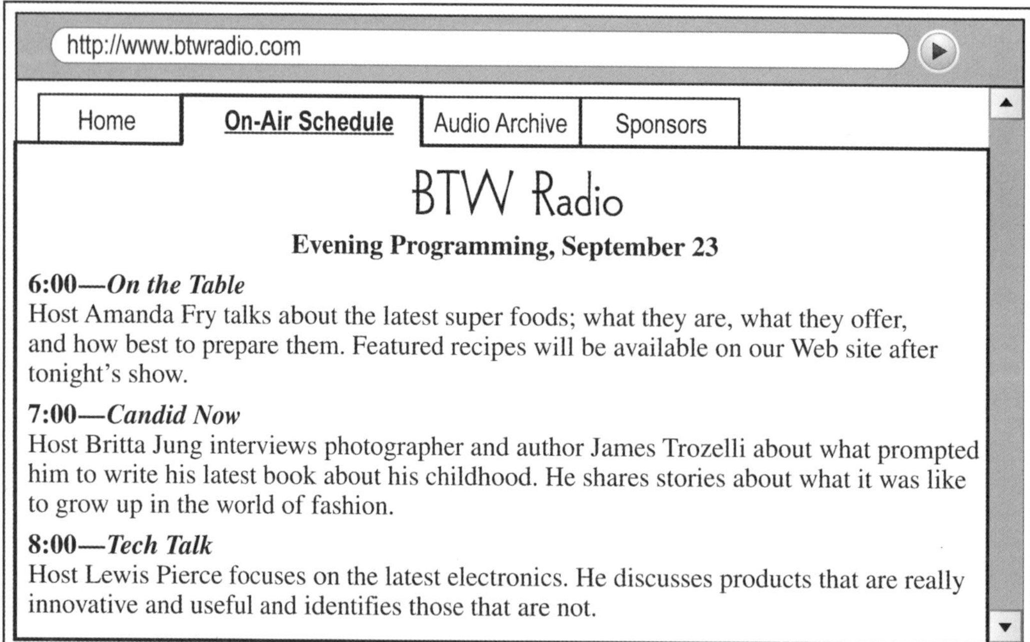

http://www.btwradio.com

Home | **On-Air Schedule** | Audio Archive | Sponsors

BTW Radio

Evening Programming, September 23

6:00—*On the Table*
Host Amanda Fry talks about the latest super foods; what they are, what they offer, and how best to prepare them. Featured recipes will be available on our Web site after tonight's show.

7:00—*Candid Now*
Host Britta Jung interviews photographer and author James Trozelli about what prompted him to write his latest book about his childhood. He shares stories about what it was like to grow up in the world of fashion.

8:00—*Tech Talk*
Host Lewis Pierce focuses on the latest electronics. He discusses products that are really innovative and useful and identifies those that are not.

E-Mail Message

To: listenercomments@btwradio.com

From: cogilvie@sunmail.net

Date: September 24

Subject: Radio Interview

I discovered BTW Radio over 20 years ago and have been a regular listener of your evening programming for at least a decade. I just want to say how much I enjoy your newest offering. I've been interested by many of the authors that have been featured on the show so far, but last evening's guest was especially entertaining. I remember James from when he was a little boy. I worked with his parents when they lived in New York, and I recall seeing James in his parents' studio most days after he got out of school. I was surprised to learn that he has written about his childhood, and I look forward to reading his new book.

Thank you for the excellent program.

Calista Ogilvie

186. What is one common feature in all of Mr. Trozelli's books?

(A) They contain fashion photographs.
(B) They focus on famous models.
(C) They are set in New York City.
(D) They follow events over multiple years.

187. What book did Mr. Trozelli discuss on BTW Radio?

(A) *The History of Jeans*
(B) *Look Past the Runway*
(C) *Growing Into Clothes: My Story*
(D) *Yards of Talent: A Decade of Style*

188. What is indicated about *Candid Now*?

(A) It is broadcast every morning at 7:00.
(B) It was recently added to BTW Radio.
(C) It is hosted by Amanda Fry.
(D) It was moved to a new time.

189. In the e-mail, the word "regular" in paragraph 1, line 1, is closest in meaning to

(A) orderly
(B) typical
(C) frequent
(D) complete

190. What is probably true about Ms. Ogilvie?

(A) She has worked in the fashion industry.
(B) She has interviewed Mr. Trozelli.
(C) She was featured on *Tech Talk*.
(D) She hosts a radio program.

Go on to the next page.

Questions 191-195 refer to the following product information, online review, and response.

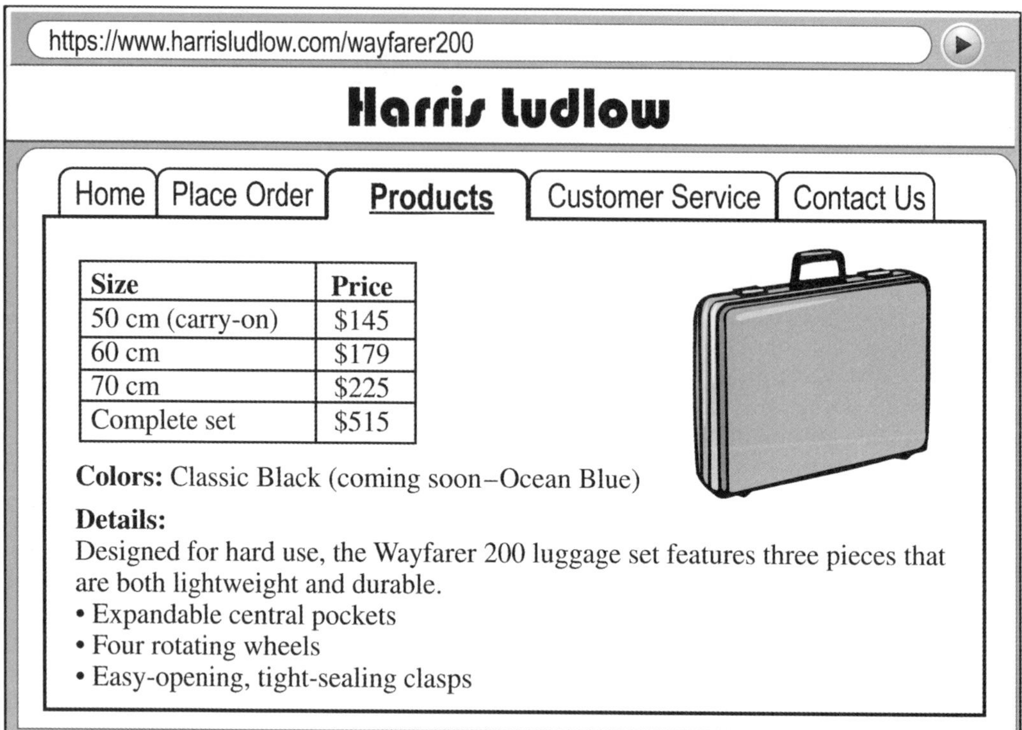

https://www.harrisludlow.com/wayfarer200

Harris Ludlow

Home | Place Order | **Products** | Customer Service | Contact Us

Size	Price
50 cm (carry-on)	$145
60 cm	$179
70 cm	$225
Complete set	$515

Colors: Classic Black (coming soon–Ocean Blue)

Details:

Designed for hard use, the Wayfarer 200 luggage set features three pieces that are both lightweight and durable.

- Expandable central pockets
- Four rotating wheels
- Easy-opening, tight-sealing clasps

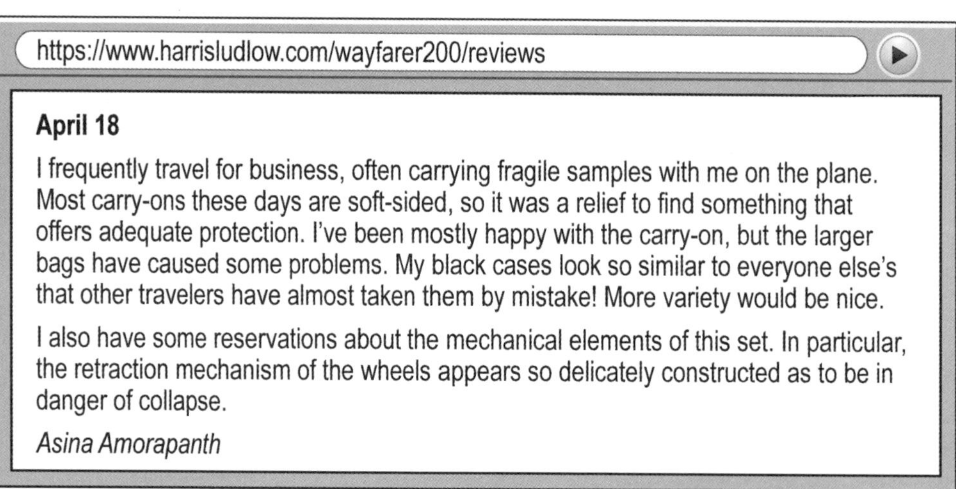

https://www.harrisludlow.com/wayfarer200/reviews

April 18

I frequently travel for business, often carrying fragile samples with me on the plane. Most carry-ons these days are soft-sided, so it was a relief to find something that offers adequate protection. I've been mostly happy with the carry-on, but the larger bags have caused some problems. My black cases look so similar to everyone else's that other travelers have almost taken them by mistake! More variety would be nice.

I also have some reservations about the mechanical elements of this set. In particular, the retraction mechanism of the wheels appears so delicately constructed as to be in danger of collapse.

Asina Amorapanth

https://www.harrisludlow.com/wayfarer200/messages 

April 20

Dear Ms. Amorapanth,

We're sorry to hear about your trouble with our product. As a result of feedback like yours, we've introduced a new color option. If you contact us at customersupport@hlluggage.com, we'll send you, in our attractive new color, a duplicate of the large suitcase to complement your Wayfarer 200 set. Note that this gift will be sent to you after you verify that you posted the April 18 review.

We also hear your concerns about our luggage components. Rest assured that our lightweight mechanism has been proven to withstand years' worth of rough treatment, retracting and extending smoothly over 10,000 times under stressful conditions in our laboratories.

Damien Cosme, Harris & Ludlow customer service

191. What does Ms. Amorapanth write about her luggage?

(A) She likes the color.
(B) The cases are too large.
(C) She purchased the bags recently.
(D) The carry-on protects her samples.

192. In the review, the word "reservations" in paragraph 2, line 1, is closest in meaning to

(A) arrangements
(B) concerns
(C) experiences
(D) features

193. What does Mr. Cosme offer to Ms. Amorapanth?

(A) A full set of blue luggage
(B) A full set of black luggage
(C) A large blue suitcase
(D) A small black suitcase

194. What must Ms. Amorapanth do in order to receive a gift from Harris Ludlow?

(A) Prove that she is the author of a product review
(B) Complete a survey about new products
(C) Retract negative feedback given on a Web site
(D) Send a package containing a defective suitcase

195. What does Mr. Cosme indicate about the wheels of the suitcases?

(A) They have been thoroughly tested.
(B) They have been redesigned to roll more easily.
(C) They are as small as possible for the size of the suitcase.
(D) They are less noisy than those of previous models.

Go on to the next page.

Questions 196-200 refer to the following notice, e-mail, and article.

Attention Everyone: Group Photo This Saturday

Exciting news—*Tasty Bites Magazine* will be featuring our restaurant in an article about Dublin's best dining establishments! They have arranged for one of their photographers to photograph us on Saturday, 4 June, at 10:00 A.M., before preparations for the day begin.

All employees will be included, so please plan to come in a bit sooner than scheduled on Saturday morning wearing your uniform. The session will take 30 minutes.

We have achieved so much since we opened, and you should all be very proud of this recognition.

To:	Herman Keel <hkeel@bentonsidebistro.net>
From:	Hilary Seaton <hseaton@hbsphotography.com>
Date:	Wednesday, 1 June
Subject:	Saturday Photography Appointment

Dear Mr. Keel,

I am writing to confirm your group photography session at 10:00 A.M. on Saturday. As discussed, this photo shoot will take place at your restaurant, and I will photograph your staff along the wall in the main dining hall. You mentioned that your waitstaff will need to start getting ready for the day at 10:30 A.M., and that should not be a problem. The shoot should be finished by 10:30 A.M.

Please let me know if you have any questions. Otherwise I will see you on Saturday!

Hilary Seaton
HBS Photography

Bistro Pleases

Enter Bentonside Bistro any day for lunch or dinner, and you'll hear the sounds of clinking forks and chattering patrons. "That's the sound of happy diners," says Herman Keel, the restaurant's owner.

Opened two years ago, the bistro has exceeded expectations. The menu features traditional Irish dishes prepared by chef Deirdre Hanrahan. She notes, "We choose ingredients that are at the height of summer, fall, winter, and spring, and showcase these on our menu."

On a recent Wednesday afternoon, Jacinta Coelho, a visitor from Brazil, was dining at the bistro. "I can't get over the freshness and homemade taste!" exclaimed Ms. Coelho. "It's like the chef went outside and selected the ingredients just for me."

Bentonside Bistro is located at 1644 Bentonside Road and is open Tuesday through Saturday from 11:30 a.m. to 9:00 p.m. The interior is painted in bright shades of blue reminiscent of the ocean, with a rotating gallery of artwork adorning the walls. The staff is friendly and the delicious food is reasonably priced. Reservations are not required.

By Declan Mulroney, Staff Writer

TEST 1

196. Who most likely posted the notice?
(A) Ms. Seaton
(B) Mr. Keel
(C) Ms. Hanrahan
(D) Mr. Mulroney

197. What are employees instructed to do on June 4?
(A) Arrive earlier than usual
(B) Attend an awards banquet
(C) Be interviewed for a newspaper article
(D) Discuss locations for a photo shoot

198. What is indicated about the waitstaff?
(A) They have been featured in *Tasty Bites Magazine* more than once.
(B) They will be photographed against a blue background.
(C) They take turns working the morning shift.
(D) They wear brightly colored uniforms.

199. What is true about the Bentonside Bistro?
(A) It is open every day for lunch.
(B) It has recently changed ownership.
(C) It specializes in Brazilian cuisine.
(D) It revises the menu seasonally.

200. What does Ms. Coelho say about her meal?
(A) She is impressed with the quality of it.
(B) She would like to prepare one like it at home.
(C) She saw it featured in a magazine.
(D) She thought it was reasonably priced.

Stop! This is the end of the test. If you finish before time is called, you may go back to Parts 5, 6, and 7 and check your work.

TEST 2

91-171

LISTENING TEST

In the Listening test, you will be asked to demonstrate how well you understand spoken English. The entire Listening test will last approximately 45 minutes. There are four parts, and directions are given for each part. You must mark your answers on the separate answer sheet. Do not write your answers in your test book.

PART 1

Directions: For each question in this part, you will hear four statements about a picture in your test book. When you hear the statements, you must select the one statement that best describes what you see in the picture. Then find the number of the question on your answer sheet and mark your answer. The statements will not be printed in your test book and will be spoken only one time.

Statement (C), "They're sitting at a table," is the best description of the picture, so you should select answer (C) and mark it on your answer sheet.

TEST 2

1.

2.

Go on to the next page.

3.

4.

TEST 2

5.

6.

Go on to the next page.

 98

PART 2

Directions: You will hear a question or statement and three responses spoken in English. They will not be printed in your test book and will be spoken only one time. Select the best response to the question or statement and mark the letter (A), (B), or (C) on your answer sheet.

7. Mark your answer on your answer sheet.

8. Mark your answer on your answer sheet.

9. Mark your answer on your answer sheet.

10. Mark your answer on your answer sheet.

11. Mark your answer on your answer sheet.

12. Mark your answer on your answer sheet.

13. Mark your answer on your answer sheet.

14. Mark your answer on your answer sheet.

15. Mark your answer on your answer sheet.

16. Mark your answer on your answer sheet.

17. Mark your answer on your answer sheet.

18. Mark your answer on your answer sheet.

19. Mark your answer on your answer sheet.

20. Mark your answer on your answer sheet.

21. Mark your answer on your answer sheet.

22. Mark your answer on your answer sheet.

23. Mark your answer on your answer sheet.

24. Mark your answer on your answer sheet.

25. Mark your answer on your answer sheet.

26. Mark your answer on your answer sheet.

27. Mark your answer on your answer sheet.

28. Mark your answer on your answer sheet.

29. Mark your answer on your answer sheet.

30. Mark your answer on your answer sheet.

31. Mark your answer on your answer sheet.

PART 3

Directions: You will hear some conversations between two or more people. You will be asked to answer three questions about what the speakers say in each conversation. Select the best response to each question and mark the letter (A), (B), (C), or (D) on your answer sheet. The conversations will not be printed in your test book and will be spoken only one time.

32. What does the woman ask for?
(A) A bill
(B) A recipe
(C) A photograph
(D) A menu

33. Who is David Wilson?
(A) A magazine editor
(B) A television producer
(C) A food critic
(D) A restaurant chef

34. What does the man offer to do?
(A) Send an e-mail reminder
(B) Make a video
(C) Reserve a book
(D) Arrange a banquet

---

35. What is the man invited to do?
(A) Watch a product demonstration
(B) Try a free sample
(C) Sign up for a newsletter
(D) Fill out a survey

36. What problem does the man mention?
(A) He is in a hurry.
(B) He has forgotten his receipt.
(C) A product is not in stock.
(D) A parcel has been damaged.

37. What does the woman suggest?
(A) Returning a purchase
(B) Trying a different product
(C) Completing a task online
(D) Visiting another store

---

38. What is the man asking about?
(A) The deadline for a project
(B) The status of a delivery
(C) The location of a meeting
(D) The amount of an invoice

39. Why is the man concerned?
(A) He cannot print some documents.
(B) Some files are missing.
(C) The wrong items were sent.
(D) A shipment was canceled.

40. What does the woman offer to send the man?
(A) A model number
(B) A cost estimate
(C) A tracking number
(D) A brochure

---

41. What does the man say about the concert?
(A) It has been moved.
(B) It is sold out.
(C) It received good reviews.
(D) It has already started.

42. Why is the woman in Vancouver?
(A) To look for a new house
(B) To take part in a seminar
(C) To go to a party
(D) To attend a sports game

43. What does the man recommend doing?
(A) Seeing a museum exhibit
(B) Going on a walking tour
(C) Trying a popular café
(D) Visiting a historic site

Go on to the next page.

44. What does the man ask the woman to do?
(A) Give him a ride to work
(B) Write a letter of recommendation
(C) Come in to work on her day off
(D) Pick up a prescription

45. Why is the woman unavailable?
(A) She is having her car repaired.
(B) She is giving a presentation.
(C) She is out of town.
(D) She has a doctor's appointment.

46. What does the woman suggest?
(A) Contacting a colleague
(B) Postponing a meeting
(C) Changing a workshop location
(D) Finding a different vendor

---

47. What project is the woman working on?
(A) Training new employees
(B) Recruiting new staff
(C) Researching a competitor
(D) Finding potential clients

48. What did the woman do on Tuesday?
(A) Reviewed applications
(B) Interviewed job candidates
(C) Met with company managers
(D) Attended promotional events

49. What does the man say has recently happened at the company?
(A) The computer equipment has been upgraded.
(B) The departments have been restructured.
(C) The regional headquarters has moved.
(D) The workload has increased.

---

50. Why does the man postpone the project?
(A) A permit is delayed.
(B) The weather will be bad.
(C) A coworker is unavailable.
(D) Some materials have not arrived.

51. What does the woman say she will do on Thursday?
(A) Leave for a trip
(B) Start a new job
(C) Meet with a supplier
(D) Volunteer at a public park

52. Why does the woman say, "If you wouldn't mind"?
(A) To suggest a solution
(B) To ask for permission
(C) To make a complaint
(D) To accept an offer

---

53. Where most likely is the conversation taking place?
(A) At a job fair
(B) At a meeting
(C) In an office kitchen
(D) In a coffee shop

54. What does Tom suggest about the company?
(A) It needs to hire more people.
(B) It treats its employees well.
(C) It will soon be renovated.
(D) It is buying some new equipment.

55. What does the woman say about Anil?
(A) He has recently joined the company.
(B) He applied for her position.
(C) He will be reporting to Tom.
(D) He has just returned from vacation.

---

56. What are the speakers mainly discussing?

(A) Factory policies
(B) Employee training
(C) Monthly results
(D) Client requests

57. What does the woman mean when she says, "I have a meeting soon"?

(A) She is not looking forward to a meeting.
(B) She cannot speak with the man for long.
(C) She is inviting the man to a meeting.
(D) She wants the man to give her a document.

58. What does the woman want to know?

(A) If deadlines have been missed
(B) If product quality is satisfactory
(C) If clients have increased their orders
(D) If machines need to be replaced

---

59. How do the speakers know each other?

(A) They live in the same area.
(B) They met at a professional conference.
(C) They used to work together.
(D) They went to the same university.

60. What does the woman say she likes about her job?

(A) Using her creativity
(B) Specializing in one area
(C) Earning bonus pay
(D) Having the chance to travel

61. What does the woman agree to do?

(A) Apply for a promotion
(B) Describe a career change
(C) Print out some business cards
(D) Look at a property for sale

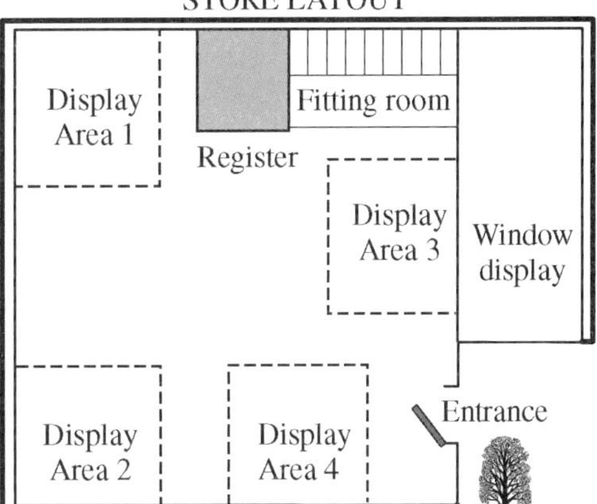

62. What did the man recently do?

(A) He transferred to another city.
(B) He attended a meeting.
(C) He purchased a new store.
(D) He signed up for a training program.

63. What is the man surprised by?

(A) The availability of staff
(B) The cost of advertising
(C) The change to a catalog
(D) The timing of a move

64. Look at the graphic. Where does the man suggest putting the shoe department?

(A) In Display Area 1
(B) In Display Area 2
(C) In Display Area 3
(D) In Display Area 4

TEST 2

Go on to the next page.

Nutrition Information

Serving size: 200 grams

Calories: 150

	Amount per serving
Fat	5 grams
Protein	11 grams
Sugar	32 grams
Sodium	40 milligrams

65. Why is the man looking for a certain product?

(A) He wants to eat healthy foods.
(B) He is allergic to a particular ingredient.
(C) He has a coupon for a discount.
(D) He has a favorite brand.

66. Look at the graphic. Which of the ingredients does the man express concern about?

(A) Fat
(B) Protein
(C) Sugar
(D) Sodium

67. What does the woman suggest that the man do?

(A) Try a free sample
(B) Go to a larger branch
(C) Speak with his doctor
(D) Purchase a different item

Jerry's Department Store

Discount Coupon

$15 off clothing purchase of $50 or more

Expires May 8

68. What is the woman doing?

(A) Assisting a customer
(B) Handing out coupons
(C) Arranging some clothing
(D) Restarting a computer

69. Look at the graphic. Why is the coupon rejected?

(A) It has expired.
(B) It is for a different department.
(C) It must be approved by a manager.
(D) It is for purchases of at least $50.

70. What does the woman offer to do?

(A) Hold some items at the register
(B) Find a product for the man
(C) Call another staff member
(D) Add the man's name to a mailing list

PART 4

Directions: You will hear some talks given by a single speaker. You will be asked to answer three questions about what the speaker says in each talk. Select the best response to each question and mark the letter (A), (B), (C), or (D) on your answer sheet. The talks will not be printed in your test book and will be spoken only one time.

71. What is the radio broadcast mainly about?
(A) Local traffic conditions
(B) An annual celebration
(C) An agricultural report
(D) A town-meeting schedule

72. What does the speaker say will happen on Elm Street?
(A) Produce will be sold.
(B) Street repairs will be completed.
(C) A new shop will open.
(D) A parade will take place.

73. What does the speaker suggest listeners do on Saturday?
(A) Avoid parking on Elm Street
(B) Visit an amusement park
(C) Prepare for rain
(D) Listen to a radio news report

---

74. Where is the talk taking place?
(A) At an art studio
(B) At a construction site
(C) At a hotel
(D) At an energy plant

75. Who most likely are the listeners?
(A) Architects
(B) Scientists
(C) Hotel managers
(D) Event planners

76. What is mentioned about the materials used?
(A) They are produced locally.
(B) They are inexpensive.
(C) They are environmentally friendly.
(D) They are hard to find.

---

77. Who most likely is the speaker?
(A) A news reporter
(B) A movie director
(C) A real estate agent
(D) A town official

78. What is Dougherty Films looking for?
(A) Movie title suggestions
(B) Additional funding
(C) A lead actor
(D) A filming location

79. What does the speaker imply when she says, "But this is Santiago Diaz we're talking about"?
(A) She has never heard of Santiago Diaz.
(B) She had previously mentioned the wrong name.
(C) Santiago Diaz is very famous.
(D) Santiago Diaz will be interviewed next.

---

80. What is the purpose of the speech?
(A) To motivate team members
(B) To announce a retirement
(C) To inaugurate a company
(D) To accept an award

81. What most likely is the speaker's job?
(A) Technology specialist
(B) Bank teller
(C) Financial analyst
(D) Marketing manager

82. Why does the speaker say, "I couldn't have done it without my team"?
(A) She does not have the skills for a task.
(B) She wants to thank her colleagues.
(C) She is requesting additional staff.
(D) She has not worked on a team before.

Go on to the next page.

83. What most likely is being advertised?
(A) A vision correction center
(B) A computer repair shop
(C) A medical school
(D) A shopping center

84. According to the speaker, why should listeners choose this business?
(A) It has an experienced staff.
(B) It has reasonable rates.
(C) It has a large selection of items.
(D) It is open seven days a week.

85. What special offer is being made?
(A) An extended warranty
(B) Sample merchandise
(C) A free consultation
(D) Next-day delivery

---

86. What is the company preparing to do?
(A) Open another branch
(B) Improve customer service
(C) Research marketing trends
(D) Launch a new product

87. What goal does the speaker set for the listeners?
(A) To create a software program
(B) To get customers to meet with them
(C) To provide high-quality support
(D) To reduce production costs

88. What will listeners most likely do next?
(A) Meet the company president
(B) Call potential customers
(C) Listen to recordings
(D) Rehearse a presentation

---

89. What problem does the speaker mention?
(A) Some staff members must be reassigned.
(B) A shipment of equipment will be delayed.
(C) A building will be without power.
(D) Some computers must be replaced.

90. What does the speaker imply when he says, "you might want to wait until later to come in"?
(A) Employees should take the day off.
(B) A due date has been pushed back.
(C) Staff should not come to the office in the morning.
(D) A meeting is at an inconvenient time.

91. What does the speaker say he will do?
(A) Ask for volunteers
(B) Send colleagues a message
(C) Run a software check
(D) Meet with team leaders

---

92. What is the purpose of the call?
(A) To respond to an inquiry
(B) To confirm a reservation
(C) To apologize for an error
(D) To ask about business hours

93. What does the speaker mention about the Andrews Museum?
(A) It is being renovated.
(B) It is located next to the hotel.
(C) The current show is very good.
(D) Admission is free of charge.

94. What does the speaker offer to do?
(A) Issue a refund
(B) Reschedule a meeting
(C) Arrange a city tour
(D) Purchase tickets in advance

Order form 489275 Customer: Pennington Technology	
Item	**Quantity**
Sandwich Trays	2
Green Salad Bowls	3
Fruit Juice Bottles	15
Plate and Utensil Sets	20

95. What type of event is being catered?
(A) An academic lecture
(B) A retirement party
(C) A product launch
(D) A business meeting

96. Look at the graphic. Which quantity on the original order form is no longer accurate?
(A) 2
(B) 3
(C) 15
(D) 20

97. What is the listener asked to do tomorrow?
(A) Pick up an identification badge
(B) Give a speech
(C) Arrive early to set up a room
(D) Bring additional staff

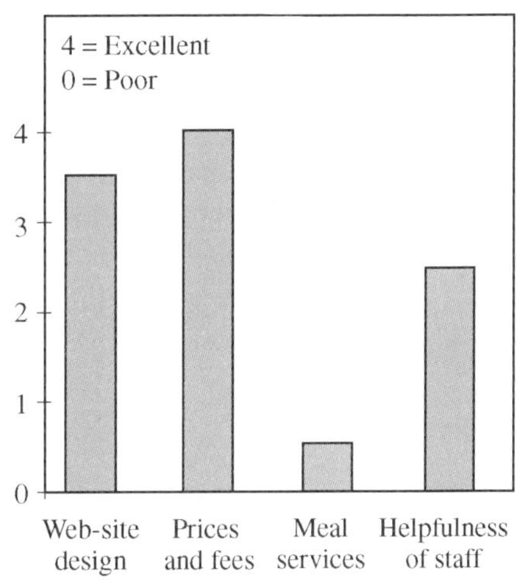

98. Where does the speaker most likely work?
(A) At a post office
(B) At an airline
(C) At a travel agency
(D) At an Internet company

99. Look at the graphic. What does the speaker want the listeners to discuss?
(A) Web-site design
(B) Prices and fees
(C) Meal services
(D) Helpfulness of staff

100. What will the speaker do after the discussion?
(A) Review some résumés
(B) Book some tickets
(C) Contact a customer
(D) Create a summary

This is the end of the Listening test. Turn to Part 5 in your test book.

Go on to the next page.

TEST 2

READING TEST

In the Reading test, you will read a variety of texts and answer several different types of reading comprehension questions. The entire Reading test will last 75 minutes. There are three parts, and directions are given for each part. You are encouraged to answer as many questions as possible within the time allowed.

You must mark your answers on the separate answer sheet. Do not write your answers in your test book.

PART 5

Directions: A word or phrase is missing in each of the sentences below. Four answer choices are given below each sentence. Select the best answer to complete the sentence. Then mark the letter (A), (B), (C), or (D) on your answer sheet.

101. Busan Cosmetics is pleased to ------- Jin-Sook Kim, a new team member in product development.

(A) welcoming
(B) welcome
(C) welcomed
(D) welcomes

102. The seminar will be attended ------- professionals in the food service industry.

(A) of
(B) over
(C) as
(D) by

103. The Human Resources Department will ------- request that employees update their personal contact information for the company's records.

(A) occasionally
(B) previously
(C) recently
(D) lately

104. All staff members should log in to their time and labor ------- daily to record their hours worked.

(A) accounts
(B) accounted
(C) accountant
(D) accountable

105. The Humson Company has just started a lunchtime fitness program, and employees are encouraged to -------.

(A) win
(B) order
(C) collect
(D) join

106. To enroll in any course, either complete the online form ------- register in person at the Greerson Learning Center.

(A) if
(B) and
(C) or
(D) but

107. Mr. Yamagata is prepared to assist Ms. Hahn's clients while ------- conducts a training seminar in New York.

(A) hers
(B) she
(C) herself
(D) her

108. Please return the signed copy of the ------- agreement to the apartment manager's office in the enclosed envelope.

(A) rental
(B) rentable
(C) rented
(D) rents

109. Employees who are affiliated with Corman Corporation will be seated ------- the third row of the auditorium.

(A) except
(B) to
(C) among
(D) in

110. Yesterday's festival featured some of the most ------- dancers that the Palace Theater has ever hosted.

(A) live
(B) liveliness
(C) lively
(D) livelier

111. Fulsome Flowers' delivery vans must be returned promptly to the store ------- the scheduled deliveries have been completed.

(A) once
(B) soon
(C) often
(D) usually

112. To ensure stability and safety, it is important to follow the instructions ------- when assembling the office bookshelves.

(A) exactly
(B) exact
(C) exactness
(D) exacting

113. At the Podell Automotive plant, Ms. Krystle ------- workers who install rebuilt engines in vehicles.

(A) conducts
(B) explains
(C) invests
(D) oversees

114. Yakubu Logistics will expand the warehouse loading area in preparation for an ------- in shipping activity.

(A) increased
(B) increase
(C) increases
(D) increasingly

115. The High Performance weather gauge is ------- accurate in measuring the level of humidity in the air.

(A) surprising
(B) surprisingly
(C) surprised
(D) surprises

116. Ms. Oh's proposal highlights a ------- strategy for decreasing the company's transportation costs in the coming year.

(A) surrounding
(B) securing
(C) relative
(D) comprehensive

117. To receive ------- updates regarding your journal subscription status, please provide an e-mail address on the order form.

(A) period
(B) periods
(C) periodicals
(D) periodic

118. ------- when they are away conducting business, members of the sales team are usually available by e-mail.

(A) Both
(B) Even
(C) Ahead
(D) Whether

119. There is a coffee machine ------- located on the second floor of the Tabor Building.

(A) conveniently
(B) slightly
(C) considerably
(D) eventually

120. The editor granted Ms. Porter a deadline ------- so that some information in her building renovations report could be updated.

(A) extend
(B) extensive
(C) extension
(D) extends

Go on to the next page.

121. Youssouf Electronics' annual charity fund-raising event ------- next Saturday at Montrose Park.

(A) will be held
(B) to hold
(C) to be held
(D) will hold

122. The buildings in the Jamison Complex are open until 7:00 P.M. on workdays, but staff with proper ------- may enter at any time.

(A) reinforcement
(B) participation
(C) competency
(D) authorization

123. Kochi Engineering has proposed the construction of a drainage system ------- to keep the Route 480 highway dry during heavy rain.

(A) was designed
(B) designed
(C) designer
(D) designing

124. Customers can obtain coverage for replacement and repair of printers ------- the purchase of an extended warranty.

(A) although
(B) because
(C) since
(D) through

125. We regret to announce that Mr. Charles Appiah has resigned his position as senior sales manager, ------- next Monday.

(A) effect
(B) effected
(C) effectiveness
(D) effective

126. The Epsilon 3000 camera allows beginning photographers to enjoy professional-quality equipment, as it is ------- sophisticated yet inexpensive.

(A) gradually
(B) technologically
(C) annually
(D) productively

127. Yee-Yin Xiong held interviews with numerous clients to determine ------- Echegaray Consulting, Inc., can improve customer service.

(A) unless
(B) in order to
(C) how
(D) as if

128. Several letters of reference from local community organizations are required for ------- into the Cypress Beach Business Association.

(A) acquisition
(B) acceptance
(C) prospects
(D) improvement

129. Rather than wearing business attire on Thursdays, staff may choose to wear casual clothing -------.

(A) enough
(B) despite
(C) instead
(D) in case

130. Your ------- registration card provides proof of ownership in case this product is lost or damaged.

(A) frequent
(B) indicative
(C) validated
(D) dispersed

PART 6

Directions: Read the texts that follow. A word, phrase, or sentence is missing in parts of each text. Four answer choices for each question are given below the text. Select the best answer to complete the text. Then mark the letter (A), (B), (C), or (D) on your answer sheet.

Questions 131-134 refer to the following information.

The Fern Lake Community Center is an entirely volunteer-run organization serving the Fern Lake community. -------131. known among locals as "the Fern," our center offers high-quality after-school care for local children of working parents. We also -------132. educational programs for all ages in our buildings on Quentin Street. -------133..

In addition, the community center offers several -------134. events throughout the year. The largest and most famous is our annual Fern Fair. All residents are invited to join us on April 12 this year on the Broad Street Pier to enjoy the area's best food, crafts, and musical performances while savoring the cool spring breeze.

For more information, visit www.fernlakecc.com/fair.

131. (A) Cooperatively
(B) Mutually
(C) Popularly
(D) Essentially

132. (A) participate
(B) claim
(C) enroll
(D) host

133. (A) We are not currently looking for volunteers.
(B) Contact our office to rent our main hall.
(C) Most of these programs are no longer available.
(D) These include classes in dancing and painting.

134. (A) outdoor
(B) exclusive
(C) athletic
(D) formal

Go on to the next page.

Questions 135-138 refer to the following information.

Rowes Atlantic Airways Baggage Policy

Each passenger -------(135.) to carry one piece of hand baggage onto the plane without charge. The carry-on item must not exceed the dimensions 56 cm x 45 cm x 25 cm, including the handle and wheels. No carry-on bag should weigh more than 23 kg. Passengers should be -------(136.) to lift bags into the overhead storage bins unaided. These -------(137.) do not apply to bags that are checked in at the service desk.

A laptop computer bag, school backpack, or handbag may also be brought on board.

-------(138.).

135. (A) allowed
(B) is allowed
(C) allowing
(D) had been allowed

136. (A) able
(B) ably
(C) abled
(D) ability

137. (A) transfers
(B) suggestions
(C) duties
(D) restrictions

138. (A) Please inquire at the service desk if it will be permitted on your flight.
(B) It should be stored under the seats when not in use.
(C) Thank you for becoming a member of the flight crew.
(D) Therefore, they will be available for a small additional fee.

Questions 139-142 refer to the following article.

LONDON (18 May) – Ubero Hotels announced today that Mr. Jeffrey Pak has been promoted to vice president of global brand marketing for the worldwide hotel chain. Mr. Pak's promotion will become effective as of 2 June. His new -------- (139.) involves overseeing worldwide marketing strategies, which includes all advertising and brand promotions. -------- (140.).

Mr. Pak was previously Ubero Hotels' regional director of business development for Southeast Asia. He -------- (141.) his career at the front desk of the Ubero Queen Sydney Hotel. Mr. Pak has stated that he believes this early experience, going back 23 years, of connecting with guests and coworkers has contributed to his hands-on -------- (142.) style.

139. (A) trend
(B) facility
(C) supervisor
(D) position

140. (A) He will also be responsible for a staff of 25.
(B) Similarly, he will be relocating to London.
(C) For example, he will be training new employees.
(D) As a result, he will keep his home in Sydney.

141. (A) begins
(B) began
(C) is beginning
(D) will begin

142. (A) manage
(B) manages
(C) managed
(D) management

Go on to the next page.

Questions 143-146 refer to the following e-mail.

To: Karen Karl, Staff Writer

From: Liz Steinhauer, Editor in Chief

Date: January 2

Re: Cover Article Assignment

Hi Karen,

Thank you for agreeing to work on an article about Veronica Zettici's ------- (143.) role in her recent film as actress and director. By the end of the week, please submit an overview explaining how you plan to focus the interview with her. Once our editors approve your ------- (144.), make sure to confirm the interview day and time with one of our staff photographers. It would be ideal if the article ------- (145.) the two roles Ms. Zettici played in the production of the film. ------- (146.).

I will be available throughout the week if you have any questions.

Liz

143. (A) double
(B) doubles
(C) doubling
(D) to double

144. (A) drawing
(B) hiring
(C) proposal
(D) edition

145. (A) comparing
(B) compared
(C) to compare
(D) were compared

146. (A) For example, you might ask her about the next project on her schedule.
(B) Furthermore, it should discuss the distinct skills she brought to each aspect.
(C) In short, your work should be completed in two weeks.
(D) In addition, the article will be published in the April issue.

PART 7

Directions: In this part you will read a selection of texts, such as magazine and newspaper articles, e-mails, and instant messages. Each text or set of texts is followed by several questions. Select the best answer for each question and mark the letter (A), (B), (C), or (D) on your answer sheet.

Questions 147-148 refer to the following coupon.

Thank you for enrolling your daughter or son in the training session at T-Star Tennis Clinic! We hope your child enjoyed the lessons and comes back to T-Star Tennis Clinic again.

Use this coupon at

Great Angle Tennis Shop

to receive 30 percent off any adult- or junior-size tennis racket or 20 percent off any other tennis equipment.

For an online purchase, enter discount code **RW445**.

Valid through June 30. Cannot be combined with any other coupon. Excludes clothing, bags, and shoes.

147. What is suggested about T-Star Tennis Clinic?

(A) It is owned by a famous athlete.
(B) It operates in several countries.
(C) It runs a program for children.
(D) It manufactures tennis equipment.

148. What is true about the coupon?

(A) It expires at the end of the year.
(B) It applies only to purchases over $30.
(C) It is not valid for online purchases.
(D) It cannot be used on tennis shirts.

Go on to the next page.

Questions 149-150 refer to the following text message chain.

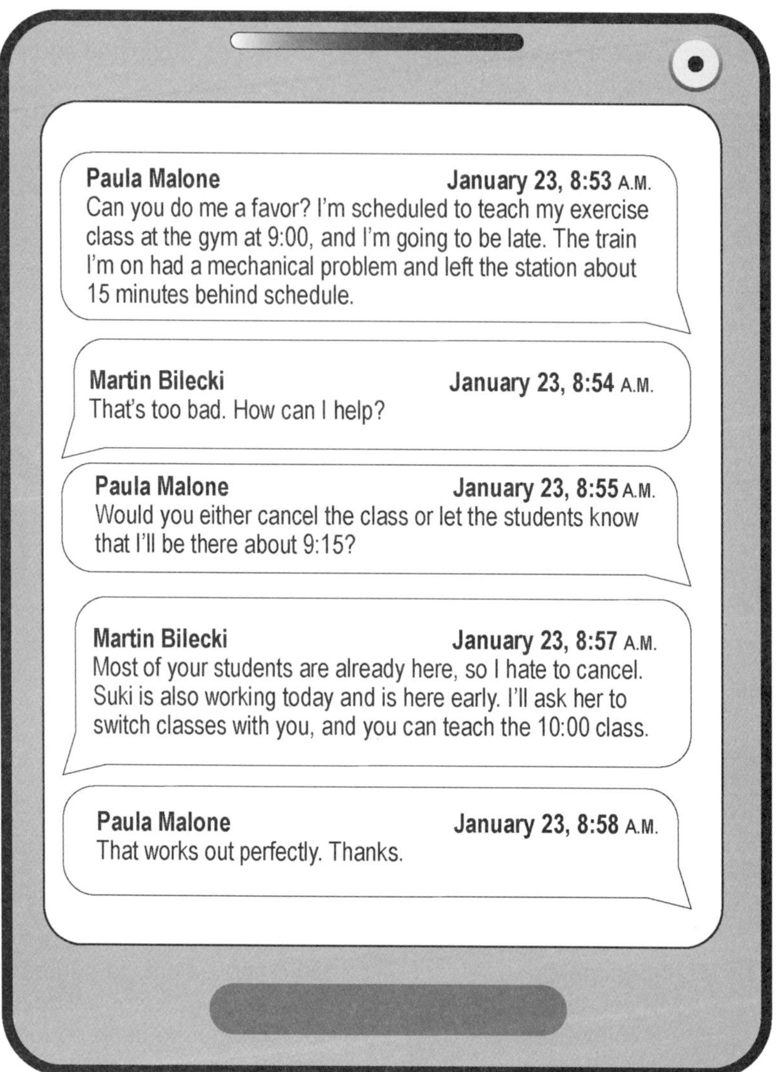
Paula Malone January 23, 8:53 A.M.
Can you do me a favor? I'm scheduled to teach my exercise class at the gym at 9:00, and I'm going to be late. The train I'm on had a mechanical problem and left the station about 15 minutes behind schedule.
Martin Bilecki January 23, 8:54 A.M.
That's too bad. How can I help?
Paula Malone January 23, 8:55 A.M.
Would you either cancel the class or let the students know that I'll be there about 9:15?
Martin Bilecki January 23, 8:57 A.M.
Most of your students are already here, so I hate to cancel. Suki is also working today and is here early. I'll ask her to switch classes with you, and you can teach the 10:00 class.
Paula Malone January 23, 8:58 A.M.
That works out perfectly. Thanks.

149. What does Mr. Bilecki indicate he will do?

(A) Arrive late to the gym
(B) Teach a class
(C) Cancel a class
(D) Change the instructors' schedules

150. At 8:58 A.M., what does Ms. Malone most likely mean when she writes, "That works out perfectly"?

(A) She likes Mr. Bilecki's idea.
(B) She likes exercising in the morning.
(C) She is excited about her new job.
(D) She is happy that she has the day off.

Questions 151-152 refer to the following notice.

Dear Atrium Hotel Guests:

We would like to apologize for the warm temperatures in the hallways and elevators. The hotel is currently undergoing work to upgrade our air-conditioning system. The new system will improve our energy efficiency and increase the comfort of our common areas.

Please note that this work does not affect the air-conditioning units in guest rooms. If there is anything we can do to make your stay more enjoyable, please feel free to contact any of our staff by dialing "0" from your room.

151. Where would the notice most likely appear?

(A) In an airport terminal
(B) In a hotel lobby
(C) In an office building
(D) In a shopping plaza

152. What is being replaced?

(A) The air-conditioning system
(B) The telephone system
(C) The furniture
(D) The elevators

Go on to the next page.

Questions 153-154 refer to the following e-mail.

E-mail

To: m.agrawal@indiatip.net
From: pritidoshi@hscot.in
Date: 17 May
Subject: IndiaTip

Dear Ms. Agrawal,

My name is Priti Doshi, and I'm an avid cyclist in Bangalore, India. While browsing online for cycling clubs, I came across IndiaTip.net. Your Web site appears to be a very comprehensive resource for travel articles and related news about India.

I would like to call your attention to an electronic guidebook I recently published. It describes all of my favourite cycling routes in Bangalore and is complete with maps, kilometre markers, and detailed descriptions about points of interest. I noticed that you have a specific page dedicated to bicycle travel in India; a mention of my guide would be an ideal addition to this page.

The book is titled *Bangalore by Bike,* and it can be purchased through www.bangalorebybike.com/AS3XK. If you could share this information with your readership, I would appreciate it.

Thank you and have a great day.

Priti Doshi

153. What is suggested about Ms. Agrawal?
(A) She lives in Bangalore.
(B) She leads guided tours.
(C) She enjoys bicycling.
(D) She runs a travel Web site.

154. Why is Ms. Doshi writing to Ms. Agrawal?
(A) To recommend a travel partner
(B) To promote a book
(C) To critique an article
(D) To update a news story

Questions 155-157 refer to the following form.

STARR Transportation

Thank you for using Starr Transportation. In a concerted effort to better serve our customers, we'd like your opinion about your most recent experience with us. Please take a moment to fill out the following survey and mail it to us in the enclosed self-addressed, stamped envelope by May 28.

Date: May 20 **Customer Name:** V.N. Chen **Phone:** 603-555-0143

Date and description of service:
April 12-transport from Carroll Corporation to Franklin Airport.
April 25-transport from Franklin Airport to my home in Centerville, NH.

Please rate the following on a scale of 1 to 4, 1 being "poor" and 4 being "excellent."

Service				
Friendliness	1	2	3	(4)
Reservation Process	1	2	(3)	4
Vehicle				
Spaciousness	1	2	(3)	4
Cleanliness	1	2	3	(4)

Would you use our services again? YES NO (MAYBE)

Would you recommend our services to others? YES NO (MAYBE)

Comments:
I use Starr Transportation often for business travel and have always been satisfied. This time, when I arrived at Franklin Airport after a long flight from Lima, Peru, the driver was nowhere to be found. The airplane had arrived at a different terminal than scheduled, but the driver should have checked the flight's arrival status well beforehand. I ended up waiting for him when I could have taken a bus.

155. How will Starr Transportation most likely use information they collect from the form?
(A) To create effective marketing materials
(B) To plan time-saving driving routes
(C) To determine employee promotions
(D) To improve customer service

156. What does Mr. Chen indicate about the vehicle?
(A) It was a bus.
(B) It was very clean.
(C) It was too large.
(D) It was difficult to drive.

157. What does Mr. Chen indicate about the service he received?
(A) The trip from Centerville took too long.
(B) The reservation process was confusing.
(C) The driver arrived later than scheduled.
(D) The vehicle was too small to fit his luggage.

Go on to the next page.

Questions 158-160 refer to the following advertisement.

Manchester Trader 29 May

Bright, clean, 300-square-metre flat for rent on the third floor of the historic Blythe House near the centre of Manchester. Available 1 July, £800 per month.

- Recently updated kitchen
- Reserved parking spot in front of the building
- One bathroom with a standing shower
- One bedroom, living room, kitchen, and separate dining area
- Cable television and wireless Internet service included in rent
- Cost of electricity shared among residents of the other three flats in the building
- No pets allowed
- Dining table and chairs stay with the apartment

One month's rent plus two months' security deposit due upon signing of the lease.

Contact owner and landlord Abigail Brown at 077 4300 6455 or at abrown@teleworm.uk.

158. What is indicated about Blythe House?

(A) It is occupied by more than one resident.
(B) It is located near public transportation.
(C) It is immediately available for a new tenant.
(D) It is suitable for residents with cats and dogs.

159. What is included in the rental fee?

(A) Electricity costs
(B) Security surveillance
(C) Internet service
(D) Cleaning services

160. According to the advertisement, what are renters required to do?

(A) Sign a one-year contract
(B) Pay some money before moving in
(C) Provide references from previous landlords
(D) Participate in an interview

Questions 161-163 refer to the following article.

Swansea Business News

(3 August) A spokesperson for Riester's Food Markets announced yesterday that it will open five new stores over the next two years, starting with one in downtown Swansea this December. —[1]—. The company, known for its reasonable prices, will next open a Liverpool store in May. —[2]—. The location of the final store has not yet been determined.

The number of Riester's locations has certainly been growing rapidly throughout the U.K. Shoppers seem pleased with the wide selection of items that include packaged goods, fresh produce, and hot ready-made meals. According to Donald Chapworth, director of marketing, the latter are particularly popular with working parents. —[3]—. "Many of these customers in particular have limited time to cook but still want their families to eat wholesome food," says Chapworth. Last March Riester's hired chef Gabriella Pierangeli, famed for her London restaurant Gabriella's on Second, to craft their signature home-style dishes. —[4]—.

161. What is the article about?

(A) The expansion of a chain of stores
(B) Families cutting their food budgets
(C) The relocation of a popular restaurant
(D) Grocery stores changing their prices

162. What does Mr. Chapworth mention that customers like about Riester's?

(A) Its friendly customer service
(B) Its inexpensive pricing
(C) Its home-delivery service
(D) Its prepared foods

163. In which of the positions marked [1], [2], [3], and [4] does the following sentence best belong?

"Two more will open at sites in Manchester and Edinburgh by summer of next year."

(A) [1]
(B) [2]
(C) [3]
(D) [4]

TEST 2

Go on to the next page.

Questions 164-167 refer to the following letter.

28 April

Maria Ortiz
Hayes Polytechnic University
19 Chamsboro Road
TOORAK VIC 3142

Dear Ms. Ortiz,

The Melbourne Groundwater System Corporation, MGSC, has approved your request for a two-year grant of $65,000 to research the impact of industry on groundwater resources in the Melbourne region. Please note that there are a few requirements that must be met before we can release these funds to you.

First, your proposal indicated that the balance of the funding needed to complete your project will be provided by Akuna Allied Bank, and that you expected the loan approval by 15 April. Please provide us with a copy of the loan agreement you have with this bank.

Also, on or about 5 May we will send the standard MGSC contract to you. This document stipulates that you will submit a quarterly status report throughout the course of this project and that MGSC will not supply any additional funds beyond the initial grant amount. Please sign and return the contract to us.

Please note that MGSC requires a detailed list of all personnel directly involved in the project, their résumés and certifications, and their estimated fees. All documentation requested must be received in one packet no later than 1 June.

Congratulations on the receipt of your grant. Do not hesitate to contact my office at 20 6501 8240 if you have any questions or concerns. I will be out of the office from 6 May to 13 May, but in my absence you may speak with Ms. Mita Kulp.

Sincerely,

Albert Johnson

Albert Johnson
Vice President
Melbourne Groundwater System Corporation

164. Why was the letter written?

(A) To ask for research proposals
(B) To announce that funds have been awarded
(C) To report the results of industry studies
(D) To offer employment

165. When is a copy of the bank agreement due to MGSC?

(A) On April 15
(B) On May 5
(C) On May 13
(D) On June 1

166. What is indicated about the MGSC contract?

(A) It includes an itemized list of costs.
(B) It will be reviewed once a year.
(C) It requires the submission of reports.
(D) It is included with the letter.

167. What is suggested about Ms. Kulp?

(A) She is in charge of approving grant applications.
(B) She has conducted research similar to that of Ms. Ortiz.
(C) She is an employee of Akuna Allied Bank.
(D) She works with Mr. Johnson.

Questions 168-171 refer to the following online chat discussion.

Sarah Lo [9:38 A.M.]	Hi all. I'd like your input. Jovita Wilson in sales just told me that her client, Mr. Tran, wants us to deliver his order a week early. Can we do that?
Alex Ralston [9:40 A.M.]	If we rush, we can assemble the hardwood frames in two days.
Riko Kimura [9:41 A.M.]	And my department needs just a day to print and cut the fabric to cover the cushion seating.
Mia Ochoa [9:42 A.M.]	But initially you need the designs, right? My team can finish that by end of day today.
Sarah Lo [9:43 A.M.]	OK. Then we'll be ready for the finishing steps by end of day on Wednesday. Alex, once you have the fabric, how long will it take to build the cushions, stuff them, and attach them to the frames?
Alex Ralston [9:45 A.M.]	That will take two days—if my group can set aside regular work to do that.
Sarah Lo [9:46 A.M.]	I can authorize that. Bill, how long will it take your department to package the order and ship it?
Bill Belmore [9:48 A.M.]	We can complete that on Monday morning.
Sarah Lo [9:49 A.M.]	Great. Thanks all. I'll let Jovita know so she can inform the client.

SEND

TEST 2

168. At 9:38 A.M., what does Ms. Lo mean when she writes, "I'd like your input"?

(A) She needs some numerical data.
(B) She needs some financial contributions.
(C) She wants to develop some projects.
(D) She wants to gather some opinions.

169. For what type of company does Ms. Lo most likely work?

(A) A package delivery business
(B) A furniture manufacturer
(C) An art supply store
(D) A construction firm

170. According to the discussion, whose department must complete their work first?

(A) Mr. Belmore's department
(B) Ms. Kimura's department
(C) Ms. Ochoa's department
(D) Mr. Ralston's department

171. What will Ms. Wilson most likely tell Mr. Tran?

(A) That she can meet his request for rush work
(B) That there will be an extra charge for completing his order
(C) That his order will be ready for delivery on Friday
(D) That she will meet him at her office next Monday

Go on to the next page.

Questions 172-175 refer to the following letter.

Highbrook Library
42 Doring Street
Norwich, CT 06360
860-555-0110

April 23

Mr. Jack Vogel
Ellicott Office Supplies
181 Foss Street
Norwich, CT 06360

Dear Mr. Vogel:

On behalf of the Highbrook Library, I would like to offer my sincere thanks for your generous gifts. The three computers you donated from your store, along with the extra paper and ink, have helped us to better serve our users. — [1] —. We now have five computers and they are almost always in use. In our last conversation you had asked how the library staff would control use. We have decided to allow library members to use a computer for free for two hours. Nonmembers pay $2 for one hour of use. We also ask all patrons to book a computer in advance because of the high demand. — [2] —.

In addition, your monetary donation has allowed us to extend our hours. The library is now open until 8:00 P.M., Monday-Thursday, which has led to a growth in membership by permitting more people to visit when their workday is over. — [3] —. We have even had several book clubs form that meet in the evenings. Perhaps you would like to join one? — [4] —.

Next year we will be investigating the possibility of adding a small café on the first floor near the community meeting room. We hope you will consider contributing to this project as well, if it seems promising. You will receive more information in the future about it.

Thank you again for your generous support of the Highbrook Library!

Sincerely,

Annabeth Hendley

Annabeth Hendley
Director, Highbrook Library

172. Why is Ms. Hendley writing to Mr. Vogel?
(A) To invite him to become an honorary library member
(B) To request advice about computer installation
(C) To ask him to purchase new books for the library
(D) To express appreciation for his donations

173. What is suggested about the Highbrook Library?
(A) It is going to close for renovation.
(B) It has increased the hours it is open.
(C) It will be hosting a fund-raising event.
(D) It is considering adding a meeting room.

174. What is indicated about the computers at Highbrook Library?
(A) They are for library members only.
(B) They need to be updated.
(C) They are free for members to use.
(D) They cannot be reserved.

175. In which of the positions marked [1], [2], [3], and [4] does the following sentence best belong?
"This policy also helps students who want to use library resources after school."
(A) [1]
(B) [2]
(C) [3]
(D) [4]

Go on to the next page.

Questions 176-180 refer to the following e-mail and report.

To:	Product Development Staff
From:	Sauda Dawodu
Date:	10 June
Subject:	Product Expansion

Dear Product Development Team,

As you may know from recent sales reports for Aswebo Toys, our products are enjoying great success in international markets. The response to our electronic and handcrafted wooden toys has been very favorable. We have, in fact, had several requests from a few of our principal clients to expand the number of wooden toys we currently make for children from birth to age five.

Consequently, in an effort to assess the prospects for Aswebo Toys' future growth in this area, the management team has decided that our company will, as a preliminary step, produce one new item intended for the early-childhood market. Belinobo Consulting has been hired to conduct market research on the type of toy that we will introduce. Using the results of their product study, the prototype will be refined and put on the market as soon as it is feasible to do so.

This plan presents our company with an exciting opportunity. I'm certain that we can count on your dedication and initiative.

Sauda Dawodu
Senior Director

RESULTS—NEW PRODUCT SURVEY
Prepared for Aswebo Toys
By Belinobo Consulting

Toy Prototype	General Preference	After presented with prototype example
Puzzle	23	25
Doll/action figure	17	15
Building set	11	10
Educational game	36	39
Board game	33	31

Survey responses were collected from 120 participants, all of whom are parents of children in the focus age group. Participants were first asked which toy they would be most likely to purchase. They were then presented with one prototype from each category and asked the same question a second time.

176. What is the purpose of the e-mail?
(A) To ask for market research volunteers
(B) To inform employees of an upcoming project
(C) To share the details of a sales report
(D) To promote a consulting firm

177. In the e-mail, the word "response" in paragraph 1, line 2, is closest in meaning to
(A) answer
(B) reaction
(C) recognition
(D) confirmation

178. What is NOT mentioned about Aswebo Toys?
(A) It sells products made by hand.
(B) It operates internationally.
(C) It will introduce a new electronic toy next year.
(D) It is a growing company.

179. What is suggested about the toys that were used in the research?
(A) They are designed for use by children up to five years old.
(B) They are currently manufactured by competitor companies.
(C) They were given to survey participants to keep.
(D) They were shown to children.

180. According to the report, what toy were the research participants the least enthusiastic about?
(A) The puzzle
(B) The educational game
(C) The building set
(D) The board game

Go on to the next page.

Questions 181-185 refer to the following information from a Web page and e-mail.

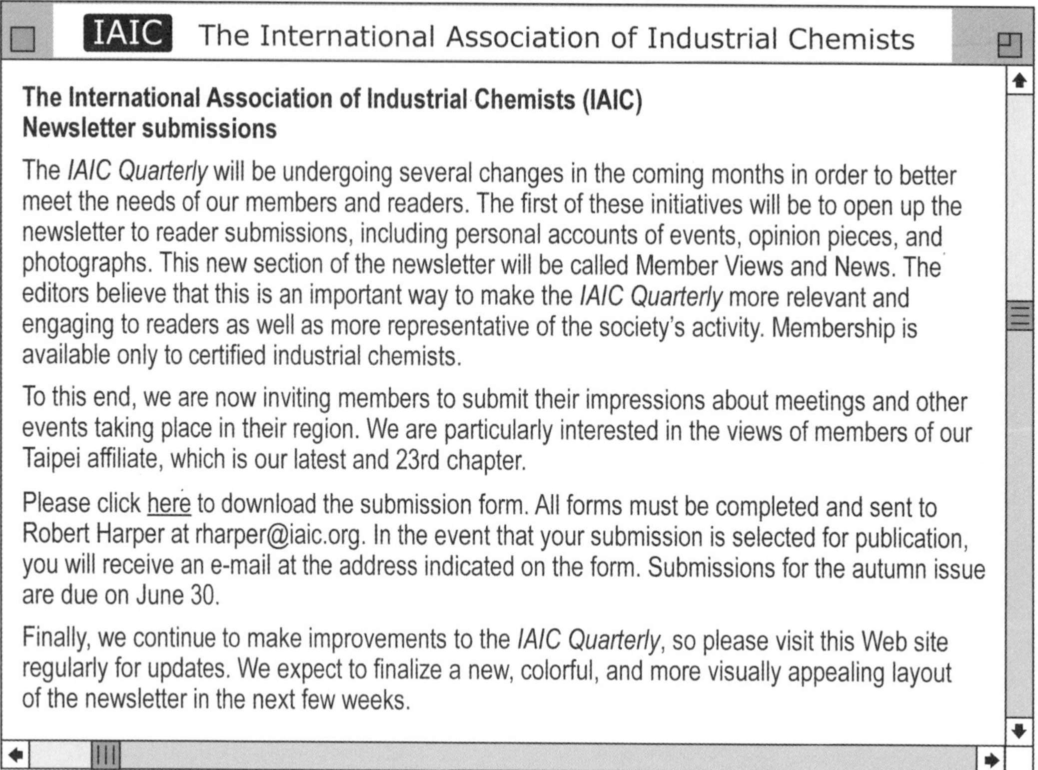

IAIC The International Association of Industrial Chemists

The International Association of Industrial Chemists (IAIC)
Newsletter submissions

The *IAIC Quarterly* will be undergoing several changes in the coming months in order to better meet the needs of our members and readers. The first of these initiatives will be to open up the newsletter to reader submissions, including personal accounts of events, opinion pieces, and photographs. This new section of the newsletter will be called Member Views and News. The editors believe that this is an important way to make the *IAIC Quarterly* more relevant and engaging to readers as well as more representative of the society's activity. Membership is available only to certified industrial chemists.

To this end, we are now inviting members to submit their impressions about meetings and other events taking place in their region. We are particularly interested in the views of members of our Taipei affiliate, which is our latest and 23rd chapter.

Please click here to download the submission form. All forms must be completed and sent to Robert Harper at rharper@iaic.org. In the event that your submission is selected for publication, you will receive an e-mail at the address indicated on the form. Submissions for the autumn issue are due on June 30.

Finally, we continue to make improvements to the *IAIC Quarterly*, so please visit this Web site regularly for updates. We expect to finalize a new, colorful, and more visually appealing layout of the newsletter in the next few weeks.

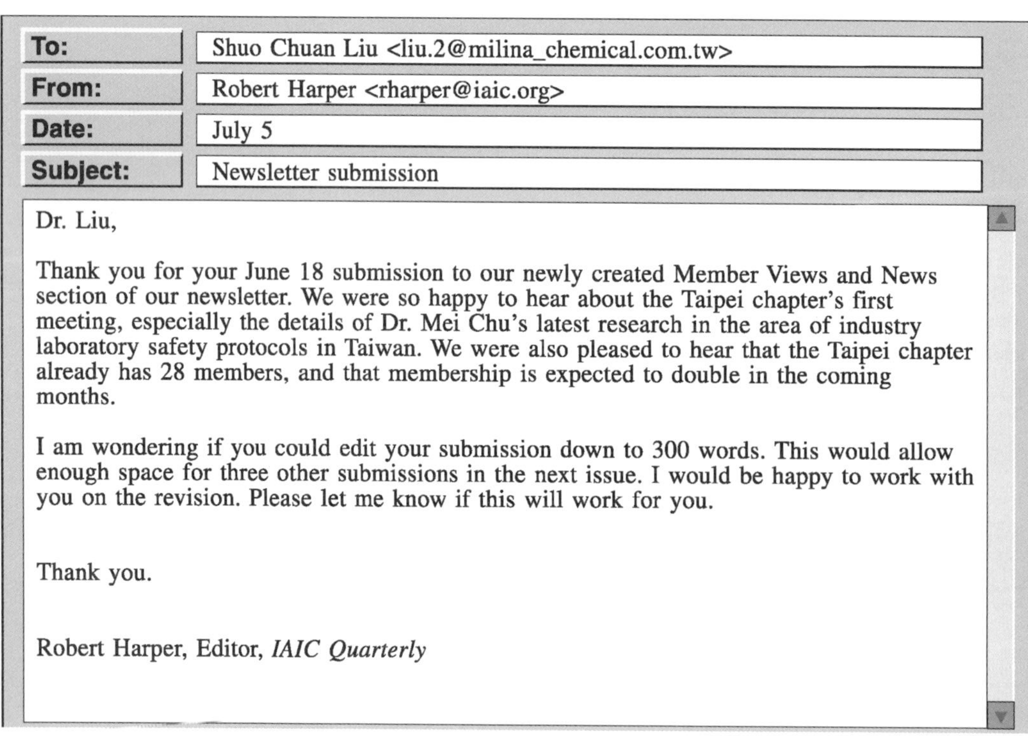

To:	Shuo Chuan Liu <liu.2@milina_chemical.com.tw>
From:	Robert Harper <rharper@iaic.org>
Date:	July 5
Subject:	Newsletter submission

Dr. Liu,

Thank you for your June 18 submission to our newly created Member Views and News section of our newsletter. We were so happy to hear about the Taipei chapter's first meeting, especially the details of Dr. Mei Chu's latest research in the area of industry laboratory safety protocols in Taiwan. We were also pleased to hear that the Taipei chapter already has 28 members, and that membership is expected to double in the coming months.

I am wondering if you could edit your submission down to 300 words. This would allow enough space for three other submissions in the next issue. I would be happy to work with you on the revision. Please let me know if this will work for you.

Thank you.

Robert Harper, Editor, *IAIC Quarterly*

181. For whom is the Web page information most likely intended?

(A) IAIC members
(B) Newsletter editors
(C) Publication directors
(D) Students of industrial chemistry

182. According to the Web page information, what is true about the newsletter?

(A) A section of it will be discontinued.
(B) Larger print will be used.
(C) It will be issued every month.
(D) It will be published in color.

183. On the Web page, the word "impressions" in paragraph 2, line 1, is closest in meaning to

(A) characteristics
(B) imitations
(C) feelings
(D) effects

184. What is suggested about Dr. Liu's submission?

(A) It explains how to become an IAIC member.
(B) It will appear with one other submission.
(C) It will appear in the autumn issue of the newsletter.
(D) It was sent to Mr. Harper on June 30.

185. What is Dr. Liu asked to do?

(A) Provide details about a meeting
(B) Shorten his submission
(C) Include contact information with an article
(D) Arrange a chapter meeting

Go on to the next page.

Questions 186-190 refer to the following notice, e-mail, and comment form.

Waikiki Orchid Hotel

Scheduled guest activities in February
All activities begin at 10:00 A.M. at the Guest Services desk in the lobby.

Activity and instructor/guide	Description
Every Monday Surfing lesson Conducted by Kekoa Kalena	Learn to surf the waves of Waikiki. Must be a good swimmer. $50 per person. Participants must be at least 12 years old.
Every Tuesday Hawaiian flower crafts Conducted by Jessica Agbayani	Your instructor will guide you in the making of a lei: a beautiful Hawaiian flower garland or necklace. All supplies included. $10 per person.
Every Wednesday History tour Conducted by Lani Okimoto	In this 90-minute walking tour, participants will learn the history of Waikiki. No charge.
Every Thursday Hawaiian cookery class Conducted by head chef Sarah Wang	Learn how to cook traditional local Hawaiian dishes. (Lesson can be tailored to include vegetarian recipes only.) Participants must be at least 12 years old. $20 per person.

Go to the Guest Services desk for further information and to sign up.

To:	Guest Services Staff <gsstaff@waikikiorchidhotel.com>
From:	Ji-Min Choi <jmchoi@waikikiorchidhotel.com>
Date:	February 7
Subject:	Update

Hi all,

I need to update this month's program of guest activities. Jessica Agbayani and Sarah Wang will be away February 10–16. I will lead Jessica's activities and Tom Anaya will lead Sarah's. Everything will return to normal on February 17, when Jessica and Sarah both return.

Sincerely,

Ji-Min Choi
Guest Services Director, Waikiki Orchid Hotel

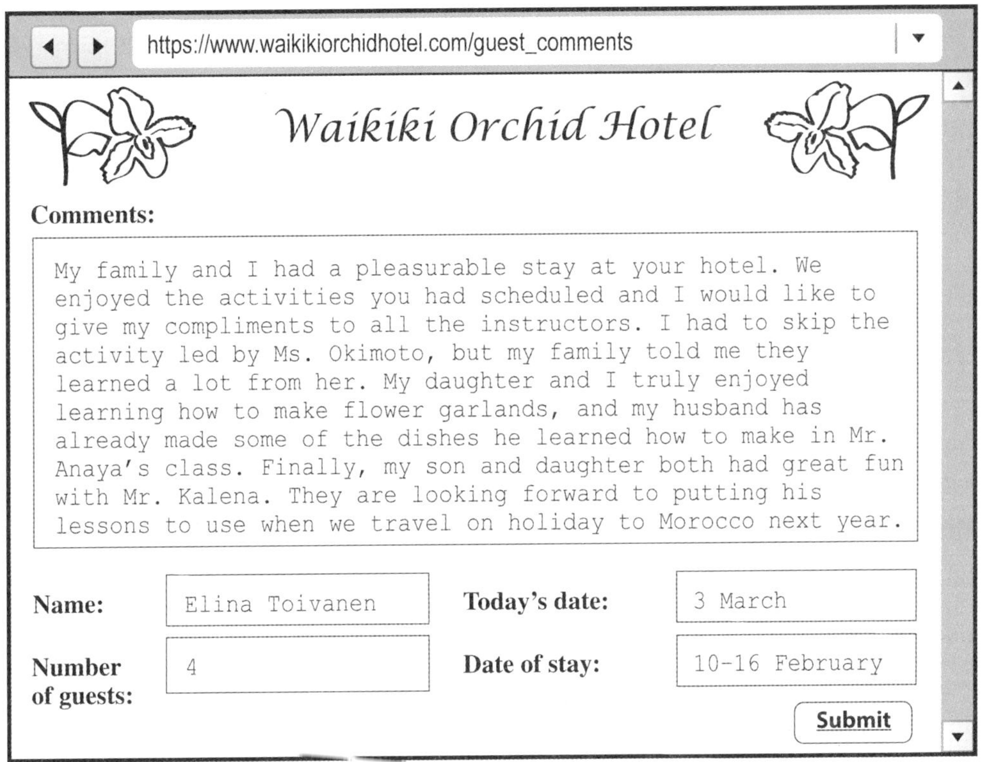

https://www.waikikiorchidhotel.com/guest_comments

Waikiki Orchid Hotel

Comments:

My family and I had a pleasurable stay at your hotel. We enjoyed the activities you had scheduled and I would like to give my compliments to all the instructors. I had to skip the activity led by Ms. Okimoto, but my family told me they learned a lot from her. My daughter and I truly enjoyed learning how to make flower garlands, and my husband has already made some of the dishes he learned how to make in Mr. Anaya's class. Finally, my son and daughter both had great fun with Mr. Kalena. They are looking forward to putting his lessons to use when we travel on holiday to Morocco next year.

Name: Elina Toivanen
Today's date: 3 March
Number of guests: 4
Date of stay: 10-16 February

Submit

186. What activity can be customized?

(A) Monday's activity
(B) Tuesday's activity
(C) Wednesday's activity
(D) Thursday's activity

187. What is the purpose of the e-mail?

(A) To introduce two new employees
(B) To respond to a guest inquiry
(C) To make changes to a schedule
(D) To arrange training courses for staff

188. In the comment form, the word "skip" in paragraph 1, line 3, is closest in meaning to

(A) jump
(B) miss
(C) pay for
(D) look over

189. Who guided guests in making flower crafts?

(A) Mr. Kalena
(B) Ms. Choi
(C) Ms. Okimoto
(D) Ms. Wang

190. What are Ms. Toivanen's children planning to do in Morocco?

(A) Go surfing
(B) Learn Moroccan crafts
(C) Take a tour
(D) Make Moroccan food

Go on to the next page.

Questions 191-195 refer to the following notice, review, and article.

Taste of Italy

Dear Valued Customers,

After 25 years in business, Taste of Italy will be closing its doors on April 23. During the week of April 17–23, please join us for a celebration of the store's history. All customers will receive a free cupcake with the purchase of any fresh bread or pastry item.

Please keep an eye out for Taste of Italy pastry chef Salvator Ribisi. He will be opening his own bakery within the coming months, where customers will be able to order custom pastries and cakes for parties and weddings.

It has been a pleasure to serve our wonderful Pineville City customers.

Sincerely,

Benito Giordano, owner

http://www.pinevillerestaurants.com

Sweet Occasions

HOME	MENUS	**REVIEWS**	LOCATIONS

I was sad that Taste of Italy closed—I had wanted them to make my wedding cake. So, I was excited when their former pastry chef opened Sweet Occasions in the Plaza Shopping Center. He made our cake, and it was perfect! Our guests kept commenting on how much they liked the cake. I would recommend Sweet Occasions to anyone.

–*Edith Costello*

★★★★★

The Evolution of a City

When the Plaza Shopping Center opened on River Road in July of last year, Pineville City mayor Angela Portofino predicted that it would benefit the city by bringing shoppers from nearby towns to the area. Based on a 25 percent increase in the city's sales tax receipts over the last six months, Ms. Portofino appears to have been correct.

However, less frequently mentioned was the potential effect of such commercial development on the city's downtown business district, which includes a number of small, family-owned stores and restaurants. In the past two months, three of these businesses—Quality Books, Ashley's Beauty Salon, and Taste of Italy—have either closed or announced plans to close, all citing a decline in customers since the Plaza's opening.

Still, the mayor believes that the overall effects of new developments such as the Plaza are positive. "It's certainly disappointing when a beloved business like Quality Books closes," she said. "But new businesses bring new opportunities for all residents of Pineville City, including new jobs."

191. Why most likely is Mr. Giordano closing his business?

(A) Because he wants to retire
(B) Because he lost business to a new shopping center
(C) Because he cannot afford to make needed repairs
(D) Because he plans to open a different kind of business

192. What is indicated about Mr. Ribisi's bakery?

(A) It opened on April 23.
(B) It was once owned by Mr. Giordano.
(C) It made Ms. Costello's wedding cake.
(D) It is giving away free pastries.

193. In the review, the word "kept" in paragraph 1, line 3, is closest in meaning to

(A) held
(B) continued
(C) saved
(D) gave

194. What is suggested about the Plaza Shopping Center?

(A) It has generated a lot of income for Pineville City.
(B) It has attracted business for local family-owned stores.
(C) It was financed by Mayor Portofino.
(D) It was built in downtown Pineville City.

195. According to her statement, why does Ms. Portofino have a positive view of the Plaza Shopping Center?

(A) Because it has a good bookstore
(B) Because it was completed ahead of schedule
(C) Because it offers discounts on expensive products
(D) Because it provides city residents with jobs

Go on to the next page.

Questions 196-200 refer to the following notice and e-mails.

The London Center of Contemporary Art presents...

Time Travel

By Conner Goodman

1-15 May

Mr. Goodman is a painter and sculptor who lives in London.

Conner Goodman's work will occupy our entire museum, with each museum hall representing a time period in English history, specifically focusing on the city of London. Mr. Goodman commemorates less commonly known moments in London's history taken from literature and film.

Upon entering the museum, visitors will experience London as it was 2,000 years ago, in the time of the ancient Romans. Each succeeding gallery that visitors encounter will portray younger versions of the city up to present-day London. Mr. Goodman's art makes use of a range of media, including paint, video, and even recycled material. All pieces in this exhibition are Mr. Goodman's original creations.

Tickets:

Museum entrance: £15 per person

Conner Goodman will discuss his exhibition at Cornwall Hall on Saturday, 9 May, at 6:00 PM. Tickets are £20 and half of all proceeds will be donated to the Historic Building Conservation Society. Please call (020) 7946 0609 for more information.

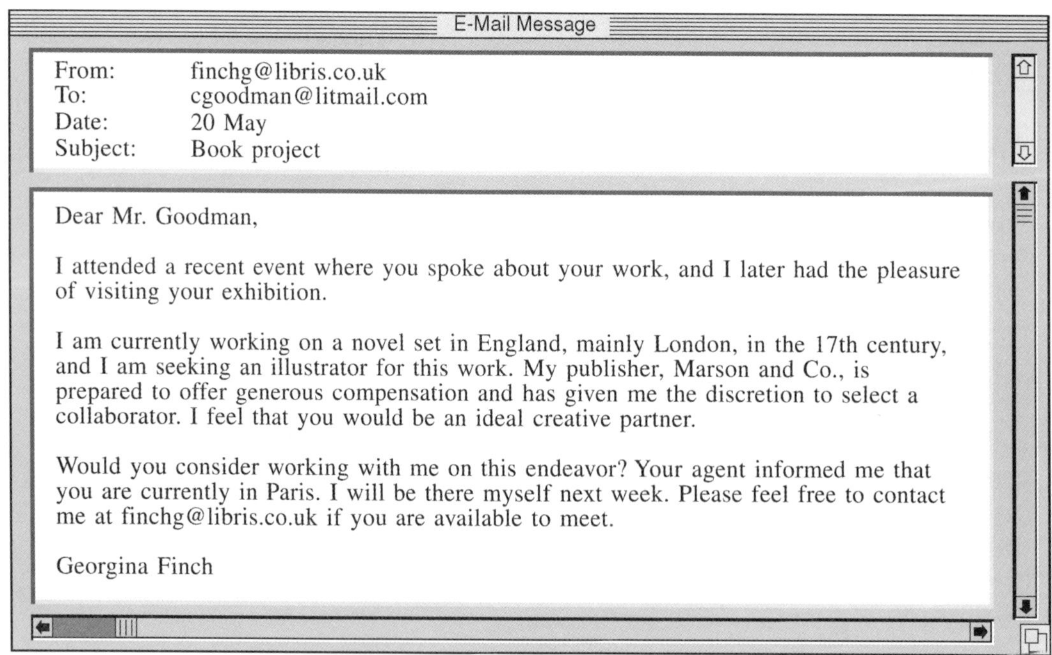

E-Mail Message

From: finchg@libris.co.uk
To: cgoodman@litmail.com
Date: 20 May
Subject: Book project

Dear Mr. Goodman,

I attended a recent event where you spoke about your work, and I later had the pleasure of visiting your exhibition.

I am currently working on a novel set in England, mainly London, in the 17th century, and I am seeking an illustrator for this work. My publisher, Marson and Co., is prepared to offer generous compensation and has given me the discretion to select a collaborator. I feel that you would be an ideal creative partner.

Would you consider working with me on this endeavor? Your agent informed me that you are currently in Paris. I will be there myself next week. Please feel free to contact me at finchg@libris.co.uk if you are available to meet.

Georgina Finch

E-mail

From:	cgoodman@litmail.com
To:	finchg@libris.co.uk
Date:	22 May
Re:	Book project

Dear Georgina,

I am intrigued by your invitation and would be more than happy to discuss the project you describe. I am preparing to travel to Brussels next Friday, but let me know where you will be staying and when, and we will find the time to explore your proposal further.

Best wishes,

Conner Goodman

196. What does the notice suggest about the exhibition?

(A) It portrays a city from a unique perspective.
(B) It is made entirely of recycled materials.
(C) It includes historical artifacts.
(D) It is inspired by a popular novel.

197. What is implied in the notice?

(A) The museum exhibition will open with a lecture.
(B) Guided audio tours of the exhibition are available for an additional fee.
(C) Visitors to the exhibition are encouraged to experience it in a particular order.
(D) Mr. Goodman is supervising a building restoration project.

198. Where most likely did Ms. Finch hear Mr. Goodman speak?

(A) At a meeting of the Historic Building Conservation Society
(B) At the Center of Contemporary Art
(C) At Marson and Co. headquarters
(D) At an event at Cornwall Hall

199. What is suggested about Mr. Goodman?

(A) He has agreed to a contract with Ms. Finch.
(B) He will meet with Ms. Finch in Paris.
(C) He is returning from Brussels next week.
(D) He is selling some of his paintings.

200. In what field do Ms. Finch and Mr. Goodman share some expertise?

(A) English history
(B) Creative writing
(C) Contemporary art
(D) Museum management

Stop! This is the end of the test. If you finish before time is called, you may go back to Parts 5, 6, and 7 and check your work.

解答篇

★參考分數計算方法、分數換算表及分數計算範例為 Test 1、Test 2 共用

★聽力題解中各國旗代表的口音分別為：美國 英國 加拿大 澳洲

參考分數計算方法

TOEIC® 聽力與閱讀測驗分數是使用統計的方法，將原始分數轉換成評量分數。藉由換算程序，即使是不同測驗，所得出的分數意義是相同的。因此，某次測驗得分 550 分，和另外一次測驗得分 550 分，表示英語能力相當。

完成練習測驗後，依照下列步驟可計算出參考分數：

步驟一：請參考第 125 及 257 頁的答案表，分別計算出聽力測驗與閱讀測驗的答對題數，各部分的答對題數，即為原始分數。

步驟二：請用第 123 頁的分數換算表，找到原始分數對應的評量分數範圍。例如：聽力測驗的原始分數是 45，換算出來的評量分數範圍就是 140 分到 225 分。

步驟三：各部分換算出來的評量分數範圍加總後，就是 TOEIC 聽力與閱讀測驗的總分。

此分數換算表是為了練習測驗而製作，不能使用於實際TOEIC聽力與閱讀測驗的分數計算。

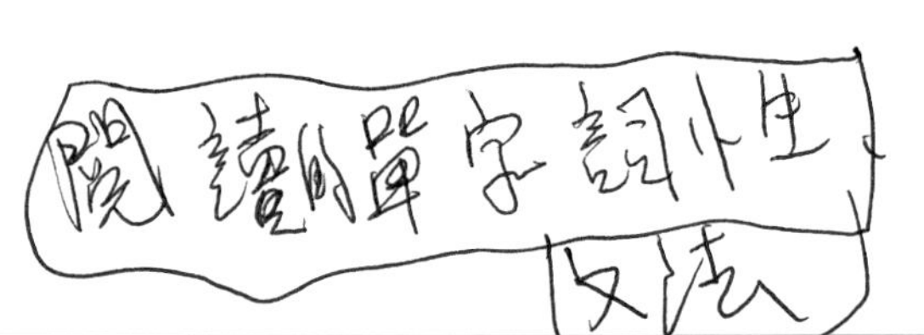

分數換算表

聽力測驗		閱讀測驗	
原始分數範圍	評量分數範圍	原始分數範圍	評量分數範圍
96 – 100	485 – 495	96 – 100	455 – 495
91 – 95	445 – 495	91 – 95	410 – 490
86 – 90	400 – 475	86 – 90	380 – 455
81 – 85	360 – 450	81 – 85	350 – 430
76 – 80	330 – 420	76 – 80	315 – 405
71 – 75	300 – 385	71 – 75	290 – 380
66 – 70	265 – 355	66 – 70	260 – 355
61 – 65	235 – 330	61 – 65	235 – 325
56 – 60	210 – 305	56 – 60	205 – 300
51 – 55	185 – 275	51 – 55	175 – 270
46 – 50	165 – 250	46 – 50	155 – 235
41 – 45	140 – 225	41 – 45	125 – 205
36 – 40	115 – 195	36 – 40	105 – 170
31 – 35	95 – 165	31 – 35	85 – 140
26 – 30	80 – 135	26 – 30	65 – 115
21 – 25	65 – 110	21 – 25	55 – 90
16 – 20	35 – 90	16 – 20	45 – 75
11 – 15	10 – 70	11 – 15	30 – 55
6 – 10	5 – 60	6 – 10	10 – 45
1 – 5	5 – 50	1 – 5	5 – 30
0	5 – 35	0	5 – 15

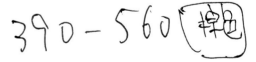

分數計算範例

聽力測驗的原始分數為 45，閱讀測驗的原始分數為 64，將其數字填到以下空欄：

步驟一

	原始分數	**評量分數範圍**
聽力測驗	**45**	
閱讀測驗	**64**	
	總分範圍	

步驟二～三

接下來，在分數換算表找出對應的評量分數範圍，將其數字記下，並算出合計值。

	原始分數	**評量分數範圍**
聽力測驗	**45**	**140-225**
閱讀測驗	**64**	**235-325**
	總分範圍	**375-550**

得出測驗總分範圍在 375 分至 550 分之間。

TEST 1 答案表

題號	正解	題號	正解	題號	正解	題號	正解
1	B	51	D	101	B	151	C
2	C	52	B	102	C	152	B
3	B	53	A	103	C	153	A
4	D	54	B	104	D	154	C
5	C	55	B	105	D	155	A
6	C	56	B	106	A	156	D
7	C	57	C	107	C	157	B
8	A	58	D	108	D	158	C
9	B	59	D	109	B	159	C
10	A	60	C	110	D	160	D
11	C	61	B	111	C	161	C
12	B	62	B	112	A	162	B
13	A	63	A	113	D	163	D
14	A	64	D	114	D	164	D
15	C	65	C	115	C	165	D
16	B	66	C	116	A	166	A
17	A	67	A	117	B	167	D
18	B	68	C	118	A	168	D
19	A	69	D	119	C	169	B
20	C	70	B	120	B	170	A
21	A	71	A	121	A	171	C
22	A	72	C	122	C	172	D
23	B	73	B	123	B	173	A
24	B	74	B	124	C	174	C
25	C	75	D	125	D	175	B
26	C	76	C	126	C	176	C
27	B	77	B	127	A	177	D
28	C	78	C	128	B	178	B
29	B	79	D	129	A	179	C
30	A	80	B	130	C	180	A
31	A	81	A	131	B	181	C
32	A	82	D	132	A	182	D
33	C	83	D	133	C	183	D
34	B	84	B	134	A	184	B
35	C	85	C	135	B	185	C
36	C	86	A	136	A	186	D
37	A	87	B	137	D	187	C
38	B	88	D	138	D	188	B
39	A	89	C	139	D	189	C
40	D	90	C	140	B	190	A
41	B	91	A	141	C	191	D
42	D	92	B	142	A	192	B
43	D	93	C	143	D	193	C
44	C	94	C	144	A	194	A
45	C	95	C	145	B	195	A
46	A	96	A	146	A	196	B
47	B	97	D	147	A	197	A
48	B	98	C	148	C	198	B
49	A	99	D	149	B	199	D
50	D	100	A	150	A	200	A

題目 / 中文翻譯	重點解說

1

(A) She's filing papers.
(B) She's using a photocopier.
(C) She's turning on some lights.
(D) She's closing a cabinet.

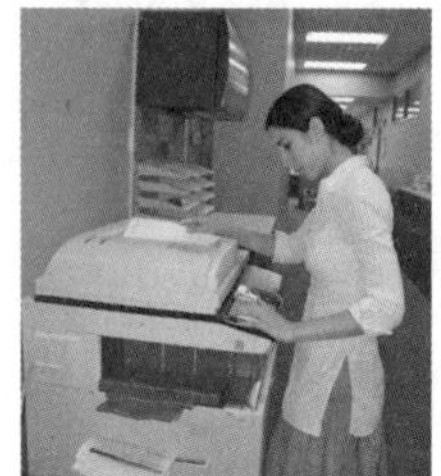

(A) 她正在歸檔。
(B) 她正在使用影印機。
(C) 她正在開燈。
(D) 她正關起櫥櫃。

正解 (B)
照片中的女士正在使用 photocopier「影印機」。文中 She's 是 She is 的縮寫。

2

(A) The man's wrapping boxes in plastic.
(B) The man's repairing an air-conditioning unit.
(C) The man's sitting in the driver's seat.
(D) The man's unlocking a gate.

(A) 男士正在用塑膠紙包裝紙箱。
(B) 男士正在修理空調機件。
(C) 男士正坐在駕駛座上。
(D) 男士正在開大門的鎖。

正解 (C)
照片中的男士坐在堆高機的 driver's seat「駕駛座」上面。文中 man's 是 man is 的縮寫。

3

(A) A towel is hanging on a fence.
(B) Some plants have been placed in pots.
(C) Some chairs have been set around a table.
(D) The door to a house has been left open.

(A) 籬笆上掛著毛巾。
(B) 植物種在花盆裡。
(C) 椅子環桌擺設。
(D) 屋門是開著的。

正解 (B)
籬笆前的 plant「植物」都種在 pot「花盆」裡。< have been + 過去分詞 >表示「(東西)被…的狀態」。place「放置…」。

題目 / 中文翻譯	重點解說

4

(A) A woman is putting away a mobile phone.
(B) A cashier is collecting a payment.
(C) A man is discarding a newspaper.
(D) Some diners are seated across from each other.

(A) 女士將手機收好。
(B) 收銀員正在收取付款。
(C) 男士丟掉報紙。
(D) 用餐者正坐在彼此對面。

正解 (D)

diners「用餐者」，指的是照片上的男、女客人。across from each other 表示「面對面」的位置關係。be seated 為「就座」。

5

(A) A customer is choosing some floor tiles.
(B) A shop assistant is unfolding a pair of jeans.
(C) A woman is checking her appearance in a mirror.
(D) Some shoes are being lined up under a bench.

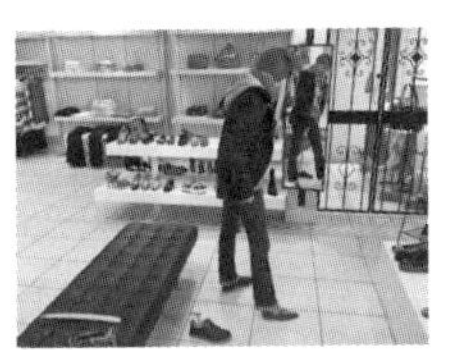

(A) 顧客正在挑選地板磁磚。
(B) 店員攤開一件牛仔褲。
(C) 女士在鏡前檢查儀容。
(D) 長凳下擺放著幾雙鞋子。

正解 (C)

照片中的女士照鏡子檢查自己的 appearance「儀容、外表」。check 指「檢查…」。
(B) unfold 是「攤開（折好的東西）」

6

(A) Signs are being posted at an intersection.
(B) Bricks are being replaced on a walkway.
(C) A man is using a lawn mower to cut the grass.
(D) A man is loading supplies into a wheelbarrow.

(A) 號誌牌放置在十字路口。
(B) 正在更換人行道的磚塊。
(C) 男士正在使用除草機割草。
(D) 男士將生活用品放到獨輪手推車上。

正解 (C)

照片中男士推著 lawn mower「除草機」。grass 指的是「草、草地」。
(A) intersection「十字路口」；(D) wheelbarrow「（載運沙土的）獨輪手推車」。

題目 / 中文翻譯

重點解說

7 Q： A：

Will you translate an e-mail into Spanish for me?
(A) Three more chapters.
(B) No, I haven't sent it yet.
(C) Sure, let me see it.

您能幫我將這封電子郵件翻譯成西班牙文嗎？
(A) 還有三個章節。
(B) 不，我還沒寄出。
(C) 當然，讓我看一下。

正解 (C)

translate A into B 指「將 A 翻譯成 B」。Will you...? 是詢問對方「可以…嗎？」用 Sure「當然」回答後，再要求對方給自己看電子郵件。

---

8 Q： A：

How many tables did you reserve?
(A) Twelve of them.
(B) I'll be right there.
(C) For the awards dinner.

您預訂了幾張桌子？
(A) 12 桌。
(B) 我馬上到。
(C) 為了頒獎晚宴。

正解 (A)

reserve a table 指「預約餐廳桌位」。How many...? 詢問「幾個…？」因此回答數量的 (A) 是正確回應。(A) 的 them 指的是問題中的 tables。

---

9 Q： A：

Where can I mail this letter?
(A) I don't have an envelope.
(B) At the post office down the street.
(C) No, not right now.

我可以去哪裡寄信？
(A) 我沒有信封。
(B) 沿著這條街走，有間郵局。
(C) 不，現在不行。

正解 (B)

mail「把…投進郵筒、郵寄…」。Where...? 詢問「在哪裡？」回答地點的 (B) 為正解。這裡的 down the street 是「沿著街道往下走」的意思。

題目 / 中文翻譯	重點解說

10 Q: A:

Why did you come to the office early today?
(A) Because I had to finish a report.
(B) Usually at eight-thirty in the morning.
(C) I'm sorry, but I can't.

你今天為何這麼早到辦公室？
(A) 因為我得完成一份報告。
(B) 通常是早上八點半。
(C) 很抱歉，但我不能。

正解 (A)

Why...? 詢問「為什麼⋯？」以 Because... 說明原因的選項 (A) 是正解。report「報告」。

---

11 Q: A:

Have you opened the front entrance yet?
(A) I left it in the back.
(B) I saw them.
(C) No—I don't have a key.

你打開前方入口了嗎？
(A) 我把它留在後面了。
(B) 我看見他們了。
(C) 不，我並沒有鑰匙。

正解 (C)

front「前方的」; entrance「入口」。
對於詢問「入口是否已經打開」，選項 (C) 回答 No，並補充說明還沒打開的原因。

---

12 Q: A:

You went to that museum last weekend, didn't you?
(A) I saw him on Sunday.
(B) I didn't have time.
(C) For a few months.

你上個週末去了那間博物館對吧？
(A) 我星期日見到他。
(B) 我沒時間。
(C) 已經幾個月了。

正解 (B)

句末的 ..., didn't you? 是確認對方「已經⋯了吧？」意在問對方是否已經去過博物館，選項 (B) 表示沒去的理由是「沒有時間」，是適當的回應。

題目 / 中文翻譯	重點解說

13 Q：(Canada) A：(USA)

How many interns do we need this summer?
(A) I think five will be enough.
(B) We'll place an advertisement.
(C) I'm well, thank you.

這個夏天，我們需要多少位實習生？
(A) 我想五位就夠了。
(B) 我們會打廣告。
(C) 我很好，謝謝你。

正解 (A)

intern「工讀生」。
對於 How many...? 的問題，選項 (A) 回答數量「五位就夠了」為正解。enough「足夠的」。

---

14 Q：(UK) A：(Australia)

What shift are you working on Saturday?
(A) The morning one.
(B) I can meet you there.
(C) Yes, we booked it in April.

你星期六上什麼班？
(A) 早班。
(B) 我可以去那裡找你。
(C) 是的，我們四月預訂的。

正解 (A)

shift「輪班制的工作時間、工作班次」。
對於「哪一個班次」的問題，選項 (A) 回答早班是正解。(A) 的 one 是指問題中的 shift。

---

15 Q：(Canada) A：(USA)

My coworkers and I are going out for lunch tomorrow.
(A) It launched at three.
(B) I had the chicken.
(C) That sounds nice.

我和我的同事明天會去吃午餐。
(A) 三點發表。
(B) 我吃了雞肉。
(C) 聽起來很棒。

正解 (C)

coworker「同事」；go out for...「外出」。
對於陳述明天預定做的事，選項 (C) That sounds nice.「聽起來很棒。」這種慣用句是正解。

題目 / 中文翻譯	重點解說

16 Q: A:

When does the plane to Seoul leave?
(A) No, I've never been.
(B) It's an hour behind schedule.
(C) From Gate 52, I think.

往首爾的飛機何時起飛？
(A) 不，我從來沒去過。
(B) 比預定時間晚了一個小時。
(C) 我想是從 52 號登機門。

正解 (B)

leave「出發」。
對於 When...?「何時…？」的問題，選項 (B) 回答出發時間「比預定時間晚了一小時」，因此是正解。behind schedule「比預定時間晚」。

---

17 Q: A:

How will I know if the baseball game is canceled?
(A) You could look on the team's Web site.
(B) Yes, I knew that.
(C) Because you chose a different date.

我該如何得知棒球賽是否會取消？
(A) 你可以上該隊的網站查詢。
(B) 是的，我知道。
(C) 因為你選擇不同的日期。

正解 (A)

對於 How...?「如何…？」的問題，選項 (A) 回答「看該隊的網站」這種方法，因此是正解。這裡的 could 指的是「可以…」，表示提議。

---

18 Q: A:

Should we get the changes to this agreement in writing?
(A) Sorry, I don't have change.
(B) That's probably a good idea.
(C) I'll write each day.

我們需要以書面方式寫下同意書的更動內容嗎？
(A) 抱歉，我沒有零錢。
(B) 這也許是個好主意。
(C) 我每天都會寫。

正解 (B)

change「更動」；agreement「同意書、合約」；in writing「書面方式」。
對於「是否需要以書面方式寫下同意書的更動內容」這個問題，選項 (B)「這也許是個好主意」，是適當的回應。probably「也許、可能」。
(A) change「（不可數名詞）零錢、找錢」。

題目 / 中文翻譯	重點解說

19 Q： A：

Will you create a chart to track our expenses this quarter?
(A) Yeah, I'll do that now.
(B) A quarterly fee.
(C) Try track 46.

你是否能製作一張本季經費的追蹤紀錄表？
(A) 好的，我現在馬上做。
(B) 一季的經費。
(C) 試試看編號 46。

正解 (A)

chart「圖表」; track「追蹤（進度）、跟蹤」; expense「經費」; quarter「季度」。
對於 Will you...? 這樣的請求，回答「馬上做」的選項 (A) 是正解。(A) 的 do that 指的是問題中的 create a chart。

---

20 Q： A：

Where can I donate some old office equipment?
(A) Because it starts at nine o'clock.
(B) No, don't eat in here.
(C) What kind of equipment is it?

我可以將舊的辦公室設備捐去哪裡？
(A) 因為九點就開始了。
(B) 不，這裡請勿飲食。
(C) 是什麼樣的設備呢？

正解 (C)

donate「捐贈」; office equipment「辦公室設備、用品」。
對於「能夠將舊的辦公室設備捐去哪裡」這個問題，選項 (C) 接著詢問設備的類型，是適當的回應。

---

21 Q： A：

I'll lose my registration fee if I can't attend the workshop, right?
(A) I'm afraid so.
(B) Just over there, on the right.
(C) Check the lost and found.

如果我無法出席工作坊，就不能拿回報名費，對嗎？
(A) 恐怕是的。
(B) 就在那裡，在右邊。
(C) 到失物招領處確認一下。

正解 (A)

registration fee「報名費」；attend「參加」；workshop「工作坊」。
句末的..., right? 是確認「是…吧？」。選項 (A) 回答I'm afraid so.「恐怕是的」，是自然且合理的回覆。

題目 / 中文翻譯	重點解說

22 Q : A :

Didn't Daniel accept the job offer?
(A) He'll let us know tomorrow.
(B) We expect a large crowd.
(C) Yes, I will.

Daniel 不願意接受該項工作職缺嗎？
(A) 他明天會告知我們。
(B) 我們預期會有大批人潮。
(C) 是的，我會。

正解 (A)

accept「接受」; job offer「工作職缺」。
對於 Didn't...?「沒有…嗎？」這種否定疑問句，選項 (A) 回答「他明天會告知我們」，是自然且合理的回應。
(B) crowd「人潮、擁擠」。

---

23 Q : A :

That building's still under construction, isn't it?
(A) Maybe the site manager.
(B) Yes, it's due to be finished in October.
(C) Yes, it's on level six.

那棟建築物仍在施工，對吧？
(A) 可能是現場經理。
(B) 是的，預計十月完工。
(C) 是的，正在第六個階段。

正解 (B)

句中 building's 是 building is 的縮寫。under construction「仍在施工」。句末的 ...,isn't it? 是確認「…是吧？」。選項 (B) 先回答 Yes，再敘述預定完工時間，因此為正解。be due to do「預定要…」。
(A) site「現場」。

---

24 Q : A :

Have we changed our paper supplier?
(A) A large inventory.
(B) I'm not sure.
(C) In the cupboard there.

我們的紙類供應商換人了嗎？
(A) 大量庫存。
(B) 我不確定。
(C) 在櫥櫃裡。

正解 (B)

supplier「供應商」。
對於 Have we...?「我們…了嗎？」這個問題，選項 (B) 不是回答 Yes ／ No，而是回答 I'm not sure.「我不確定」，是適當的回覆。
(A) inventory「庫存」。

題目/中文翻譯	重點解說

25 Q：A：

Who's exhibiting in the Central Art Gallery next month?
(A) Yes, it opens at seven P.M.
(B) My friend Aziz is coming, too.
(C) It's a group of young Japanese artists.

下個月，誰即將在 Central Art Gallery 舉辦展覽？
(A) 是的，晚上七點開館。
(B) 我的朋友 Aziz 也會到場。
(C) 一群年輕的日本藝術家。

正解 (C)

句中 Who's 是 Who is 的縮寫。exhibit「舉辦展覽」。
對於 Who...?「誰…？」這個問題，選項 (C) 回答是「一群年輕藝術家」，故為正解。

---

26 Q：A：

Shall we repaint the lobby or the boardroom?
(A) There's some in the closet.
(B) It has plenty of room.
(C) We can afford to do both.

我們應該重新粉刷大廳還是會議室？
(A) 衣櫃裡還有一些。
(B) 還有很多空間。
(C) 我們有經費可以兩處都做。

正解 (C)

repaint「重新粉刷」; boardroom「會議室」。Shall we...? 是提議做某件事。對於大廳或會議室其中一處重新粉刷的提議，選項 (C) 回答「有經費可以兩處都做」是正解。(C) 的 both「兩者」，指的是問句中的 the lobby 和 boardroom。afford「有（錢或時間的）餘裕可以做…」。

---

27 Q：A：

Are you riding your bike to work today?
(A) Alfonso's writing the book.
(B) Only if the weather's nice.
(C) Yes, I'd like to work there.

你今天會騎腳踏車去上班嗎？
(A) Alfonso 正在寫書。
(B) 如果天氣好的話。
(C) 是的，我想要去那裡工作。

正解 (B)

＜ Are you ＋ Ving? ＞「打算…嗎？」是詢問預定行程，對於這樣的問題，選項 (B) 回答 only if...「只有…才」的回答是合理的回應。
Only if the weather's nice 之後，省略了 I'm riding my bike to work today。

題目/中文翻譯

重點解說

28 Q: A:

When do you think we'll hear if we've won the Jones account?
(A) I lost my accounting manual.
(B) One of our biggest clients.
(C) Ms. Watson might already know.

你覺得我們何時才會知道我們是否成功擄獲 Jones 這名大客戶的芳心？
(A) 我的會計手冊遺失了。
(B) 我們最大的客戶之一。
(C) Watson 女士可能已經知道了。

正解 (C)
win an account「贏得交易」。
在 When...? 問句插入 do you think。對於這個詢問，選項 (C) 告知可能已經知道答案的人物，因此為適當的回應。do you think 在這裡是插入句，後方接＜主詞＋動詞＞ we'll hear。

---

29 Q: A:

You'd better call the technician to repair the photocopier.
(A) Yes—overnight delivery.
(B) Hopefully it won't take him too long.
(C) Double-sided copies, please.

你最好打電話請技術人員來修理影印機。
(A) 是的，隔天送達。
(B) 希望他不會花太多的修理時間。
(C) 煩請雙面影印。

正解 (B)
You'd better 是 You had better 的縮寫，用來表達強烈建議某事「應該…」。
對於委託別人修理的建議，選項 (B) 回應「希望不會花太多（時間）」，是適當的回答。(B) 的 him 指的是 technician「技術人員」。hopefully「希望」。

---

30 Q: A:

I don't know which computer model to buy.
(A) What features are most important to you?
(B) Because mine stopped working.
(C) No, I won't get it for a while.

我不知道該買哪一款的電腦機型。
(A) 對你來說，最重要的功能是什麼？
(B) 因為我的壞掉了。
(C) 不，我還要過陣子才會買。

正解 (A)
對於「不知道應該買哪一款」這句話，選項 (A) 反問「對你來說，哪種功能最重要」，這樣是適當的回答。feature「功能」。

題目/中文翻譯

31 Q：🇺🇸 A：🇨🇦

Didn't you see the review of our restaurant?
(A) I haven't had time to read it yet.
(B) There's a great view from the dining room.
(C) A reservation for lunch on Saturday.

您沒讀過我們餐廳的評論嗎？
(A) 我還沒有時間拜讀。
(B) 餐廳外景色絕佳。
(C) 週六的午餐預約。

重點解說

正解 (A)

review「批評、評論」。
對於使用 Didn't...? 這種否定疑問句，問對方「是否沒讀過」，選項 (A) 回答尚未拜讀的原因是「沒時間」，這是適當的回應。

題目 / 中文翻譯

Questions 32 through 34 refer to the following conversation.

請參考以下的對話回答第 32 題至第 34 題。

男：🇨🇦 女：🇺🇸

W: ❶ I love this jacket! Do you have another one just like it?

女：我好喜歡這件外套！你們還有其他同款外套嗎？

M: I'm afraid that's the last one we have in medium. Is there something wrong with it?

男：恐怕這是我們最後一件 M 號了。外套有什麼問題嗎？

W: ❷ There's a small tear on the seam of the left sleeve. But I really like it a lot!

女：左袖口接縫處有個小裂痕。但我真的很喜歡這件外套！

M: Well, if you buy the jacket as it is, then ❸ I can offer you a deal because of the tear. ❹ How does a 20% discount sound?

男：嗯，如果您買下這件，那麼我會因為這個小裂痕給您打折。您覺得八折優惠價聽起來如何？

單字註釋：tear「撕裂處」; seam「接縫」

題目 / 中文翻譯

32

Where most likely is the conversation taking place?

(A) In a clothing store

(B) In a furniture factory

(C) In a restaurant

(D) In a dry-cleaning shop

該對話最有可能發生在何處？

(A) 服飾店

(B) 家具工廠

(C) 餐廳

(D) 乾洗店

重點解說

正解 (A)

女士在❶中說「我好喜歡這件外套！你們還有其他同款外套嗎？」之後對話繼續，談外套的尺寸和購買。

題目 / 中文翻譯	重點解說

33

What is the problem?
(A) Some merchandise has been lost.
(B) Some clothing is the wrong size.
(C) An item is damaged.
(D) An order has not arrived.

發生什麼問題？
(A) 商品遺失。
(B) 服飾尺寸不合。
(C) 品項有瑕疵。
(D) 訂單尚未送達。

正解 (C)

女士在❷中說 There's a small tear on the seam of the left sleeve.「左袖口接縫處有個小裂痕」。a small tear 表示 damaged「受損」，因此選 (C)。

34

What does the man offer to do?
(A) Issue a refund
(B) Reduce a price
(C) Speak to a manager
(D) Check the inventory

男士的提議為何？
(A) 發還退款
(B) 減價
(C) 找店長談
(D) 查看庫存

正解 (B)

男士在❸中提出I can offer you a deal because of the tear.「我會因為這個小裂痕給您打折」後，說 How does a 20% discount sound?「您覺得八折優惠價聽起來如何？」
reduce「降低（數量等）、減少」。
(A) issue「發行」。

題目 / 中文翻譯

Questions 35 through 37 refer to the following conversation.

請參考以下的對話回答第 35 題至第 37 題。

男： 女：

M: Hi, ❶I'm calling to book a train ticket from London to Edinburgh, please. I'd like to leave around ten o'clock on Tuesday morning.

男：嗨，我是為了訂購從倫敦到愛丁堡的火車票而致電給您。我打算星期二上午十點左右出發。

W: Certainly, sir. ❷I can reserve a seat for you on the train departing for Edinburgh at ten-thirty. The cheapest fare is eighty-five pounds.

女：沒問題，先生。我可以幫您預訂十點三十分前往愛丁堡的火車座位，最便宜的票價是 85 英鎊。

M: OK, I'd like to buy that ticket, please. ❸I'd also like to find out whether there's room on the train for passengers to take bicycles.

男：好的，我想要訂購那張車票。我也想知道火車上面是否有讓旅客停放單車的空間。

W: Yes, there is, but ❹it'll cost three pounds more to reserve a space for your bike.

女：有的，不過您必須多花三英鎊才能預訂單車放置空間。

單字註釋：fare「票價」

題目 / 中文翻譯

35

Where most likely does the woman work?
(A) At an airport
(B) At a bicycle shop
(C) At a train station
(D) At a taxi stand

女士最有可能在哪裡工作？
(A) 機場
(B) 自行車店
(C) 火車站
(D) 計程車服務站

重點解說

正解 (C)

男士在❶中說I'm calling to book a train ticket「我是為了訂購火車票而致電給您」，女士回答❷ I can reserve a seat for you on the train「我可以幫您預訂火車座位」。

題目 / 中文翻譯	重點解說

36

Why is the man calling?
(A) To find out the hours of operation
(B) To schedule a service
(C) To reserve a ticket
(D) To inquire about a delay

男士為何來電？
(A) 查明營業時間
(B) 排定服務時間
(C) 預訂車票
(D) 詢問誤點

正解 (C)

男士在❶中說I'm calling to book a train ticket「我是為了訂購火車票而致電給您」。book「預約」換另一種說法是 (C) reserve「預約、保留」。

37

What does the woman say will cost extra?
(A) Transporting a bicycle
(B) Traveling during rush hour
(C) Changing a reservation
(D) Upgrading to business class

女士表明需要額外付費的項目為何？
(A) 單車運送
(B) 尖峰時段的旅程
(C) 更改預訂內容
(D) 升等為商務艙

正解 (A)

男士在❸中詢問「火車上是否有停放單車的空間」，女士指引說❹ **it'll cost three pounds more to reserve a space for your bike**「單車需要額外支付三英鎊才能預訂單車放置空間」。transport「運送」。

題目 / 中文翻譯

Questions 38 through 40 refer to the following conversation.

請參考以下的對話回答第 38 題至第 40 題。

男：🇨🇦 女：🇺🇸

M: Excuse me, I'm sorry to disturb you— ❶I came to use a library computer, but I forgot my library card and I can't log on without it.

男：不好意思，很抱歉打擾您——我是來使用圖書館電腦的，但是我忘記帶圖書證，因此我無法登入。

W: Oh, that's alright. ❷Let me look up your account in our database. Do you have any other identification with you?

女：喔，不要緊。讓我調閱您在我們資料庫的帳戶。您身上是否有其他身分證明呢？

M: Well, I have my driver's license. It has my name and address on it.

男：嗯，我有駕照，上面有我的姓名和住址。

W: Okay, that's fine. ❸I'll give you a password so you can access the computer now, but ❹ you won't be able to use it after today.

女：好的，這樣就可以了。我會給您一組密碼，您現在可以使用電腦，但今天過後就無法使用。

題目 / 中文翻譯

38

What does the man want to do?
(A) Sign up for membership
(B) Use a computer
(C) Make a telephone call
(D) Borrow some materials

男士想要做什麼？
(A) 註冊會員資格
(B) 使用電腦
(C) 打電話
(D) 借用資料

重點解說

正解 (B)

男士在❶說 I came to use a library computer「我是來使用圖書館電腦的」。

題目/中文翻譯	重點解說

39

Who most likely is the woman?
(A) A librarian
(B) A security guard
(C) A software developer
(D) A salesperson

女士最有可能的身分為何？
(A) 圖書館員
(B) 警衛
(C) 軟體開發人員
(D) 銷售員

正解 (A)

對於忘記帶圖書證、無法使用圖書館電腦的男士，女士說❷ **Let me look up your account in our database.**「讓我調閱您在我們資料庫的帳戶」，可由此判斷她是圖書館員。

40

What does the woman say she will give the man?
(A) An application form
(B) An Internet address
(C) A business card
(D) A temporary password

女士表示會給男士什麼東西？
(A) 申請表
(B) 網址
(C) 名片
(D) 臨時密碼

正解 (D)

女士在❸中說 I'll give you a password「我會給您一組密碼」，接著又說❹ **you won't be able to use it after today.** 補充說明「今天過後密碼就無法使用。」由此可判斷密碼只供暫時使用，因此正確答案為 (D)。

題目 / 中文翻譯

Questions 41 through 43 refer to the following conversation.

請參考以下的對話回答第 41 題至第 43 題。

男：　女：

W: Hello, Selwin Office Manufacturers. You've reached customer service. How may I help you today?

女：Selwin Office Manufacturers 您好，這裡是客服部門。今天有哪裡需要為您服務的嗎？

M: Yes, hello. ❶I recently bought a used Selwin 6 label maker. ❷The person I got it from no longer had the instructions, though, and I'm not sure how the machine works.

男：是的，您好。我最近剛購入一台二手的 Selwin 6 標籤製作機，但賣給我的人手上並沒有說明書，所以我不確定要怎麼操作機器。

W: Unfortunately, ❸that's an earlier model that we no longer produce.

女：很不幸的，這是較早期的機型，所以我們已經不再製造了。

M: Oh, no. That's a problem.

男：喔，不。這下問題大了。

W: No, it's OK, because the Selwin 10 has a similar design, and the instructions should be nearly the same.

女：不，沒關係，因為 Selwin10 有類似的設計，說明書內容應該幾乎一樣。

M: Great! ❹Could you send me the instructions? My address is ...

男：太棒了！您可以將說明書寄給我嗎？我的地址是……

W: Actually, ❺the manual for Selwin 10 is on our Web site. ❻I can send you the link so you can download it.

女：事實上，我們的網站上就有 Selwin10 的操作手冊。我可以將連結寄給您，您可以自行下載。

單字註釋：manufacturer「製造商」

題目 / 中文翻譯

41

What does the woman mention about the Selwin 6?

(A) It is easy to use.
(B) It is an earlier model.
(C) It is well designed.
(D) It is very popular.

女士提到關於 Selwin 6 的內容為何？

(A) 便於使用。
(B) 是較早期的機型。
(C) 設計良好。
(D) 相當熱門。

重點解說

正解 (B)

男士說 ❶ I recently bought a used Selwin 6 label maker.「我最近剛購入一台二手的 Selwin 6 標籤製作機」，女士回應說 ❸ that's an earlier model「這是較早期的機型」。

題目/中文翻譯	重點解說

42

What does the man request?
(A) A warranty
(B) A reimbursement
(C) A replacement part
(D) An instruction manual

男士提出何種要求？
(A) 保固書
(B) 核銷費用
(C) 替換零件
(D) 操作說明手冊

正解 (D)

男士在❷說 The person I got it from no longer had the instructions「賣給我的人手上並沒有說明書」，並要求❹ **Could you send me the instructions?**「您可以將說明書寄給我嗎？」。
(D) manual「手冊、指南」。

43

What does the woman offer to do?
(A) Reset a password
(B) Explain a policy
(C) Check part of an order
(D) Send a link to a Web site

女士的建議為何？
(A) 重設密碼
(B) 說明政策
(C) 檢查訂單的部分內容
(D) 發送網站的連結網址

正解 (D)

女士在❺針對類似機款 Selwin 10 提到「網站上有操作手冊」，以及❻ **I can send you the link**「我可以將連結寄給您」。

題目 / 中文翻譯

Questions 44 through 46 refer to the following conversation.

請參考以下的對話回答第 44 題至第 46 題。

男： 女：

M: Thanks for meeting with me ❶to revise the company budget, Georgia.

男：Georgia，非常感謝妳和我碰面一起修改公司預算。

W: No problem.

女：小事一樁。

M: ❷With the increase in rent for office space this year, we're definitely over budget right now.

男：由於今年辦公室的租金上漲，我們現在確實超出預算了。

W: Yes, we'll have to find areas to cut back on. What about parking?

女：沒錯，我們得找出一些能夠刪減的項目。停車費如何？

M: Mmm.

男：嗯。

W: ❸It's nice that we provide free passes to the nearest parking garage, but that does cost us a lot.

女：我們提供員工可至離我們最近的停車場免費停車，這雖然是件好事，但對公司來說卻是很大一筆開銷。

M: Good point. ❹We could split the cost and have employees pay half. That'd nearly cover the difference in rent.

男：有道理。我們可以請員工支付一半的費用來攤平支出。這樣就幾乎能夠補足租金的差額了。

單字註釋：split「分配、分擔」

題目 / 中文翻譯

44

What are the speakers discussing?
(A) A real estate loan
(B) A ride-sharing initiative
(C) A company budget
(D) A hiring plan

談話者正在討論什麼？
(A) 房地產貸款
(B) 共乘的提議
(C) 公司預算
(D) 聘用計畫

重點解說

正解 (C)

關於碰面的目的，男士說是❶ to revise the company budget「修改公司預算」，並在整段會話中，談論辦公室租金上漲和刪減費用的方法。budget 指的是「預算（案）」。
(B) initiative「提議」。

題目/中文翻譯	重點解說

45

What does the man say about the office space?
(A) It has become too small.
(B) It is in a good location.
(C) The rent has gone up.
(D) The lobby is outdated.

男士談到關於辦公室的什麼事情？
(A) 空間太小。
(B) 位置良好。
(C) 租金調漲。
(D) 大廳太過老氣。

正解 (C)

男士在❷ 中說 With the increase in rent for office space this year「由於今年辦公室使用空間的租金漲價」。
(D) outdated「過時的」。

46

What would the speakers like employees to do?
(A) Help pay for parking
(B) Work a weekend shift
(C) Vote on a policy change
(D) Create training materials

談話者希望員工做什麼事情？
(A) 協助支付停車費
(B) 週末輪班
(C) 投票表決政策的改變
(D) 製作培訓資料

正解 (A)

女士在❸ 中說，免費停車對公司來說負擔很重，因此男士提議❹ **We could split the cost and have employees pay half.**「我們可以請員工支付一半費用來攤平支出」。

題目 / 中文翻譯

Questions 47 through 49 refer to the following conversation.

請參考以下的對話回答第 47 題至第 49 題。

男：加拿大　女：美國

W: You know the music festival that's starting this weekend?

女：你知道這個週末音樂祭就要開始了嗎？

M: Um…someone mentioned it. Is it any good?

男：嗯……有人提過。有什麼好玩的嗎？

W: It's great! Mostly small folk groups, but they have well-known bands too. ❶Some of us go every year— ❷you want to join us?

女：簡直棒極了！大部分是小型的民謠樂團，但也有知名樂團。我們有些人甚至年年報到——你想跟我們一起去嗎？

M: But…isn't it too late to get tickets?

男：但是……現在買票不會已經太遲了嗎？

W: Well, the way it works is...about six o'clock on Friday, people start lining up in the park. We all bring something to sit on—and food—so the wait's not bad. ❸As long as you're at the park close to six, you'll get a ticket—but you have to be there to get one.

女：嗯，購票的方式是這樣的……星期五大約 6 點左右，人們就會開始在公園裡排隊。我們會自己帶座椅，還有食物，所以等待時間也不至於心情不好。只要你大約 6 點左右出現在公園裡，就能拿到票——但你人得到現場才能索票。

M: OK—I think I can get there by six. ❹Count me in!

男：好——我想我六點應該能夠抵達。算我一份！

題目 / 中文翻譯

47

Why does the woman talk to the man?

(A) To offer him a ride
(B) To invite him to an event
(C) To discuss a work assignment
(D) To ask for his assistance

為什麼女士要和男士說話？

(A) 讓他搭便車
(B) 邀請他去某項活動
(C) 討論工作任務分配
(D) 請求協助

重點解說

正解 (B)

女士一開始提到音樂祭，說❶我們有人年年報到，並提出邀約❷ you want to join us?「你想跟我們一起去嗎？」。invite「邀請、招待」。

題目 / 中文翻譯	重點解說

48

What does the woman say is important?
(A) Reviewing a schedule
(B) Arriving by a certain time
(C) Parking nearby
(D) Checking a ticket

女士在談話中表示重要的事情為何？
(A) 審查行程
(B) 在特定時間抵達
(C) 到附近停車
(D) 驗票

正解 (B)

女士在❸說「只要你 6 點左右出現在公園裡，就能拿到票。但你人得到現場才能索票」，因此正解為 (B)。

49

What does the man agree to do?
(A) Join a group
(B) Help with some work
(C) Calculate a cost
(D) Reserve some seats

男士同意做什麼事情？
(A) 參與某個團體
(B) 協助工作
(C) 計算費用
(D) 預約席次

正解 (A)

女士提出❷ **you want to join us?** 的邀約，男士知道可以索票後說❹ **Count me in!**「算我一份！」(A) 的 a group 指的是女士和一起去音樂祭的朋友。

題目 / 中文翻譯

Questions 50 through 52 refer to the following conversation.

請參考以下的對話回答第 50 題至第 52 題。

男： 女：

M: Hi, I'm Eddy Burgess. I'm opening a new law firm and I'm looking for ways to advertise it. ❶**Your company designed a Web site** for my friend's jewelry store, and she suggested I contact you.

男：嗨，我是 Eddy Burgess。我開了一間新的法律事務所，而我正在尋找宣傳方式。貴公司幫我朋友的珠寶店設計了一個網站，所以她建議我與你聯絡。

W: Thanks for calling, Mr. Burgess. This is a great way to advertise your business. ❷**Our experienced consultants can design a Web site** that will help you to stand out from other firms.

女：Burgess 先生，感謝您的來電。這是幫您的業務打廣告的最佳辦法。我們有經驗豐富的顧問群，能夠打造出讓您從其他同業中脫穎而出的網站。

M: That's great! ❸**Could I set up an appointment for tomorrow to discuss ideas with a consultant?**

男：太好了！我可以約明天跟顧問會面討論想法嗎？

W: I think so. I'll transfer you to one, but before I do that, ❹**could you tell me the name of your friend?** We like to thank people who recommend our services.

女：我想可以的。我幫您轉接一位顧問，不過在轉接之前，能否請您告訴我那位朋友的大名？我們想要向推薦本公司服務的人士道謝。

單字註釋：transfer「轉接（電話）」

題目 / 中文翻譯

50

What type of service does the woman's company provide?
(A) Career counseling
(B) Home improvement
(C) Garden landscaping
(D) Web site design

女士的公司提供何種服務？
(A) 就業輔導
(B) 居家改造
(C) 花園造景
(D) 網站設計

重點解說

正解 (D)

男士對女士說❶ **Your company designed a Web site**「貴公司設計了網站」，女士回答❷ **Our experienced consultants can design a Web site**「我們有經驗豐富的顧問群能夠打造網站」，可推知正確解答為 (D)。

題目 / 中文翻譯	重點解說

51

What does the man say he wants to do tomorrow?
(A) Make a payment
(B) Review a document
(C) Redecorate an office
(D) Meet with a consultant

男士表示他明天想要做哪件事情？
(A) 付款
(B) 審查文件
(C) 改裝辦公室
(D) 與顧問會面

正解 (D)

男士詢問 ❸**Could I set up an appointment for tomorrow to discuss ideas with a consultant?**「我可以約明天跟顧問會面討論想法嗎？」

52

What information does the woman request?
(A) The size of a room
(B) The name of the man's friend
(C) The number of people in a group
(D) The start date of renovations

女士詢問什麼資訊？
(A) 房間大小
(B) 男士友人的姓名
(C) 團體人數
(D) 改裝的起始日期

正解 (B)

女士為了向推薦自己公司的男性友人致謝，提出請託，❹**could you tell me the name of your friend?**「能否請您告訴我朋友的大名？」

題目 / 中文翻譯

Questions 53 through 55 refer to the following conversation.

請參考以下的對話回答第 53 題至第 55 題。

男：(加拿大) 女：(英國)

M: Hi—my name's Tom Wilson. ❶I'm visiting family here in Miami for three months, and I'm hoping to earn a bit of money while I'm in town. ❷Does your restaurant happen to have any short-term job openings?

男：嗨，我的名字是 Tom Wilson。接下來三個月我會至邁阿密探親，我想要在市區找分工作賺點錢。不知您的餐廳是否碰巧需要短期兼職人員呢？

W: Actually, I think we could use some help in the kitchen, ❸since it's the beginning of the tourist season now. But do you have any restaurant experience?

女：事實上，因為現在旅遊旺季開始了，我想我們的廚房可能需要點人手。不過你有任何餐廳工作的經驗嗎？

M: Um, I worked for a couple of years in a French restaurant in New Orleans. I'm sure the manager there would give me a recommendation.

男：嗯，我在紐奧爾良的一間法國餐廳工作過好幾年。我很確定餐廳經理會願意推薦我。

W: OK—that sounds promising. If you wait here a second, ❹I'm going to go to the kitchen to see if our chef's available to talk with you.

女：好的，聽起來相當可靠。請你稍待片刻，我去廚房看看主廚有沒有空能和你談談。

題目 / 中文翻譯

53

Why did the man come to Miami?
(A) To see some relatives
(B) To open a business
(C) To do some sightseeing
(D) To take cooking classes

男士為何來到邁阿密？
(A) 拜訪親友
(B) 開展事業
(C) 觀光
(D) 修習料理課程

重點解說

正解 (A)

男士說 ❶ I'm visiting family here in Miami「我來邁阿密探親」。family 的意思很廣泛，也可以表示「家族、親屬」等。relative「親戚」。

題目/中文翻譯	重點解說

54

What does the woman mean when she says, "we could use some help in the kitchen"?
(A) She enjoys her work in the kitchen.
(B) She may have work to offer the man.
(C) The restaurant is undergoing changes.
(D) Some staff need further training.

女士提到「we could use some help in the kitchen」的用意為何？
(A) 她很喜歡廚房的工作。
(B) 她可以提供男士職缺。
(C) 餐廳正在經歷許多改變。
(D) 有些員工需要進一步培訓。

正解 (B)

男士在❷詢問「不知您的餐廳是否碰巧需要短期兼職人員呢？」，底線部分則是女士的回答「我們的廚房可能需要點人手」。而且❸說明理由是「因為現在旅遊旺季開始了」，餐廳需要人手，因此選項 (B) 為正解。

55

What will the woman do next?
(A) Make a reservation
(B) Look for an employee
(C) Show the man a menu
(D) Take a customer's order

女士接下來要做什麼？
(A) 預約
(B) 尋找某位員工
(C) 給男士看菜單
(D) 幫顧客點餐

正解 (B)

女士在❹說 I'm going to go to the kitchen to see if our chef's available to talk with you.「我去廚房看看主廚有沒有空能和你談談」。在 (B) 中以 an employee 取代 our chef。

題目 / 中文翻譯

Questions 56 through 58 refer to the following conversation.

請參考以下的對話回答第 56 題至第 58 題。

男：🇨🇦 女：🇺🇸

W: Hi, Girolamo. I just got an e-mail from T-H-Y Incorporated. They're wondering ❶ **when we can begin building their new headquarters.** They want a start date.

女：嗨，Girolamo。我剛收到一封來自 T-H-Y 公司的電子郵件。他們想知道我們何時可以開始建造他們的新總部大樓。他們想要知道開工日期。

M: I've been meaning to contact them, but I'm waiting to confirm some results from the soil analysis. There's a patch of ground that might be too moist and unstable to build on. Our analysts are doing a few more tests.

男：我一直想要聯絡他們，但是我還在等待土壤分析的確認結果。有一塊地可能因為太潮濕而造成地質不穩定，因此無法施工。我們的分析師還要再做一些測試。

W: Yeah, it's probably best to wait for those results to come in before setting a definite date. In the meantime, ❷**I'll write back and let T-H-Y know what's going on.**

女：好的，我想最好還是等到所有結果出來再訂出明確的日期。同時，我會回信給 T-H-Y 公司，讓他們知曉整個情況。

單字註釋：soil「土壤」; analysis「分析」

題目 / 中文翻譯

56

Where do the speakers most likely work?
(A) At a research laboratory
(B) At a construction company
(C) At a nature park
(D) At a real estate agency

談話者最有可能在哪裡工作？
(A) 實驗研究室
(B) 建設公司
(C) 自然公園
(D) 房地產仲介

重點解說

正解 (B)

女士說 ❶ **when we can begin building their new headquarters.**「我們何時可以開始建造他們的新總部大樓」，而且男士談的是建造大樓的土壤分析，因此可判斷出正解為 (B)。

題目/中文翻譯	重點解說

57

What does the man mean when he says, "I've been meaning to contact them"?
(A) He is looking forward to discussing a project.
(B) He needs to clarify a statement.
(C) He is aware he needs to do something.
(D) He has forgotten to contact a client.

男士提到「I've been meaning to contact them」的用意為何？
(A) 他很期待能夠討論計畫。
(B) 他需要澄清某個論點。
(C) 他察覺自己需要做某件事情。
(D) 他忘記跟客戶聯繫。

正解 (C)

mean to do 意指「一直想要做…」，而男士原本打算和他們聯絡。換句話說，男士知道需要做某些事，因此 (C) 是正解。be aware (that)...「察覺…」。
(B) clarify「澄清（意思等）」。

58

What will the woman include in her e-mail?
(A) An updated list of assignments
(B) Results from a recent customer survey
(C) An estimate of additional costs
(D) An explanation for a delay in setting a date.

女士在電子郵件中會提及哪件事情？
(A) 任務分配表更新版
(B) 近期顧客調查結果
(C) 額外成本預估
(D) 說明遲遲無法決定日期的原因

正解 (D)

從對話的前半部開始可以知道目前的狀況是，T-H-Y 公司想知道開工日，但是因土壤分析尚未出爐而無法決定。此外，女士說 ❷ **I'll write back and let T-H-Y know what's going on**「我會回信給 T-H-Y 公司，讓他們知曉整個情況」，因此正解為 (D)。delay「延遲」；set a date「決定日期」。

題目 / 中文翻譯

Questions 59 through 61 refer to the following conversation with three speakers.

請參考以下三人的對話回答第 59 題至第 61 題。

男：🇦🇺 / 🇨🇦　女：🇺🇸

M: I can't believe ❶the Vancouver convention's so soon!

男（澳洲）：我簡直無法相信溫哥華會議這麼快就來了！

W: I know. It should be great, with all those big-name speakers. ❷Are we all set for transportation?

女：我懂。一定很棒吧，會場中有許多大名鼎鼎的演講者。我們的交通方式都安排好了吧？

M: Uh— ❸the plane tickets are already taken care of, and you arranged for the rental car while we're there—right, Mike?

男（加拿大）：喔——機票已經處理好了，而你是負責我們抵達之後的租用汽車事宜——對吧，Mike？

M: Uh-oh. ❹I completely forgot to make the car reservation! I've been so busy getting my workshop materials ready!

男（澳洲）：喔，糟了。我竟然完全忘記要預約租車！我一直忙於準備工作坊的資料。

M: All right... We're only two days away from leaving—it might be hard to get a car now!

男（加拿大）：好吧……我們只剩兩天就要出發了，現在一定很難訂到車了！

W: Let's not stress out about it. I saw something about a bus service to and from the hotel. ❺Let's talk to the hotel receptionist and see.

女：我們先別緊張。我曾看過往返飯店的公車服務。我們先找飯店接待人員談談，再看怎麼辦吧。

題目 / 中文翻譯

59

What are the speakers mainly discussing?
(A) Ways to reduce a travel budget
(B) Places to visit in Vancouver
(C) Possible locations for a conference
(D) Plans for an upcoming business trip

談話者主要談論的內容為何？
(A) 減低旅遊預算的方法
(B) 溫哥華的景點
(C) 會議的可能地點
(D) 規畫即將到來的出差行程

重點解說

正解 (D)

這是三個人的對話（兩男一女）。❶ 裡面提到 the Vancouver convention's so soon「溫哥華會議這麼快就來了」。convention's 是 convention is 的縮寫。接著女士詢問交通工具，❷ 之後三人談論如何安排。upcoming「即將到來的」。

題目 / 中文翻譯	重點解說

60

What problem do the speakers have?
(A) Their business cards have not arrived.
(B) Their reservations are for the wrong dates.
(C) Their transportation arrangements are not complete.
(D) Their client in Vancouver is unavailable.

談話者遇到什麼問題？
(A) 他們的名片尚未送達。
(B) 他們的預約日期錯誤。
(C) 他們尚未完成交通方式的安排。
(D) 他們在溫哥華的客戶沒有時間。

正解 (C)

❷詢問交通工具如何安排，❸回答機票已經處理好了，但 Mike 說❹ **I completely forgot to make the car reservation!**「我竟然完全忘記要預約租車！」transportation「運輸(工具)」; arrangements「安排」。

61

What does the woman suggest they do?
(A) Cancel an order
(B) Contact a hotel
(C) Prepare a speech
(D) Postpone a decision

女士建議他們做什麼事情？
(A) 取消訂單
(B) 聯絡飯店
(C) 準備演講
(D) 延遲決定

正解 (B)

女士曾看過往返飯店的公車服務，提議❺ **Let's talk to the hotel receptionist and see.**「我們先找飯店接待人員談談，再看怎麼辦吧。」

題目 / 中文翻譯

Questions 62 through 64 refer to the following conversation and coupon.

請參考以下的對話和折價券回答第 62 題至第 64 題。男：　女：

W: Excuse me, ❶I need to replace the color ink in my printer, but I see only black ink cartridges on the shelf. Do you have color cartridges?

女：不好意思，我的印表機需要更換彩色墨水，但我在櫃子上只看見黑色墨水匣。請問有彩色墨水匣嗎？

M: Oh, ❷we just reorganized that part of the store. You'll find the color ink on the other side of the aisle. I'll show you.

男：喔，本店才剛重新整理過那個區域。您在走道的另一側就會發現彩色墨水匣。我帶您去。

W: OK, great. And I brought this discount coupon with me. It's valid for Hinton printer cartridges too, right?

女：好，太好了。我還帶了折價券。Hinton 印表機墨水匣也適用對吧？

M: Yes, we accept those coupons. Just make sure you give it to the cashier when you get to the checkout counter.

男：是的，我們店裡接受折價券。請記得在結帳時，把折價券交給收銀人員即可。

題目 / 中文翻譯

62

What problem does the woman mention?
(A) An item she purchased is defective.
(B) She cannot locate a product.
(C) A sale price seems incorrect.
(D) An expiration date has passed.

女士提到什麼問題？
(A) 購買的品項有缺陷。
(B) 她找不到某個商品。
(C) 售價似乎有誤。
(D) 超過有效期限。

重點解說

正解 (B)

女士在❶提到「我需要更換彩色墨水，但我在櫃子上只看見黑色墨水匣。」locate「查找（物品的場所等）」。
(A) defective「有缺陷的」；(D) expiration date「有效期限」。

題目 / 中文翻譯	重點解說

63

What does the man say recently happened?
(A) Merchandise was rearranged.
(B) Flyers were distributed.
(C) An order was delayed.
(D) A service was discontinued.

男士表示最近發生什麼事情？
(A) 商品重新擺設。
(B) 派發傳單。
(C) 訂單延誤。
(D) 停止服務。

正解 (A)

男士在❷說明 we just reorganized that part of the store「本店才剛重新整理過那個區域」。reorganize 和 (A) 的 rearrange，都是「重新整理、重新排列」的意思。merchandise「(集合詞) 商品」。
(D) discontinue「無法繼續 (之前的動作或一直持續的事)」。

64

Look at the graphic. What discount will the woman most likely receive?

(A) $2
(B) $5
(C) $7
(D) $10

請看此圖。女士最有可能獲得多少折扣金？
(A) 2 元
(B) 5 元
(C) 7 元
(D) 10 元

正解 (D)

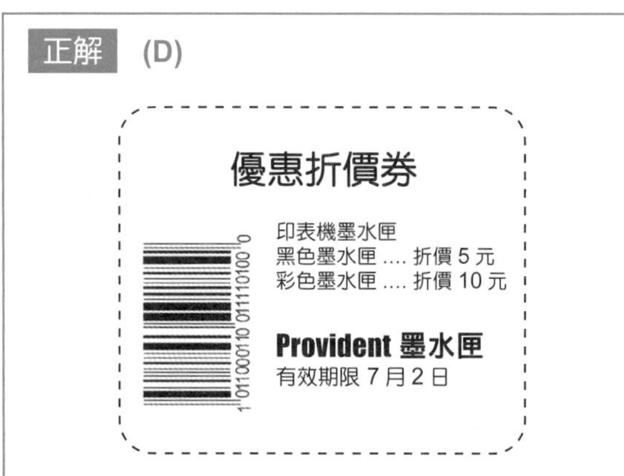

根據❶可知女士要買彩色墨水。優惠折價券上，印著彩色墨水匣的折扣金額是「10 美元」優惠。

題目 / 中文翻譯

Questions 65 through 67 refer to the following conversation and sign.

W: Hi, Barry. I'm just checking in. How's everything going up here? ❶ **Are you finished cleaning the Romano Construction offices yet?**

M: ❷ **No, it's taking longer than expected.** I vacuumed the carpet, but there are a lot of stains. So I decided to shampoo it. But then I had to go down and get the steam-cleaning machine and bring it up here.

W: Well, before you start shampooing, ❸ **could you come downstairs? I need some help moving a big table** in one of the conference rooms.

M: Sure, I'll be right down. This is a good time for me to take a break from these carpets, anyway.

請參考以下的對話和標示圖回答第 65 題至第 67 題。 男： 女：

女：嗨，Barry。我剛打卡簽到。這裡一切都好吧？Romano 建設公司辦公室的打掃工作已經完畢了嗎？

男：還沒，這比原先預期的時間還要久。我吸了地毯，但上面有許多污漬，因此我決定用洗滌劑清洗，但我得先下樓把蒸氣清洗機拿上樓。

女：好吧，在你開始清洗前，你可以先下樓一趟嗎？我需要你幫我移開其中一間會議室裡面的大桌子。

男：沒問題，我馬上下去。正好我也可以遠離這些地毯，先休息一下。

題目 / 中文翻譯

65

Who most likely are the speakers?
(A) Carpet installers
(B) Interior designers
(C) Cleaning staff
(D) Office receptionists

談話者最有可能的身分是？
(A) 地毯鋪設業者
(B) 室內設計師
(C) 清潔人員
(D) 辦公室接待人員

重點解說

正解 (C)

女士在❶詢問男士「Romano 建設公司辦公室的打掃工作已經完畢了嗎？」，接著男士詳細說明打掃工作的進度，由此可得知正確解答為 (C)。

題目 / 中文翻譯

重點解說

66

Look at the graphic. Where is the man currently working?

Office Directory
1st FL: HLT Company
2nd FL: Noble Incorporated
3rd FL: Romano Construction
4th FL: Grayton and Sons

(A) On the first floor
(B) On the second floor
(C) On the third floor
(D) On the fourth floor

請看此圖。男士目前的工作地點在何處？
(A) 1 樓
(B) 2 樓
(C) 3 樓
(D) 4 樓

正解 (C)

辦公室配置圖
1 樓：HLT 公司
2 樓：Noble 公司
3 樓：Romano 建設
4 樓：Grayton and Sons 公司

女士在❶中詢問男士，「Romano 建設公司辦公室的打掃工作已經完畢了嗎」，男士回答❷ **No, it's taking longer than expected.**「不，比原先預期的時間還要久」，並說明具體的作業內容，因此可以判斷男士在 Romano 建設。這張圖中寫著 3rd FL：Romano Construction。FL 是 floor 的縮寫。

67

What are the speakers probably going to do next?
(A) Move a table
(B) Fix a machine
(C) Look at some plans
(D) Make a conference call

談話者接下來可能做什麼事情？
(A) 移動桌子
(B) 修理機器
(C) 檢視某些計畫
(D) 進行電話會議

正解 (A)

女士在❸提到「希望男士下樓幫她搬桌子」，男士回答 Sure「當然」，因此正確解答為 (A)。

題目 / 中文翻譯

Questions 68 through 70 refer to the following conversation and card.

請參考以下的對話和圖表回答第 68 題至第 70 題。男：🇨🇦 女：🇬🇧

W: I hear that we've had some unhappy customers recently.

女：聽說最近有顧客對我們很不滿。

M: Yes, I'm afraid that's true. In fact, I've just been talking with one of them.

男：是的，恐怕這是真的。事實上，我才剛結束跟其中一位的談話。

W: Oh. Well, uh, what did the customer say?

女：喔，好吧，呃，客人說什麼？

M: She wasn't at all happy. ❶**Our driver picked her up on time**, but ❷**there was heavy traffic on the way to the airport, and she nearly missed her flight.**

男：她非常不高興。我們的司機準時接她，但是往機場的路上嚴重塞車，害她幾乎錯過班機。

W: Mmm. We should probably take a look at roadwork scheduled in the area. It might be affecting traffic more than we realized.

女：嗯，或許我們應該檢視這個區域排定的道路工程。這可能比我們原先所瞭解的交通影響程度更深。

M: Right. And we have some other issues to consider as well. ❸**Look at the rest of these comments—we'll need to decide what to do.**

男：好的。我們還有其他需要考量的事項。我們來看看其餘的評論——我們得決定該怎麼處理。

題目 / 中文翻譯

68

Where do the speakers most likely work?
(A) At a shipping company
(B) At an engineering firm
(C) At a taxi company
(D) At a railway station

談話者最有可能在哪裡工作？
(A) 貨運公司
(B) 工程公司
(C) 計程車行
(D) 火車站

重點解說

正解 (C)

男士說到❶**Our driver picked her up on time**「我們的司機準時接她」，因此可以判斷說話的人們在計程車行工作。

題目 / 中文翻譯

重點解說

69

Look at the graphic. Which customer are the speakers discussing?

Name	Comment
1. Carol Lee	Dirty seat
2. Jean Harvey	No discount
3. Eun-Jung Choi	Web site down
4. Kinu Iizuka	Late to destination

(A) Carol Lee
(B) Jean Harvey
(C) Eun-Jung Choi
(D) Kinu Iizuka

請看此表。談話者正在討論的是哪一位顧客？
(A) Carol Lee
(B) Jean Harvey
(C) Eun-Jung Choi
(D) Kinu Iizuka

正解 (D)

姓名	評論
1. Carol Lee	座位髒亂
2. Jean Harvey	無折扣優惠
3. Eun-Jung Choi	網站故障
4. Kinu Iizuka	延遲抵達目的地

男士說❷ **there was heavy traffic on the way to the airport, and she nearly missed her flight**「往機場的路上嚴重塞車，害她幾乎錯過班機」。在這張表格中，可以看出這位顧客應該是 Late to destination「延遲抵達目的地」的 (D) Kinu Iizuka。

70

What will the speakers do next?
(A) Look at fuel prices
(B) Review customer complaints
(C) Update staffing schedules
(D) Organize training programs

談話者接下來要做什麼事情？
(A) 查看燃料價格
(B) 檢視客訴
(C) 更新人員配置行程表
(D) 規畫培訓課程

正解 (B)

談話者提到不滿的顧客後，男士說❸「看看其餘的評論——我們得決定該怎麼處理」，因此可以判斷接下來要檢視顧客客訴內容。complaint 是「抱怨」。
(A) fuel「燃料」。

題目 / 中文翻譯

Questions 71 through 73 refer to the following telephone message.

Hello, Mr. Mohan, ❶**this is Suzanna Garcia calling from Garcia Catering.** I have a question about the food that we're preparing for your son's graduation party next week. ❷**Your order form indicates that you'd like fifty-five appetizer trays** —all cheese, vegetable, and fruit combos. ❸ **I'm thinking that this might be a mistake, and that you'd meant to order only five trays.** ❹**We open at nine tomorrow morning, so why don't you give me a call then—** ❺**we want to make sure we have your order right.**

請參考以下的電話留言回答第 71 題至第 73 題。

Mohan 先生您好，我是 Garcia 外燴公司的 Suzanna Garcia。我來電是要詢問您關於下周我們將在您兒子畢業典禮上所準備的食物。您的訂單指明您想要 55 份的開胃菜拼盤——而且全是起司、蔬菜和水果組合。我想可能有哪裡出錯，您訂購的應該只有五份開胃菜拼盤。我們明天上午九點開始營業，到時煩請您撥個電話給我——我們得確定您的訂單內容正確無誤。

題目 / 中文翻譯

71

What type of service does the speaker provide?

(A) Food preparation
(B) Cooking lessons
(C) Grocery delivery
(D) Nutritional counseling

說話者提供哪種服務？

(A) 準備食物
(B) 烹飪課程
(C) 雜貨配送
(D) 營養諮詢

重點解說

正解 (A)

說話者說❶ **this is Suzanna Garcia calling from Garcia Catering.**「您好，我是 Garcia 外燴公司的 Suzanna Garcia。」Catering 是餐飲提供、外燴公司。之後她也詢問宴會上的食物準備事宜。

(D) Nutritional「營養的」。

題目/中文翻譯	重點解說

72

What information does the speaker need from the listener?
(A) The time of a lunch
(B) The location for a delivery
(C) The size of an order
(D) The theme of a banquet

說話者需要得知聽取留言者的哪些資訊？
(A) 午餐時間
(B) 配送地點
(C) 訂單數量
(D) 宴會主題

正解 (C)

❷和❸可以得知，說話者認為對方不小心點了很多前菜。❺ **we want to make sure we have your order right**「我們得確定您的訂單內容正確無誤」，因此選 (C)。
(D) banquet「宴會」。

73

When should the listener return the call?
(A) Later today
(B) Tomorrow
(C) Next week
(D) In one month

聽取留言者應該何時回電？
(A) 今日稍晚
(B) 明天
(C) 下週
(D) 一個月內

正解 (B)

❹ **We open at nine tomorrow morning, so why don't you give me a call then**「本店明天上午九點開始營業，到時煩請您撥個電話給我」。

題目 / 中文翻譯

Questions 74 through 76 refer to the following telephone message.

Hi, this is Jackie Gross, from Human Resources. ❶Congratulations on your promotion to manager of our Thailand office! I'm calling because ❷I've been asked to assist you with your move overseas. ❸The first thing I'll do is get in touch with a moving company to estimate the cost of the move. ❹I also need to confirm your passport number for your work visa; I want to make sure your paperwork is in order as soon as possible. Please call me back at your earliest convenience.

請參考以下的電話留言回答第 74 題至第 76 題。

您好，我是人資部的 Jackie Gross。恭喜您榮升泰國辦公室的經理！我來電是因為我被任命協助您的海外調任事宜。首先我必須聯絡搬運公司，估算一下搬遷費用。我也必須確認您的護照號碼，以便辦理您的工作簽證。我想確保您的文件作業能夠儘快就緒。若您方便的話，煩請儘早回電給我。

題目 / 中文翻譯

74

Why is the listener going overseas?
(A) To attend a sales conference
(B) To manage an office
(C) To meet some clients
(D) To go on a tour

聽取留言者為何要出國？
(A) 參加業務會議
(B) 管理辦公室
(C) 會見客戶
(D) 旅遊

重點解說

正解 (B)

說話者提到❶Congratulations on your promotion to manager of our Thailand office!「恭喜您榮升泰國辦公室的經理！」而且在❷中說明「我被任命協助您的海外調任事宜」。由此可知聽取留言者將以 manager「經營者、管理者」的身份在外國工作。

題目 / 中文翻譯	重點解說

75

What does the speaker plan to do first?
(A) Organize a business dinner
(B) Reserve airline seats
(C) Purchase some merchandise
(D) Contact a moving company

說話者計畫首先要做什麼？
(A) 安排商務晚宴
(B) 預約航班機位
(C) 購買商品
(D) 聯絡搬運公司

正解 (D)

❸ 提到 The first thing I'll do is get in touch with a moving company「首先我必須聯絡搬運公司」。get in touch with... 和 (D) 的 contact，都是「和…聯絡」的意思。

76

What does the speaker have to confirm?
(A) Travel dates
(B) Account information
(C) A passport number
(D) Vaccination requirements

說話者必須確認哪件事情？
(A) 旅遊日期
(B) 帳戶資訊
(C) 護照號碼
(D) 疫苗接種必要條件

正解 (C)

❹ **I also need to confirm your passport number**「我也必須確認您的護照號碼」。
(D) vaccination「疫苗接種」。

題目 / 中文翻譯

Questions 77 through 79 refer to the following broadcast announcement.

Good evening, and thank you all for attending tonight's fashion show here at JC Design School. ❶We're holding this special event to show off the beautiful garments created by our most recent group of trainees. ❷These talented young people participated in a six-month training course, where they learned to create the clothing items you'll see here tonight. ❸Many of these garments were made with unconventional fabrics, ❹which you can read about in the leaflets that are being passed around. And ❺after the show, you're welcome to stay and talk with our graduating trainees. ❻They'll answer any questions you may have about their designs and creations.

請參考以下的廣播內容回答第 77 題至第 79 題。

晚安，非常感謝各位參與今晚在 JC 設計學校舉辦的時裝秀。我們之所以舉辦這項特殊活動，是為了展示由本校最近一期的學員所設計的美麗服飾。這些才華洋溢的年輕人在為期六個月的訓練課程中，學會製作今晚呈現在您眼前的每件服飾。其中許多的服飾是使用創新布料製成，您可以在我們發送的宣傳手冊裡讀到這個訊息。在時裝秀結束後，歡迎您留下與我們的準畢業生們聊聊。若您對於他們的設計或作品有所疑惑，他們都會一一回答。

單字註釋：garment「衣服、服飾」；unconventional「不因循守舊的、不落俗套的」

題目 / 中文翻譯

77

What is the main purpose of the event?
(A) To celebrate successful sales
(B) To exhibit course projects
(C) To advertise a clothing store
(D) To recruit new teachers

活動的主要目的為何？
(A) 慶祝銷售成功
(B) 發表課堂成果
(C) 宣傳服飾店
(D) 招募新任教師

重點解說

正解 (B)

❶ We're holding this special event to show off the beautiful garments created by our most recent group of trainees.「我們之所以舉辦這項特殊活動，是為了展示由本校最近一期的學員所設計的美麗服飾。」而且❷「這些才華洋溢的年輕人在為期六個月的訓練課程中，學會製作今晚呈現在您眼前的每件服飾」，因此知道活動的目的是為了發表課程的成果。

題目 / 中文翻譯	重點解說

78

According to the speaker, what can be found in the leaflet?
(A) Dates of future shows
(B) Names of event organizers
(C) Information about materials
(D) Instructions for enrollment

根據說話者表示，在宣傳手冊裡可以找到什麼？
(A) 未來展演的日期
(B) 活動策畫者的姓名
(C) 關於材料的資訊
(D) 招生說明

正解 (C)

❸ 敘述的是 Many of these garments were made with unconventional fabrics「其中有許多的服飾是使用創新布料而製成」，然後 ❹ **which you can read about in the leaflets that are being passed around**「宣傳手冊裡有材料的相關資訊」。fabric「布料」在 (C) 中，可以換成 material「原料、材料」。

79

What is scheduled to happen at the end of the event?
(A) A celebrity will appear on stage.
(B) Some creations will be sold at auction.
(C) A reception will be held in a different room.
(D) Students will answer questions about their work.

活動結束後，預計會發生什麼事情？
(A) 有位名人將會登場。
(B) 作品將進行拍賣。
(C) 在另外的房間舉辦歡迎會。
(D) 學生將會回答關於他們作品的提問。

正解 (D)

❺ 提到「在時裝秀結束後，歡迎您與我們的學員們聊聊」，然後說 ❻ **They'll answer any questions you may have about their designs and creations.**「若您對於他們的設計或作品有所疑惑，他們都會一一回答」。(A) celebrity「名人」。

題目 / 中文翻譯

Questions 80 through 82 refer to the following announcement.

Welcome to this month's all-staff meeting. To begin, I have some great news. As the editor in chief of *Science and You* magazine, **❶I am pleased to announce the finalization of our company's merger with Stonewell Publishing. ❷This means many exciting things for us, namely that we can take advantage of Stonewell's incredible technology department so we can make the online version of our magazine better.** And why wouldn't we? Our data shows that sixty percent of our magazine subscribers use their mobile phones to read articles online. Now, Stonewell has already granted all of us access to their publications. So, **❸please use some time over the next few weeks to familiarize yourselves with their Web sites.**

請參考以下的公告回答第 80 題至第 82 題。

歡迎參與本月全體職員會議。首先，我有一些好消息。身為《Science and You》雜誌總編輯，我很高興地宣布本公司與 Stonewell 出版社合併事宜終於拍板定案。這對我們而言代表著許多振奮人心的事情，比方說我們能夠運用 Stonewell 出版社出色的科技部門，讓我們的雜誌擁有更好的網路版本。我們何樂而不為呢？我們的資料顯示，有六成的雜誌訂戶都會使用行動電話在線上閱讀文章。現在，Stonewell 讓我們全體員工有權使用他們的出版品。因此，接下來幾週請大家利用時間熟悉他們的網站。

題目 / 中文翻譯

80

What is the purpose of the announcement?
(A) To review a budget proposal
(B) To discuss an upcoming merger
(C) To explain some survey results
(D) To introduce new staff members

該公告的目的為何？
(A) 審查預算提案
(B) 討論即將進行的合併案
(C) 說明調查結果
(D) 介紹新進職員

重點解說

正解 (B)

❶ **I am pleased to announce the finalization of our company's merger with Stonewell Publishing.**「我很高興地宣布本公司與 Stonewell 出版社合併事宜終於拍板定案。」之後也在❷提到合併的好處。

題目/中文翻譯 | 重點解說

81

What does the woman mean when she says, "And why wouldn't we"?
(A) She supports a decision.
(B) She hopes to relocate.
(C) She wants listeners to share their opinions.
(D) She feels concerned about a shipment.

女士提到「And why wouldn't we」的用意為何?
(A) 她支持某項決定。
(B) 她希望搬離現址。
(C) 她想要聽眾分享他們的意見。
(D) 她十分關切託運貨物。

正解 (A)

❷ 提到合併的好處後,底線部份說「我們何樂而不為呢」,由此可知女士對於公司合併這個決定持正面看法,因此選 (A)。

82

What does the woman ask listeners to do?
(A) Attend a training
(B) Sign some paperwork
(C) Gather a list of questions
(D) Review some information online

女士要求聽眾做什麼事情?
(A) 參與培訓
(B) 簽署文件
(C) 蒐集問題
(D) 檢閱線上資訊

正解 (D)

❸ 說的是please use some time over the next few weeks to familiarize yourselves with their Web sites.「接下來幾週請大家利用時間熟悉他們的網站」,故選 (D)。
familiarize oneself with...「讓…熟悉」。

題目 / 中文翻譯

Questions 83 through 85 refer to the following advertisement.

Are you thinking about getting a degree in business? Then ❶Hamson College, the school for business management, is for you. ❷Our specialized courses focus on all aspects of running your own company. With both on-site and online courses, Hamson College offers courses that can fit into anyone's schedule. In fact, ❸Hamson was ranked by students as having the most scheduling flexibility of any college. ❹Come to an information session on August seventeenth to find out if Hamson College is right for you. You'll be able to meet with professors and talk with other students. To find out more, visit us at www.hamsoncollege.edu.

請參考以下的廣告回答第 83 題至第 85 題。

您是否正在考慮取得商業學位？那麼 Hamson 企業管理學院絕對是您的首選。本校的專業課程著重全方位的公司經營之道。Hamson 學院同時擁有實體與線上教學，提供適合每個人時間表的各項課程。事實上，Hamson 學院也被學生們評為所有大學中，課程安排上最有彈性的學校。歡迎您前來 8 月 17 日的說明會，您就會知道 Hamson 學院是否適合您。您將能夠和教授們見面，並與其他學生聊聊。更多詳情請上 www.hamsoncollege.edu 查詢。

題目 / 中文翻譯

83

What does Hamson College specialize in?
(A) Teacher training
(B) Industrial design
(C) Computer programming
(D) Business management

Hamson 學院的專長為何？
(A) 教師培訓
(B) 工業設計
(C) 電腦程式設計
(D) 企業管理

重點解說

正解 (D)

❶ Hamson College, the school for business management「Hamson 企業管理學院」，以及 ❷ Our specialized courses focus all aspects of running your own company「本校的專業課程著重全方位的公司經營之道」，因此可以判斷 (D) 為正解。

題目/中文翻譯

重點解說

84

According to the advertisement, what do students like about Hamson College?
(A) The quality of the instruction
(B) The flexible scheduling
(C) The low tuition costs
(D) The work experience opportunities

根據廣告，學生喜歡 Hamson 學院哪一點？
(A) 教學品質
(B) 排課彈性
(C) 學費低廉
(D) 實務工作機會

正解 (B)

❸Hamson was ranked by students as having the most scheduling flexibility of any college「Hamson 學院被學生評為所有大學中，課程安排上最有彈性的學校」。flexible「有彈性的」。

85

What will happen on August 17?
(A) A reading group will meet.
(B) Students will graduate.
(C) An information session will be held.
(D) The registration period will end.

8 月 17 日會發生什麼事情？
(A) 讀書會聚會。
(B) 學生畢業。
(C) 舉行說明會。
(D) 報名期間截止。

正解 (C)

❹Come to an information session on August seventeenth 是「歡迎您前來 8 月 17 日的說明會」。information session「說明會」。

題目 / 中文翻譯

Questions 86 through 88 refer to the following telephone message.

Anwei! ❶Thank you so much for helping set up for the party after last night's theater performance. I couldn't have done it without you, and ❷the spicy dish you brought was delicious! You have got to tell me where you found the recipe! ❸Everyone really liked it, and it didn't look too complicated. Anyway, ❹I guess I'll see you Monday. ❺I think we have rehearsal together for Elia Grande's new play. ❻I'm really excited to get started.

請參考以下的電話留言回答第 86 題至第 88 題。

Anwei！非常感謝你昨晚在劇場公演結束後協助安排派對事宜。如果沒有你，我絕對辦不到，而且你帶來的辛辣料理實在太美味了！請務必告訴我，你上哪找到這個食譜的！每個人都好喜歡這道料理，而且看起來也不是太複雜。總之，我想我們星期一會見面吧。我記得我們要一起彩排 Elia Grande 的新劇碼。我非常興奮我們要準備開始了。

題目 / 中文翻譯

86

Why is the woman calling?

(A) To express her gratitude
(B) To ask for a favor
(C) To discuss an assignment
(D) To report some good news

女士為何來電？

(A) 表達感激
(B) 請求協助
(C) 討論作業
(D) 報告好消息

重點解說

正解 (A)

❶是說 Thank you so much for helping set up for the party after last night's theater performance.「非常感謝你昨晚在劇場公演結束後協助安排派對事宜。」express one's gratitude「表達感謝（人）之意」。

題目/中文翻譯	重點解說

87

What does the woman imply when she says, "You have got to tell me where you found the recipe"?
(A) She wonders if some ingredients are local.
(B) She would like to make the dish herself.
(C) She needs a restaurant recommendation.
(D) She cannot find a recipe in a cookbook.

女士提到「You have got to tell me where you found the recipe」的用意為何？
(A) 她想知道有些食材是不是本地出產的。
(B) 她想要自己製作料理。
(C) 她需要餐廳推薦。
(D) 她找不到烹飪書裡的一項食譜。

正解 (B)

have got to do 是「務必做…」的口語表現，底線部份意思是「請務必告訴我，你上哪找到這個食譜的」。❷是「你帶來的辛辣料理實在太美味了」。❸是「每個人都好喜歡這道料理，而且看起來也不是太複雜」，因此可推知女士想要試著自己製作這道料理。
(A) ingredient「材料」。

88

Why is the woman looking forward to Monday?
(A) She is going to see a play.
(B) She is taking a friend to lunch.
(C) Some results will be available.
(D) A new project will start.

女士為何期待星期一的到來？
(A) 她打算去看戲。
(B) 她要帶朋友去吃午餐。
(C) 某些結果出爐。
(D) 新的計畫開始。

正解 (D)

❹ 是「我想我們星期一會見面」。❺ **I think we have rehearsal together for Elia Grande's new play.**「我記得我們要一起彩排 Elia Grande 的新劇碼。」而且 ❻ 說「我非常興奮我們要準備開始了」。(D) 的 a new project 指的是 Elia Grande's new play。

題目 / 中文翻譯

Questions 89 through 91 refer to the following news report.

This is Charlie Swift from Channel 14 News. ❶I'm standing outside Granger Electronics this morning, where hundreds of people have spent hours waiting to buy ❷the new Aria 7D mobile phone—available starting today. ❸Some began waiting in line as early as four A.M. From the look of it, you'd think they were giving the phones away. Now, the Aria 7D is a significant upgrade from previous phone models, but ❹the feature consumers are most excited about is its water-protective coating. The new phone's design ensures that it is still fully functional if it comes in contact with water.

請參考以下的新聞報導回答第 89 題至第 91 題。

這是 Channel 14 新聞記者 Charlie Swift 的報導。今天上午，我站在 Granger 電器行的外面，已經有好幾百位民眾為了購買今天上市的新 Aria 7D 手機，在這裡守候數個小時。有些人甚至凌晨 4 點就已經來排隊了。光看這個陣仗，你會以為手機是店家免費發送的。現在的 Aria 7D 是以往機種的卓越升級版，不過讓顧客最興奮的功能在於它的防水外層。這款新手機的設計是，即使手機接觸到水，也能夠正常使用。

單字註釋：give...away「免費發送…」

題目 / 中文翻譯

89

According to the speaker, what is happening today?

(A) An ad campaign is being launched.
(B) A store is opening a new branch.
(C) A product is being released in stores.
(D) A clearance sale is beginning.

根據說話者表示，今天發生了什麼事情？

(A) 廣告宣傳活動開始。
(B) 店家開了新分店。
(C) 產品開始在店家販售。
(D) 清倉大拍賣開始。

重點解說

正解 (C)

說話者在❶中說 Granger 電器行外面有人潮守候，接下來說❷ the new Aria 7D mobile phone— available starting today「今天上市的新 Aria 7D 手機」，因此可得知 Granger 電器行今天有新產品發售。release「發售」。

題目/中文翻譯	重點解說

90

What does the speaker mean when he says, "From the look of it, you'd think they were giving the phones away"?
(A) The store's advertising is misleading.
(B) Some products are no longer in stock.
(C) There are a lot of customers waiting at the store.
(D) There are many good bargains at the store.

說話者提到「From the look of it, you'd think they were giving the phones away」的用意為何？
(A) 店家的宣傳令人誤解。
(B) 某些商品已經沒有庫存。
(C) 許多顧客在店外守候。
(D) 店內有許多不錯的特價品。

正解 (C)
底線部份意思是「光看這個陣仗，你會以為手機是店家免費發送的」。從❶和❷ 可以得知，很多人等著買新上市的手機。❸也說「有些人甚至凌晨 4 點就已經來排隊了」。從這些內容看來，可以判斷底線部份要說的是「人潮多到你會以為店家免費發送商品」。you'd 是 you would 的縮寫，they 指的是 Granger 電器行。

91

According to the speaker, what feature of the Aria 7D is most attractive?
(A) Its water resistance
(B) Its affordable price
(C) Its colorful patterns
(D) Its slim design

根據說話者表示，Aria 7D 最吸引人的功能為何？
(A) 防水性
(B) 可負擔的價格
(C) 彩色樣式
(D) 超薄設計

正解 (A)
❹ **the feature consumers are most excited about is its water-protective coating.**「讓顧客最興奮的功能在於它的防水外層」。(A) 把 water-protective coating「防水外層」置換成 water resistance「防水性」。❹ consumers are most excited about 修飾句中的主詞 the feature。

題目 / 中文翻譯

Questions 92 through 94 refer to the following excerpt from a meeting.

Let's talk about this year's financial goals. So, Sandala Rentals and Wilmington Limited are still our biggest sources of income. And that's great. But our other accounts are important too. They could bring in a lot more money than they do now. And ❶this is what I want to emphasize: we have to get our smaller clients to sign on for bigger advertising campaigns. That's where you come in. ❷I'd like each of you to tell me how much your clients paid for the advertisements we created for them over the past year. ❸I'll send out an e-mail with an example so you can see exactly what information to include in your report.

請參考以下會議節錄內容回答第 92 題至第 94 題。

我們來談談今年的財務目標。好的，Sandala 租賃公司和 Wilmington 股份有限公司仍是我們兩大收入來源。這雖然很好，不過我們其他的客戶也非常重要。他們可以帶來遠比現在更多的金錢。這也正是我想要強調的地方：我們必須設法讓小型客戶與我們簽署更大型的宣傳活動合約。那就是你們該著手的地方。我希望你們每個人都能告訴我，你的客戶去年總共支付多少廣告費給我們。我會發送電子郵件給大家，裡面有參考範例，好讓你們瞭解報告內容需要包含哪些資訊。

題目 / 中文翻譯

92

What does the speaker want to focus on this year?
(A) Increasing staff numbers
(B) Targeting smaller businesses
(C) Reducing operating costs
(D) Attracting new clients

何者是說話者今年想要著重的事情？
(A) 增加員工人數
(B) 以小型企業為商業目標
(C) 減低營運成本
(D) 吸引新客戶

重點解說

正解 (B)

❶說的是 this is what I want to emphasize: we have to get our smaller clients to sign on for bigger advertising campaigns.「這也正是我想要強調的地方：我們必須設法讓小型客戶與我們簽署更大型的宣傳活動合約。」target「以…為對象」。

題目 / 中文翻譯	重點解說

93

What does the speaker request help with?
(A) Greeting clients
(B) Collecting payments
(C) Gathering data
(D) Locating résumés

說話者需要哪項協助？
(A) 問候客戶
(B) 收取款項
(C) 蒐集資料
(D) 查找履歷

正解 (C)

❷提到 I'd like each of you to tell me how much your clients paid for the advertisements we created for them over the past year.「我希望你們每個人都能告訴我，你的客戶去年總共支付多少廣告費給我們」。也就是說，說話者要蒐集支付金額的資料，因此答案應為(C)。gather「蒐集」。

94

What will the listeners receive by e-mail?
(A) A work schedule
(B) A confirmation number
(C) A sample report
(D) An employee roster

聽眾收到的電子郵件裡面有什麼？
(A) 工作時程表
(B) 確認號碼
(C) 報告範本
(D) 員工名冊

正解 (C)

❸提到 I'll send out an e-mail with an example so you can see exactly what information to include in your report.「我會發送電子郵件給大家，裡面有範例參考，好讓你們瞭解報告內容需要包含哪些資訊」，因此聽眾會收到夾帶參考範本的電子郵件。
(D) roster「名冊」。

題目 / 中文翻譯

Questions 95 through 97 refer to the following talk and map.

Hello—❶welcome to the Visitors Center at Mountainside Park. My name's Josephine and ❷I'll be guiding your hike today. Normally we'd be taking the Heron Trail to the Picnic Area, but ❸the second part of that trail is closed for maintenance this week. So instead, ❹we'll be starting out on the Heron Trail and changing over midway to the Pine Trail, as you can see here on the map. We'll break for our lunch at the end of the Pine Trail, and then we'll take the Sunset Trail back to our starting point. It's supposed to be sunny today, so ❺it's a good idea to put on some sunscreen and wear a hat.

請參考以下談話和地圖回答第 95 題至第 97 題。

你好——歡迎光臨 Mountainside Park 遊客中心。我的名字是 Josephine，是您今天的健行活動導覽人員。通常我們會由蒼鷺步道前往野餐區，不過登山步道的第二段路程本週因維修而關閉。因此，我們採取另外方案，我們從蒼鷺步道出發，中途接松樹步道，一如您在地圖上所看見的情況。我們走完松樹步道後，會休息吃午餐，之後我們再行經日落步道回到出發點。今天預計是晴朗的好天氣，因此大家最好擦防曬乳液並戴上帽子。

題目 / 中文翻譯

95

Who most likely are the listeners?
(A) Maintenance workers
(B) Bus drivers
(C) Tourists
(D) Park rangers

聽眾最有可能的身分為何？
(A) 維修工作人員
(B) 公車司機
(C) 觀光客
(D) 公園管理員

重點解說

正解 (C)

說話者表示 ❶ welcome to the Visitors Center at Mountainside Park「歡迎光臨 Mountainside Park 遊客中心」，以及 ❷ I'll be guiding your hike today「我是您今天的健行活動導覽人員」，可知這群聽眾是健行活動的參加者。

題目 / 中文翻譯

重點解說

96

Look at the graphic. Where will the listeners be unable to go today?

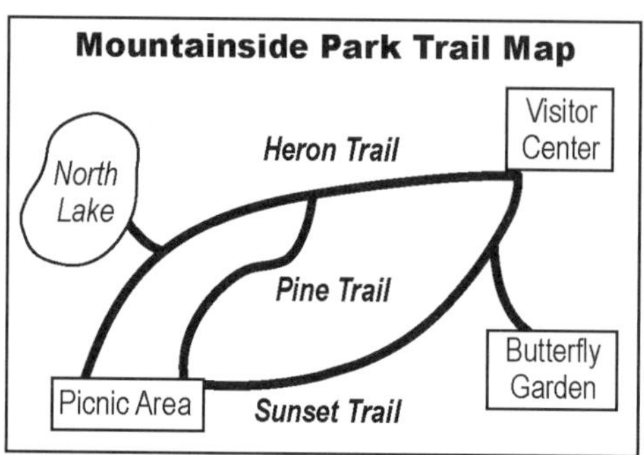

(A) The North Lake
(B) The Picnic Area
(C) The Butterfly Garden
(D) The Visitor Center

請看此圖。聽眾今天可能無法前往何處？
(A) 北湖
(B) 野餐區
(C) 蝴蝶庭園
(D) 遊客中心

正解 **(A)**

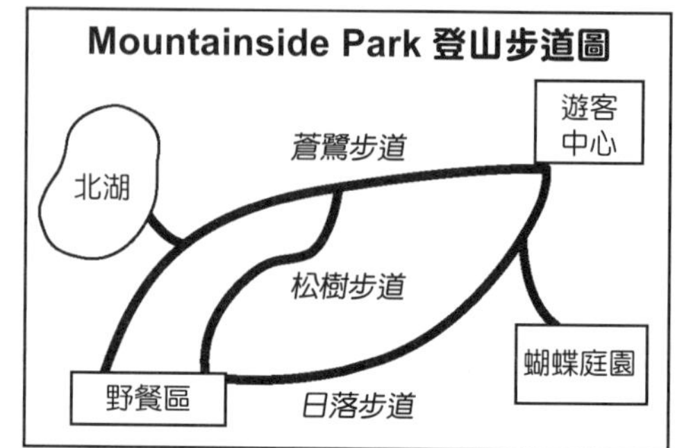

Mountainside Park 登山步道圖。
從❶得知女士和聽眾在公園遊客中心。女士說❸蒼鷺登山步道的第二段路程因維修而封閉，並說❹因此要從蒼鷺步道出發，中途接松樹步道。對照圖可以看出，不經過蒼鷺步道後半段路程就不能前往的是 (A) 北湖。

97

What does the woman encourage the listeners to do?
(A) Bring a map
(B) Check the weather forecast
(C) Store their belongings
(D) Use sun protection

女士鼓勵聽眾做什麼事情？
(A) 攜帶地圖
(B) 確認天氣預報
(C) 保管自身行李
(D) 使用防曬乳

正解 **(D)**

❺建議 It's a good idea to put on some sunscreen「最好塗上防曬乳」。sunscreen 和 (D) 的 sun protections，兩者都是「防曬乳」。protection「保護品」。

題目 / 中文翻譯

Questions 98 through 100 refer to the following telephone message and order form.

Hi, Wendy—❶I'm calling about the purchase orders we received for office furniture. The Accounting Department's going to need more of everything to accommodate all their new employees. But luckily, ❷the Human Resources Department just wants more chairs; they said everything else is OK. ❸Before you place these orders though, be sure to check the inventory. ❹If we're still short, then we'll order the necessary items. Please remember that ❺ only I, as your manager, can make changes to orders you've already submitted. So ❻let me know if you spot an error that needs to be updated. Thanks.

請參考以下的電話留言和訂購單回答第 98 題至第 100 題。

哈囉，Wendy——我打電話是想要談談關於我們收到的辦公家具採購訂單。會計部門將會需要各種能夠提供新進員工使用的用具。幸運的是，人資部門只需要更多的椅子，他們說其他的都還堪用。不過在下訂單之前，請你先確認庫存。如果仍然有缺，那麼我們就訂購必要的品項。請記得只有我，也就是你的主管，才能修改妳已經交出去的訂單。因此，如果妳發現有錯誤需要更新，請告知我。謝謝。

題目 / 中文翻譯

98

Look at the graphic. Which department filled out the order form?

ORDER FORM

Item	Order more?	Quantity to Order
Drafting tables		—
Whiteboards		—
Desk chairs	✓	9
Adjustable lamps		—

(A) Maintenance
(B) Accounting
(C) Human Resources
(D) Public Relations

請看此表。這是由哪個部門填寫的訂購單？
(A) 維修部
(B) 會計部
(C) 人資部
(D) 公關部

重點解說

正解 (C)

訂購單

項目	訂購更多	訂購數量
繪圖桌		—
白板		—
辦公椅	✓	9
可調整型檯燈		—

從圖表可以看出，填寫這張採購訂單的部門只需要辦公椅。❷ the Human Resource Department just wants more chairs; they said everything else is OK「人資部門只需要更多的椅子，他們說其他的都還堪用」，因此可以得知，填寫這張訂單的是人資部門。

題目/中文翻譯	重點解說

99

What does the speaker anticipate may happen?
(A) A project may not be completed on time.
(B) Some measurements may be incorrect.
(C) An order may be too small.
(D) There may not be enough available items.

說話者預期會發生哪件事？
(A) 計畫可能無法如期完成。
(B) 某些測量可能有誤。
(C) 有張訂單的量太小。
(D) 用品可能不足。

正解 (D)

anticipate「預期」。
說話者表示打電話是想要談談關於辦公家具採購訂單，❸和❹繼續說「下訂單之前，請先確認庫存。如果仍然有缺，那麼我們就訂購必要的品項」，因此可以得知，說話者預期辦公室家具可能不足。
(B) measurements「測量」。

100

What is the listener asked to do if she finds an error?
(A) Contact her manager
(B) Submit a form
(C) Make a correction
(D) Keep a record

聽取留言者被要求在發現錯誤時，必須做什麼事情？
(A) 聯絡主管
(B) 呈交表格
(C) 修正
(D) 做紀錄

正解 (A)

❺提到 only I, as your manager「只有我，也就是你的主管」，可以知道說話者是聽取留言者的主管。另外❻提到 let me know if you spot an error that needs to be updated.「如果妳發現有錯誤需要更新，請告知我。」因此(A)為正解。

題目 / 中文翻譯

101 正解 (B)

New patients should arrive fifteen minutes before ------- scheduled appointments.

初診患者需於預定約診時間前 15 分鐘抵達。

(A) themselves
(B) their
(C) them
(D) they

(A) 他們自己（反身代名詞）
(B) 他們的（所有格）
(C) 他們（受格）
(D) 他們（主格）

重點解說 空格後接名詞 scheduled appointments「預定約診時間」，因此空格應選能修飾名詞的所有格 (B) their「他們的」。

---

102 正解 (C)

The ------- version of the budget proposal must be submitted by Friday.

預算案最終定案版需於星期五前提交。

(A) total
(B) many
(C) final
(D) empty

(A) 全部的
(B) 許多的
(C) 最終的
(D) 空洞的

重點解說 選項全部都是形容詞。空格應填入修飾單數名詞 version「版本」的形容詞，因此最貼切的答案應為 (C) final「最終的」。budget proposal 指「預算案」。

---

103 正解 (C)

Ms. Choi offers clients ------- tax preparation services and financial management consultations.

Choi 女士提供客戶報稅服務與財務管理諮詢。

(A) only if
(B) either
(C) both
(D) not only

(A) 除非
(B)（兩者之中）任一個
(C)（兩者）都
(D) 不只

重點解說 空格後以對等連接詞 and 連接 A（= tax preparation services）和 B（= financial management consultations），兩者為並列關係。由於 both A and B 意思是「（兩者）都」，故正解為 (C) both。

題目 / 中文翻譯

104 正解 (D)

Maya Byun ------- by the executive team to head the new public relations department.

(A) chose
(B) choose
(C) was choosing
(D) was chosen

Maya Byun 獲執行團隊選為新任公關部門領導人。

(A) 選擇（過去式）
(B) 選擇（原形動詞）
(C) 正在選擇（過去進行式）
(D) 被選（過去式被動語態）

重點解說 選項都是動詞 choose「選擇」的變化形。空格後接的是沒有受詞的前置詞 by the executive team「被執行團隊」，因此被動語態 (D) was chosen 最適當。head 是「以…為首」。

---

105 正解 (D)

Belvin Theaters will ------- allow customers to purchase tickets on its Web site.

(A) yet
(B) since
(C) ever
(D) soon

Belvin 劇院不久後便會開放顧客在網站上購票。

(A) 尚未
(B) 自從
(C) 曾經
(D) 不久後

重點解說 選項都是副詞。空格之前是 will，之後是＜ allow ＋人＋ to do ＞「讓人能夠去做…」，表示未來時間。因此最適當的是修飾謂語動詞 will allow 的副詞 (D) soon「不久後」。

---

106 正解 (A)

AIZ Office Products offers businesses a ------- way to send invoices to clients online.

(A) secure
(B) securely
(C) securest
(D) secures

AIZ 辦公用品公司提供企業線上寄送發票給客戶的安全途徑。

(A) 安全的（形容詞）
(B) 安全地（副詞）
(C) 最安全的（形容詞最高級）
(D) 確保（現在式單數動詞）

重點解說 冠詞 a 之後，應接可以修飾名詞 way 的形容詞原級 (A) secure「安全的」。invoice「發票、發貨單」。

題目 / 中文翻譯

107 正解 (C)

Because several committee members have been delayed, the accounting report will be discussed ------- than planned at today's meeting.

(A) late
(B) latest
(C) later
(D) lateness

由於好幾名委員會的委員有所耽擱，所以本日會議的會計匯報時間將比原先計畫的更晚進行。

(A) 遲到的（形容詞）；遲到地（副詞）
(B) 最新的（形容詞）；最新地（副詞最高級）
(C) 更晚的（形容詞）；更晚地（副詞比較級）
(D) 遲到（名詞）

重點解說 由空格前 will be discussed 可知空格內應填入副詞作為修飾。空格後有 than，因此應該用 late「遲到的」比較級 (C) later。committee「委員會」; delay「延遲」。

---

108 正解 (D)

According to the revised schedule, the manufacturing conference will begin at 9:00 A.M. ------- 8:00 A.M.

(A) now
(B) when
(C) due to
(D) instead of

根據修改過的行程表顯示，製造會議將於上午 9 點開始，而不是 8 點。

(A) 現在
(B) 當…的時候
(C) 因為
(D) 而不是

重點解說 空格前為「會議將於上午 9 點開始」。連接空格後的 8:00 A.M，適當的意思是 (D) instead of「是…而不是…」。

---

109 正解 (B)

While the station is undergoing repair, the train will proceed ------- Cumberland without stopping.

(A) aboard
(B) through
(C) quickly
(D) straight

當車站正在進行整修時，火車將不會靠站，而是直行通過 Cumberland。

(A) 登（船／機）
(B) 通過
(C) 迅速地
(D) 直直地

重點解說 空格後是 without stopping「不停靠」。proceed「行進」和介係詞 (B) through「通過」放在一起，有「直接通過車站」的意思。undergo「歷經」。

題目 / 中文翻譯

110 正解 (D)

Dr. Morales, a geologist from the Environmental Institute, plans to study the soil from the mountains ------- Caracas.

環境研究所的地質學家 Morales 博士計畫研究 Caracas 週邊山脈的土壤。

(A) out
(B) next
(C) onto
(D) around

(A) 在外面（副詞）
(B) 緊鄰的（形容詞或副詞）
(C) 到…之上（介係詞）
(D) 在…附近（介係詞或副詞）

重點解說 空格前的名詞 the mountains 與空格後的專有地名 Caracas 之間，能插進的是介係詞，因此符合文意的是 (D) around「在…附近」。geologist「地質學家」；institute「研究所」；soil「土壤」。

---

111 正解 (C)

If you have already signed up for automatic payments, ------- no further steps are required.

若您已經註冊自動付款系統，那麼便無需再進行任何步驟。

(A) even
(B) additional
(C) then
(D) until

(A) 甚至（副詞）
(B) 額外的（形容詞）
(C) 那麼（副詞）
(D) 直至（連接詞）

重點解說 前半句表示「如果已經註冊」的條件，空格後的意思是「無需再進行任何步驟」，因此可知此選 (C) then「那麼」。further「進一步的」。

---

112 正解 (A)

Confident that Mr. Takashi Ota was ------- more qualified than other candidates, Argnome Corporation hired him as the new vice president.

Argnome 公司確信 Takashi Ota 先生遠比其他候選人更符合資格，便聘請他擔任新任副總裁。

(A) much
(B) very
(C) rarely
(D) along

(A) …得多（加強比較級）
(B) 非常地
(C) 很少地
(D) 沿著

重點解說 選項全部是副詞。要修飾空格後的形容詞比較級 more qualified「更符合資格」，強調比較程度的 (A) much「…得多」最為恰當。candidate「候選人」；vice president「副總裁」。

題目/中文翻譯

113 正解 (D)

Poleberry Local Marketplace takes pride in carrying only ------- processed dairy products from the region.

讓 Poleberry 本地市集相當自豪的是，他們只販售當地自產且天然加工的奶製品。

(A) nature
(B) natures
(C) natural
(D) naturally

(A) 自然（不可數名詞）
(B) 本質（可數名詞）
(C) 自然的（形容詞）
(D) 天然地（副詞）

重點解說 空格後接過去分詞 processed「經加工」，此處應以副詞修飾，故選 (D) naturally「天然地」。processed 修飾後面的名詞 dairy products「奶製品」。take pride in「以…自豪」；carry「出售（貨品）」。

---

114 正解 (D)

All of Molina Language Institute's ------- have three or more years of experience and a valid teaching credential.

Molina 語言學校的全體講師皆具有三年或以上的教學經驗，以及有效的教師證。

(A) instructed
(B) instruction
(C) instructing
(D) instructors

(A) 教授（過去式）
(B) 教學（名詞）
(C) 教授（現在分詞）
(D) 講師（名詞）

重點解說 空格後接複數動詞 have，因此可知空格前為主詞，而空格必須是名詞的複數。此外，空格後寫著「具有三年或以上的教學經驗以及有效的教師證」，因此正確答案為 (D) instructors「講師」。valid「有效的」；credential「證書」。

---

115 正解 (C)

The restaurant critic for the *Montreal Times* ------- the food at Corban's Kitchen as affordable and authentic.

《Montreal Times》的餐廳評論家形容 Corban's Kitchen 餐點價格親民且口味道地。

(A) ordered
(B) admitted
(C) described
(D) purchased

(A) 訂購
(B) 承認
(C) 形容
(D) 購買

重點解說 選項全部是動詞的過去式。describe A as B 的意思是「將 A 描述成 B」，因此選 (C)。critic「評論家」；affordable「可負擔的」；authentic「道地的」。

題目 / 中文翻譯

116 正解 (A)

The Merrywood Shop will hold a sale in January to clear out an ------- of holiday supplies.

(A) excess
(B) overview
(C) extra
(D) opportunity

Merrywood 商店將在一月舉辦過剩的節慶用品清倉大拍賣。

(A) 過剩
(B) 概述
(C) 額外的
(D) 機會

重點解說 選項全部是名詞。hold a sale in January to clear out「將在一月舉辦清倉大拍賣」，符合文意的是表示 an excess of...「過剩」的 (A) excess。(C) extra 指的是一般產品外加的東西，例如報紙特刊（newspaper extra）。clear out「清除」；holiday supplies「節慶用品」。

---

117 正解 (B)

Zoticos Clothing, Inc., has acquired two other retail companies as part of a plan to expand ------- Europe and Asia.

(A) each
(B) into
(C) here
(D) already

Zoticos 服飾公司已經購得其他兩家零售公司，完成進軍歐亞開拓計畫的部分環節。

(A)（兩個或兩個以上）各個（形容詞）
(B) 進入（介係詞）
(C) 這裡（副詞）
(D) 已經（副詞）

重點解說 空格前的動詞 expand「進軍、拓展（事業等）」，與空格後的名詞句 Europe and Asia 能連接的是介係詞 (B) into「進入」。expand into「進軍…」；acquire「購得」。

---

118 正解 (A)

According to the city planning director, Adelaide's old civic center must be ------- demolished before construction on a new center can begin.

(A) completely
(B) defectively
(C) plentifully
(D) richly

根據都市計畫主任表示，Adelaide 老舊的市民中心必須在開始建造新的中心前先徹底拆除。

(A) 徹底地
(B) 缺乏地
(C) 豐富地
(D) 富裕地

重點解說 選項全部是副詞。這裡要選擇修飾空格前後 be demolished「被拆除」的詞。demolished 後面接的是「在開始建造新的中心前」，因此從文意判斷是 (A) completely「徹底地」最貼切。civic center「市民中心」；construction on「…的建造」。

題目 / 中文翻譯

119 正解 (C)

An accomplished skater -------, Mr. Loewenstein also coaches the world-champion figure skater Sara Krasnova.

Loewenstein 先生本身是位傑出的溜冰高手，也是花式溜冰世界冠軍 Sara Krasnova 的指導教練。

(A) he
(B) him
(C) himself
(D) his

(A) 他（主格）
(B) 他（受格）
(C) 他自己（反身代名詞）
(D) 他的（所有格）

重點解說 逗點前的部分不是主詞加動詞，而是使用分詞構句句型，省略 Being 表示 Mr. Loewenstein 這個主詞和後半部一樣。Mr. Loewenstein 本身是 An accomplished skater「傑出的溜冰高手」，因此最適當的是反身代名詞 (C) himself「他自己」。

---

120 正解 (B)

Sefu Asamoah is an innovative architect who is ------- the traditional approach to constructing space-efficient apartment buildings.

Sefu Asamoah 是一位富有創新精神的建築師，他為打造節省空間的公寓，挑戰傳統建築方式。

(A) challenge
(B) challenging
(C) challenged
(D) challenges

(A) 挑戰（原形動詞）
(B) 挑戰（現在分詞）
(C) 受到挑戰的（過去分詞）
(D) 挑戰（第三人稱單數動詞）

重點解說 以關係代名詞 who 開始的句子中，空格後是受詞 the traditional approach「傳統做法」，因此能和 is 一起做為動詞的是 (B) challenging，為現在進行式的「挑戰」。who 的先行詞為 an innovative architect「富有創新精神的建築師」。space-efficient「節省空間的」。

---

121 正解 (A)

Because of ------- regarding noise, the hotel manager has instructed the landscaping staff to avoid operating equipment before 9:30 A.M.

由於噪音相關的抱怨，飯店經理已經指示景觀美化人員避免在上午 9 點半前操作機器設備。

(A) complaints
(B) materials
(C) opponents
(D) symptoms

(A) 抱怨
(B) 材料
(C) 反對者
(D) 症狀

重點解說 選項全部是名詞的複數形。空格後的 regarding noise「噪音相關」修飾空格的字。逗號後說的是「避免在上午 9 點半前操作機器設備」，因此符合文意的是 (A) complaints「抱怨」。landscaping「景觀美化」。

題目 / 中文翻譯

122 正解 (C)

For 30 years, Big Top Prop Company has been the premier ------- of circus equipment for troupes around the world.

三十年來，Big Top Prop 公司一直是在全世界巡迴展演團體的首要馬戲團設備供應商。

(A) providing
(B) provision
(C) provider
(D) provides

(A) 供應（現在分詞）
(B) 供應（名詞）
(C) 供應者（名詞）
(D) 供應（第三人稱單數動詞）

重點解說 空格前為形容詞 premier「首要的」，後面是介係詞 of，因此空格應填入名詞。句子的主詞是 Big Top Prop 公司，因此符合文意的是 (C) provider「供應商」。troupe「（馬戲團等）巡迴演出的劇團」。

---

123 正解 (B)

Chris Cantfield was ------- the outstanding candidates considered for the Thomas Award for exceptional police service.

在所有的傑出候選人中，Chris Cantifield 被認為是榮獲 Thomas 卓越警察獎的不二人選。

(A) on
(B) among
(C) during
(D) up

(A) 在…上面
(B) 在…之中
(C) 在…期間
(D) 在…之上

重點解說 選項全部是介係詞。後面的 the outstanding candidates「傑出候選人」，是複數名詞，因此適當的答案是 (B) among，表示「在…之中」。exceptional「卓越的」。

---

124 正解 (C)

Please instruct employees with questions concerning the new payroll policy to contact ------- or Ms. Singh directly.

請指示對於新式薪資政策有所疑問的員工直接與我或是 Singh 女士聯繫。

(A) my
(B) mine
(C) me
(D) I

(A) 我的（所有格）
(B) 我的（所有格代名詞）
(C) 我（受格）
(D) 我（主格）

重點解說 空格後是 or，用以連接和 Ms. Singh 相同詞性的字，而且是 contact「聯繫」的受詞，因此適當的答案是 (C) me「我」。句中的 with questions concerning the new payroll policy 修飾 employees。payroll「薪資（名冊）」。

題目 / 中文翻譯

125 正解 (D)

Although the author ------- presents the purchase of real estate as a safe investment, she later describes times that it might be risky.

(A) highly
(B) afterward
(C) quite
(D) initially

雖然作者起初提出購買不動產是安全的投資，但稍後也說明在該時間購買可能具有風險。

(A) 高度地
(B) 之後
(C) 相當地
(D) 起初地

重點解說 選項全部是副詞，要選擇適當修飾空格後動詞 presents「提出」的詞。關於購買不動產，前半句說是安全的投資，後半句則說可能有風險，兩者互相對照，用連接詞 Although「雖然」來連接。後半句的 later「稍後」，與 (D) initially「起初」的意思互相對照，因此是正解。

---

126 正解 (C)

The research released by Henford Trust ranked automobile companies according to sales ------- and financial position.

(A) performed
(B) performing
(C) performance
(D) performer

Henford 信託發表的研究報告依據銷售業績表現與財務狀況來列出行動電話公司排名。

(A) 表現（過去分詞）
(B) 表現（現在分詞）
(C) 表現（名詞）
(D) 表演者（名詞）

重點解說 空格前的 according to...「依據…」後面接 sales 和 financial position「財務狀況」，是用 and 連接的並列關係，因此空格要填名詞。從文意判斷，(C) performance「業績表現」是正解。sales performance「銷售業績表現」；rank 為動詞「排名」。

---

127 正解 (A)

An insightful ------- in the *Boston Daily Post* suggests that offering opportunities for professional development is a valuable method of motivating employees.

(A) editorial
(B) novel
(C) catalog
(D) directory

一篇刊載於《Boston Daily Post》的精闢社論指出，提供專業人才發展機會是能夠激勵員工的寶貴方法。

(A) 社論
(B) 小說
(C) 目錄
(D) 電話簿

重點解說 選項全部是名詞。空格後接著 in the *Boston Daily Post*「*Boston Daily* 報紙上的」，因此選擇刊載於報上的內容。動詞 suggests 之後接的是「激勵員工的寶貴方法」，由此判斷適當的選項應是 (A) editorial「社論」。insightful「精闢的」；motivate「激勵（人）」。

題目 / 中文翻譯

128 正解 (B)

The Web site advises customers to review their orders carefully as it is difficult to make changes ------- an order is submitted.

該網站建議顧客仔細檢視訂單，因為一旦提交訂單之後便難以更改。

(A) following
(B) once
(C) right away
(D) by means of

(A) 接下來的
(B) 一旦
(C) 立即
(D) 藉由

重點解說 本題從 as 之後表示前半句內容的理由。as 連接的子句除了主詞 it 和動詞 is 之外，在空格後還接著<主詞＋動詞>，因此空格內應該填上能連接這兩個部份的連接詞 (B) once「一旦」。

---

129 正解 (A)

Well-known journalist Kent Moriwaki published a book in May ------- a compilation of quotes from interviews with various artists.

著名記者 Kent Moriwaki 在五月時出版一本書籍，該書特色為一部包含眾多藝術家的訪談。

(A) featuring
(B) featured
(C) feature
(D) features

(A) 以…為特色（現在分詞）
(B) 以…為特色（過去分詞）
(C) 特色（名詞單數或複數動詞）
(D) 特色（名詞複數或單數動詞）

重點解說 選項全部是動詞 feature「以…為特色」的變化。空格前提到「Kent Moriwaki 在五月出版一本書籍」，空格後是 a book 的說明。空格後接受詞，因此修飾 a book 的 (A) featuring 最適當。a compilation of...「…的總集」。

---

130 正解 (C)

------- delays in the entryway construction, the Orchid Restaurant in Chongqing will reopen and provide an alternative entrance until all work is complete.

儘管入口建築工事延期，位於重慶的蘭花餐廳仍然重新開幕，並在所有工程完成前另開出入口。

(A) Furthermore
(B) Assuming that
(C) Regardless of
(D) Subsequently

(A) 此外（副詞）
(B) 假設（副詞子句）
(C) 儘管（介係詞片語）
(D) 接著（副詞）

重點解說 空格接的是名詞句 delays in the entryway construction「入口建築工事延期」，因此介係詞片語 (C) Regardless of「儘管」最適當。alternative「替代選擇」。

題目 / 中文翻譯

Questions 131-134 refer to the following e-mail.

To: Sunil Pai <sp8410@xmail.co.uk>
From: Fabrizio Donetti <customerservice@palazzadesign.co.uk>
Date: Friday, 1 July
Subject: Order #491001

Dear Mr. Pai:

Thank you for your recent order. ------- (131.) the tan linen suit you ordered is unfortunately not available in your size at this time, we do have the same style in stock in light gray. ------- (132.).

If you order now, we can offer you a 15% discount on the suit, as well as free shipping on your ------- (133.) order, so you could have the items by next week. If you are interested, please e-mail our customer service department and reference the order number above.

We apologize for any inconvenience this may cause you. We ------- (134.) forward to serving you and providing you with fashionable apparel in the future.

Sincerely,

Fabrizio Donetti
Customer Service Representative

請參考以下的電子郵件回答第 131 至 134 題。

收件者：Sunil Pai <sp8410@xmail.co.uk>
寄件者：Fabrizio Donetti <customerservice@palazzadesign.co.uk>
寄件日期：7 月 1 日週五
主旨：訂單編號 #491001

敬愛的 Pai 先生您好：

非常感謝您日前的訂購。雖然很不幸地，目前您訂購的褐色麻料西裝並沒有您的尺寸，但我們的庫存裡確實還有淺灰色同款西裝。* 我們可以立即寄送其中一套給您。

若您現在訂購的話，我們會提供您西裝 85 折的優惠，而且整筆訂單可享免運，好讓您在下週就能收到這些品項。如果您有興趣，請寄電子郵件給我們的客服部門，並註明上述的訂單編號。

若有造成您任何不便之處，我們深感抱歉。期待未來能夠再次為您服務，並為您提供流行時尚服飾。

客服代表
Fabrizio Donetti 敬上

* 為132 題的內文翻譯

單字註釋：tan「褐色的」；linen「麻料的」；reference「（動詞）參照、參考」

題目 / 中文翻譯

131 正解 (B)

(A) After
(B) Although
(C) Even
(D) When

(A) 在…之後
(B) 雖然
(C) 即使
(D) 當…的時候

重點解說 空格後接的是「很不幸地，目前您訂購的褐色麻料西裝並沒有您的尺寸」，逗號後是「庫存還有淺灰色同款西裝」，這兩句需要連接詞連接，從文意來看，適合的是 (B) Although「雖然」。

---

132 正解 (A)

(A) We could send you one of these right away.
(B) Thank you for returning them.
(C) These will be available early next season.
(D) You may exchange your new suits for a larger size.

(A) 我們可以立即寄送其中一套給您。
(B) 感謝您退回產品。
(C) 這些產品要等到下個季初才能取得。
(D) 您的新西裝可以換成更大的尺碼。

重點解說 空格之前，告知「您訂購的西裝並沒有您的尺寸，但是有不同色的同款西裝」，接下來告知立刻訂購的優惠和送達時間。因此適當的答案是 (A)「能夠立即寄出其中一套」。these 指的是 the same style in stock in light gray「庫存的淺灰色同款西裝」。

---

133 正解 (C)

(A) ready
(B) general
(C) entire
(D) thorough

(A) 準備就緒的
(B) 一般的
(C) 整個的
(D) 徹底的

重點解說 選項都是形容詞。空格應該是修飾後方名詞 order「訂單」的形容詞，因此根據文意選出 (C) entire「整個的」。

---

134 正解 (A)

(A) look
(B) looked
(C) were looking
(D) had been looking

(A) 看著（原形動詞）
(B) 看著（過去式）
(C) 看著（過去進行式）
(D) 一直看著（過去完成進行式）

重點解說 選擇原形動詞 look 為適當的形態。包含空格的這一句是要給顧客的郵件，表示希望將來繼續交易，因此不應該用過去式。正解是 (A) look。look forward to + Ving「期盼…」。

題目 / 中文翻譯

Questions 135-138 refer to the following notice.

For the first time, the Oakville Library is conducting a survey to learn how it can better -------135. the needs of the public. The information gathered from the survey responses will help guide -------136. five-year plan. -------137. .

The survey can be completed online at www.oakvillelibrary.org/survey. Visitors can also pick up a -------138. of this form at the circulation desk on the first floor. Library patrons are strongly encouraged to complete the survey. The Oakville Library is open Monday to Friday from 10:00 A.M. to 8:00 P.M. and Saturday and Sunday from 1:00 P.M. to 5:00 P.M. For more information, call 555-0130.

請參考以下公告回答第 **135** 至 **138** 題。

為了瞭解如何更加滿足民眾需求，Oakville 圖書館首度實施調查。由調查結果所蒐集而成的資訊將能夠協助指導圖書館的五年計畫。* 該項計畫包含計畫制訂、服務項目與資料內容。

您可透過 www.oakvillelibrary.org/survey 完成線上調查。訪客亦可於一樓流通櫃台處取得調查表格。強烈建議圖書館愛用者完成這項調查。Oakville 圖書館的開館時間為週一至週五上午 10 點至晚上 8 點，週六和週日下午 1 點至 5 點。欲知詳情，請撥打 555-0130 洽詢。 * 為 137 題的內文翻譯

單字註釋：conduct a survey「實施（問卷）調查」；circulation desk「（圖書館借還書的）流通櫃台」；patron「常客、（圖書館設施的）愛用者」

題目 / 中文翻譯

135 正解 (B)

(A) met
(B) meet
(C) meeting
(D) meetings

(A) 滿足（過去式）
(B) 滿足（原形動詞）
(C) 滿足（現在分詞）
(D) 會議（複數名詞）

重點解說 這裡要選擇的是，以 how 開始的分句主詞 it 後面跟的動詞。這個 it 指的是 the Oakville Library。空格前有助動詞 can，因此應選動詞原形 (B) meet。副詞 better「更好的」修飾空格裡的 meet。

題目 / 中文翻譯

136 正解 (A)

(A) its
(B) his
(C) your
(D) theirs

(A) 它的（所有格）
(B) 他的（所有格）
(C) 你的（所有格）
(D) 他們的（所有格代名詞）

重點解說 實施問卷調查的是 Oakville 圖書館，因此蒐集問卷調查資訊有助於五年計畫，可以判斷答案為「圖書館的」。能代表「圖書館的」這個意思的，是指「物」的代名詞的所有格 (A) its。

---

137 正解 (D)

(A) The questions are the same as those used five years ago.
(B) Patrons of the library are welcome to the event.
(C) Membership will be renewed after five years.
(D) **This plan covers programming, services, and materials.**

(A) 這些問題與五年前所使用的問題一模一樣。
(B) 歡迎圖書館愛用者參加這項活動。
(C) 會員資格可於五年後再更新。
(D) 這項計畫包含規畫、服務與內容資料。

重點解說 空格前的段落文意為，對 Oakville 圖書館使用者實施問卷調查，而問卷調查結果對圖書館的五年計畫會有幫助。空格中放進 (D)，補充說明這個計畫的內容，符合文意。This plan 指的是前面的 its five-year plan「五年計畫」。

---

138 正解 (D)

(A) placement
(B) showcase
(C) magazine
(D) copy

(A) 配置
(B) 陳列櫃
(C) 雜誌
(D) 份；本

重點解說 選項全部是名詞。包含空格的句子意思是「訪客亦可於一樓流通櫃台處取得…調查表格」。a copy of... 是指「（書或雜誌等）…的一份」，因此選 (D)。

題目 / 中文翻譯

Questions 139-142 refer to the following notice.

-------- (139.) Starting this April, the North-South express train will no longer be stopping at Green Street Station. This will affect the express service only; local train service will continue uninterrupted to all stations on the North-South line, -------- (140.) Green Street Station. Please speak with a conductor or visit our Web site if you have any questions.

Additionally, we would like to remind passengers to be -------- (141.) to others at all times. An increasing number of passengers are expressing irritation with the level of -------- (142.). Please remain mindful of those around you and keep mobile phone use at a minimum when you ride the train.

Thank you for your cooperation and for riding Montego Metro.

請參考以下公告回答第 139 至 142 題。

* 在此通知您列車行駛服務將有所變動。從這個四月開始，North-South 特快列車不再停靠 Green Street 車站。這項改變僅會影響特快列車服務，行經 North-South 線各車站——包含 Green Street 車站——的區間車行駛服務則保持暢通。若您有任何疑問，請洽詢車掌或是造訪我們的網站。

另外，我們想提醒各位乘客要隨時注意對他人的禮貌。越來越多的乘客反映對於噪音的程度感到不悅。請顧慮您周遭乘客的感受，乘坐火車期間，請將行動電話用量降至最低。

感謝您的配合與搭乘 Montego Metro。

* 為 139 題的內文翻譯

單字註釋：uninterrupted「連續的、不間斷的」；conductor「車掌」；irritation「不悅、不滿」；at a minimum「最低限度的」

題目 / 中文翻譯

139 正解 (D)

(A) Montego Metro is announcing fare increases.
(B) Note that Green Street Station will soon close.
(C) New station facilities are available on this line.
(D) Please be advised of a change to train service.

(A) Montego Metro 正在宣佈調漲運費。
(B) 請注意 Green Street 車站即將關閉。
(C) 這條路線的新式車站設施可供使用。
(D) 在此通知您列車行駛服務將有所變動。

重點解說

空格後的句子是，Starting this April, the North-South express train will no longer be stopping at Green Street Station.「這個四月開始，North-South 特快列車不再停靠 Green Street 車站」。這是知會乘客關於列車行駛服務的變動，因此文章開頭選 (D) 最符合文意。Please be advised... 是「在此通知…」的意思。

題目 / 中文翻譯

140 正解 (B)

(A) regarding	(A) 關於
(B) including	(B) 包含
(C) added to	(C) 增加
(D) given that	(D) 既然

重點解說 從空格文句的前文，得知 Green Street 車站是 North-South 線的車站。從含有空格的文句中，可知「North-South 線各車站的區間車行駛服務保持暢通」，因此意思是「包括 Green Street 車站在內的 North-South 線各車站」，應該選 (B) including「包含」。

---

141 正解 (C)

(A) adjacent	(A) 鄰近的
(B) incompatible	(B) 矛盾的
(C) polite	(C) 有禮的
(D) frequent	(D) 頻繁的

重點解說 選項全部是形容詞。含有空格的文句意思是「我們想提醒各位乘客要隨時注意…」。接下來說「越來越多的乘客感到不悅」，後面再要求乘客顧慮周遭旅客的感受。從文意來看，應該選 (C) polite「有禮的」。

---

142 正解 (A)

(A) noise	(A) 噪音
(B) expense	(B) 費用
(C) precision	(C) 精確
(D) personnel	(D) 人員

重點解說 選項全部是名詞。含有空格的文句意思是「越來越多的乘客反映對於…的程度感到不悅」。此外，空格後的文句也拜託各位「顧慮周遭乘客的感受，將行動電話用量降至最低」，從文意來看，最適當的是 (A) noise「噪音」。

題目

Questions 143-146 refer to the following letter.

Ms. Seema Nishad
Yadav Engineering Ltd.
7100 B-4 Pratap Bazar
Ludhiana 141003

Dear Ms. Nishad:

I am writing to invite you to participate in the India Materials Engineering Association's (IMEA) trade show this year. As always, the event will provide ------- (143.) opportunities for networking.

Many vendors have already reserved booths. However, there are other ways to ------- (144.) your company. Those who sponsor a meeting or provide refreshments receive special acknowledgment in the program.

Enclosed please find information regarding the trade show. It includes pricing ------- (145.) for reserving a booth, placing ads, and sponsoring an event, in addition to a list of past participants.

------- (146.). If you have questions, please contact me by e-mail.

Sincerely,

Manik Chaudhary
IMEA Vendor Coordinator
chaudhary@matengineer.org.in

Enclosure

中文翻譯

請參考以下信件回答第 143 至 146 題。

Seema Nishad 女士收
Yadav Engineering 公司
7100 B-4 Pratap Bazar
Ludhiana 141003

敬愛的 Nishad 女士您好：

在此敬邀您參加今年由印度材料工程協會（IMEA）所舉辦的貿易展。與往年一樣，此次的展覽將會提供給您各種建立人脈的機會。

許多攤販商都已經預訂好攤位。不過呢，仍然有其他能夠宣傳貴公司的方法。贊助會議或提供點心的公司都將會在活動中獲得我們的特別致謝。

隨信謹附上本次貿易展相關資訊，除了以往參與者名單之外，也包含預約攤位、打廣告以及活動贊助等費用細節。

* 希望您今年可以加入我們。若您仍有其他疑問，請透過電子郵件與我聯繫。

IMEA 攤販商協調員
Manik Chaudhary 敬上
chaudhary@matengineer.org.in

隨函附件　　　　* 為 146 題的內文翻譯

單字註釋：networking「建立（工作上的）人脈」；refreshments「點心」；acknowledgment「致謝」；place an ad「打廣告」；enclosure「附件」

題目 / 中文翻譯

143 正解 (D)

(A) extend	(A) 延長（原形動詞）
(B) extends	(B) 延長（單數動詞）
(C) extensively	(C) 廣泛地（副詞）
(D) extensive	(D) 廣泛的（形容詞）

重點解說 provide 的受詞是空格後的名詞，也就是 opportunities「機會」，應該填入可修飾這個名詞的形容詞，因此正解是 (D) extensive「廣泛的」。

題目 / 中文翻譯

144 正解 (A)

(A) promote　(A) 宣傳
(B) monitor　(B) 監管
(C) construct　(C) 建造
(D) negotiate　(D) 談判

重點解說 選項全部是動詞。空格上一句提到「許多攤販商都已經預訂好攤位」，接著包含空格的文句意思是「可是仍然有其他能夠…貴公司的方法」，並且在下面的文句中，舉例說明它的方法，包括贊助會議或提供點心等。這些都可以說是宣傳該企業的方法，因此適當的是 (A) promote「宣傳」。

---

145 正解 (B)

(A) markets　(A) 市場
(B) details　(B) 細節
(C) labels　(C) 標籤
(D) receipts　(D) 收據

重點解說 選項全部是名詞的複數形。含有空格的文句主詞是 it，指的是 information regarding the trade show「關於貿易展的資訊」。後面提到「包括預約攤位、打廣告以及活動贊助等關於價格的…」，因此空格內應選 (B) details「細節」。

---

146 正解 (A)

(A) We hope you decide to join us this year.　(A) 希望您今年可以加入我們。
(B) We have placed your ad in the brochure.　(B) 我們已經將您的廣告放入手冊。
(C) Your participation in the event will be at no cost.　(C) 您可以免費參與這項活動。
(D) Your presentation is scheduled for the first day.　(D) 您的發表時間預定為第一天。

重點解說 這封信是要鼓勵對方參與今年的貿易展，其中介紹了出展、贊助等，並提到這些價格的訊息。(A) 適合當做這封信的總結。

題目 / 中文翻譯

Questions 147-148 refer to the following job announcement.

CORPORATE TRAINER WANTED

San Francisco-based Logistos Advisors, Inc., is seeking an energetic person with strong public-speaking skills to serve as a temporary replacement for an employee who is away on leave. Logistos delivers training classes on Internet security to large financial institutions and retail businesses worldwide. The successful applicant will be responsible for assisting with training sessions throughout Latin America. Although the sessions are delivered in English, proficiency in Spanish is necessary for the job. At least one year of experience as a corporate trainer in any field is highly desirable. The work assignment is for six months, the first two weeks to be spent at the Logistos headquarters for initial training. Interested candidates should submit a cover letter and résumé to hr@logistosadvisors.com by March 1.

請參考以下的徵才啟事回答第 **147** 至 **148** 題。

徵求企業培訓師

位於舊金山的 Logistos 顧問公司正在尋求活力十足且具備極佳群眾演講能力的人才，來暫代休假員工的職務。Logistos 公司提供網路安全課程，授課對象為大型金融機構與全球零售業者。成功錄取的應徵者將會負責協助拉丁美洲各地的培訓課程。儘管培訓課程為英語授課，這項工作的必要條件之一即是精通西班牙語。強力徵求在任何領域具備至少一年以上工作經歷的企業培訓師。工作任期為半年，前兩週先於 Logistos 公司總部進行初步培訓。感興趣的求職者需繳交求職信與個人履歷，並於三月一日前寄至 hr@logistosadvisors.com。

題目/中文翻譯

147 正解 (A)

What is NOT a stated requirement for the job?

(A) Experience working at a financial institution
(B) Ability to speak more than one language
(C) Willingness to travel internationally
(D) Public speaking skills

何者並非該職務所規定的必要條件？

(A) 金融機構的工作經驗
(B) 兩種以上的語言能力
(C) 海外出差的意願
(D) 群眾演講的能力

重點解說

(B) 可從第四句中知道，需要會英文和西班牙文。(C) 可從第一句得知，公司設在舊金山，而且第三句提到成功錄取的應徵者將會負責協助拉丁美洲各地的培訓課程，因此會要到海外工作。(D) 可從第一句中得知，要找能在群眾面前演講的能力。
(C) willingness「樂意、意願」。

---

148 正解 (C)

How long will the job last?

(A) Two weeks
(B) One month
(C) Six months
(D) One year

該工作任職期間多久？

(A) 兩週
(B) 一個月
(C) 半年
(D) 一年

重點解說

第六句說明 The work assignment is for six months「工作任期為半年」。

單字註釋：replacement「代替者」；on leave「休假中」；retail business「零售商」；proficiency「精通」；cover letter「求職信、自薦信（履歷表等上面附的信）」

題目

Questions 149-150 refer to the following text message chain.

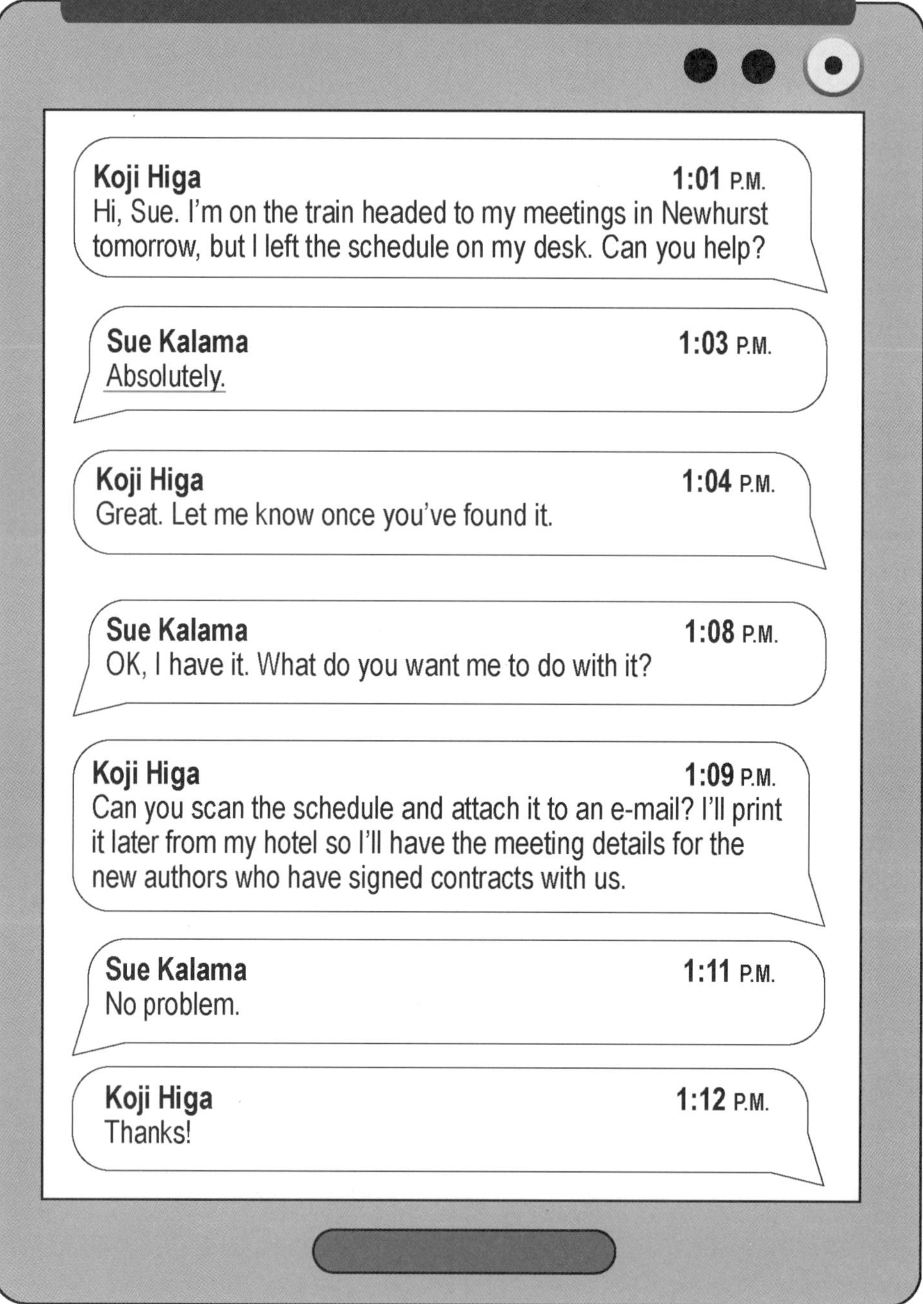
Koji Higa 1:01 P.M.
Hi, Sue. I'm on the train headed to my meetings in Newhurst tomorrow, but I left the schedule on my desk. Can you help?
Sue Kalama 1:03 P.M.
Absolutely.
Koji Higa 1:04 P.M.
Great. Let me know once you've found it.
Sue Kalama 1:08 P.M.
OK, I have it. What do you want me to do with it?
Koji Higa 1:09 P.M.
Can you scan the schedule and attach it to an e-mail? I'll print it later from my hotel so I'll have the meeting details for the new authors who have signed contracts with us.
Sue Kalama 1:11 P.M.
No problem.
Koji Higa 1:12 P.M.
Thanks!

中文翻譯

請參考以下一連串的簡訊回答第 **149** 至 **150** 題。

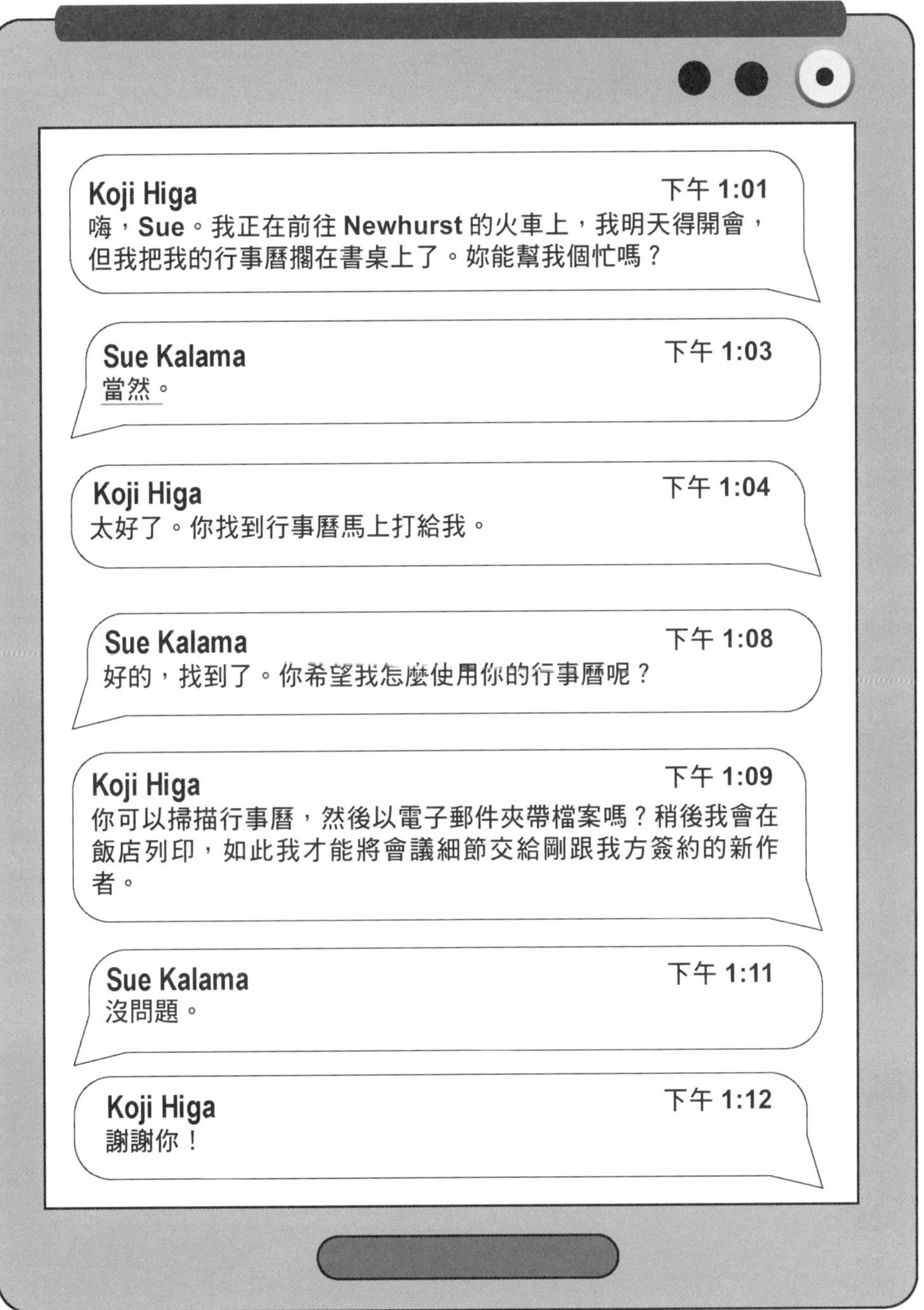

Koji Higa 下午 1:01
嗨，Sue。我正在前往 Newhurst 的火車上，我明天得開會，但我把我的行事曆擱在書桌上了。妳能幫我個忙嗎？
Sue Kalama 下午 1:03
當然。
Koji Higa 下午 1:04
太好了。你找到行事曆馬上打給我。
Sue Kalama 下午 1:08
好的，找到了。你希望我怎麼使用你的行事曆呢？
Koji Higa 下午 1:09
你可以掃描行事曆，然後以電子郵件夾帶檔案嗎？稍後我會在飯店列印，如此我才能將會議細節交給剛跟我方簽約的新作者。
Sue Kalama 下午 1:11
沒問題。
Koji Higa 下午 1:12
謝謝你！

題目 / 中文翻譯

149 正解 (B)

At 1:03 P.M., what does Ms. Kalama mean when she writes, "Absolutely"?

(A) She is happy that Mr. Higa contacted her.
(B) She is willing to assist Mr. Higa.
(C) She is certain that Mr. Higa is correct.
(D) She is leaving her meeting now.

下午 1:03 的時候，Kalama 女士寫下「Absolutely」的意圖為何？

(A) 她很高興 Higa 先生與她聯繫。
(B) 她願意協助 Higa 先生。
(C) 她很確定 Higa 先生是對的。
(D) 她正要離開會議。

重點解說　根據前文，Higa 詢問 Can you help?「妳能幫我個忙嗎？」，而接著 Kalama 回覆 Absolutely.「當然」，表示願意提供協助。be willing to...「願意…」。

---

150 正解 (A)

For what type of business does Mr. Higa most likely work?

(A) A publishing company
(B) A hotel chain
(C) A travel agency
(D) An office supply store

Higa 先生最有可能從事哪方面的職業？

(A) 出版公司
(B) 連鎖飯店
(C) 旅行社
(D) 辦公用品店

重點解說　Higa 在下午 1:09 傳來的訊息提到 the meeting details for the new authors who have signed contracts with us「將會議細節交給剛跟我方簽約的新作者」，可知和作者簽約的對象，很有可能是出版業，故選 (A)。

題目 / 中文翻譯

Questions 151-152 refer to the following document.

Browning's Shoe Repair

Order number: VG12983 **Drop-off date:** November 5

Customer: Janice Goldblatt **Contact number:** (873) 555-0143

Shoe description
Style: Lady's dress shoe **Size:** 7 **Color:** Black

Requested repair: Fix broken heel **Ready by:** November 14

Repair assigned to: Jack Burris

Notes:
Apply 10% frequent customer price reduction. Order will be picked up by Harry Silver.

請參考以下文件回答第 **151** 題至第 **152** 題。

Browning's 皮鞋修理店

訂單編號：VG12983 **送件日：**11 月 5 日

顧客姓名：Janice Goldblatt **聯絡電話：**(873)555-0143

鞋類說明：淑女鞋 **鞋碼：**7 **顏色：**黑色

需要維修處：修理破損的鞋跟 **交件日：**11 月 14 日

負責修理人員：Jack Burris

備註：
可使用九折熟客優惠價。訂單由 Harry Silver 處理。

題目 / 中文翻譯

151 正解 (C)

Who most likely is Mr. Burris?

(A) Ms. Goldblatt's assistant
(B) A department store salesperson
(C) An employee at Browning's
(D) A delivery person

Burris 先生最有可能是誰？

(A) Goldblatt 女士的助理
(B) 百貨公司銷售員
(C) Browning 的員工
(D) 送貨人員

重點解說　Jack Burris 這個名字在 Repair assigned to「負責修理的人員」的欄位中，因此可以判斷 Burris 先生在 Browning's 皮鞋修理店工作。assign A to B...「把 A 分配給 B」。

---

152 正解 (B)

What does the document indicate about Ms. Goldblatt?

(A) She is ordering a new black dress.
(B) She will receive a discount.
(C) She will visit Browning's on November 14.
(D) She is attending a special event on November 5.

該文件提到關於 Goldblatt 女士哪件事情？

(A) 她正在訂購新的黑色洋裝。
(B) 她將獲得折扣。
(C) 她將於 11 月 14 日參觀 Browning。
(D) 她將於 11 月 5 日參加一場特殊活動。

重點解說　Customer 欄上顯示 Janice Goldblatt，由此可知送修鞋子的客人是 Goldblatt 小姐。Notes「備註」的地方寫著 Apply 10% frequent customer price reduction.「將使用九折熟客優惠價」。這句話可以改用 (B) receive a discount 這種說法。

單字註釋：drop-off「交貨、卸下」；description「說明」；dress shoe「正式的鞋」

題目

Questions 153-154 refer to the following e-mail.

From:	Anton Bremen, Production Manager
To:	Andrea Lang, Director
Re:	Production cost outline
Date:	November 3

Dear Ms. Lang:

Please see the requested breakdown below. The proposed electronic truck line will be made of parts produced by our own factories unless otherwise noted. They will be appropriate for children over the age of five and controlled by small handsets. Though this is not my area of expertise, I personally envision this product selling well through department stores. Once you consider the estimated outlay, I hope we can organize a meeting to decide on the project's feasibility and next steps.

Gravitate Play, Inc., Toy Truck Planned Production Cost Outline

Arizona Factory: 1,000 units
Texas Factory: 2,000 units

Cost per unit	
Plastic Casing	= $1.50/unit
Rubber Wheels	= $2.00/unit
Electronics	= $5.00/unit
Cardboard Packaging (Devised and fabricated by supplier Promo Art)	= $0.20/unit
In-house labor (0.25 hours/unit)	= $3.80/unit

Total Direct Cost/Unit		
Direct Cost	$12.50/unit × 3,000 units	= $37,500.00
	Total Indirect Overhead	= $12,500.00
	Total Production Costs	= $50,000.00

Best Regards,
Anton Bremen, Production Manager
Gravitate Play, Inc.

中文翻譯

請參考以下電子郵件回答第 153 至 154 題。

寄件者：	Anton Bremen 生產部經理
收件者：	Andrea Lang 主任
主旨：	生產成本概算
日期：	11 月 3 日

敬愛的 Lang 女士您好，

您要求的明細表如下所示。除非另有載明，否則提案中的電動卡車產品將由我們自家工廠所生產的零件組裝而成。這些玩具適合五歲以上的孩童，並可利用遙控器操控。雖然這並非我的專業領域，但是我個人預估這項產品將會熱銷各家百貨公司。在您考量過預估成本概算後，我希望我們能夠開會決定這項企畫案的可行性，以及接下來的步驟。

Gravitate 玩具公司玩具卡車計畫生產成本概算表
亞利桑那廠：1000 單位
德州廠：2000 單位

每單位成本

塑膠外盒包裝	=1.50 美元 / 每單位
橡皮輪胎	=2.00 美元 / 每單位
電子零件	=5.00 美元 / 每單位
厚紙板包裝 (由供應商 Promo 美術社設計製造)	=0.20 美元 / 每單位
內部勞力 (0.25 小時 / 每單位)	=3.80 美元 / 每單位

直接成本總額 / 單位直接成本
12.50 美元 / 每單位 X 3,000 單位 = 37,500.00 美元
間接費用總額 = 12,500.00 美元
生產成本總額 = 50,000.00 美元

謹獻上最誠摯的敬意。
Gravitate 玩具公司生產部經理
Anton Bremen 敬上

題目 / 中文翻譯

153 正解 (A)

Why is Mr. Bremen writing the e-mail?

(A) To ask for a review of proposed costs
(B) To report a problem with product pricing
(C) To argue for increasing an existing budget
(D) To support a bid from a product manufacturer

Bremen 先生為何寫這封電子郵件？

(A) 請求檢視提案成本
(B) 報告產品定價問題
(C) 主張提高現有預算
(D) 支持某產品製造商的投標價格

重點解說

第一句寫著「您要求的明細表如下所示」，電子郵件中的表則顯示了製造費用提案的概算。第五句中寫著 Once you consider the estimated outlay「在您考量過預估成本概算後」，表示 Bremen 提交了製造成本的概算，希望對方檢視。
(C) existing「現有的」；(D) bid「投標（價格）」。

---

154 正解 (C)

What is indicated about the product packaging?

(A) It is decorated with colors appropriate for children.
(B) It is made from recycled department store packaging.
(C) It is designed and produced by an outside vendor.
(D) It is an important component of the end product.

關於產品包裝，文中提及哪件事？

(A) 適合孩子顏色的包裝。
(B) 是百貨公司包裝回收再利用的。
(C) 由外部供應商負責設計與生產。
(D) 成品的重要元件。

重點解說

product packaging「產品包裝」相關的項目為，電子郵件表中的 Cardboard Packaging「厚紙板包裝」。下一行還補充說明 Devised and fabricated by supplier Promo Art「由供應商 Promo 美術社設計製造」。Devised and fabricated 用 (C) designed and produced 置換，supplier Promo Art 則用 an outside vendor 表現。
(D) component「組成、成份」。

單字註釋：breakdown「明細表」；unless otherwise noted「除非另有載明」；handset「遙控器」；expertise「專門知識」；envision「預測」；outlay「經費」；feasibility「（實現）可能性」；casing「外殼」；devise「設計」；fabricate「製造」；overhead「間接費用」

題目 / 中文翻譯

Questions 155-157 refer to the following article.

New Tasteemix Flavor a Big Hit

By Deepanjali Jaddoo

❶ PORT LOUIS (2 February) — Three weeks ago, Helvetia Food Industries (HFI) announced the introduction of a new flavor of its popular Tasteemix breakfast cereal—coconut cream. — [1] —. HFI also announced that the product would be available for a limited time only, sending Tasteemix enthusiasts from Argentina to Zambia into a buying frenzy.

❷ All six major grocery distributors here in Mauritius confirmed that they had received a large supply of coconut cream Tasteemix shortly after the new product was introduced on 8 January. — [2] —. Both wholesalers expected it to be gone by the end of the day.

❸ "HFI's current campaign is reminiscent of the one it waged four years ago when it introduced its strawberry-cinnamon cereal," said Bina Perida, a professor of marketing at Port Louis Business College. "Then, as now, HFI announced a product as being offered for a limited time only, resulting in that item's rapid disappearance from shelves in grocery stores across the globe." — [3] —.

❹ On 5 April, HFI's accountants will review the company's first-quarter earnings. Based on the initial sales, market watchers are confident that HFI's expectations will be met. — [4] —.

請參考以下文章回答 第 **155** 至 **157** 題。

Tasteemix 新口味熱賣中

文／ Deepanjali Jaddoo

於 PORT LOUIS 報導 (2 月 2 日) – 3 週前，Helvetia 食品工業 (HFI) 宣佈推出旗下暢銷 Tasteemix 早餐麥片全新椰子奶油風味。HFI 也宣布該品項為期間限定商品，使得從阿根廷到尚比亞的 Tasteemix 愛好者都陷入購買狂熱。

Mauritus 當地最主要的六大雜貨銷售商也證實，從 1 月 8 日新品發表後不久便已經出現龐大的 Tasteemix 椰子奶油口味供貨量。* **不過昨天上午時，只剩 Vendibles 和 Foodiverse 說他們還有庫存。**兩家批發商都認為每天結束的時候將銷售一空。

Port Louis 商學院行銷教授 Bina Perida 表示：「HFI 目前的宣傳活動與四年前推出草莓肉桂口味麥片時如出一轍。當時就像現在一樣，HFI 宣布該產品為期間限量供應，結果該項商品在全球雜貨店的架上被迅速搶購一空。」

HFI 的會計師將於 4 月 5 日檢視該公司第一季收入狀況。基於首波銷售量，市場觀察家確信 HFI 將會達成預期目標。

* 為 157 題的內文翻譯

單字註釋：send A into B「使 A 變成 B 的狀態」；enthusiast「(某事的) 愛好者」；from Argentina to Zambia「這裡使用英文字母第一個字 A 開頭、和最後一個字 Z 開頭的國家名稱，表示『全世界』的意思」；frenzy「狂熱」；be reminiscent of...「引人聯想起…」；wage「 實行…」；earnings「收益」

題目 / 中文翻譯

155 正解 (A)

What is indicated about Tasteemix cereals?

(A) They are distributed internationally.
(B) They are made in a factory in Mauritius.
(C) They are HFI's main source of revenue.
(D) They were first marketed four years ago.

關於 Tasteemix 麥片，文中提及哪一件事情？

(A) 全球流通販售
(B) 在 Mauritius 的工廠製造
(C) HFI 主要的收入來源
(D) 四年前首度上市發售

重點解說 第一段第二句談到 sending Tasteemix enthusiasts from Argentina to Zambia into a buying frenzy「從阿根廷到尚比亞的 Tasteemix 愛好者都陷入購買狂熱」，由此可知 Tasteemix 這種麥片銷售全球。distribute 指「流通販售（商品等）」。(D) market「上市」

---

156 正解 (D)

What is reported about HFI?

(A) It has no more Tasteemix cereal in stock.
(B) It hired a consulting firm to do its accounting.
(C) It expects this year's earnings to be better than last year's.
(D) It previously offered a product for a limited time only.

文章報導 HFI 哪件事情？

(A)Tasteemix 麥片已經沒有庫存
(B) 聘請諮商公司負責會計事務
(C) 預估今年的收入比去年更好
(D) 之前提供過期間限定的產品。

重點解說 第三段第一句首先提到，「HFI 目前的宣傳活動與四年前推出草莓肉桂口味麥片時如出一轍。」接下來第二句說，Then, as now, HFI announced a product as being offered for a limited time only「當時也和現在一樣，HFI 宣布該產品為期間限量供應」，因此選 (D)。for a limited time only「限期」。

---

157 正解 (B)

In which of the positions marked [1], [2], [3], and [4] does the following sentence best belong?

"Yet as of yesterday morning, only Vendibles and Foodiverse reported that they had any of the item left in stock."

(A) [1]
(B) [2]
(C) [3]
(D) [4]

下面的句子最適合放在哪個位置，標示 [1]、[2]、[3] 或 [4]？

「不過昨天上午時，只剩 Vendibles 和 Foodiverse 說他們還有庫存。」

(A) [1]
(B) [2]
(C) [3]
(D) [4]

重點解說 as of...「…的時間點」。文章開始有 Yet「可是」，因此與插入句內容相反的句子應該放在前一句，以 (B) 放入 [2] 最貼切。第二段內容是「六大雜貨銷售商出現龐大的供貨量」，與插入句相連後意思是，「約一個月前，六大雜貨銷售商提供龐大的供貨量，目前卻只剩其中兩家店尚有庫存」。另外 [2] 之後句子的 Both wholesalers，和插入句中的兩家公司，以及說明 Tasteemix 高人氣的文章內容一致。

題目/中文翻譯

Questions 158-160 refer to the following memo.

MEMO

Date: May 15

❶ We would like to announce the upcoming retirement of Ken Esser. Mr. Esser began his 30-year career here at The Terra Fund as a wildlife ranger in the California Wildlife Park. He has held seven different positions, eventually becoming the general director of conservation for all West Coast Wildlife Parks. He has been in this position for the past 15 years, leading with vision and commitment. Now at the age of 65, he is leaving us for a well-deserved retirement.

❷ The board of directors has voted to give him a Lifetime Achievement Award and will present him with a commemorative plaque at the staff meeting next Friday. Following the staff meeting, we invite all employees to stay for a reception to honor Mr. Esser and his great contributions. If you would like to write a farewell note to Mr. Esser, please stop by Andrew Braun's office to sign a book that will be presented at the reception.

請參考以下備忘錄回答第 **158** 至 **160** 題。

備忘錄

日期：5 月 15 日

接著宣布 Ken Esser 先生即將退休的消息。Esser 先生在 Terra 基金會服務 30 年，一開始擔任加州野生動物公園的野生動物保育員。他歷經七個不同的職位，最後成為整個西海岸野生動物公園的總經理。Esser 先生擔任總經理長達 15 年，一直以來，他都以獨到的眼光和熱衷於工作的精神帶領著大家。現年 65 歲的他，就要光榮退休，離開我們了。

董事會已經投票表決，將頒給他終身成就獎，並在下週五員工會議時獻給他一塊紀念牌匾。開完員工會議之後，敬邀所有員工留下參加歡送會，向 Esser 先生和他的卓越貢獻表示敬意。如果你想要寫惜別感言送給 Esser 先生，請前往 Andrew Braun 的辦公室，並在將於歡送會送出的書本裡留言。

題目 / 中文翻譯

158 正解 (C)

In what field does Mr. Esser work?

(A) Youth education
(B) Historical archiving
(C) Nature conservation
(D) Urban development

Esser 先生的工作領域為何？

(A) 青少年教育
(B) 歷史檔案保管
(C) 自然保育
(D) 都市發展

重點解說 第一段第三句提到 Esser 先生，eventually becoming the general director of conservation for all West Coast Wildlife Parks「最後成為整個西海岸野生動物公園的總經理」。conservation「保育」。
(B) archive 為「（檔案等）保管」；(D) urban「都市的」。

---

159 正解 (C)

For how many years has Mr. Esser worked at The Terra Fund?

(A) 7
(B) 15
(C) 30
(D) 65

Esser 先生在 Terra 基金會工作多久？

(A) 7
(B) 15
(C) 30
(D) 65

重點解說 第一段第二句指出 Mr. Esser began his 30-year career here at The Terra Fund「Esser 先生在 Terra 基金會服務 30 年」，因此正確答案為 (C)。

---

160 正解 (D)

What will NOT be given to honor Mr. Esser?

(A) A reception
(B) An award
(C) A book
(D) A photo album

Esser 先生並不會收到哪項禮物？

(A) 歡送會
(B) 獎項
(C) 書
(D) 相簿

重點解說 (A) 是第二段第二句提到要開 reception「歡送會」。(B) 是第二段第一句要贈與 Esser 先生「終身成就獎」。(C) 是同一段第三句，要送他一本集結員工惜別感言的書。但是不曾提到 (D) 的相簿。

單字註釋：commitment「對…獻身」；well-deserved「當之無愧」；commemorative「紀念的」；plaque「匾、飾板」；farewell「告別（的）」

題目

Questions 161-164 refer to the following online chat discussion.

Kato, Yuri [9:21 A.M.]:
Hello. I'd like an update on the Mondvale Road job. Are we still on schedule to begin on Monday?

Vega, Camila [9:22 A.M.]:
No, I'm afraid that there has been some delay in getting the fabric for the drapes and bed linens. It looks like we may be held up until Wednesday.

Kato, Yuri [9:22 A.M.]:
Have you communicated this to the client?

Vega, Camila [9:23 A.M.]:
Not yet. Richard is waiting to hear from the distributor first so that we can give the client a firm date. Have you heard from them yet, Richard?

Bremen, Richard [9:34 A.M.]:
I just got off the phone with them. It looks like everything will arrive on Monday afternoon, so we could actually begin the job on Tuesday.

Vega, Camila [9:35 A.M.]:
That's good news. I'll call the client this morning and let them know.

Bremen, Richard [9:35 A.M.]:
You should also remind them that we will begin working on the guest rooms first and work our way toward the lobby and first-floor public areas last. We'll send a large crew so the work can be finished quickly.

Kato, Yuri [9:36 A.M.]:
How long do you think it will take to complete the job?

Bremen, Richard [9:37 A.M.]:
We can probably be finished by Friday, as we originally planned.

Kato, Yuri [9:38 A.M.]:
Excellent. They're a new client with several locations and a high profile in the business community, so I want things to go smoothly. I'm sure there will be more work with them in the long run if all goes well.

中文翻譯

請參考以下線上聊天討論內容回答第 **161** 至 **164** 題。

Kato, Yuri [上午 9 點 21 分]：
你好，我需要關於 Mondvale 路工作內容的更新資訊。我們仍然按照原訂計畫於星期一開工嗎？

Vega, Camila [上午 9 點 22 分]：
恐怕不行，因為窗簾跟床單的布料都被延誤了，看起來應該得擱置到下週三了。

Kato, Yuri [上午 9 點 22 分]：
你已經和顧客溝通過了嗎？

Vega, Camila [上午 9 點 23 分]：
還沒。Richard 還在等經銷商那邊的消息，這樣我們才能給顧客確切日期。Richard，你那邊有消息了嗎？

Bremen, Richard [上午 9 點 34 分]：
我剛跟他們通完電話。看起來所有的物品會在週一下午全部到齊，所以我們實際上能夠從星期二就開始作業。

Vega, Camila [上午 9 點 35 分]：
真是個好消息。我今天上午會致電客戶，並讓他們知道這件事。

Bremen, Richard [上午 9 點 35 分]：
你也必須提醒他們，我們會先從會客室的部分開始著手，然後推進到大廳，最後則是一樓公共區域。我們會派遣大量的作業人員，以便迅速完成工作。

Kato, Yuri [上午 9 點 36 分]：
你認為需要多久才能完工？

Bremen, Richard [上午 9 點 37 分]：
我們也許可以在星期五前結束，就像我們原本規畫的那樣。

Kato, Yuri [上午 9 點 38 分]：
好極了。這個客戶有好幾個據點，在業界也倍受矚目，因此我希望能夠順利進行。就長期而言，要是一切順利，我很確定未來還會有很多跟他們合作的機會。

題目 / 中文翻譯

161 正解 (C)

What kind of business does the client most likely own?

(A) A shipping company
(B) A fabric manufacturing factory
(C) A hotel chain
(D) A design firm

客戶最有可能從事哪一種業務？

(A) 貨運公司
(B) 布料製造工廠
(C) 連鎖飯店
(D) 設計公司

重點解說 這段對話是公司裡三位同事在確認工作進度。Bremen 在上午 9 點 35 分的訊息中提到 we will begin working on the guest room「從會客室的部分開始著手」，以及 the lobby and the first-floor public areas「大廳和公共區域」，由此可推測他們的客戶是飯店。而且 Kato 在上午 9 點 38 分的訊息提到 They're a new client with several locations「這個客戶有好幾個據點」，因此可以知道他們是有好幾個據點的連鎖飯店。

---

162 正解 (B)

When will the crew begin work?

(A) On Monday
(B) On Tuesday
(C) On Wednesday
(D) On Friday

工作人員何時開始作業？

(A) 星期一
(B) 星期二
(C) 星期三
(D) 星期五

重點解說 根據 Bremen 在上午 9 點 34 分的訊息結尾指出 we could begin the job on Tuesday「我們實際上能夠從星期二就開始作業」。

---

163 正解 (D)

What will Ms. Vega most likely do next?

(A) Deliver a shipment of drapes
(B) Organize a large work crew
(C) Call the fabric distributor
(D) Contact the client

Vega 女士接下來最有可能做哪件事？

(A) 運送簾布
(B) 組織大型工作團隊
(C) 致電布料經銷商
(D) 聯繫客戶

重點解說 Vega 在上午 9 點 35 分的訊息寫著 I'll call the client this morning and let them know.「我今天上午會致電客戶，並讓他們知道這件事。」

題目/中文翻譯

164 正解 (D)

At 9:38 A.M., what does Ms. Kato mean when she writes, "in the long run"?

(A) She is pleased that the client is located nearby.
(B) She is proud of her company's history of high-quality performance.
(C) She believes that the work will be more expensive than expected.
(D) She thinks that there could be additional work with the client in the future.

Kato 女士在上午 9 點 38 分時寫下「in the long run」的意圖為何？

(A) 她很高興客戶所處位置就在附近。
(B) 她以擁有高品質績效表現的公司歷史為榮。
(C) 她相信作業費用將會比預計的還要昂貴。
(D) 她認為將來可能還會有更多和顧客合作的地方。

重點解說 in the long run 意思是「就長期來看」。前一句話中，Kato 女士提到客戶時說「這個客戶有好幾個據點，在業界也倍受矚目」，接著說 I'm sure there will be more work with them「未來還會有很多跟他們合作的機會」，因此最合適的選項為 (D)。

單字註釋：drape「布簾」；bed linen「床單、被套等床上織物用品」；be held up「進退不得」；crew「一組（工作人員）」；high profile「倍受矚目的」

題目

Questions 165-167 refer to the following instructions.

Perrybridge Office Furniture

Office Workstation Installation Manual

General Notes

- Always use the tools specified in the instructions when installing.
- Use eye protection when working with tools.
- Ensure that your work area is clean and clear of any potential obstructions to the installation.
- Wash hands before beginning the installation process.
- Parts weighing more than 15 kilograms are marked Heavy. Use two or more people when lifting or moving these items.
- Elements marked DS have one or more delicate surfaces. Handle these carefully to avoid scratching.
- If you have any questions, please see our Help section on perrybridgeoffice.com before contacting us through our online form. To receive the installation instructions in a language not available in this manual, please contact us at 497-555-0101.

中文翻譯

請參考以下的指示說明回答第 **165** 至 **167** 題。

Perrybridge 辦公家具

辦公室工作站安裝操作手冊

一般注意事項

- 進行安裝時，請使用說明書載明之工具。
- 使用工具時請配帶護目鏡。
- 確認你的工作區域保持乾淨，並清除各種可能妨礙安裝的障礙物。
- 開始安裝程序前請洗手。
- 超過 15 公斤重量的零件會標示為沉重。抬起或搬動這些品項需要兩個或以上的人力。
- 標示著 DS 的零件擁有一個或以上的精緻介面。請小心處理，避免發生刮傷。
- 若您仍有其他問題，在透過線上表格與我們聯繫之前，請上我們的網站 perrybridgeoffice.com，參閱求助區域的資訊。若您想要取得此手冊並未包含在內的其他語言版本說明，請電洽 497-555-0101 與我們聯繫。

題目／中文翻譯

165 正解 (D)

What is described in the general notes?

(A) How to connect cubicle walls
(B) How to measure the office space
(C) How to operate the required tools
(D) How to prepare an area for installation

一般注意事項裡面說明哪些事情？

(A) 如何連接隔間牆面
(B) 如何測量辦公室空間
(C) 如何操作必要工具
(D) 如何準備安裝的場地

重點解說：General Notes 第三點說明的是，Ensure your work area is clean and clear of any potential obstructions to the installation.「確認你的工作區域保持乾淨，並清除各種可能妨礙安裝的障礙物」。
(A) cubicle「小隔間」。

---

166 正解 (A)

According to the instructions, what should people do before beginning to work?

(A) Wash their hands
(B) Make sure no parts are scratched
(C) Record the weight of each part
(D) Clean their tools

根據指示說明，人員在開始作業前應該先做哪件事情？

(A) 洗手
(B) 確認沒有被刮傷的部分
(C) 記錄每個部份的重量
(D) 清潔工具

重點解說：第四點是 Wash hands before beginning the installation process.「開始安裝程序前請先洗手」。

---

167 正解 (D)

Why are people advised to call the listed number?

(A) To order additional parts
(B) To schedule a product installation
(C) To report a defective product
(D) To acquire a different version of the manual

為何建議人們撥打列在上面的電話號碼？

(A) 訂購多餘料件
(B) 排定產品安裝時間
(C) 申報瑕疵品
(D) 取得不同版本的手冊

重點解說：第七點第二句是 To receive the installation instructions in a language not available in this manual, please contact us at 497-555-0101.「若您想要取得此手冊並未包含在內的其他語言版本說明，請電洽 497-555-0101 與我們聯繫」。the installation instructions in a language not available in this manual，可以置換成 (D) a different version of the manual。

單字註釋：workstation「工作站」；installation「安裝」；obstruction「妨礙」

題目

Questions 168-171 refer to the following e-mail.

From:	<DDrabik@lowmaster.co.ca>
To:	<New Employees List>
Subject:	Welcome
Date:	May 28

❶ The Lowmaster Toronto office is pleased to have such a promising group of new employees become part of our consulting team. Please review the company policies listed below and familiarize yourself with some important locations on our campus.

❷ Personal computers may not be used to complete company work. If you need to work outside your offices in Dempsey Hall, visit the Information Technology Department to request a security-enabled laptop. Their office is located in the Russ Building in R-135.

❸ The identification badges you received at orientation must be worn at all times; they provide access to the buildings on campus. If your identification badge is misplaced, contact the Security Desk immediately. The Security Desk is located in the Hadley Building in room H-290 and can be reached at extension 8645.

❹ The cafeteria is located on the first floor in the Russ Building and is open until 2:30 P.M. The lounge in D-108 in Dempsey Hall is especially convenient for your breaks. Coffee, tea, juice, and light snacks are available in the lounge until 6:00 P.M. daily.

❺ Brandt Library is located behind the Russ Building and can be accessed by way of the raised walkway connecting the two.

❻ Finally, if you expect a package or important mail, you may notify the Shipping and Receiving Office at extension 8300 or stop by room R-004 in the basement of the Russ Building.

Sincerely,

Donald Drabik

中文翻譯

請參考以下的電子郵件回答第 168 至 171 題。

寄件者：	<DDrabik@lowmaster.com.ca>
收件者：	< 新進員工名單 >
主旨：	歡迎大家
寄件日期：	5 月 28 日

Lowmaster 多倫多辦公室很榮幸擁有一群前途看好的新進員工加入我們的顧問團隊。請再次檢閱以下條列的公司政策，並熟悉園區內幾個重要地點。

請勿使用個人電腦完成公司作業。若你需要在位於 Dempsey 大樓的辦公室以外地方工作，請前往資訊科技部，取得內建安全機制的筆電。他們的辦公室位於 Russ 大樓 R-135 室。

請隨時配戴在員工訓練時獲得的身分識別證；識別證將能讓你進入園區內的各棟大樓。若你弄丟了身分識別證，請立即與安全櫃台聯繫。安全櫃台位於 Hadley 大樓 H290 室，或撥打分機 8645。

員工餐廳位於 Russ 大樓一樓，開放時間至下午 2 點 30 分。位於 Dempsey 大樓 D-108 室內的休息室是你休息的好地方。休息室每日供應咖啡、茶、果汁和小點心，開放時間至晚上 6 點。

Brandt 圖書館位於 Russ 大樓後方，可自連接兩棟大樓的高架式通道前往。

最後，若你正在等待包裹或是重要信件，你可以撥打分機 8300，告知收發室，或是前往 Russ 大樓地下室的 R-004 室。

Donald Drabik 謹誌

題目 / 中文翻譯

168 正解 (D)

What is the purpose of the e-mail?
該封電子郵件的目的為何？

(A) To assign work spaces to employees
(B) To explain employee compensation policies
(C) To arrange a company meeting
(D) To provide details to recently hired workers

(A) 分配員工工作空間
(B) 解釋員工薪資政策
(C) 安排公司會議
(D) 提供詳細資料給最近剛聘用的員工

重點解說 從收件者欄 New Employees List 和第一段第一句，可以得知這封郵件的收件人是公司的新進員工。而且第二句中寫到「請檢閱以下條列的公司政策，並熟悉園區內幾個重要地點」。第二段之後，說明公司政策和幾個重要地點，由此可知 (D) 與文意最為相符。郵件中的 new employees 可以置換成 (D) 裡面的 recently hired workers。
(B) compensation policies「薪資政策」。

---

169 正解 (B)

The word “promising” in paragraph 1, line 1, is closest in meaning to
第一段第一行的「promising」意思最接近以下何者？

(A) pledging
(B) likely to succeed
(C) suggesting
(D) recently hired

(A) 保證
(B) 很可能成功
(C) 建議的
(D) 最近聘用的

重點解說 promising 是指「有希望的、前途看好的」。這句話的意思是「公司十分歡迎前途看好的新進員工加入顧問團隊」，因此和 (B) likely to succeed「很可能成功的」最為接近。

---

170 正解 (A)

Where is the Information Technology Department located?
資訊科技部位於何方？

(A) In the Russ Building
(B) In the Hadley Building
(C) In Dempsey Hall
(D) In Brandt Library

(A) Russ 大樓
(B) Hadley 大樓
(C) Dempsey 大樓
(D) Brandt 圖書館

重點解說 第二段第二句提到 visit the Information Technology Department「前往資訊科技部」，接下來第三句說明 Their office is located in Russ Building「他們的辦公室位於 Russ 大樓」。

題目 / 中文翻譯

171 **正解** (C)

According to the e-mail, what is provided to all employees?

(A) A mailbox
(B) An approved laptop
(C) An identification badge
(D) A library card

根據電子郵件，提供給所有員工的東西是什麼？

(A) 信箱
(B) 核可的筆記型電腦
(C) 身分識別證
(D) 借書證

重點解說 第三段第一句寫著 The identification badges you received at orientation must be worn at all times「請隨時配戴在員工訓練時獲得的身分識別證」，接下來說明「識別證將能讓你進入園區內的各棟大樓」，因此可以判斷發給每位員工的東西是身分識別證。

單字註釋：familiarize oneself with...「使熟悉…」；misplace「弄丟」；raised walkway「高架式走道」

題目

Questions 172-175 refer to the following letter.

Orangedale Press
54 Thompson Street
Sausalito, CA 94965
www.orangedalepress.com

September 19

Mr. Richard Tomase
89 Moreland Drive
Portland, OR 97205

Dear Mr. Tomase:

❶ We at Orangedale Press are delighted that you have agreed to work with us again on an update of your book *Global Traveling: A Consumer's Guide*. Rest assured that we understand the ongoing paradigm shift in our field and are pleased that we can amend your previous contract with us to account for these changes. — [1] —. Since the original *Global Traveling* received such a warm reception in its target markets, we want to ensure that the updated version faithfully meets the needs and expectations of both new and returning readers. This new version will include electronic editions of your book in order for it to be more easily distributed and bring in the widest possible audience. — [2] —. All other provisions of the previous contract will remain unchanged, except for the adjustment to your royalty fees as we discussed.

❷ — [3] —. The updated agreement is enclosed. Please initial the marked paragraphs if you approve, and then sign and date it. I would appreciate it if you could return it to me by October 1. — [4] —. Also, if you have not yet returned the author information form that my assistant mailed to you, you can send that in at the same time.

❸ Thank you for attending to this matter in a timely manner and for your great contributions to the field of travel publishing. We value our authors, and we are honored to continue licensing the books we publish in both traditional and emerging formats.

❹ Please contact me if you have any questions or concerns at all.

With very best regards,

Kathryn Lloyd

Kathryn Lloyd
Director, Orangedale Press

Enclosure

中文翻譯

請參考以下信件回答第 **172** 至 **175** 題。

Orangedale 出版社
Thompson 街 54 號
Sausalito, CA 94965
www.orangedalepress.com

9 月 19 日

Richard Tomase 先生收
Moreland 大道 89 號
Portland, OR97205

敬愛的 Tomase 先生您好：

Orangedale 出版社很高興您同意再次與我們合作，並進行您的著作《全球走透透：消費者指南》更新版。您大可放心的是，我們十分瞭解這塊產業持續變動中的思維方式，也很樂意針對這些變動稍加修改之前與您簽訂的合約內容。由於原版的《全球走透透》在目標市場上獲得相當熱烈的迴響，我們想要確保這次的最新版也能忠於原味，滿足新舊讀者群的要求與期盼。這次的新版著作將納入電子版本，讓您的大作能夠更容易流通，吸引最多的潛在讀者群。* 東亞旅遊的新章節必然也會引起廣大讀者的興趣。除了我們先前談好的作品使用費有所調整之外，上一份合約的其他條文保持不變。

隨信附上合約書更新版。若您同意，請在標記的條款旁簽上姓名的首字母，接著請簽全名，並註明日期。如果您能在 10 月 1 日以前寄回文件，我將會不勝感激。此外，若您尚未寄回我助理寄給您的作者資訊，您也可以屆時一併寄回。

感謝您願意及時處理這些事宜，也感謝您對於旅遊出版業的卓越貢獻。我們相當重視我們的作者，而且能夠結合傳統與新興模式，持續發行與出版書籍，是本社的榮幸。

若您有任何問題或疑慮，請與我聯繫。

獻上最誠摯的敬意，

Kathryn Lloyd

Orangedale 出版社負責人
Kathryn Lloyd 謹誌

* 為 **175** 題的內文翻譯

題目 / 中文翻譯

172 正解 (D)

Why did Ms. Lloyd send the letter to Mr. Tomase?

(A) To request that he review a book
(B) To inquire about an itinerary
(C) To determine if he will sign some books
(D) To explain a modification to an agreement

Lloyd 女士為何寄信給 Thomase 先生？

(A) 要求他審書
(B) 徵詢旅遊路線
(C) 決定他是否要簽書
(D) 解釋合約書的修正內容

重點解說 從第一段第一、二句得知，Orangedate 出版的 Lloyd 和作者 Thomas 再度一起工作，需要修改之前簽訂的合約內容。之後同一段最後一句話提到 All the other provisions of the previous contract will remain unchanged, except for the adjustment to your royalty fees「除了我們先前談好的作品使用費有所調整之外，上一份合約的其他條文保持不變」，詳細解說了合約書修正內容，因此可以判斷這是 Lloyd 為了和 Thomas 工作，寄信說明之前合約書的修正之處。modification「修正」。

---

173 正解 (A)

What did Ms. Lloyd send with the letter?

(A) A revised contract
(B) An author information form
(C) An advance copy of a book
(D) A collection of book reviews

Lloyd 女士寄出的信件裡面夾帶了什麼？

(A) 合約書修訂版
(B) 作者資料表
(C) 新書樣本
(D) 書評集

重點解說 信中第二段開頭是 The updated agreement is enclosed.「隨信附上合約書更新版」。updated 在 (A) 中換成 revised 的說法。
(C) advance copy「新書樣本」。

---

174 正解 (C)

The phrase “attending to” in paragraph 3, line 1, is closest in meaning to

(A) planning to go to
(B) discovering of
(C) taking care of
(D) being present at

第三段第一句的片語「attending to」意義最接近下列何者？

(A) 計畫去做
(B) 發現
(C) 處理
(D) 出席

重點解說 attend to... 在這裡的意思是「處理（事情）」。後面接的 this matter，指的是第二段提到的「同意合約書並簽署後寄回」，因此和 (C) 的「處理…、照顧…」意思接近。

題目/中文翻譯

175 正解 (B)

In which of the positions marked [1], [2], [3], and [4] does the following sentence best belong?

"A new chapter on travel in East Asia is also sure to draw much interest."

(A) [1]
(B) [2]
(C) [3]
(D) [4]

下面的句子最適合放在標示 [1]、[2]、[3] 或 [4] 的哪個位置？

「東亞旅遊的新章節必然也會引起廣大讀者的興趣。」

(A) [1]
(B) [2]
(C) [3]
(D) [4]

重點解說 題目的插入句中包含 also，前一句提到 draw much interest「引起廣大讀者的興趣」。因此在前面加入敘述「吸引最多的潛在讀者群」的 (B)，是最適合的答案。

單字註釋：Rest assured that...「（因為…）請放心」；paradigm shift「典範轉移（想法或價值觀等大幅改變）」；amend「修正…」；account for...「說明…」；provision「規定」；royalty fee「權利金」；initial「標註姓名的開頭字母在…」；in a timely manner「及時」；license「授權…」；emerging「新興的」

題目

Questions 176-180 refer to the following e-mail and document.

1. 電子郵件

From:	Kana Saito <ksaito@kmail.com>
To:	Customer Service <CS@lantiauto.com>
Subject:	Request for information
Date:	September 16

To Whom It May Concern:

❶ I currently lease a car from your company. However, I recently accepted a job in Memphis City, and I am going to start taking the bus. My lease agreement is number LA508. It is a month-to-month lease that automatically renews on the same day each month.

❷ My new job starts on Tuesday, September 28, so ideally I would return the car to you on Monday, September 27. However, if the renewal date is earlier than that Monday, I would rather return the car at the end of the current month's contract and make other transportation arrangements until my new job starts.

❸ Please let me know on what exact day of the month my lease ends and when I need to return the car.

Thank you

Kana Saito

2. 文件

Lanti Auto

List of Current Month-to-Month Lease Agreements

Agreement Number	Car Model	Cost per Month	Final Contract Date for Each Month
LA502	Cartif	$199	7
LA508	Sylvon	$211	25
LA513	Thundee	$159	28
LA519	Grayley	$249	14

*For lease termination, cars must be returned by 4 P.M. on the final contract date. Otherwise, the lease will automatically be extended for one additional month.

中文翻譯

請參考以下的電子郵件和文件回答第 **176** 至 **180** 題。

寄件者：	Kana Saito <ksaito@kmail.com>
收件者：	客服部 <CS@lantiauto.com>
主旨：	詢問資訊
寄件日期：	9 月 16 日

敬啟者：

我目前承租貴公司的汽車。但是我最近接受了 Memphis 市的工作，因此我得開始搭公車。我的租賃合約書編號為 LA508，是月租費方案，每個月的同一天會自動更新合約。

我的新工作將於 9 月 28 日星期二開始，因此在理想的狀態下，我會在 9 月 27 日星期一歸還車輛。然而，若是自動更新日期比星期一當天更早，那麼我寧可在這個月租約最終日歸還車輛，在我的新工作開始上班之前另行安排交通工具。

煩請告知我本月份租期究竟何時結束，以及我該何時歸還車輛。

謝謝。

Kano Saito 敬上

Lanti 車行

現行月租費方案

合約編號	車型	月租費	每月租約最終日
LA502	Cartif	199 美元	7
LA508	Sylvon	211 美元	25
LA513	Thundee	159 美元	28
LA519	Grayley	249 美元	14

* 租賃終止時，請務必在租約最終日下午 4 點前歸還車輛。否則，租賃期限將會自動展延至下個月。

題目 / 中文翻譯

176 正解 (C)

Why did Ms. Saito send the e-mail?

(A) To request a car rental
(B) To resign from a position
(C) To get information about a lease
(D) To inquire about available parking

Saito 女士寄發電子郵件的原因為何？

(A) 要求租車
(B) 辭掉某個職位
(C) 取得租賃契約內容資訊
(D) 徵詢可用的停車位

重點解說 1 的主旨欄寫著 Request for information「詢問資訊」，第三段詢問 Please let me know on what exact day of the month my lease ends and when I should return the car.「煩請告知我本月份租期究竟何時結束，以及我該何時歸還車輛」，因此可推知寄發信件之目的為 (C)。

---

177 正解 (D)

What is suggested about Ms. Saito?

(A) She wants to sell her car.
(B) She lives near a train station.
(C) She has recently moved to a new city.
(D) She currently drives to work.

這裡暗示關於 Saito 女士的哪件事情？

(A) 她想要賣車。
(B) 她住在火車站附近。
(C) 她最近剛搬到新的城市。
(D) 她目前開車上班。

重點解說 suggest「暗示」。1 的第一段說明，目前承租 Lanti Auto 公司的汽車，但是從事新工作後打算搭公車。此外，第二段第二句敘述，「我在這個月租約最終日歸還車輛，在新工作開始上班之前另行安排交通工具」，因此可得知 Saito 女士現在開車上班。

---

178 正解 (B)

What type of car does Ms. Saito drive?

(A) A Cartif
(B) A Sylvon
(C) A Thundee
(D) A Grayley

Saito 女士開的車款是哪一種？

(A) Cartif
(B) Sylvon
(C) Thundee
(D) Grayley

重點解說 1 的第一段第三句提到 My lease agreement is number LA508.「我的合約編號為 LA508」。對照 2 合約編號的 Car Model「車型」一欄，可以知道 Saito 女士承租的是 (B) Sylvon。

題目 / 中文翻譯

179 正解 (C)

When should Ms. Saito go to Lanti Auto?

(A) On September 7
(B) On September 14
(C) On September 25
(D) On September 28

Saito 女士何時得去 Lanti 車行？

(A) 9 月 7 日
(B) 9 月 14 日
(C) 9 月 25 日
(D) 9 月 28 日

重點解說 1 的第二段提到 Saito 女士「原先預計於 9 月 27 日還車，但若到期日較早，則會在這個月租約最終日歸還車輛」。從 2 得知，Saito 女士合約編號 LA508 的租約到期日為 25 日，因此選 (C)。

---

180 正解 (A)

What is indicated about month-to-month agreements?

(A) They may expire at 4 P.M. on the final contract date.
(B) They are available for one year at most.
(C) They all cost $199 per month.
(D) They include the cost of maintenance.

這裡提到關於月租型契約的哪件事情？

(A) 可能在契約最終日下午 4 點即失效
(B) 最長的使用時間為一年
(C) 所有方案每月租金為 199 美元
(D) 包含維修費用

重點解說 2 的最下方載明，「租賃終止時，請務必在租約最終日下午 4 點前歸還車輛」，接著說「否則租賃期限將會自動展延至下個月」。換句話說，如果在租約最終日下午 4 點前還車，契約就會失效，因此選項 (A) 為正解。

單字註釋：To whom it may concern「敬啟者」; lease「（動詞）出租…、（名詞）租約」; month-to-month「按月」; renewal date「續約日期」; termination「終止、結束」

題目

Questions 181-185 refer to the following Web page and e-mail.

1. 網頁

http://www.Hardewickes.co.uk

Hardewicke's

The finest musical treasures in London!

Explore and take home some of London's rich history. The artifacts are a window into the creative minds that make up London's musical spirit.

Our collection spans musical genres from rock and roll to opera, highlighting England's great artistic contributors. The store features artists from the 1800s to rising stars seen on television today.

Click on the links below to view some of our current products. Electronic checkout is available.

Records, CDs, Tapes: £10 and up

Songbooks, signed first-edition books: £15 and up

Apparel: £30 and up

Original artwork: £50 and up

Instruments: £100 and up

We have even more in our shop, and the best pieces are often bought before they make it to the Web site! For the full experience, please visit us.

2. 電子郵件

From: Sophie Calvert

To: Hardewickes@londonloc.co.uk

Re: Mark Peckham Item

Date: February 1

To Whom It May Concern:

I have a guitar that was previously owned by Mark Peckham. I found your Web site and thought that Hardewicke's might be interested in purchasing it for resale.

The guitar was custom-made for Mr. Peckham by his close friend Elizabeth Dangerfield to celebrate the successful release of his first album. He took it on tour with him around the country as well as abroad. The guitar was purchased by my father at a charity auction hosted by Mr. Peckham 20 years ago.

Please let me know what your purchasing procedures are and whether you buy items up front or take a percentage of the transaction when you resell the item.

Thank you,

Sophie Calvert

中文翻譯

請參考以下的網頁和電子郵件回答第 181 至 185 題。

http://www.Hardewickes.co.uk 

Hardewicke's

倫敦最精緻的音樂藏寶庫！

您可以探索並將倫敦豐富的歷史帶回家。這些工藝品是一扇窗，帶您進入締造倫敦音樂精神的創作者內心世界。

我們的收藏橫跨各種音樂領域，從搖滾樂到歌劇應有盡有，聚焦全英國偉大的藝術貢獻者。從 19 世紀的藝術家到今天在電視上出現的後起之秀，都是本店的典藏對象。

請點選以下連結，即可觀看我們的最新產品。可利用電子結帳。
唱片、CD 和錄音帶：10 英鎊起
歌本和首版簽名書：15 英鎊起
服飾：30 英鎊起
原創藝術作品：50 英鎊起
樂器：100 英鎊起

店裡另有更多商品，而且通常最好的作品在登錄網站之前就已經被買走了！若您想要徹底感受一番，請來本店參觀。

寄件者：	Sophie Calvert
收件者：	Hardewickes@londonloc.co.uk
主旨：	Mark Peckham 物件
寄件日期：	2 月 1 日

敬啟者：

我有一把 Mark Peckham 之前持有的吉他。我發現你們的網站，而且認為 Hardewicke's 可能會有興趣收購這把吉他再進行轉售。

Peckham 先生的摯友 Elizabeth Dangerfield 為了慶祝他成功發行首張專輯，為他本人量身訂做這把吉他。他在國內外各地巡迴表演時總是帶著它。20 年前，我父親在 Peckham 先生主辦的慈善義賣會上購得這把吉他。

煩請告知我您的採購流程，以及您是在購入物件時預先付款，或是轉售物件之後再依照單筆收益百分比抽成。

謝謝。

Sophie Calvert 敬上

題目 / 中文翻譯

181 正解 (C)

What is NOT suggested about Hardewicke's?

關於 Hardewicke's，並未提到下列哪件事情？

(A) It has items from many different years.
(B) Its products represent numerous types of music.
(C) It guarantees the lowest prices on records and songbooks.
(D) It features products from English musicians.

(A) 擁有來自各個不同年份的物品
(B) 店內商品代表不同的音樂類別
(C) 唱片跟歌本保證最低價
(D) 商品特色為出自英國音樂家之手

重點解說

1 的第二段中，(A) 在第二句提到「從 19 世紀的藝術家到今天在電視上出現的後起之秀」。(B) 在同一段開頭則提到「從搖滾樂到歌劇應有盡有」。(D) 在同段結尾提到「聚焦全英國偉大的藝術貢獻者」。第三段寫著 Records「唱片」和 Songbooks「歌本」的價格，但並未提到保證最低價，因此正解是 (C)。
(B) represent「代表」。

---

182 正解 (D)

What is indicated about Hardewicke's?

這裡指出關於 Hardewicke's 的哪件事情？

(A) It was started by a musician.
(B) It plans to host a performance by Mr. Peckham.
(C) It advertises at concerts.
(D) It sells items directly from its Web site.

(A) 由某位音樂家所創立
(B) 打算舉辦 Peckham 先生的演出
(C) 在演唱會中進行宣傳
(D) 直接在網站上販售物品

重點解說

1 的第三段中，提到「請點選以下連結，即可觀看我們的最新產品」，接著說 Electronic checkout is available.「可利用電子結帳」。因此可知道會直接在網站上販售商品，故選 (D)。

---

183 正解 (D)

What is the lowest price Ms. Calvert's item would most likely sell for at Hardewicke's?

Calvert 女士的物件賣給 Hardewicke's 的最低價最有可能是多少？

(A) £10
(B) £30
(C) £50
(D) £100

(A) 10 英鎊
(B) 30 英鎊
(C) 50 英鎊
(D) 100 英鎊

重點解說

Calvert 女士寄出的 2，第一段提到 I have a guitar that was previously owned by Mark Peckham.「我有一把 Mark Peckham 之前持有的吉他」。如果 Hardewicke's 收購這把吉他再轉售，依照 1 的第三段最後一行 Instruments: £ 100 and up「樂器：100 英鎊起」，因此正解為 (D)。

題目 / 中文翻譯

184 正解 (B)

What is suggested about Ms. Calvert?

(A) She saw Mr. Peckham perform in England.
(B) She owns an item made by Ms. Dangerfield.
(C) She has previously worked with Hardewicke's.
(D) She would like to make a donation to her father's charity.

這裡提到關於 Calvert 女士哪件事情？

(A) 她看過 Peckham 先生在英國的表演。
(B) 她擁有 Dangerfield 女士製作的物件。
(C) 她之前曾在 Hardewicke's 工作。
(D) 她想要捐助她父親的慈善事業。

重點解說 2 的第一段第一句指出，Calvert 女士擁有 Peckham 先生的吉他。接著在第二段第一句說明，The guitar was custom-made for Mr. Peckham by his close friend Elizabeth Dangerfield「Peckham 先生的摯友 Elizabeth Dangerfield 為他量身訂做這把吉他」，因此選 (B)。

---

185 正解 (C)

What does Ms. Calvert ask about?

(A) The price of an instrument she saw at the store
(B) The procedure for renting a concert space
(C) The process for selling items to Hardewicke's
(D) The history of an item she wants to purchase

Calvert 女士詢問的事情為何？

(A) 她在店裡看到的樂器價格
(B) 租用演奏會場地的流程
(C) 販賣物件給 Hardewicke's 的程序
(D) 她想要購買的物件本身的歷史

重點解說 2 的第三段提到 Please let me know what your purchasing procedures are「煩請告知我您的採購流程」，因此答案為 (C)。

單字註釋：artifact「人造物（相對於天然物）」; make it to...「到達…」; resale「轉售、銷售二手貨」; up front「預付」; take a percentage of the transaction「收取交易手續費」

題目

Questions 186-190 refer to the following list, schedule, and e-mail.

1. 書單

Books by James Trozelli

❶ *The History of Jeans*
Where did it all begin? Trozelli visually chronicles the evolution of jeans through the centuries, from working wear to high fashion.

❷ *Look Past the Runway*
Trozelli captures the creative process of some of the top designers from New York City to Paris. Spanning almost twenty years, the book is filled with Trozelli's photographs and shows what goes on in fashion houses before designs are ready for the runway.

❸ *Growing Into Clothes: My Story*
An amusing memoir about growing up in the fashion world. Trozelli writes about his unconventional upbringing in New York City with parents who began as fashion models before launching their own design label.

❹ *Yards of Talent: A Decade of Style*
A collection of Trozelli's images spanning a decade of fashion and revealing what was in style, what was out of style, and then what was back in style again.

2. 節目表

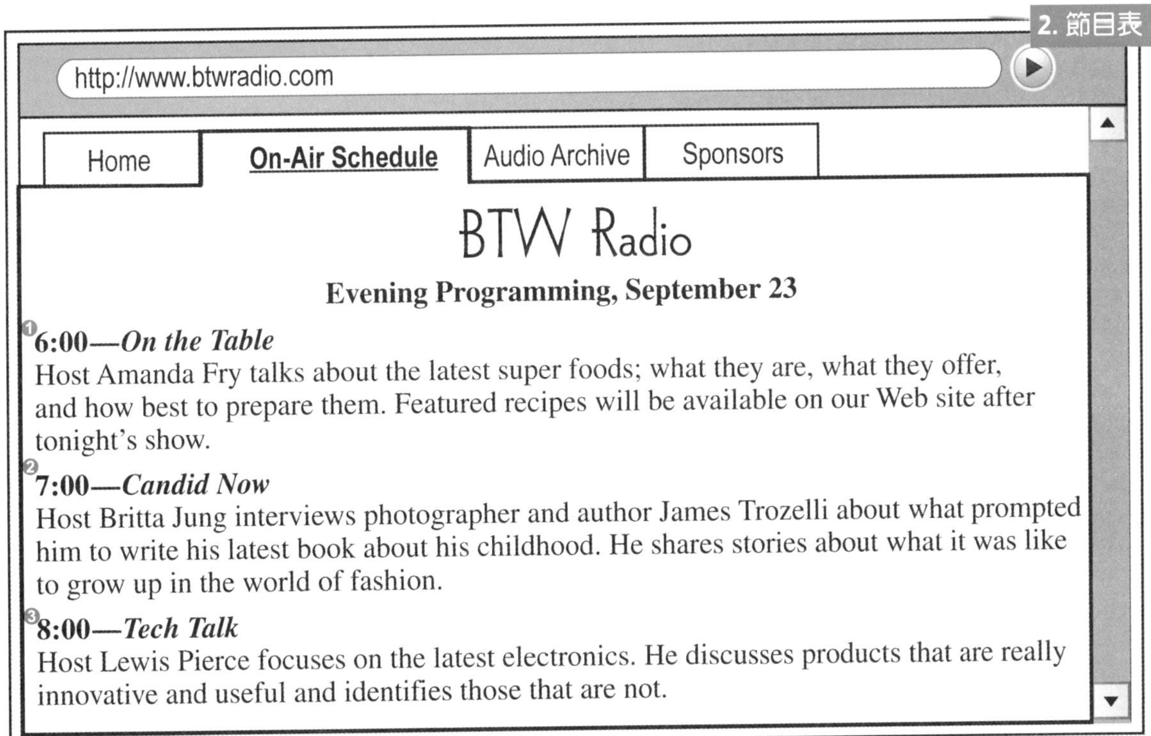

http://www.btwradio.com

Home | **On-Air Schedule** | Audio Archive | Sponsors

BTW Radio

Evening Programming, September 23

❶ ***6:00—On the Table***
Host Amanda Fry talks about the latest super foods; what they are, what they offer, and how best to prepare them. Featured recipes will be available on our Web site after tonight's show.

❷ ***7:00—Candid Now***
Host Britta Jung interviews photographer and author James Trozelli about what prompted him to write his latest book about his childhood. He shares stories about what it was like to grow up in the world of fashion.

❸ ***8:00—Tech Talk***
Host Lewis Pierce focuses on the latest electronics. He discusses products that are really innovative and useful and identifies those that are not.

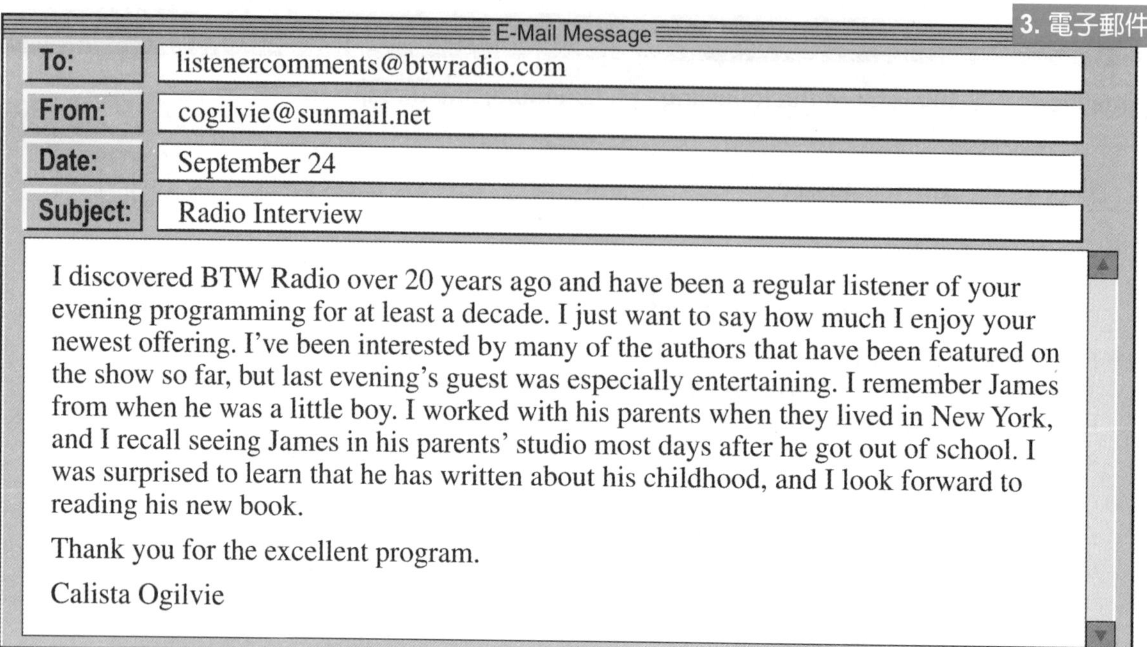
3. 電子郵件

E-Mail Message

To: listenercomments@btwradio.com
From: cogilvie@sunmail.net
Date: September 24
Subject: Radio Interview

I discovered BTW Radio over 20 years ago and have been a regular listener of your evening programming for at least a decade. I just want to say how much I enjoy your newest offering. I've been interested by many of the authors that have been featured on the show so far, but last evening's guest was especially entertaining. I remember James from when he was a little boy. I worked with his parents when they lived in New York, and I recall seeing James in his parents' studio most days after he got out of school. I was surprised to learn that he has written about his childhood, and I look forward to reading his new book.

Thank you for the excellent program.

Calista Ogilvie

中文翻譯

請參考以下的書單、節目表和電子郵件回答第 186 至 190 題。

James Trozelli 著作清單

The History of Jeans
這一切究竟是怎麼開始的？Trozelli 採用影像紀年方式，呈現牛仔褲如何在這數百年間從工作服轉變成高檔時尚。

Look Past the Runway
從紐約到巴黎，Trozelli 記錄了數名頂尖設計師的創作過程。本書耗時近 20 年，書中全是 Trozelli 拍攝的照片，並揭露時裝公司在設計成品登上伸展台之前的運作過程。

Growing into Clothes: My Story
這是一本關於在時尚界長大成人的有趣回憶錄。Trozelli 寫下他與父母住在紐約時所接受的不凡教養，他的父母起初是時尚模特兒，後來自創設計品牌。

Yards of Talent: A Decade of Style
這是 Trozelli 過去十年來的時尚寫真集，顯示目前正在流行的、過時的、以及再度流行的時尚風格。

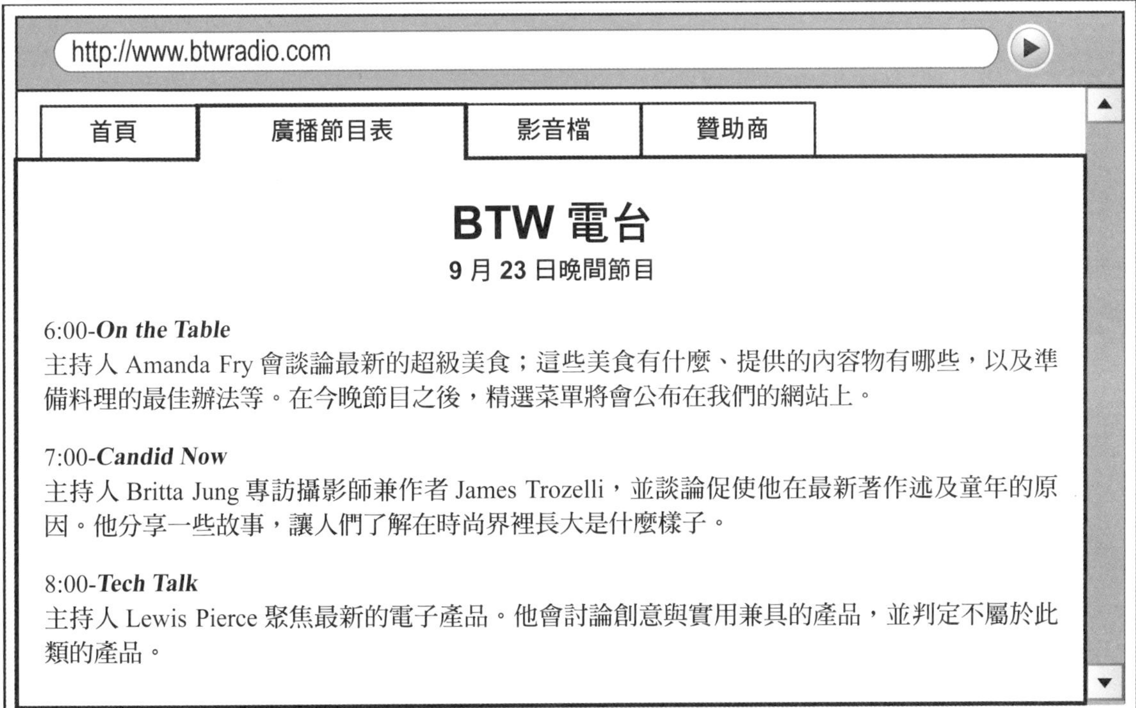

http://www.btwradio.com

首頁 | 廣播節目表 | 影音檔 | 贊助商

BTW 電台

9 月 23 日晚間節目

6:00-***On the Table***
主持人 Amanda Fry 會談論最新的超級美食；這些美食有什麼、提供的內容物有哪些，以及準備料理的最佳辦法等。在今晚節目之後，精選菜單將會公布在我們的網站上。

7:00-***Candid Now***
主持人 Britta Jung 專訪攝影師兼作者 James Trozelli，並談論促使他在最新著作述及童年的原因。他分享一些故事，讓人們了解在時尚界裡長大是什麼樣子。

8:00-***Tech Talk***
主持人 Lewis Pierce 聚焦最新的電子產品。他會討論創意與實用兼具的產品，並判定不屬於此類的產品。

E-Mail Message

收件者： listenercomments@btwradio.com

寄件者： cogilvie@summail.net

寄件日期： 9 月 24 日

主旨： 電台訪談

我在 20 多年前便發現 BTW 電台，而後成為你們晚間節目固定收聽觀眾至少十年了。我只是想說，我十分喜愛你們最新的節目內容。到目前為止，許多上過節目的重要作家都讓我深感興趣，不過昨晚的來賓特別有趣。我記得 James 還是個小男孩的模樣。當他們還住在紐約的時候，我和他的父母共事過，我還想起我總會在他父母的工作室看見放學後的他。我很驚訝他居然動筆寫下關於童年的事情，讓我很期待拜讀他的新作。

感謝您主持這麼棒的節目。

Calista Ogilvie 敬上

題目/中文翻譯

186 正解 (D)

What is one common feature in all of Mr. Trozelli's books?

Trozelli 先生所有著作的共通點為何？

(A) They contain fashion photographs.
(B) They focus on famous models.
(C) They are set in New York City.
(D) They follow events over multiple years.

(A) 內含時尚照片。
(B) 焦點為知名模特兒。
(C) 背景為紐約市。
(D) 追蹤橫跨多年的事件。

重點解說

Trozelli 先生每本書的特徵在 1 各段落都提到。第一段第二句寫著 through the centuries「在這數百年間」；第二段第二句 Spanning almost twenty years「耗時近 20 年」。及第三段第一句 memoir about growing up in the fashion world「關於在時尚界長大成人的有趣回憶錄」、第四段 spanning a decade of fashion「過去十年來的時尚寫真集」，可推知其所有著作談論的事件都橫跨好幾年。
(C) set「設定（故事背景為）…」。

---

187 正解 (C)

What book did Mr. Trozelli discuss on BTW Radio?

Trozelli 在 BTW 電台所討論的書籍是哪一本？

(A) *The History of Jeans*
(B) *Look Past the Runway*
(C) *Growing Into Clothes: My Story*
(D) *Yards of Talent: A Decade of Style*

(A) *The History of Jeans*
(B) *Look Past the Runway*
(C) *Growing Into Clothes: My Story*
(D) *Yards of Talent: A Decade of Style*

重點解說

2 的第二段可以得知，在七點開始的 *Candid Now* 節目中，James Trozelli 會接受訪問，談他最新著作述及童年的原因，第二句則提到「會告訴聽眾如何在時尚界成長」。從 1 著作清單的第三段可知，寫時尚界中的成長故事的是 (C) *Growing into Clothes: My Story*。

---

188 正解 (B)

What is indicated about Candid Now?

這裡指出關於 Candid Now 哪件事情？

(A) It is broadcast every morning at 7:00.
(B) It was recently added to BTW Radio.
(C) It is hosted by Amanda Fry.
(D) It was moved to a new time.

(A) 每日早上 7 點放送
(B) BTW 電台的最近新增節目
(C) 由 Amanda Fry 主持
(D) 節目移至新時段

重點解說

2 的節目表和 3 的第三句之後，可以得知寄送電子郵件的人，聽了專訪 James Trozelli 的 *Candid Now* 節目。3 的第二句 I just want to say how much I enjoy your newest offering.「我只是想說我十分喜愛你們最新的節目內容」，由此可知 Candid Now 是最近新增的節目。

題目 / 中文翻譯

189 正解 (C)

In the e-mail, the word "regular" in paragraph 1, line 1, is closest in meaning to

(A) orderly
(B) typical
(C) frequent
(D) complete

在電子郵件中，第一段第一行的「regular」最接近以下何意？

(A) 整齊的
(B) 典型的
(C) 經常的
(D) 完全的

重點解說 這裡的 regular 指的是「定期的、規律的」。因為提到 I have been a regular listener of your evening programming for at least a decade「成為貴電台晚間節目固定收聽觀眾至少十年了」，因此「經常的」意義上較接近 (C) frequent。

---

190 正解 (A)

What is probably true about Ms. Ogilvie?

(A) She has worked in the fashion industry.
(B) She has interviewed Mr. Trozelli.
(C) She was featured on *Tech Talk*.
(D) She hosts a radio program.

關於 Ogilvie 女士，下列何者可能是真的？

(A) 她曾在時尚業工作。
(B) 她曾訪問過 Trozelli 先生。
(C) 她曾上過 *Tech Talk* 特輯。
(D) 她主持廣播節目。

重點解說 Ogilvie 女士是 3 的電子郵件寄件者。3 的第五句提到 I worked with his parents「我曾和他的父母共事」，his parents 指的是上一句的 James 雙親。關於 James 的父母，1 的第三段第二句提到「父母起初是時尚模特兒，後來自創設計品牌」，由此得知，曾一起工作的 Ogilvie 女士曾待過時尚業。

單字註釋：chronicle「編年史」；runway「伸展台」；span「延伸到…」；memoir「回憶錄」；upbringing「教育、教養」；prompt「促使…」

題目

Questions 191-195 refer to the following product information, online review, and response.

1. 產品介紹

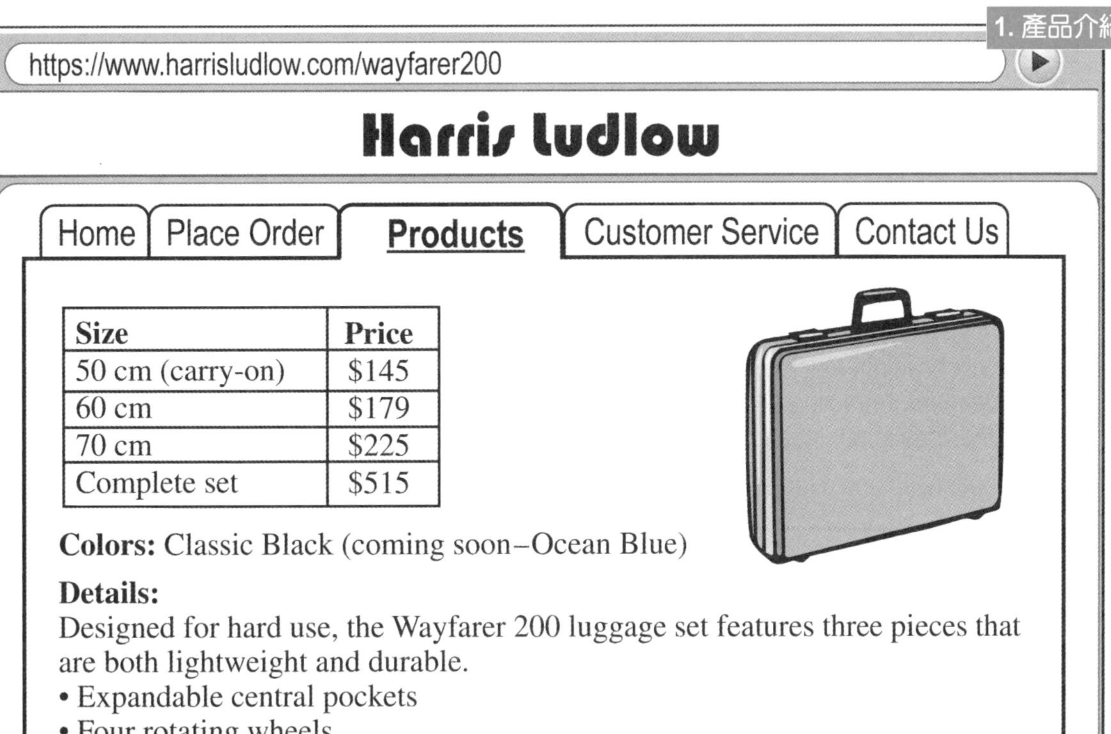

https://www.harrisludlow.com/wayfarer200

Harris Ludlow

Home | Place Order | **Products** | Customer Service | Contact Us

Size	Price
50 cm (carry-on)	$145
60 cm	$179
70 cm	$225
Complete set	$515

Colors: Classic Black (coming soon–Ocean Blue)

Details:
Designed for hard use, the Wayfarer 200 luggage set features three pieces that are both lightweight and durable.

- Expandable central pockets
- Four rotating wheels
- Easy-opening, tight-sealing clasps

2. 線上評論

https://www.harrisludlow.com/wayfarer200/reviews

April 18

I frequently travel for business, often carrying fragile samples with me on the plane. Most carry-ons these days are soft-sided, so it was a relief to find something that offers adequate protection. I've been mostly happy with the carry-on, but the larger bags have caused some problems. My black cases look so similar to everyone else's that other travelers have almost taken them by mistake! More variety would be nice.

I also have some reservations about the mechanical elements of this set. In particular, the retraction mechanism of the wheels appears so delicately constructed as to be in danger of collapse.

Asina Amorapanth

https://www.harrisludlow.com/wayfarer200/messages

April 20

Dear Ms. Amorapanth,

We're sorry to hear about your trouble with our product. As a result of feedback like yours, we've introduced a new color option. If you contact us at customersupport@hlluggage.com, we'll send you, in our attractive new color, a duplicate of the large suitcase to complement your Wayfarer 200 set. Note that this gift will be sent to you after you verify that you posted the April 18 review.

We also hear your concerns about our luggage components. Rest assured that our lightweight mechanism has been proven to withstand years' worth of rough treatment, retracting and extending smoothly over 10,000 times under stressful conditions in our laboratories.

Damien Cosme, Harris & Ludlow customer service

中文翻譯

請參考以下的產品資訊、線上評論和回應回答第 **191** 至 **195** 題。

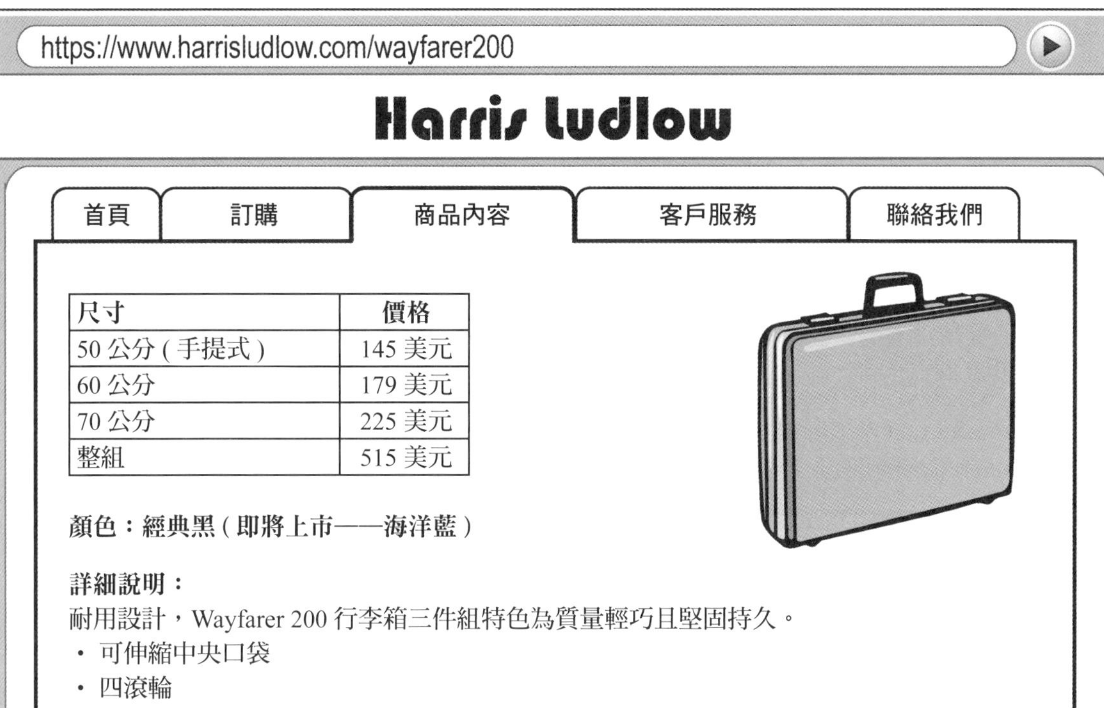

https://www.harrisludlow.com/wayfarer200

Harris Ludlow

首頁 | 訂購 | 商品內容 | 客戶服務 | 聯絡我們

尺寸	價格
50 公分（手提式）	145 美元
60 公分	179 美元
70 公分	225 美元
整組	515 美元

顏色：經典黑（即將上市——海洋藍）

詳細說明：

耐用設計，Wayfarer 200 行李箱三件組特色為質量輕巧且堅固持久。

- 可伸縮中央口袋
- 四滾輪
- 容易開啟，緊閉式拉鍊

https://www.harrisludlow.com/wayfarer200/reviews

4 月 18 日

我經常出差，常常得攜帶易碎的樣本上飛機。目前大部分的手提行李箱側邊都是軟的，因此找到能夠提供適度保護作用的產品真是讓人安心。手提行李箱讓我十分滿意，但大型行李袋卻有點問題。我的黑色外殼看起來跟每個人的都很像，結果其他旅客總是差點拿錯我的行李！有更多款式會更好。

我也很擔心這個行李箱組的某些機械器材。尤其是輪子的收縮裝置看起來相當脆弱，但似乎有倒塌的危險。

Asina Amorapanth

https://www.harrisludlow.com/wayfarer200/messages 

4 月 20 日

親愛的 Amorapanth 女士您好，

很抱歉得知您在使用我們的產品時發生問題。基於某些和您一樣的意見回饋，我們現已推出另一款顏色。若您透過 customersupport@hlluggage.com 與我們聯繫，我們將會寄給您極具魅力的新款色系，是同樣的大行李箱，讓您的 Wayfarer 200 行李箱組補足成套。請注意，在證明 4 月 18 日的評論是您所寫之後，我們才會寄送禮物給您。

我們也明白您對於行李箱零件的擔憂。請您大可放心，這些質量輕巧的機件經敝公司的實驗室證明，能夠經得起數年的嚴酷考驗，且在嚴苛的條件下仍能伸縮自如達 10,000 次以上。

Harris & Ludlow 客服人員
Damien Cosme 敬上

題目 / 中文翻譯

191 正解 (D)

What does Ms. Amorapanth write about her luggage?

(A) She likes the color.
(B) The cases are too large.
(C) She purchased the bags recently.
(D) **The carry-on protects her samples.**

Amorapanth 女士提到關於她行李的哪件事情？

(A) 她喜歡這個顏色。
(B) 外殼太大了。
(C) 她最近剛買了袋子。
(D) **隨身手提行李保護了她的樣本。**

重點解說 Amorapanth 女士的評論 2 第一段第一句提到 I frequently travel for business, often carrying fragile samples with me on the plane.「我經常出差，得攜帶易碎的樣本上飛機」，接著說 it was a relief to find something that offers adequate protection「找到能夠提供適度保護作用的產品真是讓人安心」。

---

192 正解 (B)

In the review, the word "reservations" in paragraph 2, line 1, is closest in meaning to

(A) arrangements
(B) **concerns**
(C) experiences
(D) features

在評論中，第二段第一行的「reservations」意義最接近以下何者？

(A) 安排
(B) **擔憂**
(C) 經驗
(D) 特色

重點解說 reservations 之後，接的是 about the mechanical elements of this set「這個行李箱組的某些機械器材」，然後接 the retraction mechanism of the wheels appears so delicately constructed as to be in danger of collapse「輪子的收縮裝置看起來相當脆弱，但似乎有倒塌的危險」，因此可以得知，Amorapanth 女士對於行李箱輪子的耐久性感到擔憂。這裡的 reservations about...，意思是「關於…的擔心」，意義上接近 (B)。

---

193 正解 (C)

What does Mr. Cosme offer to Ms. Amorapanth?

(A) A full set of blue luggage
(B) A full set of black luggage
(C) **A large blue suitcase**
(D) A small black suitcase

Cosme 先生提供給 Amorapanth 女士的服務為何？

(A) 藍色行李箱組
(B) 黑色行李箱組
(C) **大型藍色手提箱**
(D) 小型黑色手提箱

重點解說 Cosme 先生是寫回覆 3 的人。寄給 Amorapanth 女士的回覆 3 中，第一段第三句寫著「若您透過 customersupport@hlluggage.com 與我們聯繫，我們將會寄給您同款大行李箱的新款色系，讓您的 Wayfarer 200 行李箱組補足成套」。第二句還提到「基於某些和您一樣的意見回饋，我們現已推出另一款顏色」，再對照 1 的 Colors 欄位，得知新款色系為 Ocean Blue。因此 Cosme 先生提供的是大型行李箱，顏色則是新色 Ocean Blue，也就是藍色，選 (C)。

題目 / 中文翻譯

194 正解 (A)

What must Ms. Amorapanth do in order to receive a gift from Harris Ludlow?

(A) **Prove that she is the author of a product review**
(B) Complete a survey about new products
(C) Retract negative feedback given on a Web site
(D) Send a package containing a defective suitcase

Amorapath 女士必須做哪件事才能得到 Harris Ludlow 的禮物？

(A) 證明她是產品評論的作者
(B) 完成新品調查
(C) 撤回網站上的負評
(D) 以包裹寄回瑕疵手提箱

重點解說

3 的第一段第三句，由 Harris Ludlow 公司的 Cosme 先生向 Amorapanth 女士提出要送她大型新色行李箱。之後提到 Note this gift will be sent to you after you verify that you posted the April 18 review「請注意，在證明 4 月 18 日的評論是您所寫之後，我們才會寄送禮物給您」，所以選 (A)。
(C) retract「撤回」。

---

195 正解 (A)

What does Mr. Cosme indicate about the wheels of the suitcases?

(A) **They have been thoroughly tested.**
(B) They have been redesigned to roll more easily.
(C) They are as small as possible for the size of the suitcase.
(D) They are less noisy than those of previous models.

Cosme 先生在這裡提到手提箱滾輪的哪件事情？

(A) 經過徹底檢測。
(B) 已重新設計成更容易滾動。
(C) 就手提箱尺寸而言，已經儘可能做到最小。
(D) 比以前的款型安靜。

重點解說

3 的第二段第二句提到，「請您大可放心，這些質量輕巧的機件經敝公司的實驗室證明，能夠經得起數年的嚴酷考驗，且在嚴苛的條件下仍能伸縮自如達 10,000 次以上」。thoroughly「徹底地」。

單字註釋：rotate「旋轉」; clasp「 鉤子」; retraction「收起」; collapse「瓦解」; a duplicate of...「 …的副本」; complement「補充」; withstand「禁得起…」

題目

Questions 196-200 refer to the following notice, e-mail, and article.

1. 公告

Attention Everyone: Group Photo This Saturday

❶ Exciting news—*Tasty Bites Magazine* will be featuring our restaurant in an article about Dublin's best dining establishments! They have arranged for one of their photographers to photograph us on Saturday, 4 June, at 10:00 A.M., before preparations for the day begin.

❷ All employees will be included, so please plan to come in a bit sooner than scheduled on Saturday morning wearing your uniform. The session will take 30 minutes.

❸ We have achieved so much since we opened, and you should all be very proud of this recognition.

2. 電子郵件

To:	Herman Keel <hkeel@bentonsidebistro.net>
From:	Hilary Seaton <hseaton@hbsphotography.com>
Date:	Wednesday, 1 June
Subject:	Saturday Photography Appointment

Dear Mr. Keel,

I am writing to confirm your group photography session at 10:00 A.M. on Saturday. As discussed, this photo shoot will take place at your restaurant, and I will photograph your staff along the wall in the main dining hall. You mentioned that your waitstaff will need to start getting ready for the day at 10:30 A.M., and that should not be a problem. The shoot should be finished by 10:30 A.M.

Please let me know if you have any questions. Otherwise I will see you on Saturday!

Hilary Seaton
HBS Photography

Bistro Pleases

3. 文章

Enter Bentonside Bistro any day for lunch or dinner, and you'll hear the sounds of clinking forks and chattering patrons. "That's the sound of happy diners," says Herman Keel, the restaurant's owner.

Opened two years ago, the bistro has exceeded expectations. The menu features traditional Irish dishes prepared by chef Deirdre Hanrahan. She notes, "We choose ingredients that are at the height of summer, fall, winter, and spring, and showcase these on our menu."

On a recent Wednesday afternoon, Jacinta Coelho, a visitor from Brazil, was dining at the bistro. "I can't get over the freshness and homemade taste!" exclaimed Ms. Coelho. "It's like the chef went outside and selected the ingredients just for me."

Bentonside Bistro is located at 1644 Bentonside Road and is open Tuesday through Saturday from 11:30 a.m. to 9:00 p.m. The interior is painted in bright shades of blue reminiscent of the ocean, with a rotating gallery of artwork adorning the walls. The staff is friendly and the delicious food is reasonably priced. Reservations are not required.

By Declan Mulroney, Staff Writer

中文翻譯

請參考以下的公告、電子郵件和文章回答第 196 至 200 題。

請大家注意，本週六團拍

令人振奮的消息來了——Tasty Bites 雜誌在一篇關於都柏林最佳用餐環境的文章中，要專文特寫我們的餐廳！他們已經安排他們其中一名攝影師幫我們拍攝，時間是 6 月 4 日星期六上午十點，也就是餐廳開始準備營業之前。

所有的員工都要合照，所以請事先規畫，要比星期六上午預訂時間提早抵達，並穿著制服。拍照時間為半小時。

我們從餐廳開幕至今成果斐然，而你們都應當為這項榮譽而自豪。

收件者：	Herman Keel <hkeel@bentonsidebistro.net>
寄件者：	Hilary Seation <hseaton@hbsphotography.com>
寄件日期：	6 月 1 日星期三
主旨：	週六拍攝約定

親愛的 Keel 先生您好：

在此與您確認本週六上午十點的團拍時間。如之前所討論的，本次的照片拍攝將於您的餐廳舉行，我會以用餐大廳的牆面為您的員工拍照。您提到服務人員必須從上午 10:30 開始準備當天營業事宜，我想這並不會造成問題。上午 10:30 前就會結束拍攝。

若您尚有任何疑問，請告知我。不然我們就星期六見啦！

HBS 攝影部
Hilary Seaton

令人心滿意足的餐館

不論您哪一天踏入 Bentonside 餐館享用午餐或晚餐，都能聽到叉子碰撞的聲響與客人閒聊的話語。餐館負責人 Herman Keel 說：「這是幸福饕客的聲音。」

這間在兩年前開幕的餐館，表現遠超乎預期。這裡的特色菜單是由主廚 Deirdre Hanrahan 所準備的傳統愛爾蘭料理。她解釋說：「我們會選擇四季各自盛產的食材，然後展現在我們的菜單裡。」

最近某個星期三下午，一名叫做 Jacinta Coelho 的巴西遊客來到餐館裡用餐。「我無法忘懷料理的新鮮度與自製風味。」Coelho 女士表示：「感覺就好像主廚專為我出門挑選的食材。」

Bentonside 餐館位於 Bentonside 路 1644 號，營業時間為每週二至週六上午 11:30 至晚上 9:00。餐廳內部漆上讓人想起大海的亮藍色澤，還有擺放著藝術品的旋轉藝廊裝飾著牆面。餐廳人員十分友善，食物美味且價格合理。不需要訂位。

特約撰稿人 Declan Mulroney

題目 / 中文翻譯

196 正解 (B)

Who most likely posted the notice?

(A) Ms. Seaton
(B) Mr. Keel
(C) Ms. Hanrahan
(D) Mr. Mulroney

最有可能張貼該公告的人是誰？

(A) Seaton 女士
(B) Keel 先生
(C) Hanrahan 女士
(D) Mulroney 先生

重點解說 1 的公告提到，雜誌要報導餐廳，需要拍攝團體照，因此向工作人員告知拍攝時間等。在 2 中，拍照的攝影師告訴 Keel 先生當天的拍攝細節，因此張貼這篇公告的應該是 Keel 先生。此外，3 的第一段第二句提到，Herman Keel, the restaurant's owner「餐館負責人，Herman Keel」由此也可以知道老闆 Keel 先生張貼了這篇公告。

---

197 正解 (A)

What are employees instructed to do on June 4?

(A) Arrive earlier than usual
(B) Attend an awards banquet
(C) Be interviewed for a newspaper article
(D) Discuss locations for a photo shoot

員工被命令在 6 月 4 日做下列哪件事情？

(A) 比平常時間早到
(B) 參加頒獎宴會
(C) 接受報紙文章採訪
(D) 討論拍照地點

重點解說 關於 6 月 4 日，1 的第二段第一句提到 All employees will be included, so please plan to come in a bit sooner than scheduled on Saturday morning wearing your uniform.「所有的員工都要合照，所以請事先規畫，要比星期六上午預訂時間提早抵達，並穿著制服」，因此正確答案為 (A)。

---

198 正解 (B)

What is indicated about the waitstaff?

(A) They have been featured in *Tasty Bites Magazine* more than once.
(B) They will be photographed against a blue background.
(C) They take turns working the morning shift.
(D) They wear brightly colored uniforms.

這裡提到關於餐廳服務人員的哪件事？

(A) 他們已經多次出現在《Tasty Bites》雜誌的特輯。
(B) 他們將會在藍色背景前拍照。
(C) 他們輪流上早班。
(D) 他們穿著鮮豔的制服。

重點解說 2 的第一段第二句提到，I will photograph your staff along the wall in the main dining hall「我會以用餐大廳的牆面為您的員工拍照」。另外 3 的第四段第二句提到 The interior is painted in bright shades of blue reminiscent of the ocean「餐廳內部漆上讓人想起大海的亮藍色」，因此得知團體照背景為餐廳內部的亮藍色牆面，故選 (B)。

題目 / 中文翻譯

199 正解 (D)

What is true about the Bentonside Bistro?

(A) It is open every day for lunch.
(B) It has recently changed ownership.
(C) It specializes in Brazilian cuisine.
(D) It revises the menu seasonally.

關於 Bentonside 酒館，下列何者為真？

(A) 午餐時段每日營業。
(B) 最近剛換老闆。
(C) 特別擅長巴西料理。
(D) 每一季都會變換菜單。

重點解說
3 的第二段第三句提到廚師說，We choose ingredients that are at the height of summer, fall, winter, and spring, and showcase these on our menu.「我們會選擇四季各自盛產的食材，然後展現在我們的菜單裡」，因此正解為 (D)。seasonally「每一季」。

---

200 正解 (A)

What does Ms. Coelho say about her meal?

(A) She is impressed with the quality of it.
(B) She would like to prepare one like it at home.
(C) She saw it featured in a magazine.
(D) She thought it was reasonably priced.

Coelho 女士提到關於她的餐點哪件事情？

(A) 餐點的品質讓她留下深刻的印象。
(B) 她想要在家準備這樣的餐點。
(C) 她在某本雜誌特輯裡看過這道料理。
(D) 她認為餐點價格合理。

重點解說
3 的第三段第一句中，得知 Coelho 女士是餐館的客人。第二句的 I can't get over...「我無法忘懷…」，意思是她對食物的新鮮度和自製風味都感到驚艷。第三句的 It's like the chef went outside and selected the ingredients just for me.「感覺就好像主廚專為我出門挑選的食材」，從她這段感想，也可以看出正解是 (A)。be impressed with...「對…印象深刻」。

單字註釋：establishment「機構」；recognition「表彰」；clink「叮噹聲」；at the height of...「在…的高峰」；showcase「陳列」；exclaim「呼喊」；reminiscent of...「使人聯想…」；adorn「裝飾」

TEST 2 答案表

題號	正解	題號	正解	題號	正解	題號	正解
1	D	51	A	101	B	151	B
2	B	52	D	102	D	152	A
3	C	53	C	103	A	153	D
4	B	54	B	104	A	154	B
5	C	55	A	105	D	155	D
6	A	56	C	106	C	156	B
7	A	57	B	107	B	157	C
8	A	58	A	108	A	158	A
9	B	59	C	109	D	159	C
10	B	60	B	110	C	160	B
11	C	61	B	111	A	161	A
12	C	62	B	112	A	162	D
13	C	63	B	113	D	163	B
14	B	64	C	114	B	164	B
15	A	65	A	115	B	165	D
16	A	66	C	116	D	166	C
17	A	67	D	117	D	167	D
18	B	68	A	118	B	168	D
19	C	69	D	119	A	169	B
20	A	70	A	120	C	170	C
21	A	71	B	121	A	171	A
22	C	72	D	122	D	172	D
23	B	73	C	123	B	173	B
24	B	74	C	124	D	174	C
25	C	75	A	125	D	175	C
26	A	76	C	126	B	176	B
27	A	77	A	127	C	177	B
28	B	78	D	128	B	178	C
29	A	79	C	129	C	179	A
30	C	80	D	130	C	180	C
31	C	81	A	131	C	181	A
32	B	82	B	132	D	182	D
33	D	83	A	133	D	183	C
34	C	84	A	134	A	184	C
35	D	85	C	135	B	185	B
36	A	86	D	136	A	186	D
37	C	87	B	137	D	187	C
38	B	88	C	138	B	188	B
39	A	89	C	139	D	189	B
40	C	90	C	140	A	190	A
41	B	91	B	141	B	191	B
42	C	92	A	142	D	192	C
43	A	93	C	143	A	193	B
44	C	94	D	144	C	194	A
45	B	95	D	145	B	195	D
46	A	96	C	146	B	196	A
47	B	97	A	147	C	197	C
48	C	98	B	148	D	198	D
49	D	99	C	149	D	199	B
50	B	100	D	150	A	200	A

題目 / 中文翻譯	重點解說

1

(A) He's parking a car.
(B) He's carrying groceries.
(C) He's entering a store.
(D) He's pushing a shopping cart.

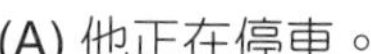

(A) 他正在停車。
(B) 他正拿著雜貨。
(C) 他正在走進商店。
(D) 他正推著購物車。

正解 (D)

照片中的男士正推著 shopping cart「購物車」。句中 He's 是 He is 的縮寫。
(B) groceries「雜貨（通常為複數形）」。

2

(A) A wall is being painted.
(B) Some plants have been placed in a row.
(C) A cement floor is being swept.
(D) Some boxes have been stacked in a corner.

(A) 牆面正在粉刷。
(B) 植物成列擺放。
(C) 水泥地板正在被清掃。
(D) 有些盒子堆放在角落。

正解 (B)

栽種在花盆裡的 plant「植物」整齊擺放著。in a row「排成一列」。
(C) swept 是動詞 sweep「清掃」的過去分詞。

3

(A) One of the women is adjusting a bicycle seat.
(B) One of the women is drinking from a cup.
(C) The women are standing by a wooden railing.
(D) The women are climbing some stairs to a porch.

(A) 其中一名女士正在調整腳踏車坐墊。
(B) 其中一名女士正在喝杯中的東西。
(C) 女士們站在木頭欄杆旁。
(D) 女士們走上通往門廊的階梯。

正解 (C)

照片中的女士們站在 wooden「木頭的」railing「欄杆」的旁邊。

題目 / 中文翻譯	重點解說

4

(A) A table has plates of food on it.
(B) A display case is located near some steps.
(C) Some chairs have been moved into a corner.
(D) Some lights are being turned off.

(A) 桌上有很多盤食物。
(B) 展示櫃位於樓梯附近。
(C) 椅子被搬至角落。
(D) 燈被關掉了。

正解 (B)

display case「展示櫃」在 step「樓梯」附近。be located「被放置於（某處）」。

5

(A) A door has been propped open.
(B) Some people are replacing some glass.
(C) Workers are cleaning large window panes.
(D) A spray bottle has been set on the ground.

(A) 門被撐開。
(B) 有些人正在換玻璃。
(C) 工人正在清潔大片的窗玻璃。
(D) 噴霧瓶放在地上。

正解 (C)

workers 指的是圖片中的男女工人。他們正在擦拭大片的 window panes「窗玻璃」。
(A) prop「以（支棍等物）支撐…」。

6

(A) Merchandise is being taken off a shelf.
(B) They're hanging some clothes on a rack.
(C) Some shirts are being packed into a box.
(D) A ladder is leaning against a wall.

(A) 從貨架上取出商品。
(B) 他們正在把一些衣服掛到架上。
(C) 有些襯衫被裝進箱內。
(D) 梯子斜倚著牆面。

正解 (A)

梯子上的女士正在從 shelf「貨架」取出 merchandise「商品」。take A off B「從 B 取出 A」。
(D) lean against...「斜倚著…」。

題目 / 中文翻譯	重點解說

7 Q： A：

Where should I meet you at the theater?
(A) In front of the box office.
(B) It got great reviews.
(C) The show starts at eight o'clock.

我要在戲院的哪個地方與你碰面？
(A) 在售票口前。
(B) 佳評如潮。
(C) 表演 8 點開始。

正解 (A)

針對 Where...? 這樣的詢問，選項 (A) 回答「售票口前」，因此是正解。in front of...「在…前面」；box office「售票口」。

---

8 Q： A：

The printer on this floor is working, isn't it?
(A) No, it's broken.
(B) Yes, there is.
(C) Fifty copies.

這層樓的印表機可供使用，對吧？
(A) 不，印表機壞了。
(B) 是的，這裡有。
(C) 50 份影本。

正解 (A)

work「運轉」，句末的 ..., isn't it?「…沒錯吧」表示確認。正解是選項 (A)，以 No 表示否定之後，再補充說明印表機故障。
(A) 的 it 指的是問題中的 The printer on this floor，選項中的 broken 為「故障」。

---

9 Q： A：

What should I prepare for the sales workshop?
(A) A group of us went.
(B) Didn't Elizabeth take care of everything?
(C) That should be fine.

關於銷售技巧的工作坊，我應該準備些什麼？
(A) 我們一群人都會去。
(B) Elizabeth 不是都安排妥當了嗎？
(C) 聽起來不錯。

正解 (B)

prepare for...「為…做準備」。
針對「應該準備什麼」的問題，不是回答應該準備哪些東西，而以選項 (B) 點出已有負責安排事宜的人員，是合理的回應。take care of... 在這裡指「負責、處理」。

題目 / 中文翻譯	重點解說

10 Q : A :

When will the town council election take place?
(A) At the town hall.
(B) At the beginning of June.
(C) Several candidates.

鎮議會選舉於何時舉行？
(A) 在鎮議會廳。
(B) 6 月初。
(C) 數名候選人。

正解 (B)

town council「鎮議會」; election「選舉」; take place「舉行（活動等）」。
針對 When...? 這樣的詢問，選項 (B) 回答「6 月初」，因此為正確解答。at the beginning of...「在…一開始」。

---

11 Q : A :

Is technical support available twenty-four hours a day?
(A) To buy a new watch.
(B) I don't have questions right now.
(C) Yes, through our Web site.

技術性的支援是 24 小時全天候都可以使用的嗎？
(A) 購買新錶。
(B) 我現在沒有問題。
(C) 是的，請上我們的網站。

正解 (C)

technical「技術性的」; available「可獲得的」; twenty-four hours a day「24 小時（全天候）」。
針對問句「可以使用…嗎？」選項 (C) 以 Yes 回答，並告知取得的方法。

---

12 Q : A :

How much does this sweater cost?
(A) It also comes in black.
(B) Cash only.
(C) It should say on the tag.

這件毛衣要價多少？
(A) 也是黑色的。
(B) 請付現金。
(C) 應該寫在標籤上。

正解 (C)

sweater「毛衣」; cost「花（錢）」。針對毛衣價格的詢問，告知標價寫在標籤上的 (C) 是適當回應。say 有「…寫在（書或佈告等）上面」的意思；tag「（寫著訊息的）標籤」。

題目 / 中文翻譯	重點解說

13 Q： A：

Who gave the presentation on company benefits?
(A) Yes, we all went.
(B) They don't fit.
(C) Someone in Human Resources.

關於公司福利的簡報是哪位做的？
(A) 是的，我們全都去了。
(B) 他們都不適合。
(C) 人事資源部的人員。

正解 (C)

give a presentation「報告簡報、發表」；company benefits「公司福利」。
對於 Who...? 這樣的人物詢問，回答「人事資源部門人員」的選項 (C) 是正解。Human Resources「人事資源（部門）」。

---

14 Q： A：

Why is there so much traffic?
(A) After the weather report.
(B) Because there's a basketball game today.
(C) No, that's enough.

為什麼這裡的交通如此壅塞？
(A) 接在氣象預報之後。
(B) 因為今天有籃球比賽。
(C) 不，這樣足夠了。

正解 (B)

對於 Why...? 這樣的詢問，回答選項 (B)「因為今天有籃球比賽」是正確解答。traffic「交通（量）」是不可數名詞，因此交通量大應該用 much。

---

15 Q： A：

Would you be interested in joining the hiring committee?
(A) Yes, I'd be honored to.
(B) Last Wednesday evening.
(C) It's an interesting article.

你有興趣加入招募委員會嗎？
(A) 是的，榮幸之至。
(B) 上週三晚上。
(C) 這是篇有趣的文章。

正解 (A)

hiring committee「招募委員會」。
Would you be interested in...?「您對…有興趣嗎？」是邀請時的禮貌性用法。回答 Yes，並且說「（如果能參加的話）榮幸之至」，選項 (A) 是正解。I'd 是 I would 的縮寫。to 之後省略了 join the hiring committee。be honored to do「對於做…榮幸之至」。

題目 / 中文翻譯	重點解說

16 Q：🇺🇸 A：🇬🇧

Are you going on vacation this month or next month?
(A) We're still deciding.
(B) A different location.
(C) I'm looking forward to it.

你是這個月還是下個月去度假？
(A) 我們尚在決定中。
(B) 別的地方。
(C) 我非常期待。

正解 (A)

go on vacation「度假」。對於度假時間的詢問，回答「尚在決定中」的選項 (A) 為適當的回應。decide「決定」。

---

17 Q：🇬🇧 A：🇦🇺

How do I get a new identification card?
(A) There's an online form to fill out.
(B) To carry in your wallet.
(C) By February 21.

我要如何取得新的身分證？
(A) 請填寫線上表格。
(B) 請攜帶你的皮夾。
(C) 到 2 月 21 日之前。

正解 (A)

identification card「身分證」。
對於 How...? 詢問方法的問題，選項 (A) 回答取得方法，也就是「填寫線上表格」，因此是正確答案。form「表格」; fill out...「填寫…」。

---

18 Q：🇨🇦 A：🇬🇧

Shall I send out the agenda for the meeting?
(A) Not in general.
(B) Uh, I have to make a revision first.
(C) Conference room C is large enough.

我需要寄發會議議程表嗎？
(A) 不是一般的。
(B) 呃，但我必須先修正內容。
(C) C 會議室的空間夠大。

正解 (B)

send out...「寄發…、發出…」; agenda「議程（表）」。Shall I...? 是詢問「是否需要寄發」，選項 (B) 回答「必須先修正（那個議程表）的內容」，是自然且通順的回應。make a revision「修正」。
(A) in general「一般來說」。

題目 / 中文翻譯	重點解說

19 Q : A :

Who was selected to work on the advertising project?
(A) A great success.
(B) It's a popular brand.
(C) I haven't heard.

誰被選為負責廣告宣傳的人員？
(A) 巨大的成功。
(B) 它是一個熱門品牌。
(C) 我沒聽說。

正解 (C)

select「選擇」; work on...「處理」; advertising「廣告宣傳」。
Who...? 是詢問人物的問題，選項 (C) 表示「我還沒聽說（誰被選上）」，是符合情境的回答。

---

20 Q : A :

The ferry to the island runs every half hour, doesn't it?
(A) Yes, there's one coming now.
(B) No thanks, that's too late.
(C) At the ticket kiosk.

開往小島的渡船每半小時發船對吧？
(A) 是的，現在有一艘船來了。
(B) 不，謝謝，太晚了。
(C) 在售票亭。

正解 (A)

island「小島」; run「(交通工具) 行駛」; every half hour「每 30 分鐘」。
結尾的 ..., doesn't it? 是用來和對方再做確認的意思。選項 (A) 回答 Yes 之後，補充說明「現在有一艘船來了」，是自然且合理的對話。(A) 的 one 指的是問題中的 ferry。

---

21 Q : A :

How should I pay the deposit on the rental car?
(A) Do you have a credit card?
(B) It's less expensive than that.
(C) Yes, there's plenty of space.

租車的訂金該如何支付？
(A) 您有信用卡嗎？
(B) 比那個還便宜。
(C) 是的，空間很充足。

正解 (A)

deposit「訂金」; rental car「租車」。
關於付款方式的詢問，對方反問「是否有信用卡」，因此選項 (A) 是合理的回應。

題目 / 中文翻譯	重點解說

22 Q： A：

Who's responsible for the packaging design?
(A) It was shipped overnight.
(B) Just sign here.
(C) Martin's team.

包裝設計的負責人是誰？
(A) 這是隔日配送。
(B) 請在此處簽名。
(C) Martin 的團隊。

正解 (C)

be responsible for...「負責…」；packaging「包裝」。
對於 Who...?這樣的詢問，回答選項 (C) 負責人「Martin的團隊」為正解。

---

23 Q： A：

Is Mr. Kim in charge of the manufacturing plant?
(A) Weren't some planted recently?
(B) I think someone else is managing it now.
(C) Just a small production defect.

Kim 先生是負責管理這間製造廠的人嗎？
(A) 最近不是栽種了些植物嗎？
(B) 我想現在已經換人管理了。
(C) 只是生產上的小缺陷。

正解 (B)

in charge of ...「管理、負責」; manufacturing plant「製造廠」。
對於「Kim 先生是否負責管理這間製造廠」的問題，回答「已經換人管理」的選項 (B)，是自然且流暢的對答。manage「管理」。
(C) production「生產」; defect「缺陷」。

---

24 Q： A：

Why don't we offer a vegetarian dish at the lunch?
(A) I've been there a few times.
(B) It may be too late to change the menu.
(C) No, let's wash the dishes later.

我們何不在午餐時段提供素食餐點呢？
(A) 我去過那裡幾次。
(B) 現在更換菜單可能太遲了。
(C) 不，我們稍後再來清洗碗盤。

正解 (B)

offer...「提供…」; vegetarian「素食主義（者）的」；dish「餐點」。
Why don't we...? 是表示建議「何不…」。對於更換午餐時段菜單的建議，回答「太晚了，可能來不及更換菜單」的選項 (B)，是合理且自然的反應。too...to...「太…以至於不能…」。

題目/中文翻譯	重點解說

25 Q： A：

Where does John usually store the extra supplies?
(A) There's one on the corner of Main Street.
(B) Sure, that might be a good idea.
(C) You'd better ask him.

John 通常把多餘的供給品存放在哪裡？
(A) 在 Main Street 的街角有一個。
(B) 當然，那可能會是個好主意。
(C) 你最好問問他。

正解 (C)

store 動詞是「存放」; extra「多餘的」; supplies「供給品、存貨」。
詢問 John 存放多餘供給品的位置，回答選項 (C)「你最好問問他」，是自然且合理的回應。You'd better 為 You had better 的縮寫句型，強烈建議「應該…」。

---

26 Q： A：

I found a new supplier for the garden fertilizer we use.
(A) Do they have good prices?
(B) In the warehouse.
(C) We sold a lot of flowers.

關於我們所使用的園藝肥料，我找到一家新的供應商了。
(A) 他們給的價格很不錯嗎？
(B) 在倉庫裡。
(C) 我們賣了很多花。

正解 (A)

supplier「供應商」; fertilizer「肥料」。
「找到新的 supplier 供應商」之後，接著選項 (A) 反問對方「覺得新供應商的價格如何？」，是自然的回應。a new supplier「新供應商」是單數名詞，但接公司等代名詞時，有時用 they。

---

27 Q： A：

How about holding a training seminar on the new database?
(A) Yes, I think we should.
(B) I've been there before.
(C) It went very well.

我們來舉辦一場新資料庫的研習講座如何？
(A) 沒錯，我想我們應該這麼做。
(B) 我以前去過那裡。
(C) 進行得非常順利。

正解 (A)

hold「舉辦…」; training seminar「研習講座」; database「資料庫」。
How about...? 對於舉辦研習講座的提議，選項 (A) 以 Yes 回答，正面肯定對方的提議，是符合情境的對話。

題目／中文翻譯	重點解說

28 Q： A：

Didn't you organize the employee picnic last year?
(A) You can use the Milton Room.
(B) I've done it the past seven years.
(C) No, it was free.

去年的員工野餐不是你策畫的嗎？
(A) 你可以使用 Milton 室。
(B) 過去七年都是我策畫的。
(C) 不，是免費的。

正解 (B)

organize「策畫、準備（活動）」；picnic「野餐」。
Didn't...? 為否定疑問句，「沒有…嗎？」。對於「去年沒策畫嗎？」這個問題，接著回答 (B)「過去七年都是我（策畫的）」是合理且適當的答案。

---

29 Q： A：

Would you take this memo to the Finance Department?
(A) Sure, I'll drop it off before the meeting.
(B) I had to pay a small fine.
(C) Right on the first page.

你能不能將這份備忘錄拿去給財務部？
(A) 當然，會議開始前我會先拿去放好。
(B) 我得償付小額罰款。
(C) 就在第一頁。

正解 (A)

memo「（公司內的）文件、備忘錄、便箋」；Finance Department「財務部」。
Would you...? 是詢問對方「能不能幫自己…？」。選項 (A) 回答 Sure，並表示會自行送過去是正解。(A) 的 it 是問句中的 this memo，drop... off「先放好…」。

---

30 Q： A：

Shall I contact you by e-mail or by phone?
(A) OK, I'll take a look at the contract.
(B) Oh, did you?
(C) Actually, I'll be seeing you tomorrow.

我應該使用電子郵件還是電話與你聯絡？
(A) 好的，我會檢視契約內容。
(B) 喔，你是嗎？
(C) 事實上，我明天會去拜訪你。

正解 (C)

contact「與…聯絡」。
問題以 A or B 的方式，確認聯絡方法是「電子郵件或是電話」。兩者皆非，選項 (C) 指出「明天會去與對方見面」是合理的回應。
actually「事實上」。
(A) contract「契約」。

題目/中文翻譯

31 Q: A:

Are you still working on the final budget?
(A) The decision was final.
(B) I usually start work at nine.
(C) I'm not, but Janet is.

你還在處理最終預算嗎?
(A) 這是最終的決策。
(B) 我通常九點開始工作。
(C) 我沒有,但 **Janet** 還在處理。

重點解說

正解 **(C)**

work on...「處理…」; budget「預算(案)」。Are you still... ? 詢問對方「是否仍在…?」選項 (C) 回答 I'm not,自己沒在處理,並且說明其他人員的名稱,因此是正確的回應。在回答 I'm not 和 Janet is 之後,皆省略了 working on the final budget。

題目 / 中文翻譯

Questions 32 through 34 refer to the following conversation.

請參考以下的對話回答第 32 題至第 34 題。

男： 女：

W: Excuse me—the chocolate cake here at your restaurant is delicious. ❶Is there any way I could get the recipe?

女：不好意思，您餐廳裡的巧克力蛋糕實在很好吃。有沒有任何辦法能夠讓我取得您的食譜呢？

M: Actually, ❷our chef, David Wilson, is publishing a cookbook that'll be out in November. And he's included the recipe for his chocolate cake. It's a customer favorite.

男：事實上，我們主廚 David Wilson 的烹飪書 11 月就會出版了。他的書中也收錄了巧克力蛋糕的食譜。巧克力蛋糕是顧客的最愛。

W: Really? That's great! Will the book be sold here?

女：真的嗎？太好了！那本書會在這裡販售嗎？

M: Yes, it will. In fact, if you leave your contact information, ❸I'll make sure a book is signed by chef David and set aside for you.

男：是的，沒錯。事實上，如果您留下您的聯絡資訊，我保證會幫您取得 David 的親筆簽名，並為您保留那本書。

題目 / 中文翻譯

32

What does the woman ask for?
(A) A bill
(B) A recipe
(C) A photograph
(D) A menu

女士詢問何事？
(A) 帳單
(B) 食譜
(C) 照片
(D) 菜單

重點解說

正解 (B)

女士因為這家餐廳的巧克力蛋糕好吃，詢問❶Is there any way I can get the recipe?「有沒有任何辦法能夠讓我取得您的食譜呢？」

題目/中文翻譯	重點解說

33

Who is David Wilson?
(A) A magazine editor
(B) A television producer
(C) A food critic
(D) A restaurant chef

誰是 David Wilson？
(A) 雜誌編輯
(B) 電視製作人
(C) 美食評論家
(D) 餐廳主廚

正解 (D)
男士說❷ **our chef, David Wilson**「我們的主廚 David Wilson」。
(C) critic「評論家」。

34

What does the man offer to do?
(A) Send an e-mail reminder
(B) Make a video
(C) Reserve a book
(D) Arrange a banquet

男士提供哪項服務？
(A) 寄發電子郵件提醒通知
(B) 錄影
(C) 保留書籍
(D) 安排宴會

正解 (C)
男士說❸ **I'll make sure a book is signed by chef David and set aside for you**「我保證會幫您取得 David 的親筆簽名，並為您保留那本書」。set aside... 和 (C) reserve 都是「保留…」的意思。

題目 / 中文翻譯

Questions 35 through 37 refer to the following conversation.

請參考以下的對話回答第 35 題至第 37 題。

男：🇨🇦 女：🇬🇧

W: OK, sir, here are your purchases. Thanks for shopping Quality First Foods. ❶**Would you like to fill out a short survey** over there at the service desk? Then you'll receive a free gift card for a future visit.

女：好的，先生，這是您訂購的物品。非常感謝您在 Quality First 食品行的消費。可否請您到服務台填寫一份簡短的調查呢？您將會免費獲贈一張可在日後消費時使用的禮品卡。

M: I would, but ❷**the problem is I'm in a rush.** I see there's a line at the service counter, and I don't have time to wait.

男：我很想，但問題是我在趕時間。我看到服務台前已經有人排隊了，可是我沒有時間可以等待。

W: That's OK. ❸**You can also fill out the survey online and submit it electronically.** Then we'll mail the gift card to you.

女：沒關係。您也可以填寫線上調查，完成電子提交後，我們便會將禮品卡寄給您。

題目 / 中文翻譯

35

What is the man invited to do?
(A) Watch a product demonstration
(B) Try a free sample
(C) Sign up for a newsletter
(D) Fill out a survey

男士被邀請做哪件事情？
(A) 觀賞產品說明會
(B) 免費試吃
(C) 註冊電子報帳號
(D) 填寫調查表

重點解說

正解 (D)

女士邀請男士說 ❶ **Would you like to fill out a short survey**「可否請您填寫一份簡短的調查呢？」survey「問卷、調查」。

題目 / 中文翻譯	重點解說

36

What problem does the man mention?
(A) He is in a hurry.
(B) He has forgotten his receipt.
(C) A product is not in stock.
(D) A parcel has been damaged.

男士提到什麼問題？
(A) 他趕時間。
(B) 他忘記拿收據。
(C) 某件產品缺貨。
(D) 包裹受損。

正解 (A)

男士說❷ **the problem is I am in a rush**「問題是我在趕時間」。be in a rush 可以置換成 be in a hurry「匆忙」。

37

What does the woman suggest?
(A) Returning a purchase
(B) Trying a different product
(C) Completing a task online
(D) Visiting another store

女士建議的事項為何？
(A) 退回購買物品
(B) 試用不同的產品
(C) 完成線上任務
(D) 參觀另一家店

正解 (C)

男士說我很想填問卷，可是沒時間，女士說❸ **You can fill out the survey on line and submit it electronically.**「您也可以填寫線上調查，並完成電子提交」。(C) 的 a task 是指填寫線上調查並完成電子提交。

題目 / 中文翻譯

Questions 38 through 40 refer to the following conversation.

M: Hi, Christine. ❶Do you know if any office supplies were delivered today? We're out of color toner for the printers.

W: I didn't see anything arrive.

M: Mmm. ❷I'm a bit worried because I can't print out my color handouts for this afternoon.

W: I have to go to a meeting in a few minutes, but ❸I have the tracking number for the order. ❹How about I forward it to you so you can follow up?

請參考以下的對話回答第 38 題至第 40 題。

男：　女：

男：嗨，Christine。今天有沒有任何辦公室用品送來呢？印表機的彩色墨水已經用完了。

女：我沒有看到任何東西送來耶。

男：嗯，我有點擔心，因為我無法列印今天下午要用的彩色講義。

女：再過幾分鐘後我還有個會議得開，不過我這裡有訂單的追蹤編號。不如我把追蹤編號轉發給你，讓你可以持續追蹤好嗎？

題目 / 中文翻譯

38

What is the man asking about?
(A) The deadline for a project
(B) The status of a delivery
(C) The location of a meeting
(D) The amount of an invoice

男士詢問的事項為何？
(A) 計畫案的截止日期
(B) 配送狀態
(C) 會議地點
(D) 發票總金額

重點解說

正解 (B)

男士詢問❶Do you know if any office supplies were delivered today?「今天有沒有任何辦公室用品送來呢？」status「狀況、狀態」。

題目 / 中文翻譯	重點解說

39

Why is the man concerned?
(A) He cannot print some documents.
(B) Some files are missing.
(C) The wrong items were sent.
(D) A shipment was canceled.

男士為何擔憂？
(A) 他無法列印文件。
(B) 有些檔案遺失。
(C) 發送錯誤項目。
(D) 取消出貨。

正解 (A)
男士說 ❷ **I'm a bit worried because I can't print out my color handouts for this afternoon.**「我有點擔心，因為我無法列印今天下午要用的彩色講義」。worried 和問題中的 concerned 都是「擔心」的意思。

40

What does the woman offer to send the man?
(A) A model number
(B) A cost estimate
(C) A tracking number
(D) A brochure

女士要寄給男士哪樣東西？
(A) 型號
(B) 預估成本
(C) 追蹤編號
(D) 小冊子

正解 (C)
女士在❸中說「有訂單的追蹤編號」，再提議❹ **How about I forward it to you so you can follow up?**「不如我把追蹤編號轉發給你，讓你可以持續追蹤好嗎？」這裡的 it 指的正是 the tracking number for the order。

題目 / 中文翻譯

Questions 41 through 43 refer to the following conversation.

請參考以下的對話回答第 41 題至第 43 題。

男：　女：

W: Hi, I'd like one ticket for the jazz concert at seven o'clock.

女：你好，我想要買一張晚上七點的爵士音樂會門票。

M: I'm sorry, but ❶there are no more tickets for tonight's concert. We do have some seats for the same performance this weekend, though. Are you interested in that show?

男：很抱歉，已經沒有今晚音樂會的門票了。不過呢，這項活動在本週末的場次裡還有一些座位。你對那場表演有興趣嗎？

W: I won't be here then. ❷I'm just in Vancouver for a friend's birthday celebration, and I fly back home tomorrow. ❸Do you have any other suggestions for things to do?

女：我到時候就不在這裡了。我只是來溫哥華參加朋友的慶生會，明天就會搭飛機回家。關於這點，你有任何建議嗎？

M: Well, ❹why don't you go to the Roussel Museum instead? It's nearby and they have a wonderful exhibit on Chinese calligraphy. I just saw it myself last weekend.

男：嗯，何不去 Roussel 博物館呢？正好就在附近，而且目前正在展覽中國書法之美。我上週末剛去看過。

單字註釋：calligraphy「書法」

題目 / 中文翻譯

41

What does the man say about the concert?
(A) It has been moved.
(B) It is sold out.
(C) It received good reviews.
(D) It has already started.

男士提到關於音樂會的哪件事情？
(A) 地點移動了。
(B) 票券全面售罄。
(C) 它（音樂會）大獲好評。
(D) 已經開始了。

重點解說

正解 (B)

男士說❶ there are no more tickets for tonight's concert「今晚音樂會的票券已經售罄」。sold out「售罄」。

題目 / 中文翻譯	重點解說

42

Why is the woman in Vancouver?
(A) To look for a new house
(B) To take part in a seminar
(C) To go to a party
(D) To attend a sports game

女士為何人在溫哥華？
(A) 尋找新家
(B) 參加研討會
(C) 前往派對
(D) 參加運動賽事

正解 (C)

女士說 ❷ **I'm just in Vancouver for a friend's birthday celebration**「我只是來溫哥華參加朋友的慶生會」。celebration「慶祝派對、慶祝會」在 (C) 用 party 取代。

43

What does the man recommend doing?
(A) Seeing a museum exhibit
(B) Going on a walking tour
(C) Trying a popular café
(D) Visiting a historic site

男士提議做什麼？
(A) 觀賞博物館展覽
(B) 徒步旅行
(C) 試吃一家人氣咖啡店
(D) 參訪歷史遺跡

正解 (A)

女士在 ❸ 中詢問「你有任何建議嗎？」，男士在 ❹ 提議 why don't you go to the Roussel Museum instead?「何不去 Roussel 博物館？」(D) historic site「歷史遺跡」。

題目 / 中文翻譯

Questions 44 through 46 refer to the following conversation.

M: Hi Victoria, it's Kwame from the clinic. ❶I know you're not scheduled to work today, but do you think you can come in? We're getting very busy over here.

W: ❷I'm afraid I can't, Kwame. ❸I'm presenting at the patient care workshop this morning.

M: Oh, I didn't realize you were a presenter. Well…good luck with that. I'm sure you'll do great.

W: Hey, ❹why don't you call Greg? ❺I know he's interested in picking up extra shifts. I'm sure he'll be happy to come in.

請參考以下的對話回答第 44 題至第 46 題。

男： 女：

男：嗨，Victoria。我是診所的 Kwame。我知道妳今天沒有排工作，不過妳方便過來一趟嗎？今天這裡真的非常忙碌。

女：Kwame，恐怕我辦不到耶。今早我得在病患照護研討會上進行簡報。

男：喔，我不知道你是講者。嗯，祝你好運。我相信你一定會做得很好。

女：對了，你為什麼不打給 Greg 呢？我知道他對額外排班有興趣。我保證他絕對會開心地加入你們。

題目 / 中文翻譯

44

What does the man ask the woman to do?
(A) Give him a ride to work
(B) Write a letter of recommendation
(C) Come in to work on her day off
(D) Pick up a prescription

男士要求女士做什麼事情？
(A) 讓他搭便車去上班
(B) 撰寫推薦信函
(C) 在休假日去診所上班
(D) 開立處方籤

重點解說

正解 (C)

男士請求說❶ I know you're not scheduled to work today, but do you think you can come in?「我知道你今天不用上班，但是你方便來診所嗎？」(C) day off 是「休假日」。(D) prescription「處方箋」。

題目 / 中文翻譯	重點解說

45

Why is the woman unavailable?
(A) She is having her car repaired.
(B) She is giving a presentation.
(C) She is out of town.
(D) She has a doctor's appointment.

女士為何沒空？
(A) 她正在修車。
(B) 她正在進行簡報。
(C) 她出城去了。
(D) 她與醫生有約。

正解 **(B)**

unavailable「沒空」。
女士在❷中拒絕了男士的請求，並說明理由是❸ **I'm presenting at the patient care workshop this morning.**「今早我得在病患照護研討會上進行簡報」。presenting 在 (B) 換成 giving a presentation「進行簡報」。

46

What does the woman suggest?
(A) Contacting a colleague
(B) Postponing a meeting
(C) Changing a workshop location
(D) Finding a different vendor

女士建議哪件事情？
(A) 聯絡同事
(B) 推遲會議
(C) 改變研討會地點
(D) 另找別的小販

正解 **(A)**

女士說❹ **why don't you call Greg?**「你為什麼不打給 Greg 呢？」之後在❺說「我知道他對額外排班有興趣」，因此可以判斷 Greg 和說話的這兩人是同事。colleague「同事」。

題目 / 中文翻譯

Questions 47 through 49 refer to the following conversation.

W: Hi, Julie. ❶**How's the recruitment project going?** What progress has been made in finding new employees?

M: Well, ❷**on Tuesday I met with department managers** to talk about what kinds of skills they'd like new team members to have. Now I'm adding this information to the job descriptions and will be posting them soon.

W: Great. The sooner you can advertise the available positions, the better. ❸**We've taken on so many new clients recently that we'll need more staff to complete all the work.**

請參考以下的對話回答第 47 題至第 49 題。

男：🇨🇦　女：🇺🇸

男：嗨，Julie。招募計畫進行得如何？尋找新進員工的進度如何？

女：嗯，星期二我和各部門主管會面時，我們討論了他們希望新進團隊人員應該具備哪些能力。現在我正要把這些資訊加進工作描述裡，而且很快就會發布內容。

男：太好了。在宣傳徵求職缺方面，請妳愈快愈好。我們最近有太多新顧客需要照料，所以需要更多職員才有辦法完成工作。

單字註釋：job description「工作描述、工作說明書」; take on...「承擔（工作等）」

題目 / 中文翻譯

47

What project is the woman working on?
(A) Training new employees
(B) Recruiting new staff
(C) Researching a competitor
(D) Finding potential clients

女士目前正在處理哪項計畫？
(A) 訓練新進員工
(B) 招募新進職員
(C) 研究競爭對手
(D) 尋找潛在顧客

重點解說

正解 (B)

男士詢問❶ **How's the recruitment project going?**「招募計畫進行得如何？」女士回答說，討論了希望新進團隊人員應該具備的能力、正在製作工作描述的文件等細節。
recruit「招募」。
(C) competitor「競爭對手」。

題目/中文翻譯	重點解說

48

What did the woman do on Tuesday?
(A) Reviewed applications
(B) Interviewed job candidates
(C) Met with company managers
(D) Attended promotional events

女士在星期二做了什麼事情？
(A) 檢閱申請書
(B) 面試求職者
(C) 與公司各主管會面
(D) 參加促銷活動

正解 (C)

❷ **on Tuesday I met with department managers**「星期二時，我和各部門主管會面」。

49

What does the man say has recently happened at the company?
(A) The computer equipment has been upgraded.
(B) The departments have been restructured.
(C) The regional headquarters has moved.
(D) The workload has increased.

男士表示最近公司發生什麼事情？
(A) 電腦設備升級。
(B) 部門重整。
(C) 區域總部遷移。
(D) 工作量增加。

正解 (D)

男士說❸ **We've taken on so many new clients recently that we'll need more staff to complete all the work.**「我們最近有太多新顧客需要照料，所以需要更多職員才有辦法完成工作」，因此可以判斷最近公司的工作量增加。workload「工作量」。

題目 / 中文翻譯

Questions 50 through 52 refer to the following conversation.

請參考以下的對話回答第 **50** 題至第 **52** 題。

男：🇦🇺 女：🇺🇸

M: Hi, Ms. Long. This is Jacob from the landscaping company. ❶I'm afraid we won't be able to start working on your garden tomorrow. ❷The weather report's showing that there'll be heavy rain.

男：Long 女士您好，我是園藝綠化公司的 Jacob。關於您的花園施工事宜，恐怕明天我們無法開始動工。天氣預報指出會下大雨。

W: Well, you know ❸I'm going to be out of town for two weeks starting this Thursday. I wanted to give you a key to the gate, so you'd be able to keep working while I'm gone.

女：嗯，你也知道從本週四開始，我將會出城兩星期。我想要把大門鑰匙給你們，當我不在家的時候，你們還是能夠繼續施工。

M: OK. Then ❹what if I come by tomorrow anyway, just to pick up the key?

男：好的。要是我明天過去找您拿鑰匙可以嗎？

W: If you wouldn't mind. I'll be at home until ten-thirty in the morning.

女：如果你不介意的話。明天上午十點半前我都會在家。

單字註釋：landscaping「園藝綠化」

題目 / 中文翻譯

50

Why does the man postpone the project?
(A) A permit is delayed.
(B) The weather will be bad.
(C) A coworker is unavailable.
(D) Some materials have not arrived.

男士為何要延遲計畫？
(A) 許可證延誤。
(B) 氣候不佳。
(C) 同事沒空。
(D) 材料尚未送達。

重點解說

正解 (B)

男士在❶說明天我們無法開始花園的施工，理由是❷ The weather report's showing that there'll be heavy rain.「天氣預報指出會下大雨」。

題目 / 中文翻譯

重點解說

51

What does the woman say she will do on Thursday?
(A) Leave for a trip
(B) Start a new job
(C) Meet with a supplier
(D) Volunteer at a public park

女士表示本週四她要做什麼？
(A) 出外旅行
(B) 開始新工作
(C) 見供應商
(D) 公共公園的志願服務

正解 (A)

女士說❸**I'm going out of town for two weeks starting this Thursday**「從本週四開始，我將會出城兩星期」。be out of town「出城、出差」。

52

Why does the woman say, "If you wouldn't mind"?
(A) To suggest a solution
(B) To ask for permission
(C) To make a complaint
(D) To accept an offer

女士提到「If you wouldn't mind」的用意為何？
(A) 提出解決辦法
(B) 徵求許可
(C) 發牢騷
(D) 接受提議

正解 (D)

男士提出❹**what if I come by tomorrow anyway**「要是我明天過去可以嗎？」女士回答 if you wouldn't mind「如果你不介意（明天請過來）」，因此可以知道女士願意接受男士的提議。

題目 / 中文翻譯

Questions 53 through 55 refer to the following conversation with three speakers.

請參考以下三人的對話回答第 53 題至第 55 題。

男：/ 女：

W: Tom, ❶can I get past you to the fridge? I need some milk.

女：Tom，能否借過一下，讓我到冰箱那裡去呢？我需要一些牛奶。

M: Sure. Have you tried this tea?

男：沒問題。你喝過這款茶嗎？
（加拿大）

W: No, I'm not big on tea. I like the coffee they give us, though.

女：沒有耶，我不是茶類愛好者，不過我挺喜歡他們提供給我們的咖啡。

M: Yeah, ❷I love working here. There are so many great benefits! Did you hear about the new vacation policy?

男：沒錯，我好愛在這裡工作，有好多非常棒的福利！妳有沒有聽說新的休假政策？
（加拿大）

W: Yes, it's great, isn't it? Oh, hello Anil. Anil, have you met Tom? ❸Anil just started this week.

女：聽說了，超棒的對吧？喔，Anil 你好。Anil，你見過 Tom 了嗎？ Anil 這週剛開始工作。

M: Nice to meet you, Tom.

男：很高興認識你，Tom。
（澳洲）

M: You too, Anil. Glad to have you with us.

男：我也是，Anil。很高興你加入我們的行列。
（加拿大）

M: Thanks. Oh, we're out of coffee?

男：謝謝。喔，沒咖啡了嗎？
（澳洲）

W: No, there's some here. Oops, I'm running late. Anil, I'll stop by later to show you how to use the time entry system.

女：不，這裡還有一點。糟糕，我快要遲到了。Anil，我晚點再過來教你怎麼使用打卡紀錄系統。

題目 / 中文翻譯

53

Where most likely is the conversation taking place?
(A) At a job fair
(B) At a meeting
(C) In an office kitchen
(D) In a coffee shop

本段對話最有可能發生在哪個地點？
(A) 就業博覽會
(B) 會議
(C) 公司茶水間
(D) 咖啡店

重點解說

正解 (C)

這段是三個人的對話。女士提到❶ can I get past you to the fridge?「能否借過一下，讓我到冰箱那裡去呢？」也提到附近有紅茶、咖啡。而且 Tom 在❷ 說 I love working here.「我好愛在這裡工作。」由此可知這段對話是在「公司茶水間」裡發生的。

題目 / 中文翻譯	重點解說

54

What does Tom suggest about the company?
(A) It needs to hire more people.
(B) It treats its employees well.
(C) It will soon be renovated.
(D) It is buying some new equipment.

Tom 談及公司的哪件事情？
(A) 需要招聘更多人員。
(B) 非常善待員工。
(C) 即將重新裝潢。
(D) 正在採購新的設備。

正解 **(B)**

Tom 說❷ **I love working here. There are so many benefits**「我好愛在這裡工作，有好多非常棒的福利」。接下來談到新的休假方針，女士回答「超棒的」，因此可以判斷公司非常善待員工。treat「對待」。

55

What does the woman say about Anil?
(A) He has recently joined the company.
(B) He applied for her position.
(C) He will be reporting to Tom.
(D) He has just returned from vacation.

女士提到 Anil 的哪件事情？
(A) 他最近剛進公司。
(B) 他申請她的職位。
(C) 他的直屬上司是 Tom。
(D) 他剛休完假回來。

正解 **(A)**

職場對話中，Tom 說❸ **Anil just started this week.**「Anil 這週剛開始工作」，可推知 Anil 最近才剛進公司。
(C) report to...「直屬於…」。

題目 / 中文翻譯

Questions 56 through 58 refer to the following conversation.

請參考以下的對話回答第 56 題至第 58 題。

男： 女：

M: Hi, Ms. Ellington. ❶Do you have a minute to talk about this month's production numbers?

男：Ellington 女士您好。請問您有時間跟我討論這個月的生產指數嗎？

W: I have a meeting soon, but go ahead.

女：我馬上就得去開會，但你可以繼續說。

M: ❷Because of problems with two machines on the assembly line, we're not producing as many plastic bottles each day.

男：由於組裝產線有兩台機器發生問題，導致我們無法每天都製造相同數量的寶特瓶。

W: Really? ❸Have any client deadlines been affected?

女：真的嗎？有沒有對哪位顧客的交貨期限造成影響？

M: Well, no, not yet. But I'm worried we won't be able to meet them next month.

男：嗯，目前沒有，但我擔心的是，下個月我們可能就無法如期交貨。

W: OK. Let's go over the figures later. I've got to get going.

女：好的。我們稍後再來確認這些數據。我得趕快離開了。

題目 / 中文翻譯

56

What are the speakers mainly discussing?
(A) Factory policies
(B) Employee training
(C) Monthly results
(D) Client requests

談話者主要討論內容為何？
(A) 工廠政策
(B) 員工訓練
(C) 每月成果
(D) 顧客要求

重點解說

正解 (C)

男士詢問❶Do you have a minute to talk about this month's production numbers?「您有時間討論這個月的生產指數嗎？」，之後談的也是關於寶特瓶製造工廠的事。(C) 的 results「成果」是指 production numbers「生產指數」。

題目/中文翻譯	重點解說

57

What does the woman mean when she says, "I have a meeting soon"?
(A) She is not looking forward to a meeting.
(B) She cannot speak with the man for long.
(C) She is inviting the man to a meeting.
(D) She wants the man to give her a document.

女士提到「I have a meeting soon」的用意為何？
(A) 她不期待開會。
(B) 她無法和男士談話太久。
(C) 她邀請男士去開會。
(D) 她想要男士給她一份文件。

正解 (B)

男士在❶中詢問「是否有時間」，女士接著回答底線的內容「我馬上就得去開會」，因此可得知女士沒有太多的時間可以和男士討論。

58

What does the woman want to know?
(A) If deadlines have been missed
(B) If product quality is satisfactory
(C) If clients have increased their orders
(D) If machines need to be replaced

女士想要知道什麼？
(A) 交貨期限是否錯過了
(B) 產品品質是否令人滿意
(C) 顧客是否增加訂單
(D) 機器是否需要淘汰

正解 (A)

男士說❷「機械問題造成每日寶特瓶製造產量不一」，女士接著問❸ **Have any client deadlines been affected?**「有沒有對哪位顧客的交貨期限造成影響？」deadline「期限」；miss「錯過、未達到」。

題目 / 中文翻譯

Questions 59 through 61 refer to the following conversation.

M: Hi, Barbara. Nice to run into you! ❶We've missed you since you left Allen Real Estate.

W: Kevin! Yes, it's been a while. That was a big decision, to change companies. But I like my new job a lot.

M: That's great. ❷How's the work different from what you did with us?

W: Well—❸I only handle commercial properties now. But I like being able to focus on one area.

M: Hey... I just had an idea. I'm organizing the annual meeting for the Real Estate Association this August, and ❹I'm sure everyone would like to hear you speak about your career move.

W: ❺I'd be happy to! Here's my business card—just let me know the details.

請參考以下的對話回答第 59 題至第 61 題。

男： 女：

男：Barbara 妳好。真高興碰巧遇見妳！自從妳離開 Allen 房地產公司後，大家都非常想念妳啊。

女：Kevin ！是啊，好久不見了。換公司可是個重大決定。不過我真的很喜歡我的新工作。

男：那太好了。現在的工作跟以前我們一起打拚的時候有什麼不同嗎？

女：嗯——我現在只處理商業物產。不過我喜歡專注在一個領域。

男：嘿，我正好有個想法。我正在協助房地產協會規畫今年八月的年度會議，我相信大家一定很想聽妳聊聊轉換職場跑道後的故事。

女：我很樂意！這是我的名片——麻煩你告訴我詳細內容。

題目 / 中文翻譯

59

How do the speakers know each other?
(A) They live in the same area.
(B) They met at a professional conference.
(C) They used to work together.
(D) They went to the same university.

談話者彼此是怎麼認識的？
(A) 他們住在同一區。
(B) 他們在一場專業會議結識。
(C) 他們過去一起工作。
(D) 他們就讀同一間大學。

重點解說

正解 (C)

男士在❶中說，自從女士離開 Allen 房地產公司後，大家對女士的思念，接著男士在❷詢問，現在的工作跟以前我們一起打拚的時候有什麼不同，可判斷出兩人之前應是 Allen 房地產公司的同事。

題目/中文翻譯	重點解說

60

What does the woman say she likes about her job?
(A) Using her creativity
(B) Specializing in one area
(C) Earning bonus pay
(D) Having the chance to travel

女士表示她喜歡工作的哪個部份？
(A) 運用創意
(B) 專精某個領域
(C) 賺取紅利
(D) 有機會去旅行

正解 (B)
女士說❸ **I only handle commercial properties now. But I like being able to focus on one area.**「我現在只處理商業物產。不過我喜歡專注在一個領域。」focus on...「專注於…」在 (B) 置換成 specialize in...「專精於…」。

61

What does the woman agree to do?
(A) Apply for a promotion
(B) Describe a career change
(C) Print out some business cards
(D) Look at a property for sale

女士同意做哪件事情？
(A) 申請升職
(B) 描述職涯的轉變
(C) 印製名片
(D) 觀看待售物產

正解 (B)
男士說❹ **I'm sure everyone would like to hear you speak about your career move**「我相信大家一定很想聽妳聊聊轉換職場跑道後的故事」，提議女士在房地產協會的年度會議上聊聊轉職的事。女士回答說 I'd be happy to!「我很樂意！」describe「描述、說明」。

題目 / 中文翻譯

Questions 62 through 64 refer to the following conversation and map.

請參考以下的對話及配置圖回答第 62 題至第 64 題。男： 女：

W: How was the meeting?

女：會議進行得如何？

M: ❶Good. We talked about ways to increase sales.

男：很好。我們討論了增加銷售的方法。

W: And? Seems like we've tried everything.

女：還有呢？我們似乎什麼都試過了。

M: Well, ❷radio advertising's pretty effective, though I can't believe how much they charge! But one guy talked about easy changes to store layout. They just moved some displays around, and it really made a difference.

男：嗯，電台宣傳相當有效，但我沒想過要價竟然這麼高！不過有人談到店面配置的小改變。他們只移動某些展示品的位置，結果真的很不一樣。

W: Hmm. I've often thought we should move the shoe department from the back of the store to the front. So it's across from the store entrance.

女：嗯，我常在想我們應該將鞋類區從店的後面移到前面，這樣就會橫跨整個店門口。

M: And here's an even better idea! ❸Put the shoes next to the fitting rooms! If people are trying on clothes in the fitting rooms, they'll probably want to get the shoes at the same time.

男：我有個更棒的想法！我們把鞋類放在試衣間旁邊！如果人們到試衣間試穿衣服，與此同時，他們很可能也會想要試穿鞋子。

題目 / 中文翻譯

62

What did the man recently do?
(A) He transferred to another city.
(B) He attended a meeting.
(C) He purchased a new store.
(D) He signed up for a training program.

男士最近做了什麼事情？
(A) 遷移到另一座城市。
(B) 參加會議。
(C) 添購新的店面。
(D) 報名培訓計畫。

重點解說

正解 (B)

女士詢問會議的事，男士回答❶ Good. We talked about ways to increase sales.「很好。我們討論了增加銷售的方法」。

題目 / 中文翻譯

重點解說

63

What is the man surprised by?
(A) The availability of staff
(B) The cost of advertising
(C) The change to a catalog
(D) The timing of a move

男士對什麼事情感到訝異？
(A) 員工可用性
(B) 廣告費用
(C) 目錄更動
(D) 移動時機

正解 (B)

男士在❷中說「電台宣傳相當有效，但我沒想過要價竟然這麼高」，可知男士被高額的廣告費用嚇到。advertising「廣告」。

64

Look at the graphic. Where does the man suggest putting the shoe department?

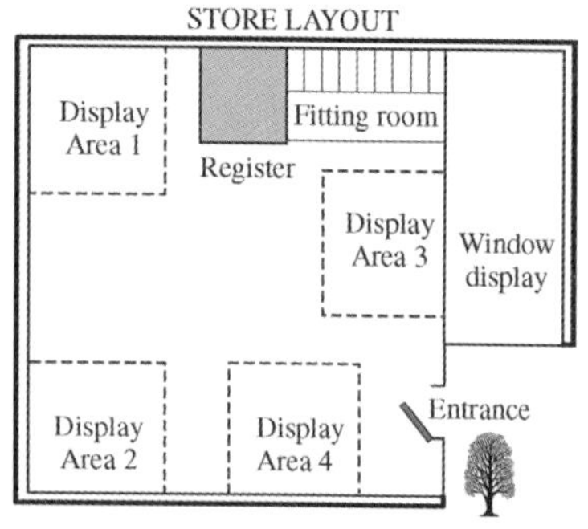

(A) In Display Area 1
(B) In Display Area 2
(C) In Display Area 3
(D) In Display Area 4

請看此圖。男士建議將鞋類區放在哪個位置？
(A) 第一展示區
(B) 第二展示區
(C) 第三展示區
(D) 第四展示區

正解 (C)

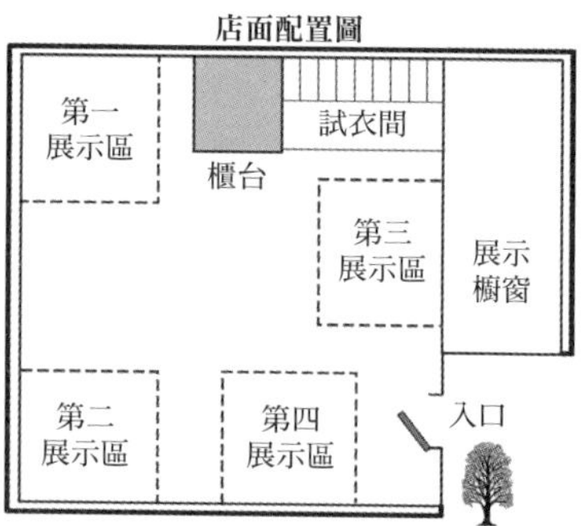

男士建議❸**Put the shoes next to the fitting rooms!**「將鞋類區放在試衣間旁邊」。對照圖表可以發現試衣間旁邊為第三展示區。

題目 / 中文翻譯

Questions 65 through 67 refer to the following conversation and label.

請參考以下的對話及標籤回答第 65 題至第 67 題。男：🇨🇦 女：🇬🇧

M: Excuse me? ❶I'm trying to change my diet and I want to eat something different for breakfast—you know, something healthier, like, maybe yogurt? Is there a yogurt that's low in calories but also has a lot of protein?

男：不好意思，我正在改變飲食習慣，所以我早餐想吃點不一樣的東西，你知道的，就是比較健康的東西，或許像是優格？這裡是否有低卡路里，但含高蛋白的優格呢？

W: We have a lot of options you might like. Here's one of our most popular brands of blueberry yogurt. See, there's a lot of protein…

女：我們擁有許多能夠讓您喜歡的選擇。這是我們最暢銷的藍莓優格品牌。請看，含有豐富的蛋白質……

M: Mmm—nice! But ❷my doctor told me I shouldn't eat a lot of sweet foods—and ❸it would put me over the daily amount he recommended. That's more than 30 grams!

男：嗯——太好了！不過我的醫生告誡我不可以吃太多的甜食——這會讓我超過他所建議的每日攝取量。這個可是超過 30 公克呢！

W: In that case, ❹I'd suggest buying a plain version of this yogurt and adding your own fresh fruit.

女：如果是這樣的話，那麼我會建議您買同款的原味優格，您可以自己添加新鮮水果。

題目 / 中文翻譯

65

Why is the man looking for a certain product?
(A) He wants to eat healthy foods.
(B) He is allergic to a particular ingredient.
(C) He has a coupon for a discount.
(D) He has a favorite brand.

男士為何要尋找特定產品？
(A) 他想要吃健康的食物。
(B) 他對特定食材過敏。
(C) 他持有折價優惠券。
(D) 他有最愛的品牌。

重點解說

正解 (A)

男士說 ❶ I'm trying to change my diet and I want to eat something... healthier.「我正在改變飲食，所以我早餐想吃點不一樣的東西，我想吃點健康的食物」。diet「（日常的）飲食、食品」。

題目／中文翻譯

重點解說

66

Look at the graphic. Which of the ingredients does the man express concern about?

Nutrition Information
Serving size: 200 grams
Calories: 150

	Amount per serving
Fat	5 grams
Protein	11 grams
Sugar	32 grams
Sodium	40 milligrams

(A) Fat
(B) Protein
(C) Sugar
(D) Sodium

請看此圖。男士表示他所擔心的食材成份為何？
(A) 脂肪
(B) 蛋白質
(C) 糖分
(D) 鈉

正解 (C)

營養成分表
每餐份量：200公克
卡路里： 150

	每份含量
脂肪	5 公克
蛋白質	11 公克
糖分	32 公克
鹽分	40 毫克

ingredient「成份、材料」。男士在❷中說明「醫生告誡我不可以吃太多的甜食」。之後提到關於優格裡的成份❸「這會超過醫生建議的每日攝取量，超過 30 公克」。對照圖表可知，超過 30 公克的是糖分。

67

What does the woman suggest that the man do?
(A) Try a free sample
(B) Go to a larger branch
(C) Speak with his doctor
(D) Purchase a different item

女士建議男士做哪件事情？
(A) 試吃免費樣品
(B) 前往更大的分店
(C) 找他的醫生談談
(D) 購買別的品項

正解 (D)

女士說❹ **I'd suggest buying a plain version of this yogurt**「我會建議您買同款的原味優格」。buy 和 (D) 的 purchase 都是「購買」的意思。(D) 的 a different item 指的是 a plain version of this yogurt。

題目 / 中文翻譯

Questions 68 through 70 refer to the following conversation and coupon.

請參考以下的對話及折價券回答第 68 題至第 70 題。男： 女：

W: OK, sir. ❶Your total for these two shirts is forty-five dollars.

女：好的，先生。這兩件襯衫的總金額為 45 美元。

M: Oh, wait—I have a discount coupon I want to use while it's still valid. I think I've got it here somewhere... Oh, here it is.

男：喔，等等——我有一張折價券，我想趁仍然有效時使用。我應該是放在某個地方……有了，在這裡。

W: OK—thanks. Hmm, it looks like the computer isn't accepting it. Let me take a look...

女：好的——謝謝您。嗯，看起來電腦似乎不接受這張折價券。讓我看一下……

M: Ah—I see the problem. Is it OK if I go back and browse a bit more to see if there's anything else that I need?

男：喔——我看到問題在哪了。我可以再回去逛逛，順便看一下我還需要什麼東西嗎？

W: Certainly. ❷I can keep these shirts here at the register for you if you'd like.

女：當然。若您願意的話，我可以將您的襯衫保留在櫃台這裡。

題目 / 中文翻譯

68

What is the woman doing?

(A) Assisting a customer
(B) Handing out coupons
(C) Arranging some clothing
(D) Restarting a computer

女士正在做什麼？

(A) 協助顧客
(B) 發放折價券
(C) 整理服飾
(D) 重新啟動電腦

重點解說

正解 (A)

從女士說❶ Your total for these two shirts is forty-five dollars.「這兩件襯衫的總金額為 45 美元」及❷ I can keep these shirts here at the register for you「我可以將您的襯衫保留在櫃台這裡」，由此可知女士正在協助顧客購物。

題目 / 中文翻譯

重點解說

69

Look at the graphic. Why is the coupon rejected?

> **Jerry's Department Store**
>
> **Discount Coupon**
>
> $15 off clothing purchase of $50 or more
>
> Expires May 8
>
> 100123456782010

(A) It has expired.
(B) It is for a different department.
(C) It must be approved by a manager.
(D) It is for purchases of at least $50.

請看此圖。折價券被拒的原因為何？
(A) 已經過期了。
(B) 適用於不同部門。
(C) 需經理核可。
(D) 至少需購物滿 50 美元。

正解 (D)

> **Jerry's 百貨公司**
>
> **折價券**
>
> 消費滿 50 美元或以上，現折 15 美元。
>
> 有效期限 5 月 8 日
>
> 
>
> 100123456782010

女士在❶說「這兩件襯衫的總金額為 45 美元」。對照圖表發現 $15 off clothing purchase of $50 or more「消費滿 50 美元或以上，現折 15 美元」，因此可知男士購物金額不足，無法使用折價券。

70

What does the woman offer to do?
(A) Hold some items at the register
(B) Find a product for the man
(C) Call another staff member
(D) Add the man's name to a mailing list

女士提供哪種服務？
(A) 將某些品項保留在櫃台
(B) 幫男士尋找商品
(C) 打電話給另一位員工
(D) 將男士姓名加入郵寄清單

正解 (A)

女士在❷說，「我可以將您的襯衫保留在櫃台這裡」。keep「保留…」可以置換成 (A) hold「保留（物品等）」。

題目 / 中文翻譯

Questions 71 through 73 refer to the following broadcast.

This is 93.9 WGKP radio, and now for the local news. ❶ **Next week is the annual Millwood County Fair.** ❷ **The annual festival celebrating Millwood's agricultural heritage will open with a parade Friday at noon on Elm Street** and end with a fireworks show on Saturday night after dark. The weather is expected to be sunny and warm most of the week, but ❸ **there could be rain showers on Saturday, so you may want to bring an umbrella.**

請參考以下的廣播內容回答第 **71** 題至第 **73** 題。

這裡是 93.3 WGKP 廣播電台，現在播送地方新聞。下週是 Millwood 鎮的年度慶典。這項慶祝 Millwood 農業傳統的年度盛事，將由星期五中午 Elm 大街的遊行揭開序幕，而由星期六晚上的夜空煙火秀畫下句點。預計本週大部分都將是晴朗且溫暖的好天氣，不過週六可能會有陣雨，因此你可能得帶雨傘出門。

題目 / 中文翻譯

71

What is the radio broadcast mainly about?
(A) Local traffic conditions
(B) An annual celebration
(C) An agricultural report
(D) A town-meeting schedule

電台廣播主要內容為何？
(A) 當地交通狀況
(B) 年度慶典
(C) 農業報告
(D) 鎮民集會行事曆

重點解說

正解 (B)

❶ **Next week is the annual Millwood County Fair**「下週是 Millwood 鎮的年度慶典」，❷ **The annual festival celebrating Millwood's agricultural heritage**「這項慶祝 Millwood 農業傳統的年度盛事」，之後所提也是關於這項慶典的事，因此正確答案為 (B)。celebration「慶典」。

題目/中文翻譯	重點解說

72

What does the speaker say will happen on Elm Street?
(A) Produce will be sold.
(B) Street repairs will be completed.
(C) A new shop will open.
(D) A parade will take place.

談話者提到在 Elm 大街會發生哪件事情？
(A) 農產品販售。
(B) 道路整修完工。
(C) 新店開張。
(D) 舉辦遊行。

正解 (D)

❷說的是 The annual festival... will open with a parade Friday at noon on Elm Street「一年一度的慶典將由星期五中午 Elm 大街的遊行揭開序幕」。take place「舉辦（活動等）」。
(A) produce「（名詞）農產品」。

73

What does the speaker suggest listeners do on Saturday?
(A) Avoid parking on Elm Street
(B) Visit an amusement park
(C) Prepare for rain
(D) Listen to a radio news report

談話者建議聽眾星期六該做哪件事？
(A) 避免到 Elm 大街停車
(B) 參觀遊樂園
(C) 為下雨做好準備
(D) 聆聽廣播新聞報導

正解 (C)

❸中建議 there could be rain showers on Saturday, so you may want to bring an umbrella「星期六可能會有陣雨，因此你可能得帶雨傘出門」。
(A) avoid「避免…」。

題目 / 中文翻譯

Questions 74 through 76 refer to the following talk.

Hello everyone, ❶welcome to the architecture conference at the West Wind Eco Inn. ❷This hotel was constructed last year using the latest energy-efficient, non-polluting materials. In addition, the lodge offers easy access to the surrounding forests and rivers that the region is famous for. ❸We're very happy to host your group of international architects. I'm sure you'll have many questions about the efficiency and cost of the materials we've used, and why you should consider using them in your own building designs.

請參考以下的談話回答第 74 題至第 76 題。

大家好，歡迎來到 West Wind 生態飯店的建築會議。這間飯店去年落成，使用最新節能、且零污染的建材所造。此外，飯店可輕鬆前往本地著名的鄰近森林與溪流。我們非常開心能夠招待各位國際建築師。我想各位一定抱持著許多關於我們所採用的建材效益度與成本的疑問，以及為什麼你們應該考慮在建築設計上面使用這些建材等。

題目 / 中文翻譯

74

Where is the talk taking place?
(A) At an art studio
(B) At a construction site
(C) At a hotel
(D) At an energy plant

該談話發生在何處？
(A) 藝術工作室
(B) 工地現場
(C) 飯店
(D) 能源廠

重點解說

正解 (C)

❶ welcome to the architecture conference at the West Wind Eco Inn「歡迎來到 West Wind 生態飯店的建築會議」，inn 指的是「(小型的) 飯店」。另外❷提到 This hotel...「這間飯店…」，可知這段談話發生在飯店裡。

題目 / 中文翻譯	重點解說

75

Who most likely are the listeners?
(A) Architects
(B) Scientists
(C) Hotel managers
(D) Event planners

誰最有可能是聽眾？
(A) 建築師
(B) 科學家
(C) 飯店經理
(D) 活動策畫人員

正解 (A)

❸提到 We're very happy to host your group of international architects.「我們非常開心能夠招待各位國際建築師」，因此得知聽眾是建築師。

76

What is mentioned about the materials used?
(A) They are produced locally.
(B) They are inexpensive.
(C) They are environmentally friendly.
(D) They are hard to find.

關於採用建材，曾提及下列哪一項？
(A) 當地生產。
(B) 價格低廉。
(C) 環保。
(D) 難以找尋。

正解 (C)

materials 指「材料、建材」。❷中說明蓋這間飯店使用的建材是 energy-efficient「節能」、non-polluting「零污染」。因此可以說使用的建材屬於 environmentally friendly「環保」。
(B) inexpensive 價格低廉。

題目 / 中文翻譯

Questions 77 through 79 refer to the following broadcast.

❶And for today's entertainment news. Renowned film company, Dougherty Films, recently announced they'll be shooting a movie right here in Brayville. In fact, ❷the crew is looking to lease a furnished apartment to film some of their main scenes in. ❸In the movie, the apartment that is chosen will be owned by the award-winning actor Santiago Diaz's character. ❹Now, if it were someone else, you might not be as enthusiastic to let a film crew into your home for several weeks. But this is Santiago Diaz we're talking about. To have your apartment considered for the film, fill out an application on the Dougherty Films Web site.

請參考以下的廣播內容回答第 77 題至第 79 題。

接下來是今天的娛樂消息。知名電影公司 Dougherty Films 最近發表要到 Brayville 這裡拍攝新電影的聲明。實際上，劇組目前想要承租內附裝潢的公寓，以進行某些主要場景的拍攝。在電影裡，這間雀屏中選的公寓將會成為 Santiago Diaz 這位獲獎無數的演員在劇中所扮演角色的家。現在，如果換做是別人，您也許不會這麼熱切地想要讓劇組人員入住您的家中達數週之久。但我們現在說的人物可是 Santiago Diaz 啊！如果您希望您的公寓能夠被列入電影的考慮名單，請上 Dougherty Films 網站填寫申請表。

單字註釋：award winning「獲獎」；enthusiastic「熱衷的、熱心的」

題目 / 中文翻譯

77

Who most likely is the speaker?

(A) A news reporter
(B) A movie director
(C) A real estate agent
(D) A town official

談話者最有可能是誰？

(A) 新聞記者
(B) 電影導演
(C) 房地產仲介
(D) 小鎮官員

重點解說

正解 (A)

從開頭的❶And for today's entertainment news.「接下來是今天的娛樂消息。」可以推知新聞記者要報導娛樂相關的新聞。

題目 / 中文翻譯	重點解說

78

What is Dougherty Films looking for?
(A) Movie title suggestions
(B) Additional funding
(C) A lead actor
(D) A filming location

Dougherty Films 正在尋找什麼？
(A) 電影標題的提案
(B) 額外資金
(C) 主角演員
(D) 拍攝場地

正解 (D)

❷ 是說明 the crew is looking to lease a furnished apartment to film some of their main scenes in「實際上，劇組目前想要承租內附裝潢的公寓，以進行某些主要場景的拍攝」。

79

What does the speaker imply when she says, "But this is Santiago Diaz we're talking about"?
(A) She has never heard of Santiago Diaz.
(B) She had previously mentioned the wrong name.
(C) Santiago Diaz is very famous.
(D) Santiago Diaz will be interviewed next.

談話者提到「But this is Santiago Diaz we're talking about」的用意為何？
(A) 她從未聽過 Santiago Diaz。
(B) 她之前提到的名字是錯的。
(C) Santiago Diaz 大名鼎鼎。
(D) Santiago Diaz 會接著受訪。

正解 (C)

❷ 和 ❸ 說明電影劇組人員想借公寓當做拍攝地點，而且是當作演員 Santiago Diaz 的家。之後在 ❹ 中說「如果換做是別人，您也許不會這麼熱切地讓劇組人員入住您的家中達數週之久」，但因為是 Santiago Diaz，大家應該會希望提供自己的公寓給劇組，因此說了底線的內容，可由底線的部份得知 Santiago Diaz 非常有名。

題目 / 中文翻譯

Questions 80 through 82 refer to the following speech.

Thank you, thank you... ❶I feel truly honored by this award for employee of the year here at Flint and Gray Banking. At the beginning of the year, ❷I was asked to develop a mobile application for our account holders that would track their bank activity and give them a summary of their spending trends over time. ❸After ten months of trial and error, we are now able to release a fully functioning application to our users. But ❹I couldn't have done it without my team of programming specialists. ❺They all did a fabulous job. ❻So for that, please join me in giving them a warm round of applause. Come on up here, everyone!

請參考以下的演講回答第 80 題至第 82 題。

非常感謝，非常感謝……能夠在這裡榮獲 Flint and Gray 銀行年度員工大獎，我感到十分榮幸。年初的時候，我受命研發一套行動應用程式，讓我們的帳戶持有人能夠追蹤他們的銀行業務，並隨時提供他們關於支出趨勢的摘要整理。歷經十個月的試驗與錯誤之後，現在我們終於能夠發行一套功能強大的應用程式提供給我們的使用者。但是，如果沒有我的團隊，沒有這群程式設計專家，我一定辦不到。他們表現得太好了。因此，請大家跟我一起給予他們最熱烈的掌聲。來吧，請大家上台！

單字註釋：fabulous「極好的」；a round of applause「熱烈的掌聲」

題目 / 中文翻譯

80

What is the purpose of the speech?
(A) To motivate team members
(B) To announce a retirement
(C) To inaugurate a company
(D) To accept an award

演講的目的為何？
(A) 激勵團隊成員
(B) 宣布退休
(C) 公司開幕
(D) 接受獎項

重點解說

正解 (D)

❶說 I feel truly honored by this award for employee of the year「能夠獲得年度員工大獎，我感到十分榮幸」，因此得知這位女士是為了接受獎項而演講。award「獎項」。
(C) inaugurate「（公司等）開幕」。

題目 / 中文翻譯	重點解說

81

What most likely is the speaker's job?
(A) Technology specialist
(B) Bank teller
(C) Financial analyst
(D) Marketing manager

談話者的工作最有可能是什麼？
(A) 科技專家
(B) 銀行出納人員
(C) 財務分析師
(D) 行銷經理

正解 (A)

❷ 說明她得獎的原因，是 I was asked to develop a mobile application「我受命研發一套行動應用程式」。之後在❹ 的後半段說「我的程式設計專業團隊」，由此可知女士的工作和科技有關。specialist「專家」。
(B) teller「（銀行的）出納人員、櫃台人員」。

82

Why does the speaker say, "I couldn't have done it without my team"?
(A) She does not have the skills for a task.
(B) She wants to thank her colleagues.
(C) She is requesting additional staff.
(D) She has not worked on a team before.

談話者為何說「I couldn't have done it without my team」？
(A) 她並沒有完成任務的才能。
(B) 她想要感謝她的同事。
(C) 她要求增加員工。
(D) 她以前從來沒有參與過團隊工作。

正解 (B)

底線部份的意思是「如果沒有我的團隊，我一定辦不到」。❸說的是「歷經十個月的試驗與錯誤之後，我們終於能夠發行應用程式」，另外關於團隊，❺中稱讚「他們表現得太好了」，並在❻希望大家給予他們掌聲，因此可得知女士想要感謝她的同事。

題目 / 中文翻譯

Questions 83 through 85 refer to the following radio advertisement.

Hi, ❶**I'm Doctor Rajesh Sharma, chief eye surgeon at the new Meadowbrook Laser Vision Correction Center.** Our center has just opened at 4 Lombard Street, next to the Townsend Supermarket. You may be asking, "Why choose one of our doctors?" ❷**Because we've performed thousands of vision correction procedures**—many more than any other surgeons in the area. If you have a vision problem, ❸**our computerized laser surgery may be able to help.** ❹**We're offering a free consultation to our first one hundred customers**, so act now! Come in and see us today!

請參考以下的電台廣告回答第 83 題至第 85 題。

大家好，我是 Rajesh Sharma 醫師，新成立的 Meadowbrook 雷射視力矯正中心眼科主治醫師。我們的中心剛開幕，地址為 Lombard 大街 4 號，就在 Townsend 超市的旁邊。您可能會問：「為什麼要選擇我們的醫生？」因為我們已經施行過數以千計的眼科矯正手術，遠超乎本地其他醫生的經驗。若您有任何視力問題，我們的電腦化雷射手術很可能會幫您一個大忙。前一百名顧客可享免費諮詢，趕快行動吧！今天就踏入我們的中心來找我們吧！

單字註釋：surgeon「外科醫生」；surgery「外科手術」

題目 / 中文翻譯

83

What most likely is being advertised?
(A) A vision correction center
(B) A computer repair shop
(C) A medical school
(D) A shopping center

廣告最有可能在宣傳什麼？
(A) 視力矯正中心
(B) 電腦維修店
(C) 醫學院
(D) 購物中心

重點解說

正解 (A)

❶ 報上名稱「我是雷射視力矯正中心眼科主治醫師」，❸ 宣傳 our computerizd laser surgery may be able to help「我們的電腦化雷射手術很可能會幫您一個大忙」。vision「視力」；correction「矯正、修正」。

題目 / 中文翻譯	重點解說

84

According to the speaker, why should listeners choose this business?
(A) It has an experienced staff.
(B) It has reasonable rates.
(C) It has a large selection of items.
(D) It is open seven days a week.

根據談話者所言，為什麼聽眾應該選這家公司？
(A) 經驗豐富的人員。
(B) 合理的價格。
(C) 選項繁多。
(D) 天天不打烊。

正解 (A)

說話者說明選擇Meadowbrook雷射視力矯正中心的理由，是 ❷ **Because we've performed thousands of vision correction procedures**「因為我們施行過數以千計的眼科矯正手術」。由此可得知該中心的醫師經驗豐富。experienced「經驗豐富的」。

85

What special offer is being made?
(A) An extended warranty
(B) Sample merchandise
(C) A free consultation
(D) Next-day delivery

在此提供哪項特殊服務？
(A) 延長保固
(B) 商品樣本
(C) 免費諮商
(D) 隔日到貨

正解 (C)

❹ 提到 We're offering a free consultation to our first one hundred customers「前一百名顧客可享免費諮詢」，因此答案為 (C)。
(A) warranty「保固、保證書」。

題目 / 中文翻譯

Questions 86 through 88 refer to the following talk.

Good afternoon. I'd like to welcome you all to today's seminar on telephone sales techniques. As you know, ❶**we're getting ready to introduce our new software program**, and we've decided to focus on telephone marketing as a way to generate interest in our product. Today we'll explain how to persuade people, during a short telephone conversation, to meet with you for a product demonstration— ❷**your goal will be to set up a face-to-face meeting.** Now, ❸**we're going to get started by listening to a few recorded conversations between potential customers and our most successful salespeople.**

請參考以下的談話回答第 **86** 題至第 **88** 題。

午安，歡迎各位來到今天的電話銷售技巧研討會。如你們所知，我們已經準備好要引進新型的軟體程式，而且我們也決定將重心擺在電話行銷，用這種方法引起對我們產品的興趣。今天我們會說明如何在短暫的電話交談中說服人們，讓你能夠進行產品展示——而你的目標就是建立面對面的會面。現在，我們就要開始了，我們先來聽一些潛在顧客與我們最成功的銷售人員之間的談話錄音內容。

題目 / 中文翻譯

86

What is the company preparing to do?
(A) Open another branch
(B) Improve customer service
(C) Research marketing trends
(D) Launch a new product

公司準備要做什麼？
(A) 開另一家分店
(B) 改善顧客服務
(C) 研究行銷趨勢
(D) 發表新產品

重點解說

正解 (D)

❶ 說明 we're getting ready to introduce our new software program「我們已經準備好要引進新型的軟體程式」。introduce「引進…」可置換成 (D) 的 launch「發表」。

題目 / 中文翻譯	重點解說

87

What goal does the speaker set for the listeners?
(A) To create a software program
(B) To get customers to meet with them
(C) To provide high-quality support
(D) To reduce production costs

談話者為聽眾所設立的目標為何？
(A) 創造軟體程式。
(B) 讓顧客與他們親自碰面。
(C) 提供高品質的支援。
(D) 減少生產成本。

正解 (B)

❷ 說 your goal will be to set up a face-to-face meeting「你的目標就是建立面對面的會面」，因此正確答案為 (B)。＜ get ＋受詞＋ to do ＞意思是「（透過說服等方式）使（人）去做…」。

88

What will listeners most likely do next?
(A) Meet the company president
(B) Call potential customers
(C) Listen to recordings
(D) Rehearse a presentation

聽眾最有可能的下一步動作為何？
(A) 與公司總裁會面
(B) 打電話給潛在客戶
(C) 聆聽錄音檔
(D) 彩排簡報

正解 (C)

❸ 提到 we're going to get started by listening to a few recorded conversations between potential customers and our most successful salespeople.「我們先來聽一些潛在顧客與我們最成功的銷售人員之間的談話錄音內容。」可得知接下來要聽的是會話的錄音檔。

題目 / 中文翻譯

Questions 89 through 91 refer to the following announcement.

Hi, everybody. Quick announcement about this weekend. ❶ **Our office building will be undergoing some repairs Saturday morning and, uh, the electricity will be off for about three hours.** ❷ **For any of you planning to come in on Saturday, power should be restored by one o'clock.** So, you might want to wait until later to come in, when everything's up and running. ❸ **I'll notify you by e-mail once the work's done.**

請參考以下的公告回答第 89 題至第 91 題。

嗨，大家好。迅速宣佈本週事項。本週六上午辦公大樓將進行整修，所以將會停電約三小時。如果有人打算在星期六來，一點之後電力才會回復。因此，你們可能得等到晚一點再來，到時一切便會就緒且恢復運作。工程一結束，我會寄發電子郵件通知大家。

題目 / 中文翻譯

89

What problem does the speaker mention?
(A) Some staff members must be reassigned.
(B) A shipment of equipment will be delayed.
(C) A building will be without power.
(D) Some computers must be replaced.

談話者提到哪個問題？
(A) 有些員工必須重新派任。
(B) 設備延誤運送。
(C) 大樓將會停電。
(D) 電腦會被淘汰。

重點解說

正解 (C)

❶ 提到「本週六上午辦公大樓將進行整修，所以將會停電約三小時」。the electricity will be off 可以置換成 (C) 的 will be without power。

(A) reassign「重新派任…」。

題目 / 中文翻譯	重點解說

90

What does the speaker imply when he says, "you might want to wait until later to come in"?
(A) Employees should take the day off.
(B) A due date has been pushed back.
(C) Staff should not come to the office in the morning.
(D) A meeting is at an inconvenient time.

談話者提到「you might want to wait until later to come in」的用意為何？
(A) 員工應該放假。
(B) 延後期限。
(C) 員工早上不該進辦公室。
(D) 開會選在一個不方便的時間舉行。

正解 (C)

might want to do 是用以表示委婉建議，底線部份的意思是「你們可能得等到晚一點再來」。❶和❷指出，「本週六上午辦公大樓將停電約三小時，約下午一點才會復電」，因此可以判斷男士和女士說的是「最好下午再進辦公室」。

91

What does the speaker say he will do?
(A) Ask for volunteers
(B) Send colleagues a message
(C) Run a software check
(D) Meet with team leaders

談話者表示他會做什麼事情？
(A) 要求自願者
(B) 發送訊息給同事
(C) 執行軟體檢查
(D) 會見團隊領袖

正解 (B)

從❶的 Our office building... 可以得知，說話者和傾聽者是在同一棟大樓工作的同事。而且說❸ **I'll notify you by e-mail once the work's done.**「工程一結束，我會寄發電子郵件通知大家」，可知正確答案為 (B)。

題目 / 中文翻譯

Questions 92 through 94 refer to the following telephone message.

Hello, Ms. Feldman. This is Geraldine Whitney at the Metropolitan Hotel. ❶You asked about the, um, art exhibitions that'll be showing while you're in the city for your sales meeting. ❷I wanted to let you know that the current contemporary art show at the Andrews Museum has had great reviews — it's really very popular right now. If you're interested, ❸the hotel can get tickets and put them aside for you — that way you'll have admission to the museum without having to wait in a long line to pay the fee. So, please let me know if you'd like me to do this, and anyway, I hope you enjoy your stay in the city.

請參考以下的電話留言回答第 92 題至第 94 題。

Feldman 女士您好，我是大都會飯店的 Geraldine Whitney。您詢問關於，呃，您來這座城市參加銷售會議時正好展出的展覽活動。我想讓您知道的是，當前正在 Andrews 博物館展出的當代藝術展深獲好評——目前大受歡迎。若您有興趣，本飯店可為您購票並將票券保留給您，如此一來，您將可以省去大排長龍購票的麻煩，直接進入博物館參觀。因此，請讓我知道您是否需要我提供此項服務，另外，祝您在本市玩得愉快。

題目 / 中文翻譯

92

What is the purpose of the call?
(A) To respond to an inquiry
(B) To confirm a reservation
(C) To apologize for an error
(D) To ask about business hours

來電的目的為何？
(A) 回覆疑問
(B) 確認預約內容
(C) 為錯誤道歉
(D) 詢問營業時間

重點解說

正解 (A)

❶ 中說的是「您詢問關於您在這座城市時，正好展出的展覽活動」，❷ 之後是關於這個問題的回覆，因此選項 (A) 為最適合的答案。respond to...「回覆…」；inquiry「查詢」。(C) apologize「道歉」。

題目 / 中文翻譯	重點解說

93

What does the speaker mention about the Andrews Museum?
(A) It is being renovated.
(B) It is located next to the hotel.
(C) The current show is very good.
(D) Admission is free of charge.

談話者提到關於 Andrews 博物館的哪件事情？
(A) 正在重新裝潢。
(B) 位於飯店旁邊。
(C) 目前的展覽非常棒。
(D) 免費入場參觀。

正解 (C)

❷中提到I wanted to let you know that the current contemporary art show at the Andrews Museum has had great reviews — it's really very popular right now.「我想讓您知道的是，當前正在 Andrews 博物館展出的當代藝術展深獲好評——目前大受歡迎」。(D) admission「入場（證）」。

94

What does the speaker offer to do?
(A) Issue a refund
(B) Reschedule a meeting
(C) Arrange a city tour
(D) Purchase tickets in advance

談話者提供哪項服務？
(A) 發放退款
(B) 重新安排會議時間
(C) 安排市區觀光
(D) 預先購買票券

正解 (D)

❸提議the hotel can get tickets and put them aside for you「本飯店可為您購票並將票券保留給您」。in advance「預先」。

題目 / 中文翻譯

Questions 95 through 97 refer to the following telephone message and order form.

Hello, this is Ellen calling from Pennington Technology. ❶**I wanted to follow up with you about the catering order form that I e-mailed you last week.** ❷**It's for the board meeting our company's holding tomorrow.** ❸**I'd like to double the number of beverages**, since it'll be a long meeting and people might get thirsty. Also, I wanted to let you know that ❹**when you arrive at our company's office, you'll have to check in at the security desk to pick up a visitor's badge.** I've already let the security guard know, so there should be a badge ready for you.

請參考以下的電話留言與訂購單回答第 95 題至第 97 題。

您好，我是 Pennington 科技公司的 Ellen。我想要跟您確認上週以電子郵件寄給您的外燴訂購單。這是為了本公司將於明天舉辦的董事會會議，所以飲料數量我想增加一倍，因為會議時間冗長，而且大家可能會覺得口渴。此外，我想要讓您知道的是，當您抵達本公司辦公室時，您必須在安檢櫃台受檢，並配戴訪客識別證。我已經知會過警衛人員，所以將會為您準備識別證件。

題目 / 中文翻譯

95

What type of event is being catered?
(A) An academic lecture
(B) A retirement party
(C) A product launch
(D) A business meeting

哪一種活動需要外燴服務？
(A) 學術演講
(B) 退休宴會
(C) 產品發表會
(D) 商業會議

重點解說

正解 (D)

cater「提供飲食」。女士說❶「我想要跟您確認上週以電子郵件寄給您的外燴訂購單」，接下來說❷ **It's for the board meeting our company's holding tomorrow.**「這是為了本公司將於明天舉辦的董事會會議」，可知是因為召開商業會議而需訂購外燴服務。

題目 / 中文翻譯

重點解說

96

Look at the graphic. Which quantity on the original order form is no longer accurate?

Order form 489275 Customer: Pennington Technology	
Item	**Quantity**
Sandwich Trays	2
Green Salad Bowls	3
Fruit Juice Bottles	15
Plate and Utensil Sets	20

(A) 2
(B) 3
(C) 15
(D) 20

請看此表。原訂購單中的哪項數量已不再正確？
(A) 2
(B) 3
(C) 15
(D) 20

正解 (C)

訂單編號 489275 客戶名稱：Pennington 科技公司	
品項	數量
三明治拼盤	2
鮮綠沙拉	3
新鮮瓶裝果汁	15
餐盤及用具組	20

❸ 中提出I'd like to double the number of beverages「飲料數量我想增加一倍」。對照圖表，可見飲料部份是 Fruit Juice Bottles「新鮮瓶裝果汁」，原先訂購數量為 15，因此正確答案為 (C)。

97

What is the listener asked to do tomorrow?
(A) Pick up an identification badge
(B) Give a speech
(C) Arrive early to set up a room
(D) Bring additional staff

聆聽者被要求明天需做哪件事情？
(A) 配戴識別證件
(B) 發表演說
(C) 提早到達，並布置室內
(D) 帶更多的人員前來

正解 (A)

關於明天送外燴的事，❹ 指出 when you arrive at our company's office, you'll have to check in at the security desk to pick up a visitor's badge.「當您抵達本公司辦公室時，您必須在安檢櫃台受檢，並配戴訪客識別證」。a visitor's badge，可以置換成 (A)an identification badge「識別（訪客等）身份的證件」。identification「識別、身份確認」。

題目 / 中文翻譯

Questions 98 through 100 refer to the following excerpt from a meeting and chart.

I'd like to start our meeting by reviewing the results of the customer feedback survey. This was given to ❶**all our passengers who took flights with us** last year. As you can see, we're doing well for the most part, but there's one area that's definitely lacking. For the rest of the meeting, ❷**I'd like everyone to think of ways we can address the area with the lowest rating.** We've got a lot of competition, and ❸**we want to make sure travelers continue to choose us as their main airline.** ❹**As you present your ideas, I'll write them on the whiteboard and send out a summary afterwards.**

請參考以下的會議節錄內容與圖表回答第 98 題至第 100 題。

在開始會議前，我想先來審視顧客回饋調查結果。這些調查的對象是去年所有搭乘本公司航線的乘客。如各位所見，大部份我們都表現得很好，但是在某個地方卻出現明顯缺失。在接下來的會議時間裡，我希望每個人都能針對顯示最低評價的區塊想出一些改進的方法。我們面臨的競爭十分激烈，而我們想要確保旅客會繼續將我們的班機視為他們的首選。當各位發表自己的想法時，我會全部寫在白板上，之後再寄發摘要整理給各位。

題目 / 中文翻譯

98

Where does the speaker most likely work?
(A) At a post office
(B) At an airline
(C) At a travel agency
(D) At an Internet company

談話者最有可能的工作地點在哪裡？
(A) 郵局
(B) 航空公司
(C) 旅行社
(D) 網路公司

重點解說

正解 (B)

❶ 中提到 all our passengers who took fights with us「所有搭乘本公司航線的乘客」，❸ 提到we want to make sure travelers continue to choose us as their main airline「我們想要確保旅客會繼續將我們的班機視為他們的首選」，由此可知談話者的工作地點應為航空公司。

題目 / 中文翻譯

重點解說

99

Look at the graphic. What does the speaker want the listeners to discuss?

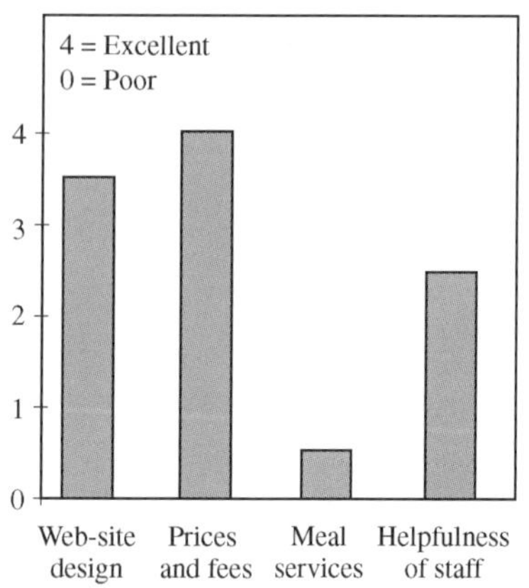

(A) Web-site design
(B) Prices and fees
(C) Meal services
(D) Helpfulness of staff

請看此圖。談話者想要聽眾討論的是哪個部份？
(A) 網站設計
(B) 價格與費用
(C) 餐點服務
(D) 人員的協助性

正解 (C)

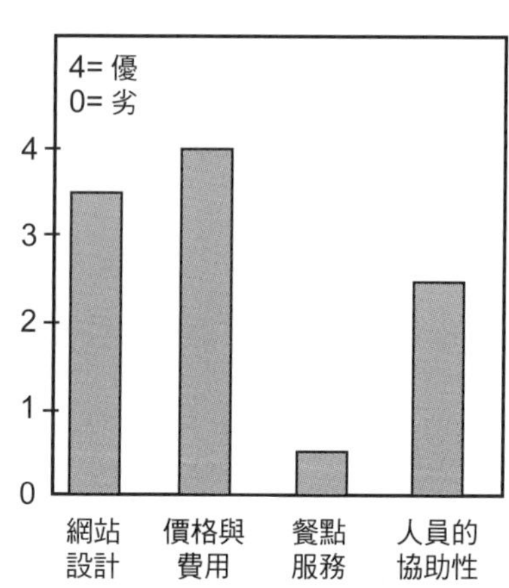

❷ 說的是 I'd like everyone to think of ways we can address the area with the lowest rating「我希望每個人都能針對顯示最低評價的區塊想出一些改進的方法」。對照圖表，可以看到最低評價的區塊為 Meal services「餐點服務」，因此正解為 (C)。

100

What will the speaker do after the discussion?
(A) Review some résumés
(B) Book some tickets
(C) Contact a customer
(D) Create a summary

談話者在討論結束後會做哪件事情？
(A) 重新審查履歷表
(B) 訂購機票
(C) 聯絡顧客
(D) 整理摘要

正解 (D)

❹ 說的是 As you present your ideas, I'll write them on the whiteboard and send out a summary afterwards.「當各位發表自己的想法時，我會全部寫在白板上，之後再寄發摘要整理給各位。」summary「摘要整理」。
(A) resume「履歷」。

題目 / 中文翻譯

101 正解 (B)

Busan Cosmetics is pleased to ------- Jin-Sook Kim, a new team member in product development.

Busan 化妝品公司很高興在此向產品開發部門新進團隊成員 Jin- Sook Kim 表示歡迎。

(A) welcoming
(B) welcome
(C) welcomed
(D) welcomes

(A) 歡迎（現在進行式或現在分詞）
(B) 歡迎（原形動詞）
(C) 歡迎（過去式或過去分詞）
(D) 歡迎（第三人稱單數）

重點解說 選項都是動詞 welcome「歡迎」的變化型態。be pleased to do「很高興去做…」，因此正解為原形動詞 (B) welcome。product development「產品開發」。

---

102 正解 (D)

The seminar will be attended ------- professionals in the food service industry.

食品服務業的專家將出席此研討會。

(A) of
(B) over
(C) as
(D) by

(A) …的
(B) 在…上面
(C) 以…的身分
(D) 被、由

重點解說 選項都是介係詞。主詞 The seminar，動詞是被動語態 will be attended。空格之後 professionals「專家們」是 attended 這個動作的主體，因此 (D) by「由…」是正解。

---

103 正解 (A)

The Human Resources Department will ------- request that employees update their personal contact information for the company's records.

人力資源處有時會要求員工更新個人聯絡資訊作為公司記錄之用。

(A) occasionally
(B) previously
(C) recently
(D) lately

(A) 偶爾
(B) 先前
(C) 最近（用於過去式或現在完成式）
(D) 最近（用於現在完成式）

重點解說 選項都是副詞。動詞 will request 表示主詞的意圖和計畫，適合用來修飾的字是 (A) occasionally「偶爾」。

題目 / 中文翻譯

104 正解 (A)

All staff members should log in to their time and labor ------- daily to record their hours worked.

(A) accounts
(B) accounted
(C) accountant
(D) accountable

全體員工必須每天必須登錄勤務管理帳號以便記錄他們的工時。

(A) 帳號（名詞複數）
(B) 解釋（過去式或過去分詞）
(C) 會計師（名詞）
(D) 應負（說明）責任的（形容詞）

重點解說 log in to...「登錄…」後面應接受詞的名詞。their time and labor 要修飾空格的詞，因此名詞 account「（電腦系統等的）帳號」的複數形 (A) accounts 最恰當。

---

105 正解 (D)

The Humson Company has just started a lunchtime fitness program, and employees are encouraged to -------.

(A) win
(B) order
(C) collect
(D) join

Humson 公司剛剛啟動午休健身計畫，並鼓勵員工參與。

(A) 獲勝
(B) 命令
(C) 收集
(D) 參與

重點解說 選項都是動詞。and 之後是主詞 employees「員工」，動詞 are encouraged，意思是「員工被鼓勵去做…」。前半段寫到「公司啟動了計畫」，因此選 (D) join「參與」最符合前後文意。

---

106 正解 (C)

To enroll in any course, either complete the online form ------- register in person at the Greerson Learning Center.

(A) if
(B) and
(C) or
(D) but

欲註冊任何課程，請完成線上表格或親至 Greerson 學習中心報名。

(A) 如果
(B) 並且
(C) 或者
(D) 但是

重點解說 選項都是連接詞。either A or B 的意思是「不是 A 就是 B」，因此正解為 (C)。either 後的 A（= complete the online form）和 B（= register in person at the Greerson Learning Center）是並列關係，舉出兩種註冊方法，分別是「完成線上表格」和「親至中心報名」。enroll「註冊」; in person「親自」。

題目 / 中文翻譯

107 正解 (B)

Mr. Yamagata is prepared to assist Ms. Hahn's clients while ------- conducts a training seminar in New York.

當 Hahn 女士人在紐約主持培訓課程期間，Yamagata 先生已做好協助 Hahn 女士客戶的準備。

(A) hers
(B) she
(C) herself
(D) her

(A) 她的東西（所有格代名詞）
(B) 她（主格）
(C) 她自己（反身代名詞）
(D) 她的（所有格、受格）

重點解說　重點在連接詞 while「當…的時候」的後面。空格後有動詞 conducts，因此空格應該選當做主詞的主格 (B) she。這裡的 she 指的是 Ms. Hahn。

---

108 正解 (A)

Please return the signed copy of the ------- agreement to the apartment manager's office in the enclosed envelope.

請將已簽名的租賃合約書放入信封封好後交回公寓管理員辦公室。

(A) rental
(B) rentable
(C) rented
(D) rents

(A) 租賃（形容詞）
(B) 可租賃的（形容詞）
(C) 已租賃（形容詞）
(D) 租金（名詞複數）

重點解說　由空格前定冠詞 the 和後面接的名詞 agreement「合約書」，可知空格內應填入形容詞加以修飾。再根據句意選出最貼切的答案應為 (A) rental「租賃的」。signed copy「已簽名文件」；enclosed「封好的」。

---

109 正解 (D)

Employees who are affiliated with Corman Corporation will be seated ------- the third row of the auditorium.

Corman 公司旗下員工請坐在觀眾席第三排的位置。

(A) except
(B) to
(C) among
(D) in

(A) 除…之外
(B) 往…的方向
(C) 在…之中
(D) 在

重點解說　選項都是介係詞。符合文意的是 (D) in the third row「在第三排」為最貼切的答案。be affiliated with...「附屬於…、和…相關聯的」；row「（座位）排」；auditorium「禮堂、觀眾席」。

題目 / 中文翻譯

110 正解 (C)

Yesterday's festival featured some of the most ------- dancers that the Palace Theater has ever hosted.

昨天的慶典特別介紹在 Palace 戲院主辦過的活動中最有活力的舞者群。

(A) live
(B) liveliness
(C) lively
(D) livelier

(A) 活著的（形容詞）
(B) 活力（名詞）
(C) 有活力的（形容詞）
(D) 更有活力的（lively 比較級）

重點解說　空格前是表示最高級的形容詞 the most，之後接名詞 dancers。對 the most 來說，最適當的是能表現最高級的形容詞 (C) lively「（人物等）有活力的」。

---

111 正解 (A)

Fulsome Flowers' delivery vans must be returned promptly to the store ------- the scheduled deliveries have been completed.

Fulsome 花店的宅配貨車一完成預定送貨行程後就必須立即折返。

(A) once
(B) soon
(C) often
(D) usually

(A) 一…就…（連接詞）
(B) 很快地（副詞）
(C) 經常地（副詞）
(D) 通常（副詞）

重點解說　空格前後都是<主詞＋動詞>，因此應該用連接詞 (A)once「一…就…」連接兩個句子。promptly「立即地」。

---

112 正解 (A)

To ensure stability and safety, it is important to follow the instructions ------- when assembling the office bookshelves.

為保障穩定度與安全性，在進行辦公室書櫃組裝時，確實遵守說明書指示是相當重要的。

(A) exactly
(B) exact
(C) exactness
(D) exacting

(A) 確實地（副詞）
(B) 確實的（形容詞）
(C) 確實性（名詞）
(D) 嚴格的（形容詞）

重點解說　為了修飾空格前的 follow the instructions「遵守說明書指示」，空格填上副詞 (A) exactly「確實地」最為合適。空格後是說明「在辦公室組裝書櫃的情況下」。ensure「保證」；stability「穩定度」；assemble「組裝」。

題目 / 中文翻譯

113 正解 (D)

At the Podell Automotive plant, Ms. Krystle ------- workers who install rebuilt engines in vehicles.

(A) conducts
(B) explains
(C) invests
(D) oversees

Krystle 女士在 Podell 車廠監督著工人們將再生引擎安裝至汽車上。

(A) 執行
(B) 解釋
(C) 投資
(D) 監督

重點解說 選項都是第三人稱單數動詞。空格內動詞的受詞是「將再生引擎安裝至汽車上的工人」，因此符合文意的是 (D) oversees「監督」。install「安裝」；rebuilt「再生的、重建的」。

---

114 正解 (B)

Yakubu Logistics will expand the warehouse loading area in preparation for an ------- in shipping activity.

(A) increased
(B) increase
(C) increases
(D) increasingly

Yokubu 物流公司將擴建倉庫儲貨區，做好應付貨運業務增量的準備。

(A) 增加（過去式或過去分詞）
(B) 增加（名詞單數）
(C) 增加（名詞複數）
(D) 漸增地（副詞）

重點解說 由空格前的冠詞 an 和空格後的介系詞片語 in shipping activity「貨運業務」，知道單數名詞 (B) increase「增加」最合適。expand「擴大」；warehouse「倉庫」；loading area「儲貨區」；in preparation for...「做好…準備」。

---

115 正解 (B)

The High Performance weather gauge is ------- accurate in measuring the level of humidity in the air.

(A) surprising
(B) surprisingly
(C) surprised
(D) surprises

High Performance 晴雨表在測量空氣濕度方面有驚人的準確度。

(A) 令人驚訝的（形容詞）
(B) 令人驚訝地（副詞）
(C) 感到驚訝的（形容詞）
(D) 讓…驚訝（第三人稱單數）

重點解說 空格前為 be 動詞 is，空格後接形容詞 accurate「精準的」，因此應選副詞用以修飾 accurate，答案為 (B) surprisingly「令人驚訝地」。gauge「測量儀器」；measure「測量…」；humidity「濕度」。

題目/中文翻譯

116 正解 (D)

Ms. Oh's proposal highlights a ------- strategy for decreasing the company's transportation costs in the coming year.

Oh 女士的企畫案強調一項削減公司來年運輸成本的全面性策略。

(A) surrounding
(B) securing
(C) relative
(D) comprehensive

(A) 周圍的
(B) 確保的
(C) 相對的
(D) 全面的

重點解說　選項都是形容詞。要修飾空格後的名詞句 strategy for decreasing the company's transportation costs「削減公司運輸成本的策略」，依文意來看，(D) comprehensive「全面的」最貼切。highlight「（動詞）強調…」；strategy「策略」。

---

117 正解 (D)

To receive ------- updates regarding your journal subscription status, please provide an e-mail address on the order form.

為取得期刊訂閱狀態的定期更新內容，請您於訂購單內提供電子郵件信箱。

(A) period
(B) periods
(C) periodicals
(D) periodic

(A) 期間（名詞單數）
(B) 期間（名詞複數）
(C) 期刊（名詞複數）
(D) 定期的（形容詞）

重點解說　空格前為動詞 receive「收到」，之後是當做受詞的名詞 updates「更新內容」，因此空格內應填入形容詞來加以修飾，故答案為 (D) periodic「定期的」。journal「期刊」；subscription「訂閱」。

---

118 正解 (B)

------- when they are away conducting business, members of the sales team are usually available by e-mail.

銷售部人員即便外出執行業務，通常亦可透過電子郵件聯繫。

(A) Both
(B) Even
(C) Ahead
(D) Whether

(A) 兩者都（副詞）
(B) 即使（副詞）
(C) 在前方（副詞）
(D) 不管是（連接詞）

重點解說　逗點前方為連接詞 when 開頭的完整子句，因此空格應填入修飾 when 用的副詞。even when 的意思是「即使」，因此正解為 (B) even「即使」。

題目 / 中文翻譯

119 正解 (A)

There is a coffee machine ------- located on the second floor of the Tabor Building.

咖啡機設置在 Tabor 大樓二樓相當便利的位置。

(A) conveniently
(B) slightly
(C) considerably
(D) eventually

(A) 便利地
(B) 輕微地
(C) 大量地
(D) 最後地

重點解說 選項都是副詞。 There is...「有…」的句中，空格後的部分修飾 a coffee machine。後面接過去分詞 located「位於」，因此空格為副詞，再由前後句意判斷，選 (A) conveniently「便利地」最為恰當。

---

120 正解 (C)

The editor granted Ms. Porter a deadline ------- so that some information in her building renovations report could be updated.

編輯同意 Porter 女士的截稿日延期，好讓她的建物修繕報告書得以更新某些資訊。

(A) extend
(B) extensive
(C) extension
(D) extends

(A) 延長（動詞）
(B) 廣泛的（形容詞）
(C) 延長（名詞）
(D) 延長（第三人稱單數）

重點解說 < grant ＋人＋…>意思是「同意（某人）…」，因此空格前是「編輯同意 Porter 女士的截稿日…是為了…」。和 a deadline 一起成為受詞的是名詞 (C) extension「延長」。

---

121 正解 (A)

Youssouf Electronics' annual charity fund-raising event ------- next Saturday at Montrose Park.

Youssouf 電子的年度慈善募款活動將於下週六在 Montrose 公園舉辦。

(A) will be held
(B) to hold
(C) to be held
(D) will hold

(A) 將被舉辦（被動式）
(B) 去舉辦（to 不定詞）
(C) 被舉辦（to 不定詞）
(D) 將舉辦（未來式）

重點解說 從 Youssouf Electronics' 到 event 是句中主詞，這句話缺少動詞，因此空格內應填入動詞。空格後沒有受詞，因此應使用被動語態，答案為 (A) will be held，意思是「（活動）將被舉辦」。fund-raising「募款」。

題目 / 中文翻譯

122 正解 (D)

The buildings in the Jamison Complex are open until 7:00 P.M. on workdays, but staff with proper ------- may enter at any time.

(A) reinforcement
(B) participation
(C) competency
(D) authorization

Jamison 綜合大樓的建築物平日開放至晚間七點，但有正當權限的員工則可隨時進入。

(A) 加強
(B) 參與
(C) 能力
(D) 權限

重點解說　選項都是名詞。逗點前的意思是「建築物平日開放至晚間七點」，but「但是」之後又說「有正當權限的員工則可隨時進入」。因此從文意來看，適合的是 (D) authorization「權限」。workday「平日」；proper「正當的」。

---

123 正解 (B)

Kochi Engineering has proposed the construction of a drainage system ------- to keep the Route 480 highway dry during heavy rain.

(A) was designed
(B) designed
(C) designer
(D) designing

Kochi 工程已經提出專為 480 號幹線道路設計的排水系統建案，目的在於確保道路在大雨期間能夠維持乾燥。

(A) 被設計（被動語態的過去式）
(B) 設計（過去分詞）
(C) 設計師（名詞）
(D) 設計（動詞的現在分詞）

重點解說　空格後的部份，修飾前面的 a drainage system「排水系統」。排水系統因為「被設計」成確保道路在大雨期間能夠維持乾燥，因此應該用過去分詞 (B) designed。highway「幹線道路」；dry「維持乾燥」。

---

124 正解 (D)

Customers can obtain coverage for replacement and repair of printers ------- the purchase of an extended warranty.

(A) although
(B) because
(C) since
(D) through

顧客可藉由購買延長保固，取得印表機更換或維修保固範圍。

(A) 雖然（連接詞）
(B) 因為（連接詞）
(C) 自從（介係詞、連接詞）
(D) 藉由（介係詞）

重點解說　空格前的意思是「顧客可取得保固」。空格後是 the purchase of an extended warranty「購買延長保固」的名詞句，因此空格要填入介係詞。因此選擇代表方法的 (D) through「藉由」。coverage「保固範圍」。

題目 / 中文翻譯

125 正解 (D)

We regret to announce that Mr. Charles Appiah has resigned his position as senior sales manager, ------- next Monday.

(A) effect
(B) effected
(C) effectiveness
(D) effective

我們非常遺憾在此宣布 Charles Appiah 先生請辭資深銷售經理乙職，並將於下週一生效。

(A) 效果；產生（名詞或原形動詞）
(B) 產生（動詞的過去式或過去分詞）
(C) 有效性（名詞）
(D) 生效的（形容詞）

重點解說 這是宣布 Mr. Charles Appiah 請辭的文句，句末標示日期為 next Monday「下週一」。空格應該填入 (D) effective，放在日期或星期幾之前，表示那一天開始生效。regret to do「遺憾地做…」；resign「請辭」。

---

126 正解 (B)

The Epsilon 3000 camera allows beginning photographers to enjoy professional-quality equipment, as it is ------- sophisticated yet inexpensive.

(A) gradually
(B) technologically
(C) annually
(D) productively

Epsilon 3000 照相機技術精巧但價格親民，讓攝影新手能夠盡情享受專業水準的設備。

(A) 逐漸地
(B) 技術上
(C) 年度地
(D) 高效地

重點解說 選項都是副詞。空格前的 it 指的是 The Epsilon 3000 camera。要修飾空格後接的形容詞 sophisticated「精巧的、高性能的」，符合文意的是 (B) technologically「技術上」。yet「儘管如此」。

---

127 正解 (C)

Yee-Yin Xiong held interviews with numerous clients to determine ------- Echegaray Consulting, Inc., can improve customer service.

(A) unless
(B) in order to
(C) how
(D) as if

為決定 Echegaray 顧問公司顧客服務改善辦法，Yee-Yin Xiong 與諸多客戶進行訪談。

(A) 除非…
(B) 為了…
(C) 如何
(D) 就好像…一樣

重點解說 空格後的部分是受語 determine「發現…，決定…」。在這個部分，主詞是 Echegaray Consulting, Inc.，後方的 can improve 是動詞。<主詞＋動詞>後，接「…的方法」，關係副詞的 (C) how 最貼切。

題目 / 中文翻譯

128 正解 (B)

Several letters of reference from local community organizations are required for ------- into the Cypress Beach Business Association.

為了獲准進入 Cypress Beach 經貿協會，必須取得地方團體組織的數封推薦函。

(A) acquisition
(B) acceptance
(C) prospects
(D) improvement

(A) 取得
(B) 接受
(C) 前景
(D) 改善

重點解說　選項都是名詞。這句話的意思是「為了…經貿協會，需要數封推薦函」。符合文意的是 (B) acceptance「接受」。acceptance into「獲准進入」。

---

129 正解 (C)

Rather than wearing business attire on Thursdays, staff may choose to wear casual clothing -------.

與其每週四穿著上班服裝，職員們反而可能會選擇穿著便服。

(A) enough
(B) despite
(C) instead
(D) in case

(A) 足夠（副詞）
(B) 儘管（介係詞）
(C) 反而（副詞）
(D) 假如（連接詞）

重點解說　句子前方提及「與其穿著上班服裝」，接著說「可以選擇穿著便服」。兩者有對照之意，因此選擇有「取代」意思的副詞 (C) instead。rather than...「與其…倒不如…」；attire「服裝」。

---

130 正解 (C)

Your ------- registration card provides proof of ownership in case this product is lost or damaged.

若本產品遺失或受損時，您的有效產品登錄註冊卡將能提供持有證明。

(A) frequent
(B) indicative
(C) validated
(D) dispersed

(A) 頻繁的
(B) 指示的
(C) 有效的
(D) 分散的

重點解說　選項都是形容詞。關於 registration card「註冊卡」的描述是，「證明是產品的持有人」，修飾 registration card 而且又和文意相符的是 (C) validated「有效的」。proof「證明」；ownership「所有權」。

題目 / 中文翻譯

Questions 131-134 refer to the following information.

The Fern Lake Community Center is an entirely volunteer-run organization serving the Fern Lake community. -------- (131.) known among locals as "the Fern," our center offers high-quality after-school care for local children of working parents. We also -------- (132.) educational programs for all ages in our buildings on Quentin Street. -------- (133.).

In addition, the community center offers several -------- (134.) events throughout the year. The largest and most famous is our annual Fern Fair. All residents are invited to join us on April 12 this year on the Broad Street Pier to enjoy the area's best food, crafts, and musical performances while savoring the cool spring breeze.

For more information, visit www.fernlakecc.com/fair.

請參考以下資訊回答第 131 至 134 題。

Fern Lake 社區中心是一座完全由義工自營的組織，為 Fern Lake 社區提供服務。本中心被在地人普遍稱為「the Fern」，這裡為上班族爸媽提供高品質的在地兒童課後照顧服務。我們位於 Quentin 街的大樓也有適合各個年齡層的教育課程。* 這些課程包括舞蹈課和繪畫課。

此外，社區中心整年提供多種戶外活動。最大型且最有名的就是年度 Fern 社區市集。今年 4 月 12 日在 Broad 街碼頭，每位居民都將受邀與我們一邊品嚐春日微風的涼意，一邊享用本區最棒的食物、工藝品，以及音樂表演。

更多訊息請上 www.fernlakecc.com/fair 查詢。

* 為 133 題的內文翻譯

單字註釋：local「(名詞) 本地人」；savor「品味…」

題目 / 中文翻譯

131 正解 (C)

(A) Cooperatively	(A) 合作地
(B) Mutually	(B) 互相地
(C) Popularly	(C) 普遍地
(D) Essentially	(D) 本質上

重點解說 選項都是副詞。空格後接「在地人稱為『the Fern』」，可知適合修飾的是 (C) Popularly「普遍地」。

題目 / 中文翻譯

132 正解 (D)

(A) participate　(A) 參與
(B) claim　(B) 主張
(C) enroll　(C) 登記
(D) host　(D) 主辦

重點解說 選項都是動詞。空格的受詞是 educational programs「教育課程」，主詞的 We 指的是 the Fern Lake Community Center。之前的句子是「提供高品質的在地兒童課後照顧服務」，包含空格的句子有 also，因此可以判斷教育課程也和「提供…」有一樣的意思，選 (D) host「主辦」最符合文意。

---

133 正解 (D)

(A) We are not currently looking for volunteers.　(A) 我們目前並不需要招募志工。
(B) Contact our office to rent our main hall.　(B) 租用大廳請聯繫我們的辦公室。
(C) Most of these programs are no longer available.　(C) 大部分的課程都已經無法使用。
(D) These include classes in dancing and painting.　(D) 這些課程包括舞蹈課和繪畫課。

重點解說 前一句提到教育課程，接下來的第一行也提到「社區中心整年還提供多種戶外活動」，因此可以知道空格的內容和社區中心提供的計畫或活動內容有關。空格前一句的 educational programs 接在 These 後，因此選擇詳細說明的 (D) 是合理的。

---

134 正解 (A)

(A) outdoor　(A) 戶外的
(B) exclusive　(B) 獨有的
(C) athletic　(C) 運動的
(D) formal　(D) 正式的

重點解說 選項全部是形容詞。空格修飾 events，空格後面接的句子是活動的具體內容，關於社區中心提供的 Fern 社區市集，說明這是 while savoring the cool spring breeze「品嚐春日微風的涼意」，因此可知修飾活動適當的字是 (A) outdoor「戶外的」。

題目 / 中文翻譯

Questions 135-138 refer to the following information.

Rowes Atlantic Airways Baggage Policy

Each passenger ------- (135.) to carry one piece of hand baggage onto the plane without charge. The carry-on item must not exceed the dimensions 56 cm x 45 cm x 25 cm, including the handle and wheels. No carry-on bag should weigh more than 23 kg. Passengers should be ------- (136.) to lift bags into the overhead storage bins unaided. These ------- (137.) do not apply to bags that are checked in at the service desk.

A laptop computer bag, school backpack, or handbag may also be brought on board. ------- (138.).

請參考以下資訊回答第 135 至 138 題。

Rowes Atlantic 航空公司 行李規定

每位乘客可免費攜帶一個手提行李登機。手提行李尺寸不得超過 56 公分 X 45 公分 X 25 公分，行李體積包括把手與輪子。所有手提行李袋不得超過 23 公斤。乘客必須能夠自行將袋子放置於座位上方的行李存放處。已於服務櫃台登記過的行李則不在此限。

筆記型電腦提袋、學校書包或是手提袋等亦可帶上飛機。* 不使用時，請將物品安置在座位底下。

* 為 138 題的內文翻譯

單字註釋：carry-on「手提（上飛機）的」；dimensions「尺寸」；unaided「自行、獨立的」；check in「（辦理登機手續並將行李等）託運」

題目 / 中文翻譯

135 正解 (B)

(A) allowed
(B) is allowed
(C) allowing
(D) had been allowed

(A) 允許（過去式或過去分詞）
(B) 被允許（現在式被動語態）
(C) 允許（現在分詞）
(D) 曾被允許（過去完成式被動語態）

重點解說 這個問題是要選擇動詞 allow「允許…」的正確形式。空格之後沒有受詞，因此應該使用被動語態「被允許」，也就是 (B) is allowed。這篇文章因為是航空公司的行李規定，以現在式說明事實。

題目 / 中文翻譯

136 正解 (A)

(A) able
(B) ably
(C) abled
(D) ability

(A) 能夠的（形容詞）
(B) 出色地（副詞）
(C) 身體健全的（形容詞）
(D) 能力（名詞）

重點解說 空格之前為 be，之後為 to 不定詞的 to lift。因此應該選 (A) able，表示 be able to do「能夠做…」。

---

137 正解 (D)

(A) transfers
(B) suggestions
(C) duties
(D) restrictions

(A) 轉移
(B) 建議
(C) 義務
(D) 限制

重點解說 選項都是名詞的複數形。空格前的部份說明登機手提行李的限制。關於這個限制，包含空格的句子意思是，「已經在服務櫃台登記過的行李不適用這些…」，因此選 (D)。

---

138 正解 (B)

(A) Please inquire at the service desk if it will be permitted on your flight.
(B) It should be stored under the seats when not in use.
(C) Thank you for becoming a member of the flight crew.
(D) Therefore, they will be available for a small additional fee.

(A) 請洽詢服務櫃台該項物品能否帶上您的飛機。
(B) 不使用時，請將物品安置在座位底下。
(C) 感謝您成為航班組員的一份子。
(D) 因此，只要一點點的額外費用就可以利用這些。

重點解說 空格前的句子指出，能帶上飛機的提袋種類是 A laptop computer bag, school backpack, or handbag。依照文意，空格應該用 it 來指提袋類，接著說明「不使用時，要將物品安置在座位底下」，所以選 (B)。laptop 前的冠詞 A 用以統稱單數名詞，因此下一句才會出現 It should be stored。not in use「不使用」。

題目 / 中文翻譯

Questions 139-142 refer to the following article.

LONDON (18 May) – Ubero Hotels announced today that Mr. Jeffrey Pak has been promoted to vice president of global brand marketing for the worldwide hotel chain. Mr. Pak's promotion will become effective as of 2 June. His new -------- (139.) involves overseeing worldwide marketing strategies, which includes all advertising and brand promotions. -------- (140.) .

Mr. Pak was previously Ubero Hotels' regional director of business development for Southeast Asia. He -------- (141.) his career at the front desk of the Ubero Queen Sydney Hotel. Mr. Pak has stated that he believes this early experience, going back 23 years, of connecting with guests and coworkers has contributed to his hands-on -------- (142.) style.

請參考以下文章回答第 **139** 至 **142** 題。

5 月 18 日，倫敦訊——Uberto 飯店今日宣布 Jeffrey Pak 先生榮升這家世界級連鎖飯店的全球品牌行銷副總裁。Pak 先生的晉升將於 6 月 2 日生效。他的新職務包含監督全球行銷策略，內容含括所有的廣告與品牌宣傳等。* 他也負責管理 **25** 名員工。

Pak 先生之前擔任 Uberto 飯店東南亞區域業務發展主任。他的職涯是從 Uberto Queen Sydney 飯店服務台展開的。Pak 先生曾說過，他相信這可以回溯到 23 年前的早期經驗，讓他與客人和同事之間建立緊密關聯，也造就了他邊做邊學的管理風格。

* 為 **140** 題的內文翻譯

單字註釋：hands-on「（董事等高層）實際參與（實務）的」

題目 / 中文翻譯

139 正解 (D)

(A) trend	(A) 趨勢
(B) facility	(B) 設施
(C) supervisor	(C) 監督者
(D) position	(D) 職位

重點解說 選項都是名詞。報導一開始就敘述 Pak 先生榮升負責國際品牌行銷的副總裁。包含空格的句子說明了 Pak 先生的職務內容，提到「他的新…包含監督全球行銷策略」，因此選 (D) position「職位」。

題目/中文翻譯

140 正解 (A)

(A) **He will also be responsible for a staff of 25.** (A) 他也負責管理 25 名員工。
(B) Similarly, he will be relocating to London. (B) 同樣地，他也會調至倫敦。
(C) For example, he will be training new employees. (C) 例如，他將會培訓新員工。
(D) As a result, he will keep his home in Sydney. (D) 因此，他會留著雪梨的房子。

重點解說 空格前一句說明 Pak 先生新職位的負責內容。使用 also，加上職位內容的 (A) 較符合上下脈絡。be responsible for...「負責…」。

---

141 正解 (B)

(A) begins (A) 開始（現在式第三人稱單數動詞）
(B) **began** (B) 開始（過去式）
(C) is beginning (C) 正在開始（現在進行式）
(D) will begin (D) 將會開始（未來式）

重點解說 這是選擇動詞 begin「開始…」正確時式的問題。第 2 段第 1 句「Pak 先生之前擔任…」，第三句「23 年前的早期經驗」，都是在敘述 Pak 先生之前的經歷。包含空格的句子有 his career at the front desk「服務台的經歷」，因此應該選「開始…」的過去式 (B) began。

---

142 正解 (D)

(A) manage (A) 管理（原形動詞）
(B) manages (B) 管理（第三人稱單數動詞）
(C) managed (C) 管理（過去式或過去分詞）
(D) **management** (D) 管理（名詞）

重點解說 空格後接名詞 style，表示「經營風格」的意思，故選 (D) management。his hands-on 修飾 management style。

題目/中文翻譯

Questions 143-146 refer to the following e-mail.

To: Karen Karl, Staff Writer
From: Liz Steinhauer, Editor in Chief
Date: January 2
Re: Cover Article Assignment

Hi Karen,

Thank you for agreeing to work on an article about Veronica Zettici's ------- (143.) role in her recent film as actress and director. By the end of the week, please submit an overview explaining how you plan to focus the interview with her. Once our editors approve your ------- (144.), make sure to confirm the interview day and time with one of our staff photographers. It would be ideal if the article ------- (145.) the two roles Ms. Zettici played in the production of the film. ------- (146.).

I will be available throughout the week if you have any questions.

Liz

請參考以下的電子郵件回答第 **143** 至 **146** 題。

收件者：特約撰稿人 Karen Karl
寄件者：總編輯 Liz Steinhauer
寄件日期：1 月 2 日
回覆：封面文章撰寫任務

嗨，Karen 妳好：

感謝妳同意撰寫關於 Veronica Zettici 在最新電影裡身兼女演員與導演雙重角色的專文。本週結束前，請繳交提綱並說明妳要如何將焦點集中在她的訪談上面。一旦我們的編輯同意妳的提案，請務必與我們的專屬攝影師確認訪談日期和時間。要是在文章裡能夠比較 Zettici 女士在電影製作方面的雙重角色，那就再完美不過了。* 此外，這篇專文得討論她在每個領域所發揮的卓越能力。

如果妳有任何疑問，我整個星期都有空。

Liz

* 為 **146** 題的內文翻譯

題目 / 中文翻譯

143 正解 (A)

(A) double
(B) doubles
(C) doubling
(D) to double

(A) 雙重的（形容詞）
(B) 加倍（現在式第三人稱單數動詞）
(C) 加倍（現在分詞）
(D) 加倍（to 不定詞）

重點解說

空格後的 role... as actress and director「身兼女演員與導演」，可知 Veronica Zettici 在最新的電影裡扮演「雙重角色」。另外，由空格前的所有格，及空格後接名詞，可知空格內應填入形容詞 (A) double「雙重的」。

---

144 正解 (C)

(A) drawing
(B) hiring
(C) proposal
(D) edition

(A) 繪畫
(B) 雇用
(C) 提案
(D) 版本

重點解說

選項都是名詞。前一句是 please submit an overview explaining how you plan to focus the interview with her「請繳交提綱並說明妳要如何將焦點集中在她的訪談上面」。根據文意，包含空格的句子接下來是「一旦我們的編輯同意妳的…」，因此選 (C) proposal「提案」。

---

145 正解 (B)

(A) comparing
(B) compared
(C) to compare
(D) were compared

(A) 比較（現在分詞）
(B) 比較（過去式或過去分詞）
(C) 比較（to 不定詞）
(D) 被比較（過去式被動語態）

重點解說

請選擇 if 後接子句「主詞 the article」後方應接續的正確動詞形態。自 the two roles 開始是受詞，動詞應用過去式的 (B) compared。此題包含空格的句子「It would be ideal...」，是 if 子句的假定形，意思是「如果…就再完美不過了」。

題目 / 中文翻譯

146 正解 (B)

(A) For example, you might ask her about the next project on her schedule.
(B) **Furthermore, it should discuss the distinct skills she brought to each aspect.**
(C) In short, your work should be completed in two weeks.
(D) In addition, the article will be published in the April issue.

(A) 例如說，你可以詢問她關於她排定的下個計畫。
(B) 此外，文章應該討論她在每個領域所發揮的卓越能力。
(C) 總之，你的工作必須在兩週內完成。
(D) 此外，這篇文章將會發表在四月號的期刊。

重點解說 空格前的部分，描述理想的文章內容要素。用 Furthermore「此外」來加上其他要素的 (B)，最符合前後文意。it 指的即是前句的 the article。

題目 / 中文翻譯

Questions 147-148 refer to the following coupon.

Thank you for enrolling your daughter or son in the training session at T-Star Tennis Clinic! We hope your child enjoyed the lessons and comes back to T-Star Tennis Clinic again.

Use this coupon at

Great Angle Tennis Shop

to receive 30 percent off any adult- or junior-size tennis racket or 20 percent off any other tennis equipment.

For an online purchase, enter discount code **RW445**.

Valid through June 30. Cannot be combined with any other coupon. Excludes clothing, bags, and shoes.

請參考以下的優惠券回答第 147 至 148 題。

非常感謝您幫貴子女報名 T-Star 網球教室訓練課程！
希望您的孩子喜歡 T-Star 網球教室的課程，且日後能再次回來上課。

本優惠券適用於

Great Angle 網球用品店

所有成人或兒童球拍享七折優待
或任選其他網球用品八折優惠。

線上訂購請輸入折扣代碼 RW445。

即日起至 6 月 30 日前有效。無法與其他優惠券併用。
服飾、袋子與鞋類除外。

題目 / 中文翻譯

147 正解 (C)

What is suggested about T-Star Tennis Clinic?

(A) It is owned by a famous athlete.
(B) It operates in several countries.
(C) It runs a program for children.
(D) It manufactures tennis equipment.

這裡提到關於 T-Star 網球教室的哪件事？

(A) 擁有者為知名運動選手。
(B) 在數個國家皆有營運。
(C) 設有兒童課程。
(D) 製造網球用品。

重點解說
第一句敘述「非常感謝您幫貴子女報名 T-Star 網球教室訓練課程」，並接著說「希望您的孩子喜歡 T-Star 網球教室的課程，且日後能再回來上課」，因此正解為 (C)。run「經營」。
(A) athlete「運動選手」。

---

148 正解 (D)

What is true about the coupon?

(A) It expires at the end of the year.
(B) It applies only to purchases over $30.
(C) It is not valid for online purchases.
(D) It cannot be used on tennis shirts.

關於優惠券，何者為真？

(A) 有效期限為年底。
(B) 僅適用於超過 30 美金的購物。
(C) 線上訂購無效。
(D) 無法用於網球衣。

重點解說
關於優惠券的使用條件，在最後一行清楚指出 Excludes clothing, bags and shoes.「服飾、袋子與鞋類除外」，因此選 (D)。
(A) expire「期限終止而無效」；(B) apply to...「適用於…」。

單字註釋：combine「結合…」；exclude「把…排除在外」

題目

Questions 149-150 refer to the following text message chain.

Paula Malone **January 23, 8:53 A.M.**
Can you do me a favor? I'm scheduled to teach my exercise class at the gym at 9:00, and I'm going to be late. The train I'm on had a mechanical problem and left the station about 15 minutes behind schedule.

Martin Bilecki **January 23, 8:54 A.M.**
That's too bad. How can I help?

Paula Malone **January 23, 8:55 A.M.**
Would you either cancel the class or let the students know that I'll be there about 9:15?

Martin Bilecki **January 23, 8:57 A.M.**
Most of your students are already here, so I hate to cancel. Suki is also working today and is here early. I'll ask her to switch classes with you, and you can teach the 10:00 class.

Paula Malone **January 23, 8:58 A.M.**
That works out perfectly. Thanks.

中文翻譯

請參考以下一連串的簡訊回答第 149 至 150 題。

Paula Malone 1 月 23 日，上午 8 點 53 分

幫我個忙好嗎？我原本排定健身房運動課程的授課時間是 9 點，但我快遲到了。我搭乘的火車發生機械故障，結果比原定時間晚了 15 分鐘才離開車站。

Martin Bilecki 1 月 23 日，上午 8 點 54 分

真是太糟糕了。我要怎麼幫你呢？

Paula Malone 1 月 23 日，上午 8 點 55 分

你可以幫我取消這堂課，或是告知學生我會在 9 點 15 分左右抵達嗎？

Martin Bilecki 1 月 23 日，上午 8 點 57 分

你大部分的學生都已經到了，所以我不想取消。Suki 今天也有上班，而且早就來了。我會請她和你調課，這樣你可以教 10 點那堂課。

Paula Malone 1 月 23 日，上午 8 點 58 分

這樣太好了。謝謝。

題目 / 中文翻譯

149 正解 (D)

What does Mr. Bilecki indicate he will do?

(A) Arrive late to the gym
(B) Teach a class
(C) Cancel a class
(D) Change the instructors' schedules

Bilecki 先生暗示他將會做哪件事？

(A) 晚到健身房
(B) 教授一堂課
(C) 取消課程
(D) 更改講師的授課時間表

重點解說 Bilecki 先生在上午 8 點 57 分的簡訊裡提到另一位講師 Suki 女士，並表示 I'll ask her to switch classes with you, and you can teach the 10:00 class.「我會請她和你調課，這樣你可以教 10 點那堂課」，因此答案為 (D)。

---

150 正解 (A)

At 8:58 A.M., what does Ms. Malone most likely mean when she writes, "That works out perfectly"?

(A) She likes Mr. Bilecki's idea.
(B) She likes exercising in the morning.
(C) She is excited about her new job.
(D) She is happy that she has the day off.

上午 8 點 58 分時，當 Malone 女士寫下「That works out perfectly」，她最有可能想要表達的意思為何？

(A) 她喜歡 Bilecki 先生的想法
(B) 她喜歡晨間運動
(C) 她對於新工作感到興奮
(D) 休假讓她感到開心

重點解說 That works out perfectly 意指「這樣太好了」。這是對於 Bilecki 先生提議「和 Suki 女士調課」而說的話，因此可以得知 Malone 女士喜歡 Bilecki 先生的想法，故正解為 (A)。work out「進展順利」。

單字註釋：mechanical 機械的；hate to do 不想做…；switch 交換…

題目/中文翻譯

Questions 151-152 refer to the following notice.

Dear Atrium Hotel Guests:

❶ We would like to apologize for the warm temperatures in the hallways and elevators. The hotel is currently undergoing work to upgrade our air-conditioning system. The new system will improve our energy efficiency and increase the comfort of our common areas.

❷ Please note that this work does not affect the air-conditioning units in guest rooms. If there is anything we can do to make your stay more enjoyable, please feel free to contact any of our staff by dialing "0" from your room.

請參考以下公告回答第 **151** 至 **152** 題。

各位親愛的 Atrium 飯店貴賓您好：

關於走廊和電梯的高溫，我們在此深感抱歉。目前飯店正在進行空調系統更新的工程。新的系統將會改善我們的能源使用效率，並增加公共區域的舒適度。

請注意，這項工程並不會影響客房內的空調設備。為了讓您在居住期間感到愉悅，若您有任何需要我們協助之處，歡迎使用您房間的電話，請撥 0 隨時與我們的人員聯繫。

題目 / 中文翻譯

151 正解 (B)

Where would the notice most likely appear?

(A) In an airport terminal
(B) In a hotel lobby
(C) In an office building
(D) In a shopping plaza

該公告最有可能出現在何處？

(A) 機場航廈
(B) 飯店大廳
(C) 辦公大樓
(D) 購物廣場

重點解說　由公告開頭 Dear Atrium Hotel Guests「各位親愛的 Atrium 飯店貴賓」，可知正解為 (B)。

---

152 正解 (A)

What is being replaced?

(A) The air-conditioning system
(B) The telephone system
(C) The furniture
(D) The elevators

要汰換的東西為何？

(A) 空調系統
(B) 電話設備
(C) 家具
(D) 電梯

重點解說　根據公告中第一段第二句，The hotel is currently undergoing work to upgrade our air-conditioning system.「目前飯店正在進行空調系統更新的工程」，可知答案為 (A)。

單字註釋：hallway「走廊」; undergo「經歷（變化等）」; comfort「舒適」; feel free to do「任意做…」

題目

Questions 153-154 refer to the following e-mail.

E-mail

To: m.agrawal@indiatip.net
From: pritidoshi@hscot.in
Date: 17 May
Subject: IndiaTip

Dear Ms. Agrawal,

❶ My name is Priti Doshi, and I'm an avid cyclist in Bangalore, India. While browsing online for cycling clubs, I came across IndiaTip.net. Your Web site appears to be a very comprehensive resource for travel articles and related news about India.

❷ I would like to call your attention to an electronic guidebook I recently published. It describes all of my favourite cycling routes in Bangalore and is complete with maps, kilometre markers, and detailed descriptions about points of interest. I noticed that you have a specific page dedicated to bicycle travel in India; a mention of my guide would be an ideal addition to this page.

❸ The book is titled *Bangalore by Bike*, and it can be purchased through www.bangalorebybike.com/AS3XK. If you could share this information with your readership, I would appreciate it.

Thank you and have a great day.

Priti Doshi

中文翻譯

請參考以下電子郵件回答第 153 至 154 題。

E-mail

收件者：m.agrawal@indiatip.net
寄件者：pritidoshi@hscot.in
寄件日期：5 月 17 日
主旨：IndiaTip

敬愛的 Agrawal 女士您好：

我的名字是 Priti Doshi，我是一名來自印度 Bangalore 的自行車愛好者。當我在網路上搜尋單車俱樂部時，碰巧逛到 IndiaTip.net。您的網站看起來像是非常包羅萬象的資源網，裡面都是關於印度的旅遊文章以及相關消息。

我想要請您關注一本我最近剛出版的電子版旅遊指南，內文描述所有我最愛的 Bangalore 自行車路線，且備有地圖、公里數計算器，以及名勝的詳細說明。我發現您有一個專門介紹印度單車旅遊的網頁；再加上我的旅遊指南將會使這個網頁更臻完美。

書的名稱是《Bangalore by Bike》，您可上網購買，網址為 www.bangalorebybike.com/AS3XK。若您能夠將這個訊息分享給您的讀者，我會不勝感激。

謝謝您，祝您有美好的一天。

Priti Doshi 敬上

題目 / 中文翻譯

153 正解 (D)

What is suggested about Ms. Agrawal?

(A) She lives in Bangalore.
(B) She leads guided tours.
(C) She enjoys bicycling.
(D) She runs a travel Web site.

這裡提到關於 Agrawal 女士的哪件事？

(A) 她住在 Bangalore。
(B) 她帶領觀光導覽。
(C) 她很喜歡騎單車。
(D) 她經營旅遊網站。

重點解說 電子郵件一開頭是 Dear Ms. Agrawal，顯示收件者為 Agrawal 女士。且第一段第三句提到 Your Web site appears to be a very comprehensive resource for travels article and related news about India.「您的網站看起來像是非常包羅萬象的資源網，裡面都是關於印度的旅遊文章以及相關消息」，因此選 (D)。

---

154 正解 (B)

Why is Ms. Doshi writing to Ms. Agrawal?

(A) To recommend a travel partner
(B) To promote a book
(C) To critique an article
(D) To update a news story

Doshi 女士去信 Agrawal 女士的原因為何？

(A) 建議旅遊夥伴
(B) 宣傳某本書籍
(C) 批評某篇文章
(D) 更新新聞故事

重點解說 第二段開頭說明最近出版的自著電子版旅遊指南，於第三段第一句告知書名和購書的網址。接下來第二行提到 If you could share this information with your readership，「若您能夠將這個訊息分享給您的讀者」，因此正確答案為 (B)。
(C) critique「批評…」。

單字註釋：avid「熱心的」；browse「瀏覽（網路等）」；come across...「碰到…」；comprehensive「綜合的」；resource「資源」；point of interest「名勝」；dedicate to...「專精於…」；readership「讀者群」

題目

Questions 155-157 refer to the following form.

STARR Transportation

★★★★★★★★★★★★★★

❶ Thank you for using Starr Transportation. In a concerted effort to better serve our customers, we'd like your opinion about your most recent experience with us. Please take a moment to fill out the following survey and mail it to us in the enclosed self-addressed, stamped envelope by May 28.

Date: May 20 **Customer Name:** V.N. Chen **Phone:** 603-555-0143

Date and description of service:
April 12-transport from Carroll Corporation to Franklin Airport.
April 25-transport from Franklin Airport to my home in Centerville, NH.

❷ Please rate the following on a scale of 1 to 4, 1 being "poor" and 4 being "excellent."

Service				
Friendliness	1	2	3	(4)
Reservation Process	1	2	(3)	4
Vehicle				
Spaciousness	1	2	(3)	4
Cleanliness	1	2	3	(4)

Would you use our services again? YES NO (MAYBE)

Would you recommend our services to others? YES NO (MAYBE)

❸ **Comments:**
I use Starr Transportation often for business travel and have always been satisfied. This time, when I arrived at Franklin Airport after a long flight from Lima, Peru, the driver was nowhere to be found. The airplane had arrived at a different terminal than scheduled, but the driver should have checked the flight's arrival status well beforehand. I ended up waiting for him when I could have taken a bus.

中文翻譯

請參考以下表格回答第 **155** 至 **157** 題。

STARR 運輸公司

感謝您惠顧 STARR 運輸公司。為了全力提供顧客更好的服務，我們想要請您評論最近與本公司接觸的經驗。請撥冗填寫以下調查，並放入隨附的郵資已付回郵信封，於 5 月 28 日前寄回本公司。

日期：**5 月 20 日**　顧客姓名：**V. N. Chen**　電話：**603-555-0143**

日期與服務內容：
4 月 12 日，由 Carroll 公司接駁至 Franklin 機場
4 月 25 日，由 Franklin 機場接駁至位於 NH. Centerville 的自宅

請用 **1-4** 分來評分，**1** 分表示「差」，**4** 分表示「優」。

服務

態度友善	1	2	3	(4)
預約手續	1	2	(3)	4

車輛

寬敞	1	2	(3)	4
乾淨	1	2	3	(4)

您還會再度使用我們的服務嗎？	是	否	(可能)
您會推薦別人使用我們的服務嗎？	是	否	(可能)

意見欄：
我經常因為出差而使用 STARR 運輸公司，每次都讓我很滿意。這一次，當我從秘魯利馬長途飛行抵達 Franklin 機場的時候，司機居然不見人影。飛機降落的航廈與原本預定的有所不同，但司機應該事先查清航班的到站狀態。我原本可以搭公車，但我最後卻只能等他。

題目／中文翻譯

155 正解 (D)

How will Starr Transportation most likely use information they collect from the form?

Starr 運輸公司最有可能如何使用他們藉由表格蒐集到的資訊？

(A) To create effective marketing materials
(B) To plan time-saving driving routes
(C) To determine employee promotions
(D) To improve customer service

(A) 用來創造有效的行銷素材
(B) 用來規畫省時的行駛路線
(C) 用來決定員工升職
(D) 用來改善客戶服務

重點解說 第一段第二句說明，In a concerted effort to better serve our customers, we'd like your opinion about your most recent experience with us.「為了全力提供顧客更好的服務，我們想要請您評論最近與本公司接觸的經驗」，因此 (D) 是正解。better serve our customers 可以置換成 (D) improve customer service。

---

156 正解 (B)

What does Mr. Chen indicate about the vehicle?

Chen 先生指出關於車輛的哪件事情？

(A) It was a bus.
(B) It was very clean.
(C) It was too large.
(D) It was difficult to drive.

(A) 是一台公車。
(B) 非常乾淨。
(C) 太大了。
(D) 難以駕駛。

重點解說 從第一段的顧客名稱欄位，可以得知 Chen 先生是這份問卷的回答者。Vehicle「車輛」這個項目的 Cleanliness「乾淨」得到四分的評價。四分表示 excellent「優」，故正解為 (B)。

---

157 正解 (C)

What does Mr. Chen indicate about the service he received?

對於 Chen 先生得到的服務，他指出哪件事情？

(A) The trip from Centerville took too long.
(B) The reservation process was confusing.
(C) The driver arrived later than scheduled.
(D) The vehicle was too small to fit his luggage.

(A) 從 Centerville 出發的路程耗時太久。
(B) 預約手續令人困惑。
(C) 司機比預定時間晚到。
(D) 車輛太小，無法安置他的行李。

重點解說 第三段第二句到第四句可知，「飛機降落的航廈與原本預定的有所不同，但司機居然不見人影，我最後卻只能等他」，因此答案為 (C)。

單字註釋：in concerted effort「齊心協力」; spaciousness「寬敞」; beforehand「事先」; end up doing「結果變成…」

題目

Questions 158-160 refer to the following advertisement.

Manchester Trader 29 May

1 Bright, clean, 300-square-metre flat for rent on the third floor of the historic Blythe House near the centre of Manchester. Available 1 July, £800 per month.

- Recently updated kitchen
- Reserved parking spot in front of the building
- One bathroom with a standing shower
- One bedroom, living room, kitchen, and separate dining area
- Cable television and wireless Internet service included in rent
- Cost of electricity shared among residents of the other three flats in the building
- No pets allowed
- Dining table and chairs stay with the apartment

2 One month's rent plus two months' security deposit due upon signing of the lease.

3 Contact owner and landlord Abigail Brown at 077 4300 6455 or at abrown@teleworm.uk.

中文翻譯

請參考以下廣告回答第 **158** 至 **160** 題。

Manchester 交易商

5 月 29 日

乾淨又明亮、位於鄰近 Manchester 市中心且歷史悠久的 Blythe House 三樓，佔地 300 平方公尺的空間現正出租中。7 月 1 日可入住，月租 800 英鎊。

* 最近翻新的廚房
* 位於建築物前的預留停車格
* 淋浴式衛浴一間
* 房間、客廳、廚房以及獨立用餐區各一間
* 租金含第四台和無線網路服務
* 電費與建物其他三個樓層的住戶均攤
* 不可養寵物
* 公寓附餐桌椅

簽約時，請繳納一個月租金外加兩個月押金。

欲聯繫建物所有人暨房東 Abigail Brown，請撥打 077 4300 6455 或來信 abrown@teleworm.uk。

題目 / 中文翻譯

158 正解 (A)

What is indicated about Blythe House?

(A) It is occupied by more than one resident.
(B) It is located near public transportation.
(C) It is immediately available for a new tenant.
(D) It is suitable for residents with cats and dogs.

這裡指出關於 Blythe House 的哪件事？

(A) 居住人數超過一人。
(B) 毗鄰大眾運輸。
(C) 新房客可立即入住。
(D) 居民適合養貓狗。

重點解說 第一段第六點說明 Cost of electricity shared among residents of the other three ats in the building「電費與建物其他三個樓層的住戶均攤」，可知正解為 (A)，resident「居民」。(C) tenant「房客」。

---

159 正解 (C)

What is included in the rental fee?

(A) Electricity costs
(B) Security surveillance
(C) Internet service
(D) Cleaning services

租金包含哪種費用？

(A) 電費
(B) 安全監控
(C) 網路服務
(D) 打掃服務

重點解說 第一段第五點說明 Cable television and wireless Internet service included in rent「租金含第四台和無線網路服務」，因此正確答案為 (C)。(B) surveillance「監控」。

---

160 正解 (B)

According to the advertisement, what are renters required to do?

(A) Sign a one-year contract
(B) Pay some money before moving in
(C) Provide references from previous landlords
(D) Participate in an interview

根據廣告，房客需要做哪些事情？

(A) 簽一年期的合約
(B) 入住前需要支付一些款項
(C) 提供前房東給的參考資訊
(D) 參與面談

重點解說 第二段指出 One month's rent plus two months' security deposit due upon signing of the lease.「簽約時，請繳納一個月租金外加兩個月押金」，故選 (B)。

單字註釋：square-metre「平方公尺（美國用 square-meter）」; flat「公寓房間（英國用法）」; historic「歷史上著名的」; security deposit「押金、保證金」; due「（金錢等）應得權益」; landlord「房東」

題目

Questions 161-163 refer to the following article.

Swansea Business News

❶ (3 August) A spokesperson for Riester's Food Markets announced yesterday that it will open five new stores over the next two years, starting with one in downtown Swansea this December. — [1] —. The company, known for its reasonable prices, will next open a Liverpool store in May. — [2] —. The location of the final store has not yet been determined.

❷ The number of Riester's locations has certainly been growing rapidly throughout the U.K. Shoppers seem pleased with the wide selection of items that include packaged goods, fresh produce, and hot ready-made meals. According to Donald Chapworth, director of marketing, the latter are particularly popular with working parents. — [3] —. "Many of these customers in particular have limited time to cook but still want their families to eat wholesome food," says Chapworth. Last March Riester's hired chef Gabriella Pierangeli, famed for her London restaurant Gabriella's on Second, to craft their signature home-style dishes. — [4] —.

中文翻譯

請參考以下文章回答第 161 至 163 題。

Swansea 商業新聞

（8 月 3 日報導）Riester's Food Markets 發言人昨天表示，從今年 12 月 Swansea 市區的新店面開始，明後兩年將會有 5 家全新店面開張。該公司素以親民的價格而聞名，且明年 5 月將會開設 Liverpool 的新店面。* 明年夏天將會在 Manchester 和 Edinburg 兩地再開兩家店。最後店面的位置目前尚未決定。

Riester's 的店家數量正以驚人的速度在英國各地開枝散葉。消費者似乎很開心能夠擁有琳瑯滿目的商品，包括包裝商品、新鮮農產品，以及熱騰騰的現成餐點。根據行銷主任 Donald Chapworth 表示，後者深受上班族父母歡迎。「尤其是這類的顧客群，很多人無暇煮飯，但仍想要讓家人們品嚐健康的食物，」Chapworth 說。去年 3 月，Riester's 聘請因為在倫敦開設 Gabriella's on Second 餐廳而聲名大噪的 Gabriella Pierangeli 主廚，更加用心製作招牌家庭風味料理。

* 為 163 題的內文翻譯

題目 / 中文翻譯

161 正解 (A)

What is the article about?

這篇文章關於什麼？

(A) The expansion of a chain of stores
(B) Families cutting their food budgets
(C) The relocation of a popular restaurant
(D) Grocery stores changing their prices

(A) 連鎖商店的擴張
(B) 家庭正在削減食物預算
(C) 某家人氣餐廳的搬遷
(D) 雜貨店改變價位

重點解說 第一段第一句指出 A spokesperson for Riester's Food Markets annouced yesterday that It will open 5 new stores over the next two years，意為「Riester's Food Markets 發言人昨天表示，明後兩年將會有五家全新店面開張」，因此選 (A)，expansion「擴張、進軍」。

題目/中文翻譯

162 正解 (D)

What does Mr. Chapworth mention that customers like about Riester's?

(A) Its friendly customer service
(B) Its inexpensive pricing
(C) Its home-delivery service
(D) Its prepared foods

Chapworth 先生提到顧客喜歡 Riester's 的哪一點？

(A) 親切的顧客服務
(B) 親民的價格
(C) 宅配服務
(D) 調理食品

重點解說　第二段第三句是 According to Donald Chapworth, director of marketing, the latter are particularly popular with working parents.「根據行銷主任 Donald Chapworth 表示，後者深受上班族父母歡迎」。這句話中的 the latter 指的是前一句提到的 packaged goods「包裝商品」、fresh produce「新鮮農產品」，以及 hot ready-made meals「熱騰騰的現做餐點」。hot ready-made meals 在 (D) 中置換為 prepared foods。

---

163 正解 (B)

In which of the positions marked [1], [2], [3], and [4] does the following sentence best belong?

"Two more will open at sites in Manchester and Edinburgh by summer of next year."

(A) [1]
(B) [2]
(C) [3]
(D) [4]

下面的句子最適合放在標示 [1]、[2]、[3] 或 [4] 的哪個位置？

「明年夏天將會在 Manchester 和 Edinburg 兩地再開兩家店。」

(A) [1]
(B) [2]
(C) [3]
(D) [4]

重點解說　題目中的插入句談的是關於兩個店面的開幕時間與地點。由第一段開頭可知，「Riester's 將會有五家題目中的全新店面開張」，接著在句子後半部和第二句提到「從 Swansea 市區開始鋪店」，接著提及「再來是 Liverpool 的店面」。另一方面，第三句說「最後店面的位置尚未決定」，未提到剩下的兩個店面，因此關於兩個地點的語句，適合放在第二句和第三句之間，答案為 (B) [2]。

單字註釋：spokesperson「發言人」; wholesome「有益健康的」; famed for...「以…著名的」; craft「(以手工)精心製作…」; signature「特徵」

題目

Questions 164-167 refer to the following letter.

28 April

Maria Ortiz
Hayes Polytechnic University
19 Chamsboro Road
TOORAK VIC 3142

Dear Ms. Ortiz,

❶ The Melbourne Groundwater System Corporation, MGSC, has approved your request for a two-year grant of $65,000 to research the impact of industry on groundwater resources in the Melbourne region. Please note that there are a few requirements that must be met before we can release these funds to you.

❷ First, your proposal indicated that the balance of the funding needed to complete your project will be provided by Akuna Allied Bank, and that you expected the loan approval by 15 April. Please provide us with a copy of the loan agreement you have with this bank.

❸ Also, on or about 5 May we will send the standard MGSC contract to you. This document stipulates that you will submit a quarterly status report throughout the course of this project and that MGSC will not supply any additional funds beyond the initial grant amount. Please sign and return the contract to us.

❹ Please note that MGSC requires a detailed list of all personnel directly involved in the project, their résumés and certifications, and their estimated fees. <u>All documentation requested must be received in one packet no later than 1 June.</u>

❺ Congratulations on the receipt of your grant. Do not hesitate to contact my office at 20 6501 8240 if you have any questions or concerns. I will be out of the office from 6 May to 13 May, but in my absence you may speak with Ms. Mita Kulp.

Sincerely,

Albert Johnson

Albert Johnson
Vice President
Melbourne Groundwater System Corporation

中文翻譯

請參考以下信函回答第 **164** 至 **167** 題。

4 月 28 日

Maria Ortiz 女士收
Hayes Polytechnic 大學
Chamsboro 路 19 號
TOORAK VIC 3142

敬愛的 Ortiz 女士您好：

Melbourne 地下水系統股份有限公司，簡稱 MGSC，已經同意授予您為期兩年的補助獎金，申請金額為 65,000 美元，以利研究工業對於 Melbourne 地區地下水資源所造成的影響。請注意在我們將款項發放給您之前，您必須達成幾點要求。

首先，您的計畫書表示，完成計畫所需資金的剩餘款項將由 Akuna 聯合銀行提供，且您希望可以在 4 月 15 日前取得貸款許可。請提供我們您與該銀行之間的貸款同意書影本。

另外，我們將於 5 月 5 日左右寄發 MGSC 的標準合約書給您。該文件規定，在整個計畫期間您必須繳交每季的狀況回報，且 MGSC 不再提供任何超過原本授予金額的款項。請在合約書上簽名後寄還給我們。

請注意，MGSC 需要一份該計畫所有直接參與人員的名冊清單、個人履歷和證書，以及預估薪資。所有要求文件必須於 6 月 1 日前一併繳交。

恭喜您獲得補助獎金。若您有任何問題或疑慮，請立即撥打 20 6501 8240 與我的辦公室聯繫。5 月 6 日至 5 月 13 日期間我不在辦公室，但我人不在的期間，您可以找 Mita Kulp 女士商談。

Melbourne 地下水系統股份有限公司副總經理
Albert Johnson 謹誌

題目/中文翻譯

164 正解 (B)

Why was the letter written?

(A) To ask for research proposals
(B) To announce that funds have been awarded
(C) To report the results of industry studies
(D) To offer employment

寫信的原因為何？

(A) 要求研究計畫書
(B) 宣布獲得的資金
(C) 提報產業研究結果
(D) 提供工作

重點解說 信中第一段第一句提到 The Melboume Groundwater System Corporation, MGSC, has approved your request for a two-year grant of $65,000「Melbourne 地下水系統股份有限公司，簡稱 MGSC，已經同意授予您為期兩年的補助獎金，申請金額為 65,000 美元」，可知信件主旨為 (B)。grant「補助獎金」在 (B) 中置換成 fund「資金」。

---

165 正解 (D)

When is a copy of the bank agreement due to MGSC?

(A) On April 15
(B) On May 5
(C) On May 13
(D) On June 1

MGSC 給予的銀行同意書影本繳交期限為何？

(A) 4 月 15 日
(B) 5 月 5 日
(C) 5 月 13 日
(D) 6 月 1 日

重點解說 信中第二段第二句說「請提供我們您與該銀行之間的貸款同意書影本」。第四段底線部份指示 All documents requested must be received in one packet no later than 1 June.「所有要求文件必須於 6 月 1 日前一併繳交」，因此答案為 (D)。

---

166 正解 (C)

What is indicated about the MGSC contract?

(A) It includes an itemized list of costs.
(B) It will be reviewed once a year.
(C) It requires the submission of reports.
(D) It is included with the letter.

這裡指出關於 MGSC 合約書的哪件事？

(A) 內含費用的項目明細
(B) 每年受審
(C) 需要繳交報告
(D) 附在信函裡

重點解說 信中第三段第二句提到，同意書指出，This document stipulates that you will submit a quarterly status report throughout the course of this project「該文件規定，在整個計畫期間，您必須繳交每季的狀況回報」。stipulate「規定，要求」。
(A) itemize「分項細述…」。

題目/中文翻譯

167 正解 (D)

What is suggested about Ms. Kulp?

(A) She is in charge of approving grant applications.
(B) She has conducted research similar to that of Ms. Ortiz.
(C) She is an employee of Akuna Allied Bank.
(D) She works with Mr. Johnson.

這裡提到關於 Kulp 女士的哪件事？

(A) 她負責補助獎金申請的核可事宜。
(B) 她進行和 Ortiz 女士類似的研究。
(C) 她是 Akuna 聯合銀行的行員。
(D) 她和 Johnson 先生一起共事。

重點解說

Kulp 女士在第五段被提及，寫信者 Johnson 先生在同一段第二句中指出，如果有問題或疑慮，希望和他聯繫，另外說明 5 月 6 日起至 13 日不在辦公室。此外，in my absence you may speak with Ms. Mita Kulp「我人不在的期間，您可以找 Mita Kulp 女士商談」，由此可知 Kulp 女士和 Johnson 先生一起共事。

單字註釋：grant「補助金」; balance「結餘」; personnel「人員」; certification「證明」; documentation「文件（的提供）」; packet「一批」

題目

Questions 168-171 refer to the following online chat discussion.

Sarah Lo [9:38 A.M.]	Hi all. I'd like your input. Jovita Wilson in sales just told me that her client, Mr. Tran, wants us to deliver his order a week early. Can we do that?
Alex Ralston [9:40 A.M.]	If we rush, we can assemble the hardwood frames in two days.
Riko Kimura [9:41 A.M.]	And my department needs just a day to print and cut the fabric to cover the cushion seating.
Mia Ochoa [9:42 A.M.]	But initially you need the designs, right? My team can finish that by end of day today.
Sarah Lo [9:43 A.M.]	OK. Then we'll be ready for the finishing steps by end of day on Wednesday. Alex, once you have the fabric, how long will it take to build the cushions, stuff them, and attach them to the frames?
Alex Ralston [9:45 A.M.]	That will take two days—if my group can set aside regular work to do that.
Sarah Lo [9:46 A.M.]	I can authorize that. Bill, how long will it take your department to package the order and ship it?
Bill Belmore [9:48 A.M.]	We can complete that on Monday morning.
Sarah Lo [9:49 A.M.]	Great. Thanks all. I'll let Jovita know so she can inform the client.

SEND

中文翻譯

請參考以下的線上聊天討論內容回答第 **168** 至 **171** 題。

Sarah Lo [上午 9 點 38 分]	嗨，大家好。我需要各位給點意見。銷售部的 Jovita Walson 剛剛告訴我她的客戶 Tran 先生希望我們提早一星期完成出貨。我們辦得到嗎？
Alex Ralston [上午 9 點 40 分]	如果趕工，我們可以在兩天內完成硬木框架。
Riko Kimura [上午 9 點 41 分]	我的部門只需一天就能印製並裁剪好能夠覆蓋坐墊的布料。
Mia Ochoa [上午 9 點 42 分]	但就根本而言，你需要先設計對吧？我的部門在今天以前就能完成設計。
Sarah Lo [上午 9 點 43 分]	好的。這樣我們在星期三結束前就能準備進入最後完成階段了。Alex，拿到布料後，製作坐墊、填塞作業，並黏到框架上面需要多久的時間？
Alex Ralston [上午 9 點 45 分]	需要兩天——如果我的團隊能夠先擱置一些常規工作。
Sarah Lo [上午 9 點 46 分]	這點我倒是可以授權。Bill，你的部門需要多久時間來進行訂單的包裝與運送？
Bill Bellmore [上午 9 點 48 分]	我們星期一早上就能完成。
Sarah Lo [上午 9 點 49 分]	非常好。感謝各位。我會告知 Jovita，好讓她通知客戶。

傳送

題目 / 中文翻譯

168 正解 (D)

At 9:38 A.M., what does Ms. Lo mean when she writes, "I'd like your input"?

(A) She needs some numerical data.
(B) She needs some financial contributions.
(C) She wants to develop some projects.
(D) She wants to gather some opinions.

當 Lo 女士在上午 9 點 38 分寫下「I'd like your input」時，她的意思是什麼？

(A) 她需要一些數據資料。
(B) 她需要一些財務資助。
(C) 她想要發展某些計畫。
(D) 她想要蒐集一些資訊。

重點解說

I'd like your input「我想要各位的意見」，Lo 女士說完這句話之後指出，銷售部的 Walson 女士傳達了客戶提早一星期完成出貨的希望，並詢問 Can we do that?「我們辦得到嗎？」因此選 (D)。input「意見、想法」。
(A) numerical「數字的」。

---

169 正解 (B)

For what type of company does Ms. Lo most likely work?

(A) A package delivery business
(B) A furniture manufacturer
(C) An art supply store
(D) A construction firm

Lo 女士最有可能在哪種類型的公司上班？

(A) 包裝配送業務
(B) 家具製造業
(C) 美術用品店
(D) 建築公司

重點解說

由 Ralston 先生在上午 9 點 40 分發言時的「組裝硬木框架」，Kimura 女士接著說「印製並裁剪好能夠覆蓋坐墊的布料」，而後 Lo 女士在上午 9 點 43 分發言「製作坐墊、填塞、並黏到框架上」，可以判斷 Lo 女士工作的地點應為家具公司。

---

170 正解 (C)

According to the discussion, whose department must complete their work first?

(A) Mr. Belmore's department
(B) Ms. Kimura's department
(C) Ms. Ochoa's department
(D) Mr. Ralston's department

根據討論顯示，誰的部門會先完成工作？

(A) Belmore 先生的部門
(B) Kimura 女士的部門
(C) Ochoa 女士的部門
(D) Ralston 先生的部門

重點解說

Ralston 先生和 Kimura 女士針對 Lo 女士的號召說明自己的狀況，Ochoa 女士說 But initially you need the design right?「但就根本而言，你需要先設計，對吧？」，接著說 My team can finish that by the end of day today.「我的團隊今天以前就能完成」，故正解為 (C)。

題目/中文翻譯

171 正解 (A)

What will Ms. Wilson most likely tell Mr. Tran?

(A) That she can meet his request for rush work
(B) That there will be an extra charge for completing his order
(C) That his order will be ready for delivery on Friday
(D) That she will meet him at her office next Monday

Wilson 女士最有可能告訴 Tran 先生的事情是什麼？

(A) 她能夠完成對方提出加快出貨的要求
(B) 完成他的訂單需要額外的費用
(C) 他的訂單將會在星期五進行配送
(D) 下星期一，她會在辦公室和他碰面

重點解說 根據 Lo 女士一開始的發言，可知 Wilson 女士的客戶 Tran 先生要求提早出貨一星期。經過 Lo 女士與各部門的討論之後，確認了提早出貨的可能性。Lo 女士說會和 Wilson 女士聯絡，讓她回覆 Tran 先生提早出貨的相關事宜，因此答案為 (A)。rush「緊急的」。

單字註釋：assemble「組裝…」; hardwood「硬木的」; initially「最初」; stuff「裝填…」; set aside...「撥出…」; authorize「授權給…」

題目

Questions 172-175 refer to the following letter.

Highbrook Library
42 Doring Street
Norwich, CT 06360
860-555-0110

April 23

Mr. Jack Vogel
Ellicott Office Supplies
181 Foss Street
Norwich, CT 06360

Dear Mr. Vogel:

❶ On behalf of the Highbrook Library, I would like to offer my sincere thanks for your generous gifts. The three computers you donated from your store, along with the extra paper and ink, have helped us to better serve our users. — [1] —. We now have five computers and they are almost always in use. In our last conversation you had asked how the library staff would control use. We have decided to allow library members to use a computer for free for two hours. Nonmembers pay $2 for one hour of use. We also ask all patrons to book a computer in advance because of the high demand. — [2] —.

❷ In addition, your monetary donation has allowed us to extend our hours. The library is now open until 8:00 P.M., Monday-Thursday, which has led to a growth in membership by permitting more people to visit when their workday is over. — [3] —. We have even had several book clubs form that meet in the evenings. Perhaps you would like to join one? — [4] —.

❸ Next year we will be investigating the possibility of adding a small café on the first floor near the community meeting room. We hope you will consider contributing to this project as well, if it seems promising. You will receive more information in the future about it.

❹ Thank you again for your generous support of the Highbrook Library!

Sincerely,

Annabeth Hendley

Annabeth Hendley
Director, Highbrook Library

中文翻譯

請參考以下信函回答第 172 至 175 題。

Highbrook 圖書館
Doring 街 42 號
Norwich, CT 06360
860-555-0110

4 月 23 日

Jack Vogel 先生收
Ellicott 辦公用品店
Foss 街 181 號
Norwich, CT 06360

敬愛的 Vogel 先生您好：

謹代表 Highbrook 圖書館在此衷心感謝您的慷慨贈禮。您捐出店裡的 3 台電腦，還有紙張與墨水，讓我們能夠提供使用者更好的服務。我們現有 5 台電腦，而且每台幾乎是隨時都在使用的狀態。在我們上次對談時，您問到圖書館人員控制電腦使用量的方法。我們已經決定，圖書館會員可免費使用電腦兩小時。非會員每小時則支付 2 塊美元。由於需求過大，我們也籲請所有圖書館愛好者事先預約電腦。

此外，您的捐助款項讓我們得以延長開館時數。圖書館目前開放時間為週一至週四至晚間 8 點，讓更多人可以在下班後進館參觀，帶動會員人數的成長。* 這項規定亦能協助想要在放學後使用圖書館資源的學生。我們甚至組成好幾個夜間集會的讀書會。說不定您會想要參加其中一個呢？

明年本館將會在調查一樓靠近社區集會廳處增設小咖啡館的可能性。如果看起來可行，希望您也能夠繼續支持這項計畫。未來您將會收到更多關於這項計畫的消息。

再次感謝您對於 Highbrook 圖書館慷慨解囊！

Highbrook 圖書館主任
Annabeth Hendley 敬上

* 為 175 題的內文翻譯

題目 / 中文翻譯

172 正解 (D)

Why is Ms. Hendley writing to Mr. Vogel?

(A) To invite him to become an honorary library member
(B) To request advice about computer installation
(C) To ask him to purchase new books for the library
(D) To express appreciation for his donations

Hendley女士去信Vogel先生的原因為何？

(A) 邀請他成為圖書館名譽會員
(B) 請求關於電腦安裝的建議
(C) 要求他為圖書館添購新書
(D) 對他的捐獻表示謝意

重點解說 信中第一段第一句表達感謝之意，On behalf of the Highbrook Library, I would like to offer my sincere thanks for your generous gifts.「謹代表 Highbrook 圖書館在此衷心感謝您的慷慨贈禮」。這裡的 your generous gifts 指的是第二句的「三台電腦、紙張與墨水」，以及第二段第一句的「捐助款項」。gifts 在 (D) 中以 donations 置換。
(A) honorary「名譽上的」。

---

173 正解 (B)

What is suggested about the Highbrook Library?

(A) It is going to close for renovation.
(B) It has increased the hours it is open.
(C) It will be hosting a fund-raising event.
(D) It is considering adding a meeting room.

這裡提到關於 Highbrook 圖書館哪件事？

(A) 將閉館整修。
(B) 增加開館時間。
(C) 將會舉辦募款活動。
(D) 考慮增加一間會議室。

重點解說 第二段第一句便指出 your monetary donation has allowed us to extend our hours「您的捐助款項讓我們得以延長開館時數」，接著在第二句標明具體開館時間，因此正確答案為 (B)。

---

174 正解 (C)

What is indicated about the computers at Highbrook Library?

(A) They are for library members only.
(B) They need to be updated.
(C) They are free for members to use.
(D) They cannot be reserved.

這裡提到關於 Highbrook 圖書館電腦的哪件事？

(A) 限圖書館會員使用。
(B) 需要更新。
(C) 會員可享免費使用。
(D) 無法預約。

重點解說 第一段第五句表示 We have decided to allow library members to use a computer for free for two hours.「我們已經決定，圖書館會員可免費使用電腦兩小時」，故答案為 (C)。

題目 / 中文翻譯

175 正解 (C)

In which of the positions marked [1], [2], [3], and [4] does the following sentence best belong?

"This policy also helps students who want to use library resources after school."

(A) [1]
(B) [2]
(C) [3]
(D) [4]

下面的句子最適合放在標示 [1]、[2]、[3] 或 [4] 的哪個位置？

「這項規定亦能協助想要在放學後使用圖書館資源的學生。」

(A) [1]
(B) [2]
(C) [3]
(D) [4]

重點解說

題目中 The policy also helps students 指的是「這項規定亦能協助學生」。換句話說，前一句應該也是關於可以帶來好處的規定。第二段第一句提到更改圖書館開館時間的規定，第二句則舉出好處是「讓更多人可以在下班後進館參觀」。因此 (C) 是適合的選擇。

單字註釋：sincere「衷心的」; generous「慷慨的」; monetary「貨幣的」; workday「工作日」; investigate「調查…」

題目

Questions 176-180 refer to the following e-mail and report.

1. 電子郵件

To:	Product Development Staff
From:	Sauda Dawodu
Date:	10 June
Subject:	Product Expansion

Dear Product Development Team,

1 As you may know from recent sales reports for Aswebo Toys, our products are enjoying great success in international markets. The response to our electronic and handcrafted wooden toys has been very favorable. We have, in fact, had several requests from a few of our principal clients to expand the number of wooden toys we currently make for children from birth to age five.

2 Consequently, in an effort to assess the prospects for Aswebo Toys' future growth in this area, the management team has decided that our company will, as a preliminary step, produce one new item intended for the early-childhood market. Belinobo Consulting has been hired to conduct market research on the type of toy that we will introduce. Using the results of their product study, the prototype will be refined and put on the market as soon as it is feasible to do so.

3 This plan presents our company with an exciting opportunity. I'm certain that we can count on your dedication and initiative.

Sauda Dawodu
Senior Director

2. 報告書

RESULTS—NEW PRODUCT SURVEY
Prepared for Aswebo Toys
By Belinobo Consulting

Toy Prototype	General Preference	After presented with prototype example
Puzzle	23	25
Doll/action figure	17	15
Building set	11	10
Educational game	36	39
Board game	33	31

Survey responses were collected from 120 participants, all of whom are parents of children in the focus age group. Participants were first asked which toy they would be most likely to purchase. They were then presented with one prototype from each category and asked the same question a second time.

中文翻譯

請參考以下的電子郵件和報告書回答第 176 至 180 題。

收件者：	產品研發人員
寄件者：	Sauda Dawodu
寄件日期：	6 月 10 日
主旨：	產品擴展

親愛的產品研發團隊同仁：

從 Aswebo 玩具近期銷售報告，你們可能已經得知本公司產品在國際市場上獲得巨大的成功。本公司電子類與手工木製玩具的反應非常熱烈。事實上，我們已經收到好幾位主要客戶要求我們增加目前專為出生至 5 歲孩童製作的木質玩具產量。

因此，為了評估 Aswebo 玩具在這塊領域的未來發展前景，管理團隊決定公司將準備製作一款瞄準嬰幼兒市場的新產品。我們已聘請 Belinobo 顧問公司來執行關於我們即將發表的玩具的市場調查。利用他們的產品調查結果，將能夠改善產品原型，並以最為可行的方法上市發售。

本計畫將會為公司帶來令人振奮的大好機會。我確信我們能夠仰賴各位的努力和積極主動。

資深主任
Sauda Dawodu 謹誌

結果報告－新品調查

專為 Aswebo 玩具製作
Belinobo 顧問公司執行

玩具模型	一般偏好	提供玩具模型後
拼圖	23	25
洋娃娃 / 玩偶	17	15
建築組合	11	10
教育性遊戲	36	39
棋盤遊戲	33	31

本調查由 120 名參與者回答，每位參與者都是關鍵年齡層孩童的父母。參與者一開始被問到他們最可能購買的玩具。接著為參與者展示每種類型的玩具，然後再問一次相同的問題。

題目 / 中文翻譯

176 正解 (B)

What is the purpose of the e-mail?

(A) To ask for market research volunteers
(B) To inform employees of an upcoming project
(C) To share the details of a sales report
(D) To promote a consulting firm

該封電子郵件的目的為何？

(A) 徵求市場調查志工
(B) 告知員工即將發展的計畫
(C) 分享銷售報告的詳細內容
(D) 宣傳某家顧問公司

重點解說 1 的第一段第三句提到「客戶要求我們增加商品產量」。另外第二段第一句表示「為了評估未來發展前景，決定製作瞄準嬰幼兒市場的新產品」，因此 (B) 為正解。upcoming「即將到來的」。

---

177 正解 (B)

In the e-mail, the word "response" in paragraph 1, line 2, is closest in meaning to

(A) answer
(B) reaction
(C) recognition
(D) confirmation

在電子郵件中，第1段第2句的「response」意義最接近

(A) 答案
(B) 反應
(C) 認可
(D) 確認

重點解說 包含 response 的句意是「對本公司玩具的反應非常熱烈」，因此最接近 (B) reaction「反應」。接下來的句子也舉出對商品反應熱烈的具體例子，「客戶要求我們增加商品產量」。

---

178 正解 (C)

What is NOT mentioned about Aswebo Toys?

(A) It sells products made by hand.
(B) It operates internationally.
(C) It will introduce a new electronic toy next year.
(D) It is a growing company.

這裡並未提及關於 Aswebo 玩具的哪件事？

(A) 販售手工商品。
(B) 國際化經營。
(C) 將會在明年發表新型電子玩具。
(D) 是一家成長中的企業。

重點解說 (A) 出現在 1 的第一段第二句「本公司手工木製玩具」。(B) 出現在第一段第一句「在國際市場上獲得巨大的成功」。(D) 出現在第一段第一句「獲得巨大的成功」，而且第三句「客戶要求我們增加商品產量」。只有選項 (C) 的內容完全不曾被提及。

題目 / 中文翻譯

179 正解 (A)

What is suggested about the toys that were used in the research?

(A) They are designed for use by children up to five years old.
(B) They are currently manufactured by competitor companies.
(C) They were given to survey participants to keep.
(D) They were shown to children.

關於在調查中所使用的玩具，這裡指出哪件事？

(A) 專供 5 歲以下孩童使用的設計。
(B) 目前由競爭企業製造。
(C) 送給參與調查的人員。
(D) 展示給孩童觀看。

重點解說

1 的第一段第三句提到「客戶要求我們增加目前專為出生至五歲孩童製作的木質玩具產量」。因此第二段第二句表示「已聘請 Belinobo 顧問公司來執行關於我們即將發表的玩具的市場調查」。2 是 Belinobo 顧問公司的調查報告，調查所使用的玩具產品是專為出生至五歲的孩童所設計的。
(B) competitor companies「競爭企業」。

---

180 正解 (C)

According to the report, what toy were the research participants the least enthusiastic about?

(A) The puzzle
(B) The educational game
(C) The building set
(D) The board game

根據報告，研究參與人員最不感興趣的玩具是哪一項？

(A) 拼圖
(B) 教育性遊戲
(C) 建築組合
(D) 棋盤遊戲

重點解說

enthusiastic「熱衷的」。從 2 的表格下方第二句和第三句，可以得知問題是參與調查者最想買什麼玩具。對照 2 的表格，無論是在「一般偏好」或是「提供玩具模型後」的欄位裡，Building set「建築組合」的得分都最低，因此選 (C)。

單字註釋：assess「評價」; preliminary「預備的」; refine「精鍊…」; feasible「可行的」; count on...「依靠…」; dedication「奉獻精神」; initiative「創造力」; focus group「焦點團體訪談（為了市場調查而找一群銷售對象來訪談）」

題目

Questions 181-185 refer to the following information from a Web page and e-mail.

1. 網頁

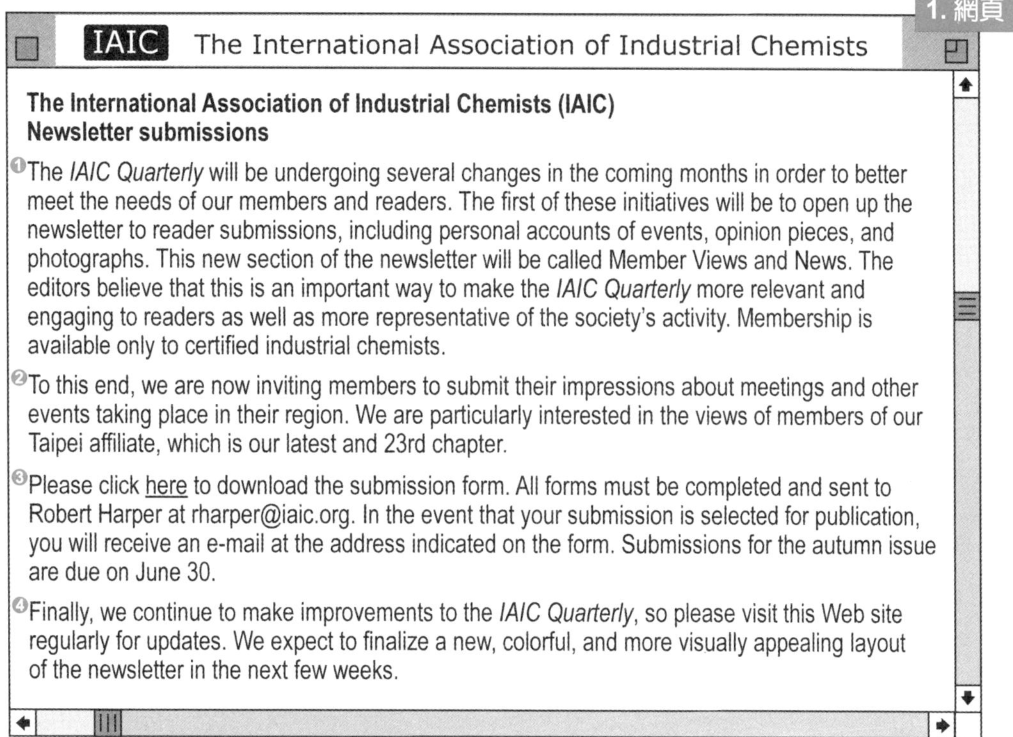

IAIC The International Association of Industrial Chemists

The International Association of Industrial Chemists (IAIC)
Newsletter submissions

① The *IAIC Quarterly* will be undergoing several changes in the coming months in order to better meet the needs of our members and readers. The first of these initiatives will be to open up the newsletter to reader submissions, including personal accounts of events, opinion pieces, and photographs. This new section of the newsletter will be called Member Views and News. The editors believe that this is an important way to make the *IAIC Quarterly* more relevant and engaging to readers as well as more representative of the society's activity. Membership is available only to certified industrial chemists.

② To this end, we are now inviting members to submit their impressions about meetings and other events taking place in their region. We are particularly interested in the views of members of our Taipei affiliate, which is our latest and 23rd chapter.

③ Please click here to download the submission form. All forms must be completed and sent to Robert Harper at rharper@iaic.org. In the event that your submission is selected for publication, you will receive an e-mail at the address indicated on the form. Submissions for the autumn issue are due on June 30.

④ Finally, we continue to make improvements to the *IAIC Quarterly*, so please visit this Web site regularly for updates. We expect to finalize a new, colorful, and more visually appealing layout of the newsletter in the next few weeks.

2. 電子郵件

To:	Shuo Chuan Liu <liu.2@milina_chemical.com.tw>
From:	Robert Harper <rharper@iaic.org>
Date:	July 5
Subject:	Newsletter submission

Dr. Liu,

Thank you for your June 18 submission to our newly created Member Views and News section of our newsletter. We were so happy to hear about the Taipei chapter's first meeting, especially the details of Dr. Mei Chu's latest research in the area of industry laboratory safety protocols in Taiwan. We were also pleased to hear that the Taipei chapter already has 28 members, and that membership is expected to double in the coming months.

I am wondering if you could edit your submission down to 300 words. This would allow enough space for three other submissions in the next issue. I would be happy to work with you on the revision. Please let me know if this will work for you.

Thank you.

Robert Harper, Editor, *IAIC Quarterly*

中文翻譯

請參考以下的網頁資訊和電子郵件回答第 181 至 185 題。

IAIC 國際工業化學家協會 (IAIC)

電子報徵文

為了更加滿足會員與讀者的需求，《IAIC 季刊》在接下來幾個月將會經歷多項改變。這些改革的第一項即是開放讀者投稿電子報，包括個人活動資訊、意見和感想，以及寫真相片等。電子報的新專欄將命名為會員觀點與消息。編輯群相信此一重要舉動將使《IAIC 季刊》更加貼近讀者、更具吸引力，且更能夠成為社會活動的代表典型。會員資格僅開放給合格的工業化學家。

為此，本協會目前正向會員邀稿，表達他們對於所在區域舉辦的會議或其他活動的感想。我們尤其對台北分會的會員投以濃厚興趣，台北分會是我們第 23 個，也是最新的分支。

請點擊此處下載徵文表格。請務必完成所有表格後，寄給 Robert Harper，電子郵件地址為 rharper@iaic.org。若您的投稿獲選刊登，您將會收到從表格載明的郵件地址發送給您的電子郵件。秋季號議題徵文截稿日期為 6 月 30 日。

最後，我們會持續改善《IAIC 季刊》，所以請定期參訪我們的網站，查看更新狀態。我們希望在接下來幾週能夠做出全新、豐富有趣，且在視覺上更加具有吸引力的電子報版面。

收件者：	Shou Chuan Liu <liu.2@milina_chemical.com.tw>
寄件者：	Robert Harper <rharper@iaic.org>
寄件日期：	7 月 5 日
主旨：	電子報徵文

Liu 博士您好：

感謝您在 6 月 18 日投稿本刊新設立的電子報會員觀點與消息版。我們非常高興聽到來自台北分會首場會議的訊息，特別是 Mei Chu 博士針對台灣工業實驗室安全協議方面的最新研究。我們也很高興得知台北分會目前已有 28 名會員，而且預計再過幾個月會員人數便會倍增。

我在想能否請您將您的投稿下修至大約 300 字左右。如此一來，下一期的期刊就能有空間刊出其他三篇稿件。我很樂意與您一起進行修改。煩請告知我這對您而言是否可行。

謝謝。

《IAIC 季刊》編輯
Robert Harper 敬上

題目 / 中文翻譯

181 正解 (A)

For whom is the Web page information most likely intended?

網頁資訊中預期的讀者群是誰？

(A) IAIC members
(B) Newsletter editors
(C) Publication directors
(D) Students of industrial chemistry

(A) IAIC 會員
(B) 電子報編輯
(C) 出版負責人
(D) 工業化學學生

重點解說 1 的第一段提到 IAIC 季刊的多項改變，第二段則提到向會員邀稿。從以上可知，網頁上的資訊是提供給 IAIC 會員的。

---

182 正解 (D)

According to the Web page information, what is true about the newsletter?

根據網頁資訊顯示，關於電子報的敘述，何者為真？

(A) A section of it will be discontinued.
(B) Larger print will be used.
(C) It will be issued every month.
(D) It will be published in color.

(A) 即將終止的專欄
(B) 將使用較大的印刷字體
(C) 每月發刊
(D) 發行彩色版本

重點解說 1 的第四段第二句是 We expect to finalize a new, colorful, and more visually appealing layout of the newsletter「我們希望能夠做出全新的、豐富有趣且在視覺上更加具有吸引力的電子報版面」，可知正確答案為 (D)。
(A) discontinue「終止」; (B) print「印刷字體」。

---

183 正解 (C)

On the Web page, the word "impressions" in paragraph 2, line 1, is closest in meaning to

網頁第 2 段第 1 行「impressions」的意義最接近

(A) characteristics
(B) imitations
(C) feelings
(D) effects

(A) 特徵
(B) 模仿
(C) 感想
(D) 效應

重點解說 1 的第一段提到，會在新專欄「會員觀點與消息」中，刊登個人的意見和感想。接下來在第二段提到，To this end, we are now inviting members to submit their impressions「為此，本協會目前正向會員邀稿，表達他們的感想」，因此與投稿的 impressions「印象、感想」最相近的詞是 (C) feelings「感想、感覺」。

題目 / 中文翻譯

184 正解 (C)

What is suggested about Dr. Liu's submission?

(A) It explains how to become an IAIC member.
(B) It will appear with one other submission.
(C) **It will appear in the autumn issue of the newsletter.**
(D) It was sent to Mr. Harper on June 30.

這裡指出關於 Liu 博士稿件的哪件事？

(A) 解釋如何成為 IAIC 會員。
(B) 將會和另一篇徵文同時刊登。
(C) 將會出現在秋季號電子報。
(D) 在 6 月 30 日寄給 Harper 先生。

重點解說 1 的第三段最後一句提到「秋季號議題的截稿期限為 6 月 30 日」，寄給 Liu 博士的電子郵件 2 的第一段第一句是 your June 18 submission「您 6 月 18 日的投稿」，由此可判斷 Liu 博士投稿將刊登於秋季號電子報。

---

185 正解 (B)

What is Dr. Liu asked to do?

(A) Provide details about a meeting
(B) **Shorten his submission**
(C) Include contact information with an article
(D) Arrange a chapter meeting

Liu 博士被要求做哪件事？

(A) 提供某場會議的細節
(B) 縮短徵文篇幅
(C) 納入文章的連結資訊
(D) 安排分會會議

重點解說 2 的第二段第一句是向 Liu 博士提出要求 I am wordering if you could edit your submission down to 300 words.「我在想能否請您將您的投稿下修至大約 300 字左右」，因此正解為 (B)。edit your submission down「將投稿編輯下修」可以換成 (B) 的說法 shorten his submission。

單字註釋：quarterly「季刊」；account「報導、描述」；opinion pieces「(專業的) 意見投書」；relevant「關係重大的」；engaging「有魅力的」；to this end「為了達到這個目的」；affiliate「分會」；chapter「(工會等) 支部」；in the event that...「萬一…的時候」safety protocol「安全公約」

題目

Questions 186-190 refer to the following notice, e-mail, and comment form.

1. 行程表

Waikiki Orchid Hotel

Scheduled guest activities in February
All activities begin at 10:00 A.M. at the Guest Services desk in the lobby.

Activity and instructor/guide	Description
Every Monday Surfing lesson Conducted by Kekoa Kalena	Learn to surf the waves of Waikiki. Must be a good swimmer. $50 per person. Participants must be at least 12 years old.
Every Tuesday Hawaiian flower crafts Conducted by Jessica Agbayani	Your instructor will guide you in the making of a lei: a beautiful Hawaiian flower garland or necklace. All supplies included. $10 per person.
Every Wednesday History tour Conducted by Lani Okimoto	In this 90-minute walking tour, participants will learn the history of Waikiki. No charge.
Every Thursday Hawaiian cookery class Conducted by head chef Sarah Wang	Learn how to cook traditional local Hawaiian dishes. (Lesson can be tailored to include vegetarian recipes only.) Participants must be at least 12 years old. $20 per person.
Go to the Guest Services desk for further information and to sign up.	

2. 電子郵件

To:	Guest Services Staff <gsstaff@waikikiorchidhotel.com>
From:	Ji-Min Choi <jmchoi@waikikiorchidhotel.com>
Date:	February 7
Subject:	Update

Hi all,

I need to update this month's program of guest activities. Jessica Agbayani and Sarah Wang will be away February 10–16. I will lead Jessica's activities and Tom Anaya will lead Sarah's. Everything will return to normal on February 17, when Jessica and Sarah both return.

Sincerely,

Ji-Min Choi
Guest Services Director, Waikiki Orchid Hotel

3. 意見欄

https://www.waikikiorchidhotel.com/guest_comments

Waikiki Orchid Hotel

Comments:

My family and I had a pleasurable stay at your hotel. We enjoyed the activities you had scheduled and I would like to give my compliments to all the instructors. I had to skip the activity led by Ms. Okimoto, but my family told me they learned a lot from her. My daughter and I truly enjoyed learning how to make flower garlands, and my husband has already made some of the dishes he learned how to make in Mr. Anaya's class. Finally, my son and daughter both had great fun with Mr. Kalena. They are looking forward to putting his lessons to use when we travel on holiday to Morocco next year.

Name:	Elina Toivanen	**Today's date:**	3 March
Number of guests:	4	**Date of stay:**	10-16 February

Submit

中文翻譯

請參考以下的行程表、電子郵件和意見欄回答第 186 至 190 題。

Waikiki Orchid 飯店

二月份房客預定活動
所有活動開始時間為上午 10 點，地點在大廳的房客服務櫃台。

活動名稱與授課教師／指導人員	活動說明
每週一 衝浪課程 由 Kekoa Kelena 帶領	學會駕馭 Waikiki 的海浪。必須是游泳高手。費用為每人 50 美元。年滿 12 歲以上者始得參加。
每週二 夏威夷花卉工藝 由 Jessica Agbayani 帶領	您的授課教師將會帶您製作夏威夷花環：這是一種美麗的夏威夷花冠或花朵項鍊。含所有材料。費用為每人 10 美元。
每週三 歷史導覽 由 Lani Okimoto 帶領	在這趟 90 分鐘的漫步之旅，參與者將會瞭解 Waikiki 的歷史。免費。
每週四 夏威夷烹飪課程 由 Sarah Wang 主廚帶領	學習如何烹煮傳統夏威夷在地美食。(課程可量身調整為僅含素食食譜。) 年滿 12 歲以上者始得參加。費用為每人 20 美元。

欲取得更進一步的資訊及報名事宜，請洽詢房客服務櫃台。

收件者：	客服人員 <gsstaff@waikikiorchidhotel.com>
寄件者：	Ji-Min Choi <jmchoi@waikikiorchidhotel.com>
寄件日期：	2 月 7 日
主旨：	更新內容

大家好：

我需要更新這個月的住宿房客活動計畫內容。2 月 10 日至 16 日期間，Jessica Agbayani 和 Sarah Wang 不在這裡。我將會帶領 Jessica 的活動，而 Tom Anaya 則帶領 Sarah 的活動。2 月 17 日起一切恢復原狀，屆時 Jessica 和 Sarah 都回來了。

Waikiki Orchid 飯店房客服務部主任
Jin-Min Choi 謹誌

https://www.waikikiorchidhotel.com/guest_comments

Waikiki Orchid 飯店

意見欄：

我的家人和我在飯店裡渡過快樂的住宿時光。我們很喜歡飯店策畫的活動，而且我要向所有的授課教師致意。我不得不缺席由 Okimoto 女士所帶領的活動，但是我的家人告訴我，他們真的從她身上學到好多。我的女兒和我非常喜歡學習製作花環，我的丈夫還做過幾道他在 Anaya 先生的課堂上學會如何烹飪的料理。最後，我的一雙兒女和 Kalena 先生玩得非常開心。他們很期待在明年我們前往摩洛哥度假的時候，能夠將他的授課內容學以致用。

姓名：	Elina Toivanen	**當天日期：**	3 月 3 日
房客人數：	4	**入住期間：**	2 月 10 日至 16 日

提 交

題目 / 中文翻譯

186 正解 (D)

What activity can be customized?

哪一項活動可為客人量身打造？

(A) Monday's activity
(B) Tuesday's activity
(C) Wednesday's activity
(D) Thursday's activity

(A) 週一的活動
(B) 週二的活動
(C) 週三的活動
(D) 週四的活動

重點解說

1 的第四段說明週四舉辦的夏威夷烹飪課程，Lesson can be tailored to include vegetarian recipes only.「課程可量身調整為僅含素食食譜」，可知答案為 (D)。tailor「(為某目的和需求) 特製」，可以換成問題句的 customize「訂做…」。

---

187 正解 (C)

What is the purpose of the e-mail?

該電子郵件的目的為何？

(A) To introduce two new employees
(B) To respond to a guest inquiry
(C) To make changes to a schedule
(D) To arrange training courses for staff

(A) 介紹兩位新進員工
(B) 回覆房客訴求
(C) 調整預定行程
(D) 安排員工培訓課程

重點解說

2 的第一句是 I need to update this month's program of guest activities.「我需要更新這個月的住宿房客活動計畫內容」，接下來敘述具體的更新內容，可知正解為 (C)。update「更新」在 (C) 中置換成 make changes to...「調整…」。
(B) inquiry「詢問」。

---

188 正解 (B)

In the comment form, the word "skip" in paragraph 1, line 3, is closest in meaning to

在意見表中，第 1 段第 3 行的「skip」意義最接近

(A) jump
(B) miss
(C) pay for
(D) look over

(A) 跳躍
(B) 未出席
(C) 支付
(D) 檢查

重點解說

skip 的受詞是 the activity led by Ms. Okimoto「由 Okimoto 女士所帶領的活動」，skip 的意思是「缺席 (上課等)」。因此 (B) miss「未出席 (上課等)」最為恰當。

題目 / 中文翻譯

189 正解 (B)

Who guided guests in making flower crafts?

(A) Mr. Kalena
(B) Ms. Choi
(C) Ms. Okimoto
(D) Ms. Wang

帶領房客進行花卉工藝製作的人是誰？

(A) Kelna 先生
(B) Choi 女士
(C) Okimoto 女士
(D) Wang 女士

重點解說 1 的週二活動欄中，花卉工藝製作的指導人員為 Jessica Agbayani。但是 2 的第二句到第三句寫著，Jessica 不在的期間，由發送電子郵件的 Jin-Min Choi 代課。因此指導花卉工藝製作的是 (B) Ms. Choi。

---

190 正解 (A)

What are Ms. Toivanen's children planning to do in Morocco?

(A) Go surfing
(B) Learn Moroccan crafts
(C) Take a tour
(D) Make Moroccan food

Toivanen 女士的孩子計畫在摩洛哥做什麼？

(A) 衝浪
(B) 學習摩洛哥手工藝品
(C) 參加遊覽行程
(D) 製作摩洛哥料理

重點解說 3 第五句開始的內容是，Toivanen 女士的小孩很喜歡 Kalena 先生的課程，第六句則提到「他們很期待在明年我們前往摩洛哥度假的時候，能夠將他的授課內容學以致用」。從 1 可得知，Kalena 先生教授的課程是衝浪的課程，因此答案為 (A)。

單字註釋：garland「花環、花冠」；give one's compliments to...「代為問候（人）」；put ... to use「利用、實踐」

題目

Questions 191-195 refer to the following notice, review, and article.

1. 公告

Taste of Italy

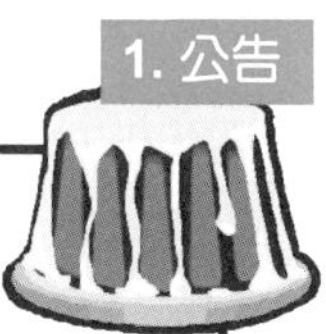

Dear Valued Customers,

❶ After 25 years in business, Taste of Italy will be closing its doors on April 23. During the week of April 17–23, please join us for a celebration of the store's history. All customers will receive a free cupcake with the purchase of any fresh bread or pastry item.

❷ Please keep an eye out for Taste of Italy pastry chef Salvator Ribisi. He will be opening his own bakery within the coming months, where customers will be able to order custom pastries and cakes for parties and weddings.

❸ It has been a pleasure to serve our wonderful Pineville City customers.

Sincerely,

Benito Giordano, owner

2. 評論

http://www.pinevillerestaurants.com

Sweet Occasions

HOME	MENUS	**REVIEWS**	LOCATIONS

I was sad that Taste of Italy closed—I had wanted them to make my wedding cake. So, I was excited when their former pastry chef opened Sweet Occasions in the Plaza Shopping Center. He made our cake, and it was perfect! Our guests kept commenting on how much they liked the cake. I would recommend Sweet Occasions to anyone.

–Edith Costello

The Evolution of a City

3. 文章

❶ When the Plaza Shopping Center opened on River Road in July of last year, Pineville City mayor Angela Portofino predicted that it would benefit the city by bringing shoppers from nearby towns to the area. Based on a 25 percent increase in the city's sales tax receipts over the last six months, Ms. Portofino appears to have been correct.

❷ However, less frequently mentioned was the potential effect of such commercial development on the city's downtown business district, which includes a number of small, family-owned stores and restaurants. In the past two months, three of these businesses—Quality Books, Ashley's Beauty Salon, and Taste of Italy—have either closed or announced plans to close, all citing a decline in customers since the Plaza's opening.

❸ Still, the mayor believes that the overall effects of new developments such as the Plaza are positive. "It's certainly disappointing when a beloved business like Quality Books closes," she said. "But new businesses bring new opportunities for all residents of Pineville City, including new jobs."

中文翻譯

請參考以下公告、評論和文章回答 第 **191** 至 **195** 題。

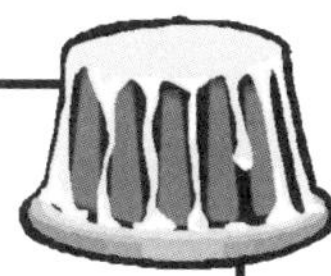

Taste of Italy

各位敬愛的貴賓：

在營業了 25 年之後，Taste of Italy 將於 4 月 23 日閉店。4 月 17 日至 23 日這週，請加入我們歡慶店家歷史的行列。所有的購買任何新鮮麵包或糕點產品的顧客都將獲得免費的杯子蛋糕。

請您將目光集中到 Taste of Italy 的糕點主廚 Salvator Ribisi 身上。再過幾個月，他自己的烘焙坊就要開幕了，顧客可前往訂購派對與婚禮專用的客製化點心和蛋糕。

很榮幸能夠為我們美好的 Pineville 市顧客服務。

店主人 Benito Giordano 敬上

http://www.pinevillerestaurants.com 

Sweet Occasions

首頁	菜單	評論	位置

我很遺憾 Taste of Italy 歇業了，我一直很想讓他們來製作我的結婚蛋糕。因此，當他們的前任糕點主廚在 Plaza 購物中心開了 Sweet Occasions 時，我感到非常興奮。他為我們製作蛋糕，而且完美極了！我們的賓客不斷表示他們有多麼喜愛那個蛋糕。我願意將 Sweet Occasions 推薦給每個人。

— *Edith Costello*

城市進化論

當 Plaza 購物中心去年 7 月於 River 大道開幕時，Pineville 市市長 Angela Portofino 便預言，購物中心將會為該區帶來臨近城鎮的消費者，因而對該市有利。基於該市過去 6 個月來的銷售稅額提升 25% ，Portofino 女士顯然是對的。

然而，鮮少被提及的是，這項商業發展對於該市鬧區商店街的潛在影響，包含一些小型家庭自營式商店和餐廳。過去兩個月以來，其中 3 間店家 Quality 書店、Ashley's 美容沙龍，以及 Taste of Italy 不是關門大吉就是宣布計畫歇業，所有店家都指稱，自從 Plaza 開幕後，店裡的來客量大為衰減。

儘管如此，市長堅信像 Plaza 購物中心這類的新發展仍具有正面的整體效益。「像 Quality 書店這樣深受喜愛的店家歇業當然令人失望，」她說，「但是新的企業將會為所有 Pineville 市的居民帶來新契機，包括新的工作職缺。」

題目 / 中文翻譯

191 正解 (B)

Why most likely is Mr. Giordano closing his business?

Giordano 先生結束營業最有可能的原因為何？

(A) Because he wants to retire
(B) Because he lost business to a new shopping center
(C) Because he cannot afford to make needed repairs
(D) Because he plans to open a different kind of business

(A) 因為他想要退休
(B) 因為他的生意被新開的購物中心搶走
(C) 因為他無法負擔需要的整修費用
(D) 因為他計畫開展不同類型的事業

重點解說：由 1 的署名可知 Giordano 先生是 Taste of Italy 的店主。3 的第二段第二句指出 Taste of Italy 的歇業原因，接著說 all citing a decline in customers since the Plaza's opening「自從 Plaza 開幕後，店裡的來客量大為衰減」，故選 (B)。lose business to...「生意被…搶走」。

---

192 正解 (C)

What is indicated about Mr. Ribisi's bakery?

這裡指出關於 Ribisi 先生烘焙坊的哪件事？

(A) It opened on April 23.
(B) It was once owned by Mr. Giordano.
(C) It made Ms. Costello's wedding cake.
(D) It is giving away free pastries.

(A) 4 月 23 日開幕。
(B) 曾經是 Giordano 先生所有。
(C) 製作了 Costello 女士的結婚蛋糕。
(D) 將贈送免費糕點。

重點解說：1 的第二段第一句和第二句指出，Taste of Italy 糕點主廚 Salvator Ribisi 先生自己的烘焙坊即將開幕。關於這家烘焙坊，在 2 的第一句到第三句提到，Costello 女士說 Taste of Italy 前糕點主廚為她製作了結婚蛋糕，因此正確解答為 (C)。
(D) give away...「免費贈送…」。

---

193 正解 (B)

In the review, the word "kept" in paragraph 1, line 3, is closest in meaning to

在評論中，第 1 段第 3 行的「kept」意義最接近

(A) held
(B) continued
(C) saved
(D) gave

(A) 舉辦
(B) 繼續
(C) 保存
(D) 給予

重點解說：keep doing 表示「持續做某件事」，意義上最接近 (B) continued「持續」。

題目 / 中文翻譯

194 正解 (A)

What is suggested about the Plaza Shopping Center?

(A) It has generated a lot of income for Pineville City.
(B) It has attracted business for local family-owned stores.
(C) It was financed by Mayor Portofino.
(D) It was built in downtown Pineville City.

這裡指出關於 Plaza 購物中心的哪件事？

(A) 為 Pineville 市帶來豐富收入。
(B) 為當地家庭自營式的店家吸引商機。
(C) 由 Portofino 市長提供資金。
(D) 建於 Pineville 市鬧區。

重點解說

3 的第一段第一句指出，市長預言 Plaza 購物中心將會對該市有利，接下來第二句說 Based on a 25 percent increase in the city's sales tax receipts over the last six months, Ms. Portofino appears to have been correct.「基於該市過去 6 個月來的銷售稅額提升 25%，Portofino 女士顯然是對的」，因此選 (A)，income「收入」。
(C) financed「提供資金給…」。

---

195 正解 (D)

According to her statement, why does Ms. Portofino have a positive view of the Plaza Shopping Center?

(A) Because it has a good bookstore
(B) Because it was completed ahead of schedule
(C) Because it offers discounts on expensive products
(D) Because it provides city residents with jobs

根據 Portofino 市長的發言，她對 Plaza 購物中心抱持正面看法的原因何在？

(A) 因為這是一家非常好的書店
(B) 因為比預定時間提早完工
(C) 因為提供昂貴商品的優惠折扣
(D) 因為提供工作給該市居民

重點解說

3 的第三段第三句提到 Portofino 市長的發言，new businesses bring new opportunities for all residents of Pinveille City, including new jobs「新的企業將會為所有 Pineville 市的居民帶來新契機，包括新的工作職缺」，可知答案為 (D)。

單字註釋：close one's doors「歇業」; keep an eye out for...「留心…」; evolution「發展、進化」; tax receipts「稅款收入」; cite「引…為證」; beloved「心愛的」

題目

Questions 196-200 refer to the following notice and e-mails.

1. 公告

The London Center of Contemporary Art presents…
Time Travel
By Conner Goodman
1-15 May
Mr. Goodman is a painter and sculptor who lives in London.

❶Conner Goodman's work will occupy our entire museum, with each museum hall representing a time period in English history, specifically focusing on the city of London. Mr. Goodman commemorates less commonly known moments in London's history taken from literature and film.

❷Upon entering the museum, visitors will experience London as it was 2,000 years ago, in the time of the ancient Romans. Each succeeding gallery that visitors encounter will portray younger versions of the city up to present-day London. Mr. Goodman's art makes use of a range of media, including paint, video, and even recycled material. All pieces in this exhibition are Mr. Goodman's original creations.

Tickets:
❸Museum entrance: £15 per person

❹Conner Goodman will discuss his exhibition at Cornwall Hall on Saturday, 9 May, at 6:00 PM. Tickets are £20 and half of all proceeds will be donated to the Historic Building Conservation Society. Please call (020) 7946 0609 for more information.

2. 電子郵件

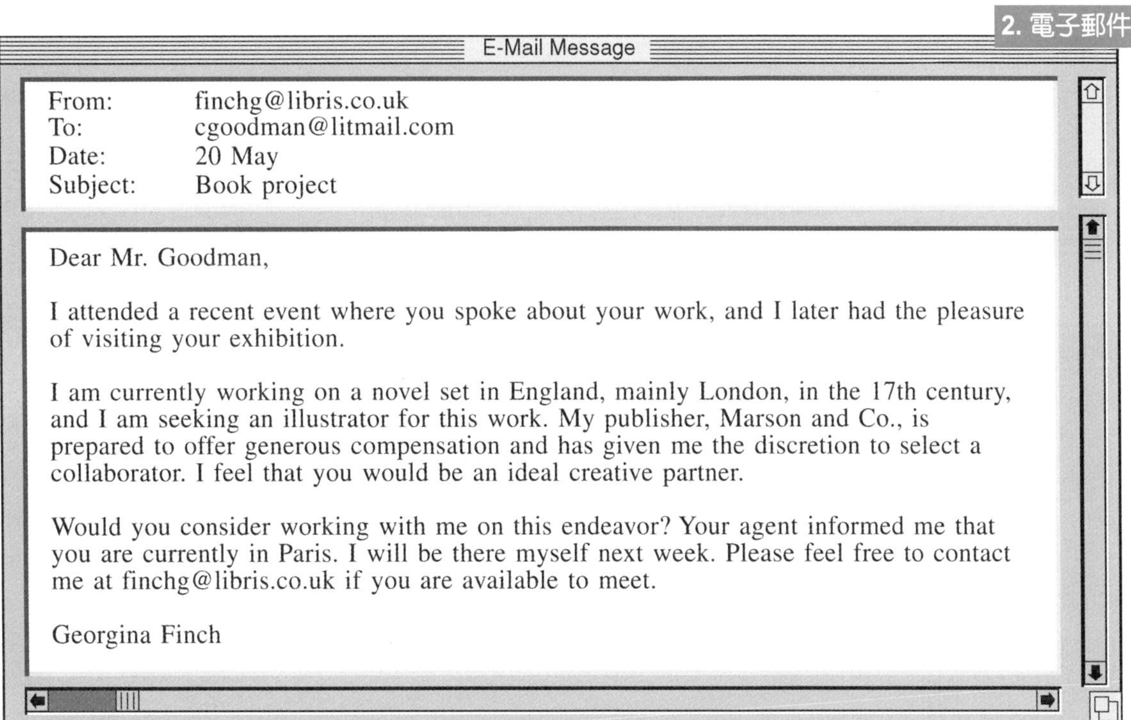

E-Mail Message

From: finchg@libris.co.uk
To: cgoodman@litmail.com
Date: 20 May
Subject: Book project

Dear Mr. Goodman,

I attended a recent event where you spoke about your work, and I later had the pleasure of visiting your exhibition.

I am currently working on a novel set in England, mainly London, in the 17th century, and I am seeking an illustrator for this work. My publisher, Marson and Co., is prepared to offer generous compensation and has given me the discretion to select a collaborator. I feel that you would be an ideal creative partner.

Would you consider working with me on this endeavor? Your agent informed me that you are currently in Paris. I will be there myself next week. Please feel free to contact me at finchg@libris.co.uk if you are available to meet.

Georgina Finch

3. 電子郵件回覆

E-mail

From: cgoodman@litmail.com
To: finchg@libris.co.uk
Date: 22 May
Re: Book project

Dear Georgina,

I am intrigued by your invitation and would be more than happy to discuss the project you describe. I am preparing to travel to Brussels next Friday, but let me know where you will be staying and when, and we will find the time to explore your proposal further.

Best wishes,

Conner Goodman

中文翻譯

請參考以下公告和電子郵件回答第 **196** 至 **200** 題。

倫敦當代美術館為您獻上……

時間旅行

Conner Goodman 作品

5 月 1 日至 15 日

Goodman 先生是畫家與雕刻家，現居倫敦。

Conner Goodman 的作品將攻陷整座博物館，每個展示廳再現每個時期的英國歷史，且特別將焦點置於倫敦市。Goodman 先生的作品紀念那些取自文學與電影，在倫敦歷史上卻罕為人知的時刻。

踏入博物館，參觀者彷彿回到 2,000 年前古羅馬時期的倫敦。參觀者巡禮每座接連的藝廊，裡面描繪著城市從年輕時期到今日的倫敦風貌。Goodman 先生的藝術運用廣泛的媒體種類，包括繪畫、影像，甚至再生材料。本次展覽的所有作品都是 Goodman 先生原創。

票券資訊：
博物館入場費：每人 15 英鎊

Conner Goodman 將於 5 月 9 日晚間 6 點，在 Cornwall 展覽廳討論他的展覽作品。票價為 20 英鎊，將捐出所有收入的一半給歷史建築保存協會。更多資訊請洽 (020)7946 0609。

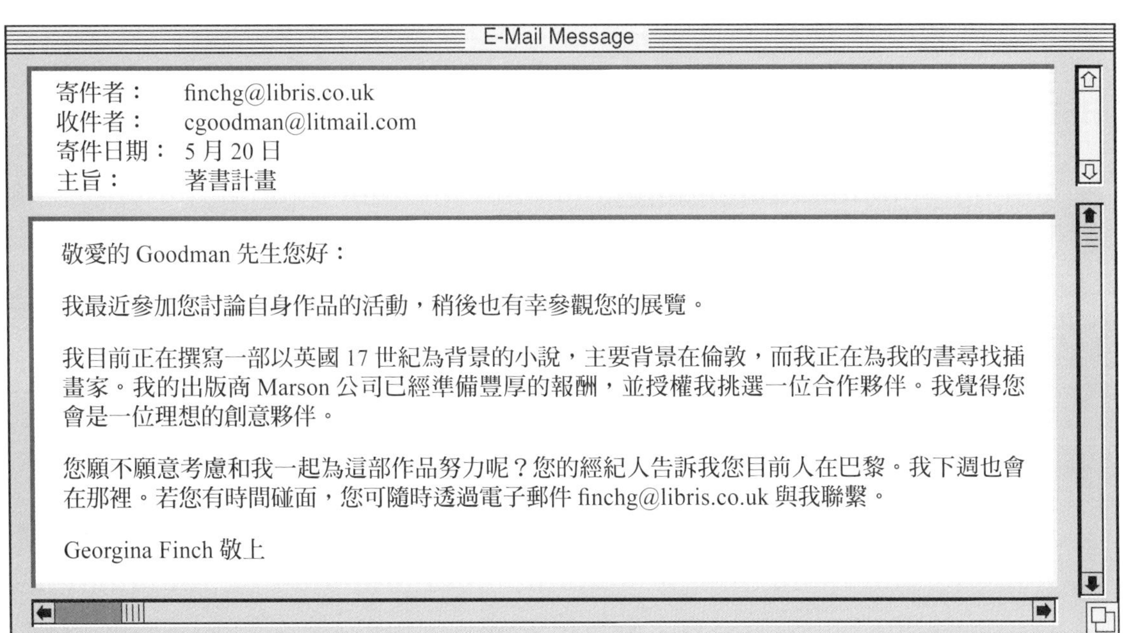

E-Mail Message

寄件者： finchg@libris.co.uk
收件者： cgoodman@litmail.com
寄件日期： 5 月 20 日
主旨： 著書計畫

敬愛的 Goodman 先生您好：

我最近參加您討論自身作品的活動，稍後也有幸參觀您的展覽。

我目前正在撰寫一部以英國 17 世紀為背景的小說，主要背景在倫敦，而我正在為我的書尋找插畫家。我的出版商 Marson 公司已經準備豐厚的報酬，並授權我挑選一位合作夥伴。我覺得您會是一位理想的創意夥伴。

您願不願意考慮和我一起為這部作品努力呢？您的經紀人告訴我您目前人在巴黎。我下週也會在那裡。若您有時間碰面，您可隨時透過電子郵件 finchg@libris.co.uk 與我聯繫。

Georgina Finch 敬上

E-mail

寄件者：	cgoodman@litmail.com
收件者：	finchg@libris.co.uk
寄件日期：	5 月 22 日
回覆：	著書計畫

Georgina 您好：

我對您的邀請感到興味盎然，且非常樂意與您討論您提到的計畫。我準備於下週五前往布魯塞爾，請讓我知道您會在哪裡停留，還有我們何時能夠碰面，以進一步討論您的提案。

謹獻上最誠摯的祝福。

Conner Goodman 敬上

題目 / 中文翻譯

196 正解 (A)

What does the notice suggest about the exhibition?

(A) It portrays a city from a unique perspective.
(B) It is made entirely of recycled materials.
(C) It includes historical artifacts.
(D) It is inspired by a popular novel.

該公告指出關於展覽的哪件事？

(A) 從獨特的角度來描繪一座城市。
(B) 完全由再生材料所製作。
(C) 包含歷史工藝品。
(D) 受到一本人氣小說的啟發。

重點解說

1 的第一段第二句提到「在倫敦歷史上卻罕為人知的時刻」。換句話說，歷史上少被提起、描繪的角度與一般不同，因此選 (A)。
(D) be inspired by...「受到…啟發」。

---

197 正解 (C)

What is implied in the notice?

(A) The museum exhibition will open with a lecture.
(B) Guided audio tours of the exhibition are available for an additional fee.
(C) Visitors to the exhibition are encouraged to experience it in a particular order.
(D) Mr. Goodman is supervising a building restoration project.

該公告暗示了哪件事？

(A) 博物館展覽由講座揭開序幕。
(B) 展覽的語音導覽需額外付費才可使用。
(C) 鼓勵訪客按照特殊順序來體驗整個展覽。
(D) Goodman 先生正在監督一項建築重建計畫。

重點解說

1 的第二段第二句提到 Each succeeding gallery that visitors encounter will portray younger versions of the city up to present-day London.「參觀者巡禮每座接連的藝廊，裡面描繪著城市從年輕時期到今日的倫敦風貌」，可知正解為 (C)。

---

198 正解 (D)

Where most likely did Ms. Finch hear Mr. Goodman speak?

(A) At a meeting of the Historic Building Conservation Society
(B) At the Center of Contemporary Art
(C) At Marson and Co. headquarters
(D) At an event at Cornwall Hall

Finch 女士最有可能在哪裡聽見 Goodman 先生的談話？

(A) 在歷史建物保存協會的會議上
(B) 在當代美術中心
(C) 在 Marson 公司總部
(D) 在 Cornwall 展覽廳的活動場合

重點解說

1 的第四段第一句宣傳 Conner Goodman will discuss his exhibition at Cornwall Hall on Saturday, 9 May, at 6:00 PM.「Conner Goodman 將於 5 月 9 日晚間 6 點，在 Cornwall 展覽廳討論他的展覽作品」。從 2 的第一段第一句可得知，Finch 女士聽過這個演講，因此答案為 (D)。

題目/中文翻譯

199 正解 (B)

What is suggested about Mr. Goodman?

(A) He has agreed to a contract with Ms. Finch.
(B) He will meet with Ms. Finch in Paris.
(C) He is returning from Brussels next week.
(D) He is selling some of his paintings.

這裡提到關於 Goodman 先生的哪件事？

(A) 他同意與 Finch 女士簽約。
(B) 他將與 Finch 女士在巴黎碰面。
(C) 他下週將從布魯塞爾返國。
(D) 他正在販售他的一些畫作。

重點解說 由寫給 Goodman 先生的電子郵件 2 第三段第二句到第四句中可得知，Finch 女士從經紀人那裡得知 Goodman 先生目前人在巴黎，她下週也會去巴黎，因此詢問 Goodman 先生能否在巴黎見面。Goodman 先生回信 3，第二句說 let me know where you wii be staying and when, and we'll find the time to explore your proposal further「請讓我知道您會在哪裡停留，還有我們何時能夠碰面，以進一步討論您的提案」，因此合適的答案為 (B)。

---

200 正解 (A)

In what field do Ms. Finch and Mr. Goodman share some expertise?

(A) English history
(B) Creative writing
(C) Contemporary art
(D) Museum management

Finch 女士和 Goodman 先生在哪個領域擁有某些共同的專業素養？

(A) 英國歷史
(B) 創意寫作
(C) 當代美術
(D) 博物館管理

重點解說 從 1 的第一段第一句，可以了解 Goodman 先生展覽的主題和倫敦的歷史有關。而且 2 的第二段第一句說 I am currently working on a novel set in England... in the 17th century「我目前正在撰寫一部以英國 17 世紀為背景的小說」，由此判斷 Goodman 先生和 Finch 女士都對英國歷史有專業素養。

單字註釋：contemporary「當代的」; sculptor「雕刻家」; occupy「占據…」; commemorate「紀念…」; succeeding「接續」; portray「描繪…」; creation「創作（品）」; compensation「報酬」; discretion「處理權」; endeavor「努力、試圖」; intrigue「激起…的興趣」

TOEIC® Listening and Reading Test Official Test-Preparation Guide Vol.6
TOEIC® 聽力與閱讀測驗官方全真試題指南 VI

發 行 人　邵作俊
作　　者　ETS®
編　　譯　TOEIC®臺灣區總代理 忠欣股份有限公司 編輯委員會
出 版 者　TOEIC®臺灣區總代理 忠欣股份有限公司
地　　址　台北市復興南路二段 45 號 2 樓
電　　話　(02) 2701-7333
傳　　真　(02) 2708-3879
網　　址　www.toeic.com.tw

初版日期／中華民國 106 年 7 月
再版日期／中華民國 111 年 6 月
定　　價／新台幣 950 元
本書如有缺頁、破損或裝訂錯誤，請寄回更換。